When our group sessions ended, I really didn't believe that the other girls wanted to be friends and keep in touch, even though we all said so....

We had all revealed so many intimate secrets to each other. Sometimes, sharing such things ties people together tightly, binds them in knots that are almost impossible to break.

Misty's mother and father had a bad divorce and her father was in a romance with a much younger woman. Her mother was trying to see other men, but was still quite self-absorbed with her pursuit of youth and beauty, and poor Misty felt so alone.

Star lived with her grandmother, her mother's mother, after her father had first deserted the family and then her mother had run off with a boyfriend. Yet Star was still the proudest and, in some ways, the strongest of the four of us.

And then there was the official president of our club, Jade, a beautiful and rich girl who lived in a Beverly Hills mansion. Her parents treated her like another possession, an asset over which to battle during their nasty divorce.

It was really the other girls who had made question why my mother had wanted to adopt me in the first place. She never seemed comfortable with me and hated the responsibilities that came along with being a mother.

The revelation was enough to make me feel sick to my stomach and even more unwanted and confused. . . .

V.C. Andrews® Books

Published by POCKET BOOKS

V.C. ANDREWS®

Into The Garden

POCKET STAR BOOKS
New York London Toronto Sydney Singapore

Following the death of Virginia Andrews, the Andrews family worked with a carefully selected writer to organize and complete Virginia Andrews' stories and to create additional novels, of which this is one, inspired by her storytelling genius.

This book is a work of fiction. Names, characters, places and incidents are products of the author's imagination or are used fictitiously. Any resemblance to actual events or locales or persons, living or dead, is entirely coincidental.

An *Original* Publication of POCKET BOOKS

A Pocket Star Book published by
POCKET BOOKS, a division of Simon & Schuster Inc.
1230 Avenue of the Americas, New York, NY 10020

ISBN: 0-671-00771-8

First Pocket Books paperback printing December 1999

10 9 8 7 6 5 4 3 2 1

V.C. ANDREWS and VIRGINIA ANDREWS are registered
trademarks of the Vanda General Partnership.

POCKET STAR BOOKS and colophon are registered
trademarks of Simon & Schuster Inc.

Front cover illustration by Lisa Falkenstern

Printed in the U.S.A.

Into The Garden

Prologue

Whenever I read stories about girls my age, I would wonder what had happened to my childhood. Sometimes it seems I was born and now here I am, Cathy Carson, seventeen. All the years before are blurred as if my memories had been kept on old film that spoiled. Faces and names, places and events, no matter how important they were at the time, are smudged and splotched so that nothing is recognizable. Of course, I know why. I don't want to remember, not after all that has happened, not after what my father did to me.

He's out of our lives, but he's not gone. He's never far away. All I have to do is close my eyes and there he is again, smiling, speaking softly, telling me how pretty I am, and then touching me, doing it all under the guise of his special lessons that would give me an advantage over other girls my age.

I shudder just the way I would if ice dripped down my back. Then I shake my head hard to rattle the images and

1

stop the flow of pain. It goes away, and for a while, I am safe.

After having spent months and months with my therapist, Doctor Marlowe, and after being with the other Orphans With Parents, Jade, Star, and Misty, in group therapy, I was able to get back into the world. I had finished my junior year at St. Jude's High School and completed the group therapy. I was supposed to have a follow-up session, but it hadn't been scheduled yet.

When our group sessions ended, I really didn't believe that the other girls wanted to be friends and keep in touch, even though we all said so and Jade took everyone's telephone number. We had all revealed so many intimate secrets to each other. Sometimes, sharing such things ties people together tightly, binds them in knots that are almost impossible to break. Each revelation is like another string wrapping around our hearts, binding us together forever.

But sometimes, after you realize what you have revealed, you can't face the listener again. It's embarrassing to know that when she looks at you, she sees your pain and your humiliation. You turn away. You wish she would go away, and you don't try to make contact. You are eager to turn her back into a stranger. You might even see each other somewhere, gaze blankly into each other's faces, and pretend you didn't see each other.

Half of me hoped that would happen, but the other half, the half that longed for friends and kindred spirits, hoped it wouldn't. No one but my father, who had his reasons, ever kept a promise to me. I didn't expect the girls would keep theirs. Each of them had her own problems, and each was surely occupied and distracted.

Misty Foster's mother and father had a bad divorce and

her father was in a romance with a much younger woman. Her mother was trying to see other men, but was still quite self-absorbed with her pursuit of youth and beauty, and poor Misty felt so alone, she came up with the idea of calling herself and the rest of us Orphans With Parents, or the OWP's. It was a funny idea, but after a while, I liked it because I had never belonged to any organization or club, had never been in a play or on a team. It wasn't the sort of club membership anyone would want, but at least there was a sense of togetherness, something shared.

Star Fisher lived with her grandmother Pearl Anthony, her mother's mother, and her eight-year-old brother, Rodney, after her father had first deserted the family and then her mother had run off with a boyfriend. Yet Star was still the proudest and, in some ways, strongest of the four of us. I was afraid of her when we first met. She seemed so hard and even mean, but after I heard her story and she heard ours, she seemed to soften, even become protective of me and the others. In so many ways, I wanted to be like her.

And then there was the official president of our club, Jade Lester, a beautiful and rich girl who lived in a Beverly Hills mansion. Her parents treated her like another possession, an asset over which to battle during their nasty divorce. They were two strong and independent people. Her father was a famous and successful architect and her mother was an executive in a cosmetic company who guarded her career with a passion, even refusing to permit her parental responsibilities to interfere with climbing the corporate ladder. At the time we ended our group therapy, her parents were approaching some sort of compromise over custody, but had still not reached it.

As bad as my story was, I ended up feeling sorry for

each of them. They seemed to feel sorrier for me than they did for themselves, and they didn't even know the whole truth about my family.

Family is such a strange word to apply to my situation. I had been adopted, but I had not discovered that until after my father began forcing himself on me. It was really the other girls who had made me question why my mother had wanted to adopt a child in the first place. She never seemed comfortable with me and hated the responsibilities that came along with being a mother. I had wondered what had made her want me, but not with the passion and the need the girls instilled in me. Finally, I confronted my mother and forced her to tell me the truth, or what I discovered was the sordid truth.

I was not really her adopted daughter. I was her half sister. Our mother had had some sort of love affair and had become pregnant in her forties. My half sister had been pressured into getting married to Howard Carson, and then pressured again into adopting me. There was still a great deal I didn't know, but that revelation was enough to make me feel sick to my stomach and even more unwanted and confused.

What was I? Who was I? To learn that you were a regretted mistake, a sin, an embarrassment, is horrible, but I still had to know more.

My half sister Geraldine (I have great difficulty now thinking of her as my mother) always warned me about getting too close to the truth. She claimed it doesn't set you free. She said, "It's like too much of any good thing. It puts you in a darker place. Don't ask so many questions."

One time when I pursued one of my endless lines of questions, telling her I had to know the truth, that the truth was important, Geraldine responded by asking me, "What if you were horribly ugly, but you lived in a world without reflections, no mirrors, no way to see yourself and know? Would you be better off if someone brought you a mirror and showed you your face? That's the truth, too, and all it brings is pain."

Was she right? Had I forced her to hold up a mirror? Was my pain my own doing? Maybe that was why she hated mirrors and caring about your looks, why she criticized most women for being narcissistic, why she censored my books and magazines when I was younger and wouldn't permit me to watch certain television programs, why she practically spit at some commercials, and why she wanted me to do all that I could to hide my breasts when they began to develop much too early.

Or maybe there was another reason, a deeper reason, one that she feared even more than the truths she had already revealed. Our house was full of secrets, unspoken dark thoughts that hovered in corners or lived like insects under rugs and in locked closets. Should I take them out? Should I do what she warned me not to do? Should I continue to cling to silence, to look away, to close my eyes?

I remembered how Star described her fantasy world, her magic carpet to take her away from her unhappiness. I was never able to do that. Make-believe was always too difficult, too thin, and easily shattered by Geraldine's voice or look. It was like a balloon that started to lift me away and always exploded or leaked its air and brought me down hard, planting me firmly in my loneliness.

Clocks ticked, day turned to night and then to day. I moved through my responsibilities as if I had been hypnotized, mechanically, never feeling any excitement, surprised at the sound of my own laughter, if it ever came, and even surprised by my own tears and sobs.

After Geraldine had reluctantly told me part of the truth, I felt even lighter, less substantial, more alienated and alone. I stared out of my window at the street and watched the cars go by, wondering who everyone was and where everyone was going. I was also looking for a sign of my stepfather. He loomed forever and ever out there.

Geraldine thought he wouldn't dare show his face, but in my secret, deepest places, I feared he would return. Maybe I would see his hands first, those familiar large palms, those long, spidery fingers, and then he would come out of the darkness, smiling, reaching for me. I would close my body like a fist and hold my breath.

And he would touch me again. Try as I would, I couldn't keep myself locked away. My cries of protest would go unheard and he would cover me like a blanket woven out of the darkness.

1

Forbidden Pleasures

When Jade called to invite me, as well as Misty and Star, to her home for our first official meeting of the OWP's, my heart seemed to wake up and beat happiness as well as blood through my veins and arteries. My whole body came alive and lifted as if some heavy chains had been broken. I could almost hear them shatter and clank at my feet.

Geraldine was busy preparing our dinner, cleaning the vegetables for our salad, inspecting every carrot, every lettuce leaf for some imperfection and then pausing to baste the roast chicken, but always listening with one ear tilted in my direction. Our downstairs phone was on the kitchen wall near the door and I had no phone in my room. The only time I could have any privacy during a personal call was when she was upstairs, out of the house, or in the bathroom. The moment I cradled the receiver, she spun on her heels, demanding to know who had called.

"It was Jade," I announced, unable to hide my excitement, "inviting me to her house for a brunch."

"Jade?" Geraldine's small eyes narrowed into suspicious slits, darkened with accusations, fears, and threats. "Isn't she one of *them?*"

Geraldine usually referred to the other girls in my group therapy as "Them." It made it sound as if they were all monstrous, alien creatures. If they were monstrous, what was I in her eyes? I wondered. She blamed everything on my father when she spoke about it, if she ever spoke about it, but deep down in my heart, I believed she blamed me as well. I could see it and feel it in the way her eyes lingered on me like two tiny spotlights of accusation.

After all, I thought, she had made me feel as if there was something polluted about me because I had been born a child out of an adulterous affair, even if the adulterer was her own mother. Sin was always something contagious in Geraldine's eyes. Why shouldn't she believe I had inherited a tendency toward it?

I couldn't remember her ever looking at me with pleasure, and certainly never with pride. She was always searching for something to criticize as if she had been given the responsibility of ensuring that I never wandered from the path of righteousness, her righteousness. My premature voluptuous figure only reinforced her tarnished image of me. Once she even told me it meant I'd be oversexed, and she always talked about sex as if it was a disease. She often tried to make me feel ashamed of what I looked like and she had even gone so far as to try to prevent me from having a female figure as long as she could, making me wear what were practically straight-jackets when my body started to develop.

"She's one of the girls, yes," I said finally, hoping she

wouldn't start criticizing Jade and the others as she had done so many times in the past.

"The girls? You mean those girls from Doctor Marlowe's clinic?" she asked, grimacing as if she had just bitten into a rotten walnut.

Geraldine never had approved of the therapy sessions. She hated the idea of strangers knowing anything intimate about us. She would have had me keep it all locked inside, no matter what damage it did to me. In her way of thinking, you swallowed the bad with the good and you locked it inside and worked, worked, worked, keeping yourself busy to forget whatever was unpleasant or ugly.

"Doctor Marlowe never referred to it as a clinic, Mother. You know we went to her office in her home. You make it sound terrible, like a hospital or a research lab or something with the four of us being treated like guinea pigs," I told her.

She grimaced again, only with more disgust this time. Geraldine could twist her mouth until it almost looked like a corkscrew. She was so thin these days, she hardly had a cheek to pull in, but it dipped in like the center of a saucer when she turned her lips.

"It's just a bunch of hocus-pocus, all this psychological mumbo-jumbo. What did people do before all this counsel and analysis, huh? I'll tell you," she said quickly. As she often did, Geraldine asked a question that she had already answered to her liking in her own mind. "They gritted their teeth and they endured. It made them stronger.

"Nowadays, you have all these moaners and groaners, crying and complaining as soon as they're in the least bit of difficulty. They're even on television—television! And why? To tell the most personal things! People have no shame anymore. They are willing to tell complete strangers their most private secrets and business, for the whole world to see and know. Disgusting.

"We're just thinning the blood with all this stupidity," she insisted, "thinning the blood, making ourselves weak and pitiful. There's no grit. People have no self-respect and these so-called doctors just encourage it all."

"Doctor Marlowe has helped us, Mother, helped all of us through very difficult times," I insisted.

"Um," she said, grinding her teeth. "Well, I don't want you associating yourself with such girls. I didn't like the idea of that doctor bringing you all together like that in the first place. It wasn't healthy."

"But I like them and they like me. We have..."

"What?" she snapped. "What do you have?"

"A lot in common," I said.

She stared at me, her eyes turning red with fear and shock.

"You mean, they...their daddies..."

"No, they each have a different problem, none of them like mine," I said quickly.

She recovered instantly, whipping her upper body ramrod straight. She hated anything that even vaguely suggested what had happened.

"What good will come of you being around girls with problems, Cathy? You're just going to poison the well some more. They can't be good influences. If you were sick with pneumonia, would it be good for you to hang around with patients sick with tuberculosis? No, of course not. If this Doctor Marlowe thought you were in need of help, why would she mix you in with other girls who were sick, too? To make more money, faster, that's why," she said.

"No, that's not true. It was a technique..."

"Technique," she spat. "They have all sorts of words, to cloud the truth and get away with their hocus-pocus. I don't want you having anything more to do with those girls, hear?"

"But—"

"No but's, Cathy. I have all the responsibility now. Always did," she spat. "You go off and get into trouble with some disturbed teenage girls and I have more to handle. It's enough running this house and making sure you get what you need."

"But I need friends, too!"

"Friends, yes, but not mental cripples," she insisted, and turned her back on me.

"They're not mental cripples. If they're mental cripples, what am I?"

She was silent.

"I'm going," I asserted.

She slammed a pot down on the counter so hard, I felt my insides jump into my throat. Then she turned toward me, wagging the pot she gripped in her hand like a club.

"You'll not be disobedient now," she warned. "I'm legally your mother and I'm still the one responsible for you, and you'll obey, hear?"

I stared at her. Suddenly, she turned from flushed red to the whitest pale and fell back against the counter.

"Mother, what's wrong?" I cried.

She waved me off.

"Nothing," she said, taking a deep, and what looked like a painful, breath. "It's just a little dizzy spell. Go tend to your own chores. I'll be calling you to set the table soon."

She clutched her stomach and chest as if to keep everything inside and turned her back to me. I waited and watched until she straightened up her bony shoulders, this time with more effort, and then returned to what she was doing. She moaned under her breath, but said no more. I watched her for a moment before leaving the kitchen.

I was determined to go to Jade's house. I wouldn't be shut out. I hadn't told Geraldine that the brunch was tomorrow. I would sneak out and go, I thought. I would just use her golden rule: what she doesn't know, won't hurt her. Hide the truth. The truth can bring pain. Why bring her any pain? Sometimes it's kinder to lie.

Because I didn't talk about the brunch anymore, Geraldine didn't mention it again and the subject drifted off like so many unpleasant thoughts and words in our house. Sometimes, when I looked around my home, I thought the already dark walls were becoming even darker as more vile, nasty, and ugly words were splattered over them.

Geraldine liked the house this way. She kept the curtains drawn tight most of the day so "people couldn't gape through our windows and snoop." As if anyone really cared what went on in our little home, I thought. We had to be the most boring people on the street. Who'd want to know about us? Geraldine never participated in any social events and rarely spoke to anyone. She liked keeping to herself, keeping the lights low, the doors shut tight, the world at bay.

After dinner, I managed to get to the phone to call Jade without Geraldine overhearing. She had gone upstairs to the bathroom. She didn't like using the downstairs bathroom. She was always afraid either I or my adoptive father when he was here could hear her. I knew that was the reason because she always yelled at me after I used the downstairs bathroom and said, "When you go, start with some tissue in the water so you don't make any disgusting noises. These walls and doors are so thin, you can hear someone's stomach gurgle."

I should have asked her if the walls and doors were so thin, why didn't you ever hear what went on behind mine? She hadn't heard me when I needed her most, and now as I reached for the phone, I hoped her voluntary deafness would continue.

"It's Cathy. I have a problem," I began, when Jade answered her phone.

"Oh no," she cried. "I knew your mother wouldn't let you come. And I'm having this great brunch prepared for us. Star and Misty are definitely coming. Please don't tell me you can't come."

"No," I said, laughing at her skepticism, "I'm coming too, only I have to keep it from my mother for now. She doesn't want me to go to your house."

"Why?" she demanded. I could hear the indignation, like some bubble, expanding in her every passing moment. Only Star could stand up to that explosion when it occurred. "Does she think she's better than me and my family?"

"She was never in favor of my going to Doctor Marlowe in the first place, remember? She thinks we're all going to be bad influences on each other."

"What about her? What about her influence or lack of it? She let all that happen to you right under her snooty nose. She's about the worst excuse for a mother—"

"Please," I pleaded, thinking if she only knew the truth.

"Well, what do you want me to do?"

"Tell your driver I'll be waiting on the corner and not at my house."

I gave her the cross street and assured her I would be there when he came.

"Great," she said. "Tomorrow, the police will come and accuse me and my chauffeur of kidnapping you. Your mother will press charges, for sure."

"No, she won't," I said, laughing.

"All right," she concluded. "At least you have the guts to do the right thing and not let her intimidate you. The girls will be proud of you," she added.

It made me feel good to hear her say that and I realized I wanted nothing as much as I wanted their respect. I wanted it much more than I wanted Geraldine's.

"Thanks. Should I bring anything?"

"Yes," she said, "you."

I laughed again and quickly hung up just as I heard Geraldine's footsteps on the stairs. I knew how good she was at seeing deceit in my eyes, so I finished putting away the dishes quickly and told her I had a headache and was going to lie down. That was the one excuse she always seemed to buy. I think that was because she had headaches so much herself.

"All right," she said, retiring to the living room to look for something "decent" on television. "Don't forget. I'll be doing the week's shopping in the morning."

I didn't volunteer to go along and she didn't ask. We did so little together. We never went to a restaurant, to the movies, or even to the mall. It made her nervous when I accompanied her to stores because she was always watching the way men looked at me and then telling me to close my coat more or hold my arms up higher so my upper body didn't swing so much. She made me so self-conscious about myself, I didn't enjoy being with her anyway.

As quickly as I could, I went upstairs to my room and closed the door. That was one of her house rules...keep your bedroom door closed, guard your privacy, and don't expose yourself and therefore make someone else uncomfortable. With my father gone and just she and I here, what did it matter now? Even though I wondered, I didn't question it. It was easier to simply let her dictate her laws of behavior and let them float on through the house like birds without eyes, bumping into everything until they settled somewhere and waited to be nudged again.

I went to sleep that night dreaming about the girls, about having friends and doing fun things together, maybe even having parties and meeting boys.

I met Misty, Star, and Jade when Dr. Marlowe put us together for group therapy. We were all so different, and yet, we were all alike in one way: we were all victimized somehow by our own parents.

It had been a while since we had last seen each other. Every time the phone rang, which it didn't do often, I was hoping it was one of them. Who else would care to call me? Geraldine had no family to speak of, no sisters or brothers, other than me, of course. Our mother and her father were long gone, and my adoptive father's family, none of whom had wanted anything much to do with him anyway, were now as much persona non grata as he was. It got so I welcomed solicitors, just to hear another voice over the phone. Geraldine was always right nearby going, "Hang up, hang up, just hang up."

But Jade had finally called. She had called!

The hardest thing for me to do was conceal my excitement the next morning. I took the easiest way out. Since Geraldine never wanted to know about my periods, she had no idea when they should be occurring. I complained about menstrual cramps and told her I didn't have much of an appetite. As usual she put her hands over her ears and shut her eyes if I said anything like that.

"If I've told you once, I've told you a hundred times, Cathy. You don't talk about those things. Those things are personal and should be kept locked up inside your own head. They're not for the ears of strangers."

"You're not a stranger, Mother," I pointed out, even though I thought she behaved like one sometimes.

She shook her head.

"That's not the point. What happens in your body is nobody's business, not even mine," she insisted.

We'd had this same discussion on and off before. Sometimes, I liked to have it just to get a rise out of her, to see and hear her say the same things. It was as if I needed constant proof that she was the way she was and she actually believed the strange things she said.

Once I said, "But what if something's wrong? How will I know if I don't tell you?"

"You'll know," she insisted. "Your body is your best judge of itself."

If that's true, I better head right for the mental hospital, I wanted to say, but sealed my lips and gave up instead.

To avoid any more discussion and especially any nitty-gritty details I might let slip from my mouth after what I had told her about my period this morning, Geraldine hurried along, diving into her chores like someone jumping into a pool to get out of the hot sun. She had already eaten her breakfast, which was usually just a piece of toast and a cup of tea, followed by one of her herbal panaceas. My father used to make fun of them, but she ignored him. I never took them and she never offered them or encouraged me to take them. It was as if she had some secret super-remedy for everything and didn't want to share it.

This morning I just had some juice and a little bowl of cereal. Before she went up to her bedroom to change into what she called appropriate clothes for the public, she told me she would like me to clean out the food pantry.

"Take everything off the shelves and dust around, and then make an inventory. I've got an idea about what we have and what we need, of course, but I want it better organized," she instructed.

Geraldine ran the house as if it was a nuclear submarine, polishing, cleaning, checking, and rechecking every nook and cranny. At times she made me feel like some sort of junior officer or worse, a grunt. While most girls my age were enjoying their summer vacation, going to the beach, to the malls, and movies, meeting friends and having parties, I was at work in our backyard, on our patio, in our house, straightening and reorganizing things I had straightened and reorganized only a week or so before. Once, while I watched a squirrel working hard to accumulate its food, going through the same motions, I thought, I'm not much different. Maybe that's why he stops, gazes at me, and goes on without any concern.

I thought the best thing to do was get right into the pantry so she would think things were clicking along just as she had expected. She came downstairs all dressed, her cloth shopping bag in hand, and looked in on me.

"Good," she said, watching me clean out one of the shelves. "Take your time and do it right. I won't be any longer than usual."

I waited until I heard the front door close and then I quickly went up to my room to choose something nice to wear. It was a warm day, but I didn't own a single pair of shorts. Geraldine wouldn't buy me any, but I had a pair of jeans I had cut at the knees without her knowing. I had them stuffed in the leg of another pair.

I put them on and found a light pink cotton sweater she hadn't thrown out. She often sifted through my meager wardrobe, searching for anything I might have grown out of, and then either donated it to the thrift shop or simply put it in the garbage. Anything that might have become slightly tight or even suggested being too short was doomed.

The girls at Doctor Marlowe's had always been critical of the way I kept my hair. It wasn't entirely my own fault. Geraldine trimmed it unevenly and wouldn't let me go to a beauty parlor. She thought that was a big waste of money.

"They call themselves stylists," she said, "and then they can charge you twice as much as they should. Most of the time, all they do is look in some magazines and try to copy what they see even if it doesn't fit you."

I didn't argue with her. She didn't even look to see if I nodded or looked like I disagreed. Geraldine always expected that whatever words of wisdom she cast my way would fall into my net and be held dearly by me. Why shouldn't she believe that? I thought. I rarely gave her any reason to doubt it. Unlike most girls my age, at least up until now, I would avoid arguments, speaking back, or being defiant.

I must say my heart was pounding so hard when I started out of the house, I thought my legs would turn to wet noodles and I would faint at the door. She would come home and find me sprawled on the floor and tell me that's what I get for trying to defy her wishes. I almost expected to feel an electric shock when I reached for the polished brass doorknob and turned it. Taking a deep breath, closing my eyes and opening them, I stepped out of the house into the bright warm sunshine.

It was a glorious day and certainly not one to spend boxed up in a food pantry, cleaning and polishing shelves and taking inventory. The clouds looked like thick smears of whipped cream over blue frosting. The sidewalk and streets glittered, and the Santa Ana breeze was warm and gentle. All of it gave me more courage.

I hurried down our narrow sidewalk and onto the street, turning right and walking quickly without looking back once. If I did, I thought, I might hesitate and hesitation might lead to my returning home.

I was hoping the limousine would be there already and I wouldn't have to wait, but it wasn't. Seconds seemed more like minutes. I strained my neck to look down the street for signs of the long black car I had seen bringing Jade to Doctor Marlowe's or waiting for her afterward. It wasn't in sight.

I glanced at my watch and looked fearfully in the direction from which Geraldine would be coming. It was far too early for her to be returning, but nevertheless, I couldn't help worrying that she might have forgotten something or simply decided to come home to check on me. She often had these spurts of paranoia, jumping up to see if doors and windows were locked or if I was doing whatever chores I was supposed to be doing.

It was surely only my imagination, but it seemed to me that every passing driver looked at me with suspicion and wondered why I was loitering at the corner. Fortunately, Geraldine had no interest in our neighbors so I didn't have to worry about any of them calling her or telling her they had seen me. She hated gossip and compared it to dogs barking at each other or cats hissing. It was all meaningless and wasteful and led only to unhappiness and trouble. Idle talk was worse than idle hands. If you had nothing of value to say, keep your lips firmly shut was Geraldine's motto.

Finally, I saw the sleek shiny black automobile turn up the street and glide toward the corner where I waited. The chauffeur slowed and pulled to the side. Before he could get out to open the door, it flew open and Misty cried, "Get your booty in here, Cat!"

I glanced once toward my house and then practically lunged into the big automobile. Star was sitting there cool and collected, her beautiful pearl black skin never looking more radiant and smooth, her eyes like black diamonds. She had her hair freshly braided and wore a khaki knee-length cotton skirt and a matching cotton blouse. I slipped in beside her and Misty closed the door.

"Onward," she cried.

The driver nodded and smiled, and we pulled away from the curb.

Misty wore a pair of leggings with an oversize T-shirt that read *How's my walking? Call 555-4545.* She was a petite girl, but complained about her figure being too boyish. I was willing to trade bodies with her anyday. Her blue eyes seemed to sparkle with impish joy at the sight of me.

"That's not your real phone number, is it?" I quickly asked, nodding at the T-shirt.

"No. It's the Motor Vehicle bureau. I had it made up on the boardwalk in Venice Beach."

"Can't you get into trouble for that?" I asked.

"Now how is she going to get into trouble for that?" Star questioned. "Cat, you're about as timid as a church mouse. I bet you only cross the street at crosswalks," she added.

"As a matter of fact, that's true," I said.

Star laughed.

"Stop picking on her," Misty ordered, and turned back to me. "How have you been?" she cried, reaching forward to squeeze my hands. "Can you believe we're really getting together? And how about this limousine?"

"You should have seen when it pulled up to my house," Star said. "The neighbors were staring and Granny kept shaking her head and muttering, 'Lordy be, Lordy be. My grandchild, riding in that chariot.'"

I could easily imagine the scene.

"What are you going to tell people when you return?" Misty asked her.

"I don't know. Maybe I'll tell them I was in a movie," she suggested.

"What happens when they find out you're not in a movie?" I followed.

"Who cares?" she replied. "They don't have any right sticking their noses in my business anyway, do they?" she demanded, her eyes wide and furious.

I shrugged.

She stared at me a moment, still looking furious, and then she smiled and laughed.

"You act like the sidewalk is thin ice and you're made of lead and heavy stones. You don't have any reason to be scared of anyone anymore. You're a member of the OWP's. Go on, tell her, Misty," she said.

"That's right," Misty said. She grew serious for a moment. "Have you gone back to see Doctor Marlowe?"

"Not yet," I said. "She called and spoke with my mother once, but no appointment has been set. What about you two?"

"I've been back to see her," Star said. "But I'm finished now."

"Me too," Misty said. "I think Jade is too. You're the only one left."

"She told me to call her any time," Star said, "but I hope I don't need to." She gazed at me. "Just go see her and finish it," she continued. "The longer you hold off doing something you're scared of doing or you don't think is pleasant, the worse it seems."

"She's right," Misty said.

"Of course I'm right. I don't need you telling everyone I'm right."

Misty just threw one of her small shrugs and pretty little smiles back at her.

"I'm hungry," she said. "I deliberately just nibbled on breakfast so I'd have a good appetite. Jade said she was making sure we had a special buffet. I can't even imagine what it will be like."

"It's just food whether a fancy cook from France prepares it or not," Star said.

"Wrong," Misty sang. She marked the air with her right forefinger, making an X.

"What's that supposed to mean?" Star demanded.

"I'm keeping track of your boo-boo's," Misty replied.

Star shifted in the seat, shook her head, and looked at me.

"So what have you been doing with yourself, huh? You're sitting there like some Buddha while we gobble like turkeys."

"Just helping around the house, reading, taking a walk sometimes. There's a lot to do in the yard. My mother fired the gardener we had. She said we have to be economical because we're going to be living only on our interest income."

"Why doesn't she go out and get a job then?" Star asked.

"She makes it all sound critical, but I know we have a good income. There was money she inherited, besides the money my father had to surrender."

"He should have had to surrender more than money," Star muttered. "And you know what I'm referring to, Cat."

I felt myself turn red, the heat rising quickly up my neck and into my face.

Misty glanced at her with a look of reprimand and Star turned to gaze out the window. We were all quiet for a moment, but Misty hated silences. They made her fidget.

"That's a nice sweater," she told me.

"Yeah," Star said. "The way it fits, I'm surprised your mother let you wear it."

"She doesn't know," I said. "She doesn't even know I have these cut-off jeans."

"You snuck out, didn't you?" Star realized. "That was why you wanted to be picked up at the corner?" she demanded.

"Yes," I said.

"What's going to happen when she finds out?" Misty said.

"I don't know."

"Nothing's going to happen," Star insisted. "Don't make her more scared than she already is." She turned to me. "She'll bitch a little and then she'll realize you can't be treated like some infant.

"Parents," she added, nodding, "have to grow up too."

"Amen to that," Misty said, imitating her.

Star gave her one of her Star looks and then smiled and shook her head.

"Well, look at this," she said, and we leaned over to gaze out the window at the security booth and the gate that led into Jade's neighborhood. "That girl does live like some princess. No wonder she's spoiled rotten."

The guard waved us through and the large gate swung open. We all gaped at the beautiful, enormous houses, each one custom-made.

"Wow," Misty said. "These make my house look like a bungalow."

"What do you think it does to my granny's? I guess I live in a dog house," Star said.

The streets in the development were wide and lined with palm trees. There was even a sidewalk. Occasionally, the houses were broken up with free space, trees, and lawn, and there was a lake at the center, around which all the houses were built. All of them had good-size yards behind them, too.

"Are we still in America?" Misty cried.

"Not my America," Star said.

The limousine slowed and then turned into a circular driveway. We continued to gape as Jade's house came into view. It was as big as she had described. I remembered how proudly she had described it.

It certainly held my attention. The limousine came to a stop and the chauffeur got out quickly to open the door for us. For a moment, none of us moved. We just stared.

"Well, what are we acting like a bunch of silly tourists for?" Star cried. "It's just a big house. C'mon," she said, and stepped out first.

Misty and I followed, neither of us able to stop gaping. As we started toward the tall double front door, it was flung open and Jade appeared.

"I'm absolutely famished," she announced to us, her hands on her hips. "I skipped breakfast waiting for you guys. At least you can walk faster," she added.

Jade was truly the most elegant looking teenage girl I knew. She had long, lush brown hair with a reddish tint that flowed gently down to her shoulders. Her eyes were green and almond shaped. Her high cheekbones gave her face an impressive angular line that swept gracefully into her jaw and perfectly shaped lips. Her nose was a little small, but also just slightly turned up and she was always stylishly dressed and perfectly made-up.

"It's not our fault you live out in the boondocks," Star quipped.

"Boondocks! This is probably the most desirable gated community in Los Angeles, maybe even the whole West Coast!" Jade bragged.

Star looked around as if deciding whether or not she wanted to move in.

"Um. No graffiti at least," she said, and Jade laughed.

"C'mon, c'mon. Everything is set up for us in the back. Did you bring bathing suits?" Jade asked.

"No one told me to," Star said.

"I didn't think of it," Misty said, shaking her head.

I was ashamed to say I didn't even own one.

"That's all right. I'll find something for each of you. Worse comes to worse," she added with a coy smile, "we'll skinny-dip."

"What?" I cried.

"Just kidding," she said, and took my hand. "Cat, stop worrying," she ordered. "We're going to have a good time for a change. You have to leave your sadness and troubles outside the door."

"She doesn't know how to stop worrying," Star said.

"Well, let that be the first commandment of the OWP's: no worries."

"Right," Misty said. "Isn't this great?" she added. "We're together, forever."

She threaded her arm through mine and squealed with delight.

"Right," Star muttered, taking my other arm, "misery loves company."

They were all around me. I looked again at the beautiful mansion. How could anyone be miserable here, especially me? I wondered, as I entered with my best friends in all the world, my only friends in all the world. We had each had our private storms and now, all our bright and hopeful smiles made one united, special rainbow.

2

Together Again

The entryway in Jade's house was almost as big as my living room. The floor glittered with rich-looking golden brown tiles. On my right was a wall-size oval mirror that caught the three of us gaping ahead at the widest, most dramatic staircase I had ever seen in real life. The steps were carpeted in red velvet.

"I feel like I just stepped into *Gone With the Wind*," Misty declared.

On the wall to the left of the stairway was an enormous oil painting of a watery meadow with some sort of mill in the background, all under a windy sky.

"That's the biggest picture I ever saw," Star said, impressed.

"It's a Jonathan Sandler. He's an American artist who worked in the late nineteenth century, imitating the Dutch landscape painters. My father got it as part of a package deal he made with some wealthy builder in Virginia. There are lots of paintings in this house," she continued.

Her matter-of-fact tone made it sound more like she was bored with it than boasting. "Some my mother bought and some my father acquired so there's a mixture of styles. They never agreed on much of anything, why should they agree on paintings?" she offered.

Misty nodded knowingly. Her parents weren't much different from Jade's in that regard.

All of the rooms in the house were large and opulent. Besides the works of art on the walls, there were vases and clocks, crystals and small statues almost everywhere. I didn't see much empty space, which made me think it was as big and as full as a museum.

We three continued to gawk as Jade led us through the house to the den, a long room with paneled walls, a built-in big-screen television and a wall of bookshelves that nearly reached the ceiling. She walked us through French doors that opened onto a large, tiled patio. To the right on the patio were long narrow tables arranged with the buffet spread over them. A maid and the butler waited to serve us.

It looked like enough food for a wedding. One table was covered with dishes of salads, framed with breads and rolls; another table had platters of meats, shrimp, and even small lobster tails. There were soft drinks, lemonade, and juices on a third table, and after that were the desserts: small cakes, cookies, two pies, and bowls of mixed fruit.

"Who all is coming?" Star asked, breathless with awe.

"Coming? No one's coming. My mother's on a business trip and my father is in Nashville talking to investors who want to build a music theater."

"You mean that this is all for us?" Star followed.

"I wasn't sure what everyone liked, so I asked them to prepare a variety."

"Variety? Some supermarkets don't have this much variety. What happens to all the food we don't eat?" Star pursued.

"I don't know," Jade said, starting to get annoyed. "The servants do things with leftovers. That's why they're here. Let's get some food and sit."

"I'm glad I didn't eat much for breakfast," Misty cried, and started for the tables. The maid handed her a dish immediately and the butler waited to hear what she wanted. He then served her.

I didn't know what to choose first. I tried taking a little of everything, but the butler put too big a portion of everything I chose on my plate.

Jade took the least of any of us. We sat around a large table under an umbrella. The butler and the maid then brought us whatever we wanted to drink. They stood back by the tables and watched, waiting to see if anyone wanted anything else.

"Do you always eat like this?" Star asked. "With servants and all?"

"No. Most of the time, I have a fruit shake or just some yogurt, but this is a special occasion."

"I'll say. I didn't know how special an occasion it was," Star said, and we all laughed, even me.

As we sat, ate, and talked, I gazed at the beautiful grounds. The grass looked more like carpet. All the bushes and flowers were arranged and trimmed to perfection. It was as if one of those famous artists whose paintings hung on the walls inside had planned the landscaping. The pool was kidney shaped with a whirlpool at the far end, over which the blue green water flowed back into the pool itself. There were heavy cushioned pink lounge chairs around the patio and a small cabana to the right with an outside shower.

"It really is beautiful here," I suddenly blurted. The others stopped talking and looked at each other and laughed.

"You sound like you just woke up," Star said.

"I don't know if I'm awake or dreaming."

"You want to make her head fatter than it already is?" Star warned, nodding at Jade.

"Don't worry about it, Star. If I stray, you'll be there to knock me back."

"That's the truth," Star said. Misty laughed and we were all silent for a long moment.

"I can't help it. It still feels like we're all back at Doctor Marlowe's," Misty said. "I keep expecting one of us to start talking about her family problems."

"Well, let's make another rule right now...no references to that stuff unless we all decide it's okay, okay?"

"What will we talk about?" Misty asked.

"There are lots of other things going on besides our miserable family lives," Jade insisted. "For starters, anyone seeing anyone?"

She gazed around the table.

"I'm not. Not yet," Star added cryptically.

"What's that supposed to mean, 'not yet'?" Jade followed, her perfectly trimmed eyebrows dipping toward each other.

"Well, I was over at Lily Porter's house the other day and I saw a picture of her cousin Larry. He's in the army and he sent her this picture of himself all dressed up in his uniform, standing by a tank. He's over in Germany, but he's coming back soon."

"So?" Jade said.

"So, I thought he was fine, and she told me as far as she knows, he's not involved with anyone back here. She's going to introduce me as soon as he's home. She said she'll have a party or something."

"Right, and he'll just topple over the moment he sets eyes on you," Jade said.

Star's eyes grew small for a moment and then she smiled.

"Well, maybe I'll borrow one of your expensive outfits and dazzle him like you dazzle every man that sees you."

Jade laughed.

"Sure. Choose anything you want. I have magic clothes, guaranteed to win you the man you love."

"What about you? Someone set your heart on fire these days?" Star challenged.

Misty and I were like observers at a verbal tennis match. Our heads turned from one to the other.

"No. My mother took me to an afternoon party over at the Nelson's two days ago just so I could meet their son Sanford, who just got home from his European studies in Paris. He's rich and very intelligent, but he's got the personality of a nose wart. Talk about being conceited. The only reason that boy looks into a girl's eyes is to see his own reflection."

We all laughed. How I wished I had some stories, some experiences to relate, but all I could do was listen and be envious.

"Are we really going to form a club?" Misty asked when we all grew quiet.

"Club sounds juvenile," Jade said. "Let's just call it something else."

"What?" Star asked.

"I don't know. Someone come up with something. I can't think of everything."

"Amazed to hear you admit it," Star muttered.

We were all quiet, thinking.

"Why don't we just call ourselves sisters," I suggested. They turned to me.

"I don't mean real sisters, but..."

"I like it," Jade said. "The OWP's, Sisters of Misfortune." She glanced at Star.

"Now what?" Misty asked. "Can I get some T-shirts made up for us?"

"How would you explain it to your mother and father?" Star asked.

"I don't know. Neither of them ever ask me what my T-shirts mean. They pretend not to see them on me. This one won't be any different."

"T-shirts won't be enough to make us sisters," Jade said.

Suddenly she looked different, darker, deeper in thought. "There's something I never told Doctor Marlowe."

"What's that?" Star said.

Jade turned to her right and looked up at the house.

"I have my own private world. It's an attic room with just a small window. I go there when I want to feel like I'm..."

"What?" Misty asked.

"Away from all this," she said with a sweep of her hands. "We'll go up there and perform the ceremony," she added.

"Ceremony? What ceremony?" Misty asked, her eyes wide.

"The ritual that will make us all feel closer, more like sisters." When she gazed at Star, I felt that the two of them might have discussed it beforehand. Star's lips relaxed into a small smile.

"Ritual?" Misty said, her face full of worry.

"You're not afraid, are you?" Jade teased.

"No, no. Of course not. What about you, Cat?" she asked me quickly.

"I don't think even Jade, even Jade and Star together," I added, "could come up with anything that would frighten me more than my own memories," I said.

Everyone grew serious and nodded.

"That's why we need this," Jade said. "It's why I invited you all here. It's why sisters is not really an exaggeration. We're more than friends. We're family."

She gazed out at the beautiful grounds.

"We might be the only real family we have."

"Then let's get to it," Star said.

"Can't we have dessert first?" Misty cried, eyeing the pies and cookies.

Everyone laughed, but it was different, it was a laugh full of nervousness, thin and as fragile as we all were.

Maybe that's what really makes us sisters, I thought.

After we had finished eating, we reentered the house, all of us speaking more softly, keeping our voices as low as we would if we had just entered a church. Jade led us back to the grand staircase, explaining how she had first discovered the attic room when she was only seven and how she just naturally began bringing her most cherished possessions into it. When her father discovered what she was doing, he thought it was amusing. He had the room fixed up for her, cleaned and wallpapered, and then he found some special furniture.

Suddenly she stopped at the base of the staircase and gave us all an ominous look.

"Let's make another rule right now and let's live by it.

Let's promise each other not to lie to each other and not to avoid saying or doing anything that might be unpleasant if we feel deep in our hearts it is the best thing for our sister. Either we're going to be different from everyone else out there, or we're not. We're either really going to be honest with each other and really become family or not," she emphasized. "Well?" She looked directly into Star's face.

"Fine with me," Star said. "I never lied to you about what's wrong with you yet."

"It goes both ways."

"It should," Star countered.

"Cat?"

I nodded although I felt I would be the biggest target for everyone else's critical arrows.

"Misty?"

"It's okay with me. I don't mind what anyone says about me," she added.

"There! That's a lie," Jade accused, her forefinger in her face. "Well?"

"Okay, it's a lie. What I meant is I won't mind what anyone here says about me. I mean, I'll mind, but I'll take it. Is that all right?"

"It's better," Jade conceded, "but it's not quite enough honesty yet. Anyway," she continued, turning away from Misty, who released a breath and shook her head at me. "My father found all these toy-like things and made me my own dollhouse up here. Sometimes, I felt like a doll in it myself. There are even small lamps and tables, small bookcases, and of course, little dishes, glasses, and cups.

"But I have other things in there, things that have had some special meaning for me and they're not all small things. I keep the room under lock and key. The maid doesn't even get in there to clean, which my mother hates. I take care of that room by myself."

"Wow," Star said, exaggerating her surprise as we continued down the upstairs hallway, "you actually clean one room yourself?"

"Okay," Jade admitted, "I'm a spoiled brat." She smiled. "But I won't deny that I've enjoyed it."

"Don't you just hate all this truth?" Star asked Misty and me.

With some hesitation, we both laughed.

As we passed Jade's mother's bedroom, we gazed through the double doors and saw an enormous bed with a headboard made out of what looked like pearls. It rose halfway to the ceiling. It was a four-poster bed, too. I could see there was a whole other room, a living room, just off to the right, with a television set. I asked about it, but Jade wasn't going to stop to show us anything at the moment.

At the end of the hallway there was a narrow stairway that took us up to the attic, Jade's dollhouse to the right and a storage area to the left. She took a key from her pocket, unlocked the padlock, and then she opened the door and stepped back for all of us to enter.

We all paused inside the doorway. It was as if we had fallen down a well into Oz or some other make-believe world. The one small window was draped in a candy red-and-white curtain. The floor was covered with a thick, cream tinted rug that also had some red streaking through it. As she had described, the room was furnished with small milk white chairs and tables, a sofa, and short pole lamps. There was even a small television set in a miniature cabinet. There were little pictures of clowns and horses, scenic views, and some cartoon characters on the white and candy apple red wallpaper. I, especially, felt like Gulliver in Lilliput, a giant among tiny people. I was afraid to move, afraid I might step on something or shatter something with a clumsy gesture.

"We don't have to sit on furniture," Jade said, as she saw us lingering in the doorway. "We can sit on the floor. That's what I usually do when I'm up here."

She closed the door behind her and went to the small area where there was a dining room table all set with toy dishes and silverware. Behind it was a miniature kitchen with cabinets, a sink, and a stove. None of us, not even Misty, could fit on those tiny kitchen table chairs, I thought. A beautiful doll with long flowing golden hair was seated at the head of the table. On the other chairs were characters from various children's stories. I recognized Pinocchio of course, and Dorothy from Oz, as well as Pocahontas.

Jade opened one of the small cabinet doors, reached in, and then turned back to us with a long, black candle in her hand. I saw her look to Star who nodded. Then Jade pulled down the shade over the small window to darken the room. She set a candle holder down on the floor and squatted beside it, inviting us to do the same. We gathered in a small circle and Jade set the candle in the holder.

"I don't mean to be so dramatic about all this, but I've been thinking about us and I've done some research on different rituals designed to bind people the way I think we all want to be bound."

"What do you mean by bound?" Misty asked.

Jade looked very thoughtful for a moment. It was very quiet. All I could hear was the tiny ticking of a small clock on a shelf behind me.

"We've all got to feel we're part of something much

greater than ourselves. If you put a teaspoon of water into a bottle of wine, the water would lose its identity. It would take on the smell and the taste of the wine. We've got to dissolve ourselves like that into each other."

"How do we do that?" Misty asked. Without realizing she was doing it, she was whispering.

Instead of answering right away, Jade lit the candle.

"We have to pledge ourselves to each other, to the sisterhood, and swear to put the interests of all of us above our own personal interests."

Misty still looked troubled and confused.

"Don't you want to do that?" Jade asked her.

Misty looked at me and then nodded.

"Sure. That's why we're here, I guess."

"We've all been brought together because people who were or are supposed to be responsible for us were more interested in their own happiness. That's why we have to be unselfish when it comes to each other," Jade said.

The candle burned brightly, the light flickering on all our faces, making our eyes look like they all had tiny candles in them as well.

"But what do we actually do? Swear on a Bible or cut an X in our palms or something and take some sort of blood oath?" Misty inquired.

"Too typical, right out of comic books," Jade replied.

"So, then what?" Misty looked at Star who looked at Jade. She nodded at the candle.

"We have to toss something into the small flame," Jade continued, "something that will prove how much we trust the OWP's."

"I don't understand," I said. "Into the flame?"

"That's just symbolic," Jade said. "Fire consumes, burns away the selfish part of ourselves. It changes one form of energy into another. That's why it's so often used in any ritual."

"But what would we toss into it? What form of energy?" I looked at Misty who didn't look worried anymore. She looked intrigued.

"We make an offering, a deep secret," Jade said, glancing at Star, which convinced me the two of them had talked a little about all this. "We change a secret into a common bond, an offering, a commitment to each other. It has to be something we didn't even tell Doctor Marlowe, something so close, so revealing, we couldn't do it. Obviously, something then, that no one else knows about us. If you've told someone, it's no good. In fact," she said, tightening her lips and making her eyes even darker, "we need something you even hate to tell yourself."

Everyone was silent. The candle licked the air, the flame snapping at each of us as if it was challenging us, calling for our secrets.

Jade finally broke the silence. "Cat, why don't you go first."

"I can't think of anything worse or more secret than what I told you all about my father and me," I said.

"Think harder," Jade ordered.

I struggled with memories. I've told them everything that matters when I was with them at Doctor Marlowe's, I thought.

"Well?" Misty asked, shaking my hand.

"Give her a chance," Star ordered.

I really did tell them almost everything about my father and me, I thought. I wanted to get all that out of my system. What could I give them now?

And then it came to me. I couldn't have told them this because I didn't know it then myself.

"My mother," I said, "is more than just my adoptive mother. She's my half sister."

Misty and Jade dropped my hands at the same time. I opened my eyes. They were all looking at me.

"Your half sister?" Jade asked. "I don't understand."

"Remember how you all kept asking me why my parents would want to adopt me, why my mother especially would take on the responsibility of a child if she was so uptight about everything? Well, that's the reason."

I told them what I knew about my real mother getting pregnant with me and how my half sister had been influenced by her father and eventually got married and was persuaded to pretend she was my adoptive mother.

"No one else but me and my mother and father knows the truth," I said. "No one but you now."

"But who's your real father then?" Misty asked.

"I don't know. There's a lot I still don't know. It's worse than pulling teeth to get my mother to tell me anything else."

"You still call her your mother?"

"It's hard not to call her that when I speak to her, but I really can't think of her like my mother anymore. It's easier for me to think of you all as my sisters than her. She wants me to call her my mother anyway, and she's always reminding me that she's legally my guardian and I've got to treat her with the same respect a parent deserves. She says sisters don't have the same reverence for each other. You know how she rules the house, how she always did.

"It's complicated," I admitted, "but up until now, I've done what Jade said, I've avoided thinking about it myself. I mean, I'd like to know more, but I don't as well. Know what I mean?"

"No," Misty said. "That's all too wild. Your whole life

you thought your sister was your mother? I don't know what I would do if I found out such a secret. Why did they keep it a secret? It's crazy."

"I know. I guess anyone would think we're a sick family," I said, and stared at the flickering candlelight. "How I wish that what Jade said would happen *could* happen," I told them.

"What do you mean?" Misty asked.

"That I could toss all this into the fire and watch it go up in smoke."

They all stared at me, and then Star shook her head.

"What?" Misty asked her.

"Just like Cat," she said, "to come up with a secret that none of us could top. Well, I guess that gets us off the hook."

"Yeah, Cat's secret makes anything I could come up with sound so stupid," Misty said, looking at Jade.

Jade sighed deeply. "I agree," she said finally, putting her stamp of approval on the decision.

3

True Confessions

The girls were shocked that I knew so little about my family and my origin. All I could say was "I don't know," and "I'm not sure," to every question they fired at me, making me feel like some criminal under the lights in a police station.

"If it was me, I'd be dying to know everything," Misty finally said. "I'd nag and nag until your mother, I mean half sister, told you every nitty-gritty detail. I'd give her no peace, not a moment."

"It's not that easy to talk to my mother," I said. "She can turn herself off like a light switch."

"I know what you said before, but I still don't understand how you can sit there and still call her your mother!" Jade cried. "You know now that she's not."

I shrugged.

"I know what she's told me, but it hasn't sunk in my head long enough I guess. It's all I've ever called her," I added when she widened her grimace.

"I wouldn't desecrate the word by calling her Mother."

"You can't just erase all these years in a few minutes," I protested.

"From what you've been telling us about her," Star said, "you'd think you'd be glad not to have to call her Mother. What's her name?"

"Geraldine. I do think of her more as Geraldine since she told me the truth."

"She'd be lucky to have me call her that. I can think of a lot of better names for her. She's got no right to keep any of it secret," she added, "not now. Misty's right. You should want to know everything."

"I guess I do want to know. It's just that…"

"You're just afraid of her," Jade concluded. She thought a moment. "Did you ever think that maybe she's lying? Maybe she made it all up just to keep you under her thumb. Just from the little we know about her from what you've told us, I think she's capable of doing something like that."

Star nodded.

"What proof do you have that she's telling you the truth?" Jade demanded.

"Proof? Nothing," I said. "Except what she has told me."

"That's no proof, girl. Jade's right. First thing you do is snoop around, look for letters, documents, pictures, anything that will tell you something."

"You mean, go look through her personal things?"

"Well sure, what else? They're your personal things too, right?"

"I don't know if I could do that. She guards her privacy religiously. I'm rarely in her room."

"You've got to find out more," Misty said, her face serious and determined. "You should be told who your real father is, for starters. It's not fair. It's not right." She looked at Star who nodded.

"Maybe she really doesn't know," I said.

"Maybe she does," Jade said. "All right," she added, straightening up and turning to them, "we have our first OWP project: to help Cat discover everything and anything about her own past."

They agreed quickly.

"What do you mean? What are you going to do?" I asked, my heart thumping. I was going to be in plenty of trouble as it was, sneaking out and coming here after Geraldine had specifically forbidden it.

"Were you born in Los Angeles?"

"I think so," I said. "I don't know."

"You don't even know where you were born?" Star cried.

"She never said where I was born."

"At least see if you can find out where and we'll see if we can check birth records, for starters," Jade plotted.

"Yeah, you have to have a birth certificate," Star said, "and your parents would be on it!"

"Maybe it was a secret birth, in a basement or an attic," Misty suggested with her eyes full of stories. "And then they forged a birth certificate. I read that in this book and—"

"Where did your real mother live?" Jade asked, waving Misty off as if she was waving away an annoying fly.

"Here, in Pacific Palisades, not far from us."

"So at least you remember her?" Misty said.

"I didn't know her very well. My mother wasn't ever all that eager to take me to see her. I don't think they got along well."

"What about your grandfather?" Jade asked. "I mean, the man you thought was your grandfather," she corrected.

"He died two years later. I remember him a little better, although he wasn't really very interested in me and I didn't see all that much of him either. He was around holidays and such, but not too often otherwise."

"No wonder," Star muttered. "He always knew you weren't his, right?"

"I guess. Geraldine said he knew I wasn't his child, but I don't know."

"Will you stop with that 'I don't know'! If I hear it one more time, I'll go mad!" Jade screeched.

"Well, I *don't*," I said, tears coming to my eyes. "It's something I just found out and I guess I'm still in some shock about it."

Jade looked up at the ceiling a moment as she regained control of herself.

"Okay," she said. "Okay. Your assignment is to search for and locate any and all information that might shed light on your past."

"My assignment?"

"As a member of the OWP's. I'm the president, remember? I can give out assignments."

"When did we decide that?" Misty asked, her head tilted like a kitten.

"Just now. Any objections?"

Misty thought for a moment and shrugged. "I guess not," she said. Then her expression changed, her face brightening "Hey—when are we going swimming? You mentioned it when we first came."

"Misty, can't you stay on the topic we're discussing?"

Misty shrugged.

"I thought we were finished."

"Oh, brother," Jade said. She looked to Star who smiled and shook her head. "All right, I guess we accomplished what we set out to do business-wise for now. Let's go to my room and I'll find bathing suits for everyone," Jade finished.

"I don't know if I want to go swimming," I said.

"We all want to go swimming so you do, too. You're not going to start being negative, are you?" she asked, her eyes narrowing slightly. "You're not going to disagree every time we decide something?" Her voice rose in pitch. My heart actually began to skip beats. I shook my head.

"No, I..."

"So? Then? What?" she asked, raising her arms.

"I don't know how to swim," I confessed.

Her mouth froze in the shape of an O.

"You don't know how to swim?" She looked at Star, who shook her head, and then turned back to me, skeptical. "How can that be? You never learned in school?"

"I had a doctor's excuse when I was younger. I once got a bad earache and my mother thought swimming would make it worse, and there isn't a pool at the parochial school I attend."

"No one ever took you to the beach or to a pool?" Star asked.

"No." I looked down. "My mother wouldn't ever buy me a bathing suit. Remember when I told you my father was thinking about building a pool?"

"Yeah, and your mother wasn't happy about it, so the idea of it went away," Star recalled.

"And with it, my hope of learning how to swim."

"All right," Jade said, lifting her shoulders, "second major OWP project is going to be teaching Cat how to swim."

"Really?" Misty said.

"Really," Jade said. "If one of us is weak in an area, we all are. That's what it means to be bound, to be one. Did you forget already?" she demanded.

"No." Misty started to smile but stopped. Jade looked like she might just explode any moment if another syllable even vaguely opposed to something she said was uttered.

"Let's go," she commanded, and leaned over to blow out the candle. Moments later, we left her secret room and headed for her bedroom and her closet, a walk-in, almost as big as my entire room.

Her room itself was three times the size of mine. She had a vanity table with a marble top and a gilded mirror that ran the length of the entire wall. I laughed to myself imagining what Geraldine would say about it if she saw it. You couldn't help but look at yourself all the time in this room.

Jade's bed, like her mother's, was also a canopy with white silk draped over posts. There were at least a half dozen huge pillows with frilly lace pillowcases that matched the beautiful bedspread. On the night table was a light red telephone shaped like a pair of lips.

Built into the wall directly across from her bed was not only a large screen television, but a stereo system.

All of her furniture had a glossy pearl finish. There were two dressers, an armoire, and a desk. The walls were a light pink. It looked like pink cloth. She had no posters, but on one wall was a painting of John Lennon of the Beatles. It looked very expensive.

When we all gazed into her walk-in closet, we could only stare at the rows and rows of garments, the shelves of shoes and the built-in dresser.

"There's more clothing here than in some stores," Star remarked.

"Every year I give away about a quarter of it to charities," Jade said.

"Put me on the list of charities," Star said, and Jade laughed.

She went directly to the dresser, opened the next-to-bottom drawer and began flinging bathing suits at us.

"This should fit Misty. I wore it only once when I was twelve," she added.

"Thanks a lot."

"Well, be happy I saved it," Jade retorted.

Misty held it up and reluctantly nodded.

"It looks like it will fit me," she said, "and it's not bad."

It was a black and gold one-piece with the black on one side of the top, streaking down over the center of the suit where it then wrapped around to the rear.

"Star is about my size so choose any of these," she ordered and heaved three at her. "Wait. This is my favorite bikini, but you can wear it today," she added and threw that as well. Star caught the top and held it up. The bottom was a thong.

"You wore this?" she asked.

"Only here, never at the beach. I'm a coward. Try it on. Go on," she urged and Star began to disrobe. Misty was already down to her bra and panties.

"Cat, I have this pair of shorts that matches my biggest bikini top," she added.

I stared at it.

"Unless you want to go topless," she added with a teasing smile.

I shook my head and took the faded pink top.

"It's going to be too small," I said. "It won't fasten in the back."

She thought a moment.

"We'll tie something to it. Here," she said and plucked a pink ribbon from the top of the dresser. "Just make a knot and it will work fine. It doesn't matter what it will look like. It's only us," she added.

Misty was already stepping into her suit. I looked at her with envy. She raised her eyebrows when she saw me staring.

"What?"

"I wish I had your figure," I said.

"What? Did you hear that? We're supposed to tell each other the truth," she reminded me.

"It is the truth," I said.

"I believe her," Jade said, picking out a suit for herself, another two piece, this one gold with a thong bottom. She started to get undressed and then stopped and looked at me. "Well?" she said. "Aren't you going to get into your bathing suit?"

"It's not a bathing suit," I moaned.

"It'll work, won't it? Later, we'll get you a real bathing suit and you can keep it here so your mother won't know," she added. Star laughed. She looked terrific in Jade's suit. What a beautiful figure she has, I thought. They all have beautiful figures. I'll look like a baby elephant out there and I can't swim either.

I stared at the shorts and top in my hands. I'll look so foolish in this, I thought. I was so ashamed of my figure that I was happy we didn't have as many mirrors at home.

"Can't I just watch you all swim?" I begged.

"No," Jade said firmly. She unbuttoned her blouse and pulled it off quickly. "You're one of us now. You do what we do. There'll be no exceptions, no excuses."

I looked down. I felt myself trembling.

"Jade," Star said. "Maybe just this one time it's okay if she doesn't want to…"

"No," Jade insisted, flashing fire back at Star. "This is the first big test for the OWP's. We need to do everything together," she asserted.

"Okay, okay. Stop fighting," I cried. "I'll put on the suit, I'll try to swim." I wanted to be part of the group more than anything, even if it meant drowning in Jade's pool, wearing nothing more than a tight pink bikini top.

I reached back, undid my bra and took it off. I quickly put on the top Jade had given me and, just as I suspected, it was about an inch too short in back. Jade stepped around and tied the ribbon, making it work.

"There," she said. "You survived. Put on the shorts and let's get to the water. I have suntan lotion out in the cabana. And music, too."

I hurried to slip into the shorts she had given me. They were snug, but they worked.

"Onward, OWP's," Jade declared.

"It won't take you any time at all to learn how to swim," Misty said, coming up beside me. "Don't worry about it."

"Thanks," I said and followed them out, thinking that after everything that had happened so far at Jade's house, swimming will be easy.

Except for a gardener working in the far corner of the property, I was grateful to see that there was no one else around. When I put my foot in the water, I realized the pool was heated. It was almost as warm as a bath.

"My mother keeps the water warmer than necessary,"

Jade explained. "I think she always did it to drive my father crazy. He was always complaining about how expensive it is. And she hardly ever goes swimming anymore."

She dove right in. Misty waded down the steps and Star followed behind her. Moments later they were splashing each other and laughing. I stood in the shallow end, my arms folded across my bosom, watching.

"Okay," Jade said, holding up her hand. "Let's help Cat."

She swam over to me and instructed me to get into deeper water and hold her hands. "Start kicking," she said. "Faster, harder. Kick! Make believe you're kicking your mother!"

Jade led me around the pool, walking backwards as I kicked.

"You cup your hands like this," Star showed me. Misty explained how to take a breath and turn your head and then take another breath.

"It's the way I was taught in physical education," she explained.

"Keep kicking," Jade cried. "Practice the breathing. Good."

She brought me into deeper water and then suddenly, she let go of my hands. I panicked and went under. When my head came up, they were all yelling for me to kick and move my arms. I gagged. In seconds Star's hands were around my waist. She held me above water for a moment.

"Let her go. She'll swim or drown," Jade said.

"Is that the way you learned?" Star countered.

"Practically," Jade said.

"We'll take it slower with her," Star insisted, and went back to leading me around, letting me go, taking hold of my hands and leading me around. Remarkably, she turned out to be the one with the most patience. Jade and Misty left the pool and sprawled out on lounges, watching Star teach me how to swim.

I did manage to swim a half dozen feet before we stopped to rest.

"You're learning," Star assured me, and we left the pool to join Jade and Misty at the lounges. Picking up the telephone beside her lounge chair, Jade called the maid and asked her to bring out lemonade and fruit for us.

"This is the best hotel I've ever been at," Star muttered as she lay back on a lounge.

I was so out of breath, I just sprawled on my back and looked up at the blue sky. I closed my eyes and drifted with the music Jade had turned on while Star and I were still in the pool. Their banter and laughter was like a lullaby putting me into a relaxed state. I didn't even hear them offer me some lemonade. The excitement, the swimming, all of it had left me more exhausted than I had imagined.

Almost a half hour later, Jade nudged me.

"We're breaking it up," she said. "Star's got to get back to help her granny and Misty promised to go to the movies with her mother tonight."

I sat up quickly. My face felt so stiff I thought it might crack.

"Ow," I said grimacing.

"Didn't you put on any sunblock?" Jade asked.

"No," I said.

"Brother. Okay, I have something that will help a little, a skin cream especially for after sun. There are *some* benefits to having a mother who heads a cosmetic company."

"Can you get me this great new lipstick?" Misty asked

as we started back for the house. "The one that makes your lips look like neon lights at night?"

"Absolutely. I have a few tubes. I can get whatever color you want."

Misty squealed with delight.

"Aren't we lucky to have each other," she cried.

As I dried my hair in Jade's bathroom, she made comments about how I could improve my looks. I stared at myself in her vanity mirror and wondered if it was possible for me to even resemble any of them in terms of being attractive. Maybe I could, I thought. Maybe I could be a lot more like them than I had ever hoped.

Before I knew it, it was time to leave and the limousine was waiting for us in front of the house. Misty had to be dropped off first because she was the closest. The driver then decided I would be next.

"The same corner?" he asked.

"No," I said, and gave him my address.

"That a girl," Star told me. "Once she sees you're going to be your own person, she'll back off."

"I don't know," I said, unable to hide my worry. It was one thing to act so brave in front of her and the others, but to face Geraldine when she was furious...I wasn't sure. She had a way of turning her eyes into gray, cold marbles and swelling her shoulders until she looked like a bird of prey. She had never spared the rod when it came to discipline either. I remembered one time when she hit me with the fireplace poker and gave me a black and blue mark across my right thigh that remained for nearly a month. And that was only because I had watched something on television she had expressly told me not to watch!

As the limousine drew closer, I felt my insides tighten

and tangle like a rusty old chain. It was actually hard to take a deep breath. My ribs seemed fragile enough to crack.

"Remember," Star said, "you've got rights. If you need help, you just call one of us. Okay?"

I nodded as the car pulled to the curb.

"So long. I had a great time," I told her. "Say hello to your granny for me."

"Don't worry, everything will be okay," she said and I closed the door. I stood there and watched the limousine drive off. Then I took a deep breath and headed for my front door.

When I opened the door, I was struck by the deep silence. There was no radio playing old music, no vacuum cleaner going, no water running. Perhaps Geraldine fell asleep in her chair, I thought as I stepped through the doorway.

The moment I crossed the threshold, I was hit with the straw end of a broom right across the back of my head. It caught me by surprise and off-balance, so that I fell forward, barely getting my hands out in time to stop myself from landing smack on my face.

Another swipe of the broom, however, caught me on the rear and I did sprawl forward.

"How dare you disobey me like this? How dare you!" she screamed. She hit me again, raising and lowering the broom with swift, sharp blows across my legs, my back, and my shoulders before I could crawl forward fast enough and get to my feet, screaming and covering my head.

"Stop!"

"Get up to your room. Get up there. I saw you get out of the limousine. Don't even try to lie to me."

She stood with the broom up on her shoulder like a baseball bat, her face flushed red, her eyes like two hot coals now.

"Look at your face, too. What were you doing there? Why are you so sunburned?"

"We went swimming," I said.

"Swimming? You don't know how to swim. Were there boys there, too?"

"No, no, it was just us and the girls taught me."

"Liar, filthy liar. After all I've been through with you to have you do this now. My heart is cracking," she said, shaking her head. She relaxed her shoulders and brought the broom around to serve as more of a cane than a rod. "Why did you disobey me? Why?"

"I want to have friends. They're my friends."

"Water seeks the lowest level," she muttered. "They're your kind now, is that it? All I've done with you, tried to teach you is wiped out, right? It's in the genes. It's in you. You're her all over again. I might as well give you over to Satan himself."

"My girlfriends are not bad. They're good. They're sensitive and concerned and we care about each other, more than our own families care about us. It's nothing like you think."

She whipped her eyes at me and filled them with such cold accusation, I couldn't help but look away. That just confirmed whatever ugly thoughts had blossomed like black weeds in her garden of fear and loathing.

"Get upstairs," she said. "You'll go without supper tonight."

"I don't care. I already ate," I muttered.

My angry words seemed to renew her energy. She lifted the broom again and started to swing it at me, but instead of backing up, I remembered Star's words of encouragement and stepped forward. Geraldine looked like she wanted to whip the skin off me, but I didn't retreat or cower as usual.

"Don't hit me again," I said firmly. "Stop it."

She froze.

I was holding my breath and even though my whole body was trembling, I held my ground. I glared at her, defiant, determined.

Then she shook her head, the tight, thin lines in her face softening.

"What's the use?" she asked herself as she lowered the broom. Her shoulders dropped like rocks in a pond. She sighed deeply, her body shuddering as if her heart had truly cracked. "You can't change what's been there since birth. It was foolish of me to even try, to ever hope."

"What's been there since birth? What are you talking about? Tell me!" I screamed.

She turned away as if I wasn't even there and headed toward the kitchen.

"I want to know more," I called after her. "I want to know the truth, all of it. I've got a right to know and you have to tell me."

She paused and looked back at me. I never saw her look so small and tired.

"You want to know the truth?" she asked, and laughed coldly. "The truth is you're truly your mother's daughter. That's the only truth that matters in this house."

She continued down the hallway.

"That's not enough. I want to know it all," I cried. She ignored me and went into the kitchen, closing the door behind her. I stood there a moment, my body shaking so much it made my teeth chatter. I embraced myself and took a deep breath. Then I went up to my room and closed my door behind me. A terrible silence rained down around me. I couldn't even hear her running water or clanging pots below. She was probably still fuming, standing there and staring at the kitchen door.

We were both shut up in our own nightmares, and lived in the same house filled with only horrid memories, I thought. Surviving them seemed to be all that mattered now. That was the only thing that really held us together. It certainly wasn't love.

Love probably never set foot on our doorstep, and if it had and come in, it would have looked around once and fled. Which was exactly what I felt like doing.

4

A Hidden Past

Geraldine didn't call me to dinner and I didn't leave my room until nearly nine o'clock. I knew she would either be listening to music, watching one of her television evangelist programs, or just dozing in her chair. I was surprised to discover she had gone up to bed. I welcomed the quiet and made myself a hot chocolate.

While I sat there, I thought about the way the girls had reacted to my secret and my ignorance concerning my past. Perhaps I should take Jade's assignment more seriously, I thought. I listened hard for the sounds of Geraldine moving about her room, but heard nothing. Then I rose, quietly put my cup and saucer into the dishwasher and went into the pantry. I turned on the light and looked up.

There was a storage area in a crawl space that was entered through a small square door in the ceiling of the pantry. On occasion I had heard Geraldine make references to it, but I couldn't recall ever seeing her open the little doorway and go up there for anything.

Now, I gazed up at it and considered. In no other room in the house, save my parents' bedroom, could anything like old documents, pictures, whatever, be stored. I had never gone into Geraldine's closets, of course, but my suspicions centered on the crawl space. We had a stepladder in the garage. I went out there and, as quietly as I could, began to bring it into the house. It was awkward going through doorways, and I knocked it against the doorjamb in the kitchen.

My heart stopped and started slowly as I listened hard for sounds that Geraldine might have heard something and gotten up to see. She often slept with an ear open for burglars because we had no alarm system. The house creaked as the ocean breezes whipped in from the sea, but I didn't hear any footsteps or any doors opening.

Feeling safe, I continued to the pantry, set up the ladder, and climbed to the ceiling. The crawl space door seemed stuck in place. As I suspected, it hadn't been opened for a very long time, maybe even years. It was difficult pushing on it without making any noise, and at one point, I almost slipped off the ladder.

Finally, the little door cracked open and gave way to my efforts. It had to be slid to the side. I practically inched it along, trying to keep the smallest sound muffled. When I looked up, I realized there was no light, so I had to go back down the ladder to a cabinet under the sink and get the flashlight. The batteries were dead. Everything in this house seemed to be conspiring against me, trying to prevent me from finding any trace of my own past. Fortunately, Geraldine's obsessive attention to household inventory paid off because there was a supply of fresh batteries in the drawers assigned to tools and hardware. I quickly got the flashlight working and returned to the ladder, practically tiptoeing my way up.

The beam of light revealed a wall of cobwebs on every side of the opening. The dust was so thick that it looked like a second layer of wood. But there, to my right, were several cartons tied up with thick string. None of them were labeled. Once again, I descended the ladder, this time to get a utility knife to cut the strings around the cartons. I went back up and, completely disregarding the cobwebs and dust, pulled myself into the crawl space and, on my hands and knees, approached the cartons.

I sat there for a moment, my whole body trembling, and listened once more to be sure I had not been discovered. It was very quiet. Even the creaking in the house seemed to have stopped as if the house itself was now holding its breath. I brought the knife to the nearest carton and cut the strings. Then I opened the carton and directed the flashlight's beam into it.

Neatly packaged, each item wrapped in cellophane, were old toys, toys for a little girl: small dolls, doll's clothing, teacups and dishes, toy furniture and a dollhouse that had been carefully taken apart. I lifted each thing out of the carton carefully and inspected it. Someone had painted tears on the cheeks of some of the doll's faces. I could tell they were painted because the tears were uneven. The face of one doll was smashed in as though someone had taken a hammer to it.

Were these dolls once mine? None of them looked familiar. Were they Geraldine's? Why were they hidden away like this? It was as if someone's childhood was to be kept secret or buried forever.

I went to the carton on my right and cut the strings, again slowly opening it and shining the light down again to see items wrapped in cellophane, only this time, the box was full of clothing. I took one article out of its packaging and held it up. It was a light yellow dress for a toddler. I went to the next garment and the next, taking each out and inspecting it to discover the same thing: clothing for a very small child. They all looked new, never worn. Whose clothes were these? Mine? Geraldine's? Why were they all stored up here instead of being given away or even thrown away, which was what Geraldine usually did with old discarded things?

I turned and slid over to my left to open the next carton, cutting the strings faster and pulling up the lids. Here I found what I would call mementoes: snippets of pretty ribbons, jeweled combs, charm bracelets for a very tiny wrist, a pair of bronzed baby shoes, a cigar box full of old pictures, and a hand-painted jewelry box that was also a music box. It didn't play anything when I opened it because it needed to be wound. I was happy about that. The music might have woken Geraldine. Everything was neatly wrapped in cellophane as well. Whose things were these?

With even more trepidation now, I turned to the last carton. I undid the strings and opened it slowly. On top was a baby's crib blanket with a scented soap placed on it. I took it out carefully and laid it aside. Underneath was a small stack of envelopes tied with thick rubber bands and nothing else. The rubber bands practically fell apart before I slipped them off. There was no address on the front of any of the envelopes, no name. They were originally pink, but time had faded them so they were a light cream color. All of them had been opened.

I took out the letter in the top envelope and unfolded it.

Dear Cathy, it began, and I sucked in my breath. Who had written to me?

> *I know you won't read my letters until you are much older than you are now. My daughter Geraldine has promised me that when you are old enough to understand, she will be sure to give you my letters. Also, by the time you are given them, you will, she assures me, be told the truth about your birth.*
>
> *What a funny way for a mother to introduce herself to her own child, but that's what these letters are meant to do. All these years before you have these letters in your hands, you will have thought of me as your grandmother. I can't begin to tell you what a strange feeling it has been and will continue to be for me to have you call me Grandmother and for me to pretend you are my granddaughter and not my daughter. I hope I can eventually get you to understand why it had to be this way.*
>
> *The most wonderful thing for a mother to do is give her daughter the benefit of her own experience and wisdom. It is really the only legacy that matters. I feel certain that money won't be a problem for you, so inheriting my jewelry or assuming the trust fund I have set aside to be given to you on your eighteenth birthday is just window dressing when it comes to the real things a mother can give a daughter.*

Trust fund? I thought. Geraldine never mentioned any trust fund to me. When was she going to do that? I had only a year to go to my eighteenth birthday. I returned to the letter.

Let me begin by telling you the first honest thing since you have been given the truth about yourself. I never had a good and happy marriage. I married for all the wrong reasons. My mother used to parade around me when I dressed for parties and chant, "Remember, sweetheart, it's just as easy to fall in love with a rich man as it is with a poor man." She had me believe that falling in love was something you had complete control over, and you could direct your deepest emotions in the direction you wanted, any time you wanted. She would laugh at the very idea that love happened miraculously, bells rang in your head or in your heart, that you could look across a room and see a perfect stranger and suddenly feel your very soul blossom with happiness. All that, she told me, was just poppycock. That was her favorite word for most things she denied or disbelieved: poppycock. It was her father's word. I hated it, hated to hear it, but I never said so to her face.

You couldn't have found a more obedient child. I was brought up in a household that was probably closer to a little monarchy than anything else. My father was the king and my mother was the queen and I was merely one of their subjects. When one or the other made a pronouncement, it thundered with godly weight on my little shoulders. My father believed that fear comes first and then, almost as an afterthought, there was love. He wanted me to be afraid of him, and he got what he wanted.

All this is preparation for telling you why I did what you will have a hard time understanding...why I gave you away. Oh, I suppose I didn't give you away as much as I shifted you to another place in our family. I knew I couldn't raise you as my daughter, yet I couldn't stand the thought of you living with complete strangers. I wanted to be able to see you whenever I wanted to see you, as many times as I wanted. Pretending to be your grandmother gave me the opportunity to show love and affection for you, something I could never have done otherwise. I hope that I'm going to be able to do that for a long, long time and one day, after you have read my letters, I hope we can meet somewhere, just the two of us, and I can hug you the way a mother should hug her daughter and you might learn to hug me as a daughter would hug her mother. Maybe that's a fantasy. We don't realize how precious and how rare fantasies can become as we get older and are forced to admit to cold realities.

Another reason I gave you to Geraldine is that Geraldine has been a more obedient daughter to my husband and me than I was to my father and mother, and I knew she would do everything she was told to do as she was told to do it. I suppose my husband and I were no better than my parents, running our family just like the monarchy in which I was raised. At least, that was how we behaved toward each other.

Geraldine is very different from me. She's more like my husband, but sometimes I think she's better off the way she is because I've suffered in ways she'll never experience. She has never truly loved and lost, not in the passionate sense of those words.

I have, and if you're reading this letter, you're probably old enough to conclude even before I tell you, that the man I loved, truly loved passionately, was your real father.

I'm looking at the clock now and I see the time it's taken me to write these thoughts. I'll have to stop for now. The man you know as your grandfather is calling for me. We're on our way to one of his business dinners and they're always so important that we can't be a minute late.

I guess I should have started writing this earlier, but (and you might find this either amusing or interesting) I looked at myself in the mirror and I suddenly saw you. I saw myself in your face and I thought what if all this time goes by and we never look at each other truthfully? It put such a pang of fear in my heart that I sat right down and began writing.

Of course, I'll write again and again. For now, I'll have to hide this letter, just as I've had to hide my real feelings. My fingers tremble as I sign this.

Love,
Mother

I sat there with the letter in my hands for a moment and then looked back over the other cartons. All these things must have been things she had given me, but I didn't recognize any of it. Geraldine kept them from me, I realized.

Surely, that was so, but why keep toys and blankets, combs and jewelry from me?

Suddenly, I heard a noise below, a loud clap of wood. My heart jumped. I turned and looked down through the crawl space door. My ladder! It was gone! I heard it being carried away.

"Mother!" I screamed. "Mother!"

She had taken the ladder back to the garage. A few minutes later, she appeared in the pantry. She was in her robe and slippers and she looked up at me.

"Why did you take away the ladder?"

"Who told you to go up there?" she replied instead.

"I wanted to see what was up here," I said. "How am I supposed to get down?"

"Since when do you go sneaking around our home like this? Since when do you go and do something without first asking me? I'll tell you since when, since you started with that psychotherapist and those wicked girls. You go and disobey me and go swimming and who knows what, and then you come home and go snooping. You think that's all just some coincidence? Huh? I don't. I told you this would happen. I warned you."

"Bring back the ladder," I pleaded. "How am I supposed to get down from here?"

"You wanted to be up there. Be up there," she said, turning away.

"It's scary up here. I can't stay up here. Stop it," I shouted.

She paused in the doorway to look up at me.

"You made your bed for the night. Sleep in it," she said.

"Wait," I called. "What are these things? Why didn't you ever give me these letters?"

She turned again and without replying, put out the pantry lights and walked out, closing the pantry door behind her.

"Mother!" I shouted, and then I looked down at the letter in my hands and screamed, "Geraldine!"

I waited, but she didn't return. Opening all the cartons and crawling about up in this tiny storage space had stirred the thick dust. It made me cough and sneeze and feel dirty all over. I leaned over the little doorway and directed the flashlight through the door. It looked to be at least ten feet to the floor. I'd have to lower myself carefully, hold on with my hands and then try to drop to my feet. How stupid. What did she think I would do, stay here until morning?

I put the letters back into the carton and closed it. Then I started to position myself at the top of the crawl space doorway. It was impossible to hold onto the flashlight at the same time. I debated dropping it to the floor below, but imagined it would break, so I decided to stuff it into my blouse. After I did that, I began to lower myself through the now very dark opening. My heart was thumping so hard, I thought I might lose my breath and fall. My fingers didn't seem strong enough to grip the sides. This is so crazy, I kept telling myself. Why did she do this?

I turned my body and with my legs shaking, continued to lower myself through the opening. With the full weight of my body on my hands and wrists, my fingers slipped badly and I felt splinters gouge into my skin. I lost hold with my left hand, and my right just seemed to fly off the wood. Screaming, I fell downward and hit the floor awkwardly, my left foot hitting first, twisting under my body and getting caught under me. I actually heard the bone snap.

My head hit the floor hard enough to roll stars through my eyes and send a sharp ache down the back of neck and shoulders. I lost my breath, gasped, and pulled my left leg out from under me but I was so full of pain, I couldn't breathe fast enough. I must have blacked out for a few seconds or even a full minute. When my eyes opened again, I saw only darkness. My ankle seemed to have a mouth of its own and screamed pain up my leg.

"Mother!" I cried. "Help me!"

Crying, I pulled myself forward. I tried, but it wasn't possible to stand on my ankle. I reached into my blouse and pulled out the flashlight. Then I dragged myself toward the door. Practically crawling and sliding through it, I braced myself on the kitchen counter and screamed again and again for her. The pain filled my eyes with hot tears that streaked down my cheeks.

Finally, the lights went on in the hallway. I heard her footsteps on the stairs and moments later, she appeared in the kitchen doorway, her hands on her hips, scowling.

"What are you howling about?"

"I fell," I cried. "I fell and I think I broke my ankle!"

She gazed down at my foot quickly.

"Nonsense," she said.

"No, it's not nonsense. I heard it crack. Why did you take away the ladder?" I shouted at her. "How could you do that? My foot feels like it's blowing up like a balloon."

She shook her head and went to the refrigerator.

"All you need is some ice on it," she said, without even looking at my foot.

She scooped out some cubes and put them in a plastic bag.

"Here," she said, thrusting it at me. "Put this on it and go to sleep. This is what comes of being disobedient.

Maybe now you'll listen and stay away from those nasty girls who poisoned you."

She turned and started away.

"It's not just swollen, I tell you. It's broken. I heard it snap."

She didn't turn back.

"Let's see how it looks in the morning," I heard her say. "If you can't get upstairs, sleep on the sofa in the living room."

I heard her footsteps on the stairs and then all was quiet, except the ringing in my ears and the screams caught in my throat. Hopping and pulling myself along, I did make it to the living room where I flopped on the sofa. I pulled off my shoe and put the ice on my ankle, but it didn't relieve the pain. All night I moaned and cried until sometime before morning, I fell asleep. When I opened my eyes, she was standing over me, gazing down at my ankle. It was all purple and swollen.

"Maybe it is broken," she decided. "Sit up and I'll help you get into the car. I guess we'll have to go to the hospital emergency room. This is a fine thing, a fine way to start a new day," she muttered, "and all because you're associating with sick people."

I was in too much pain and too tired to argue with her. She let me lean on her as we made our way to the car. Once inside, I closed my eyes and leaned against the door. She muttered her stream of complaints all the way to the emergency room. When we arrived, she went inside first and an attendant brought out a wheelchair for me. It took almost an hour for anyone to look at me and then I was sent for X-rays and it took another two hours before the doctor came to see me. All the while Geraldine sat in the waiting room with me, shaking her head at the magazines displayed on tables around the room.

"What if a child comes in here? They could read or look at any of these. Just look at this picture of this actress in her nightgown. She might as well be naked. You can look right through it and see what she had for breakfast."

I was still in too much pain to really listen or reply, but I saw the way the other patients were gaping at her and listening to the things she said. They were all whispering to each other.

Finally, the nurse had me return to the examination room where the doctor had my X-rays up on the lighted screen.

"It's a fracture," he said. "Did you try to walk on this after you injured it?"

"Yes," I said.

"Hmm. Rotation is unstable," he said, examining my foot. "You'll need a long leg cast and you'll have to have frequent X-rays to avoid delayed discovery of disastrous displacement."

Geraldine groaned as if this was all happening to her instead of me.

"Doctors and medicine," she muttered.

"Pardon me?" the doctor said.

"Nothing," she mumbled, turning to me. "This is what you get being places you're not supposed to be."

"Oh. How did this happen?" he asked.

"I fell trying to get down from the attic," I lied.

He nodded.

"You'll be all right," he added, and called the nurse to start the preparations for my cast. After another three hours, we were on our way home and I had a cast and crutches. They had given me something for the pain, too, and I felt myself starting to drift in and out of sleep.

Either Geraldine finally stopped complaining about Doctor Marlowe, the girls, and me or I simply didn't hear her anymore. The medicine was kicking in and turning off my eyes, my ears, even my thoughts.

When we got home, she had to help me out of the car. Going up the stairs to my room was an ordeal, especially because I felt so bleary-eyed. She didn't have the strength to support me and I wobbled and made her scream. Somehow we managed, and I got into bed. Almost the moment my head hit the pillow, I was asleep, and when I woke up, I could see that it was nearly twilight. My stomach rumbled. I hadn't eaten anything all day. I groaned and started to sit up, forgetting the cast. It quickly reminded me this was not a dream.

As usual the door to my room was closed. I threw my leg and cast over the side of the bed and turned myself around, reaching for the crutches. After I caught my breath, I hobbled to the door and opened it.

"Mother!" I called. A moment later she was at the foot of the stairway.

"What?"

"I'm hungry and thirsty," I said.

"Fine. Now I'll become a maid. Go back to bed. I'm bringing up your supper," she said.

"Did anyone call me?" I called after her.

"No," she shouted.

She wouldn't tell me if they had, I thought. Why did I even bother to ask?

A little while later, she came up the stairs, each of her steps sounding heavier than the one before it. She looked out of breath, even pale when she came through my bedroom door carrying the tray.

"I can come downstairs to eat," I said. She nodded.

"Next time you'll have to. I guess I'm not as young as I was. Aggravation can age you years in minutes," she added, sending a sharp, cold look my way.

She put the tray down on my desk and I hobbled over to it and sat. There were two boiled eggs, jam and toast, a glass of prune juice and some Jell-O. Usually, she cooked chicken or fish.

"It looks like a hospital meal," I said.

"Complaints? You're lucky to get anything. All this is your fault. Don't forget that," she said, wagging her long, thin finger at me.

"How is it my fault, Mother? You took the ladder away. That was cruel and stupid."

She pulled her shoulders back.

"Don't you dare call me cruel and stupid!" she shouted. She paused, pressed her lips together and made her eyes small and hateful. "Anyway, after what you did, you deserved to be punished."

"What did I do that was so terrible?" I cried, holding up my arms.

"Sneaking up there when my back was turned," she replied.

"Well, why didn't you ever give me those letters? And why are all those things hidden away in those cartons? Those things were all for me, weren't they? You never gave me any of them, did you?"

"No, and I was right not to. It was just her way to try to make up for her own sins by buying you things," she spat. That was followed by a cold smile. "She was hoping to buy your love, to get you to care more about her than you did me. It always worried her that you might," she added. "I knew that was a constant fear gnawing at her heart. Serves her right," she said with satisfaction in her smile.

"You hated your own mother?"

"No, I didn't hate her. I pitied her for her weaknesses," she said, quickly wiping the smile off her face.

"Why didn't you ever tell me I had a trust fund?" I followed, as I ate.

"What for? You can't touch it for another year," she replied.

"Still, I should have been told," I insisted. "How much is in it?"

"Oh, so now you're worrying about how much money you have, is that it?"

"No, but I'd like to know. Is that wrong?" I asked. I held the tears locked under my lids even though they were hot.

"When the time comes, you'll know," she said. "In the meantime, I'll look after the finances, thank you."

"Can't you tell me more about what happened?" I pleaded. I remembered what Jade told me to discover. "Where was I born, for example? Was it here in Los Angeles or did she go some place else to have me?"

She pressed her lips together tightly as if she was preventing her tongue from forming the answer.

"It was all a despicable mess. There's no need to rake up the dirty past and have to relive those months and weeks and days. Besides, what difference does it make? You're who you are now and you're here and that's that," she added. She took a deep breath as if her lungs were not giving her enough air on their own. Then she nodded at my tray. "I'll be back later for the dishes."

"It's my past," I said, pressing on. "I have a right to know it."

She stopped and pivoted back to glare at me.

"Right? You have a right? Who gives you any rights? I give you your rights, that's who. Who's had to suffer the most because of all this? I'm the one who had to suffer the most, not you. You were well-taken care of, weren't you? No orphanage for you even though you were born out of wedlock. No farming you out to strangers. You had a home with family right from the beginning, didn't you?"

"Family," I muttered bitterly. "Some family."

"I'll not be blamed for what he did. You could have come to me earlier."

"Oh, right," I said. "You wouldn't listen to anything that had the slightest relationship to that," I said. "You wouldn't even help me when I had my first period. He was the only one who ever pretended to care about me. That's why it all happened."

She shook her head.

"You were never this disrespectful before. It's surely those girls. They're like some sort of disease. Don't let me hear of you even talking to them, hear?"

"They are my friends," I insisted.

"We'll see," she said. She started out and stopped to look back at me. "We'll see."

She closed the door and left me choking on a piece of toast in my tightened throat. I drank some juice and pushed the plates away. I won't eat, I thought. That's what I'll do. I'll fast until she lets me talk to the girls.

An hour later she came in and saw that I had barely touched my supper.

"What's this waste of food?" she demanded. "You had to be hungry. You didn't eat all day."

"And I won't eat," I said, "not another morsel until you let me talk to Misty or Jade or Star when one of them calls me."

She stared at me a moment, almost with a look of amusement in her eyes.

"Is that so?" she said. She picked up the tray and started out. At the door she turned. "You're just like her," she said again, "selfish and stubborn. She got what she deserved and you'll get what you deserve. It won't be my fault. I have told you the right things. If you choose not to listen, you choose not to listen.

"I'll not bring up another meal. If you want to eat, go down and get it yourself. If you don't…" She shrugged. "You don't."

She closed the door again and it was quiet except for the heavy sound of her footsteps as she descended.

I hugged my pillow. The pain had returned. It thumped up my leg and added to my thick pool of misery.

I should have brought those letters down from the crawl space with me, I thought. Now it would be some time before I could go back up there and finally learn the differences between all the lies and the truth. That is if Geraldine didn't destroy them first.

I lay back and recalled the first letter. I had committed practically the whole document to memory. I replayed it in my mind. She sounded so regretful, so sorry, and so eager to have me love her. Why couldn't she have raised me? The world might have been so different for me. I wouldn't have had my father doing the things he had done to me. I wouldn't have Geraldine tormenting me with her anger and hate. The shadows would disappear.

What had I done to deserve this except be born? Right now, I thought, if I had been given the chance to decide, I would have said, no thanks. Leave me where I am. Keep your world, your earth, your air and water, trees and flowers. Let me stay here, behind some cloud waiting for another chance, the chance to really be someone's daughter instead of someone's mistake.

My first cry of life would have brought smiles instead of tears and worry.

Most of all, I would have known who I was right from the beginning instead of having to spend most of my life tracing the clues backward, through the darkness, behind the locked doors, into the vault that held my name under lock and key.

5

The Prisoner

Geraldine didn't stop by in the morning to see how I was. I heard her pass by my door on her way downstairs without even hesitating to see if I was up. I was very hungry, but very determined not to be treated like a child and a prisoner in my own home, shut off from friends. I rose and drank some water. Then I lay there waiting. Soon, I thought, soon she'll realize I'm serious about not eating unless she lets me have my friends and she'll come upstairs.

Instead of her footsteps on the stairway and in the hall, however, I heard her vacuuming below. I knew it could go on for hours and hours. Every day she went over the house from top to bottom. It was her whole life and I realized if I did what she wanted, lived the way she wanted me to live, it wouldn't be long before it would be my life, too.

Pouting, I folded my arms and hunkered down, glaring at the door. There was a continuous dull ache traveling up my leg. That, combined with the gurgling in my stomach, made me feel very uncomfortable. How did people like Ghandi do this? I wondered. How do you stop your body from screaming for food? Try as I would, I couldn't prevent myself from thinking about cereal and fruit, eggs, toast and jam, juice, cookies, all sorts of sandwiches. All of it paraded before my eyes. Things in my room even started to resemble foods. A ribbon on the dresser turned into a banana. Beside it, a sheet of paper became a slice of turkey.

Reluctantly, I got up and went to my door, opening it slightly. The vacuum cleaner was off. I heard a window being opened. She was airing out a room now. Soon, she could be washing the kitchen floor and it would be off limits for an hour or so until she was convinced it was dry. Then, I heard the phone ringing. I hobbled to the top of the stairway to listen.

"Hello," she said. She was quiet and then she said, "No, she can't talk on the phone," and cradled the receiver hard. It had to have been one of the girls, I thought.

"Mother?"

There was silence.

"Mother?"

The silence was louder. Then I heard the garbage can in the kitchen being moved. It was funny how I could identify every sound in this house. I had grown up with them as my listening vocabulary. I could be blind and I'd know exactly what she was doing her every waking moment.

I returned to my room, put on my robe, got the crutches, and made my way downstairs. She had just started to dip the mop into a pail with water and floor detergent when I appeared in the hallway.

She turned and straightened up when she saw me.

"Well, well. Has the princess finally put an end to her temper tantrum and decided to come down to apologize?" she asked.

"I don't think I have done anything I have to apologize for," I said.

She nodded.

"I'm not surprised."

"Was that phone call for me?" I asked.

"If you want something to eat, you better get it now. I'm about to do the floor," she replied instead.

"Someone called me, right?"

"No," she lied. "Are you getting yourself some breakfast or not? I don't have all day. I have to complete the pantry inventory that you failed to do, remember?"

"You can't stop me from having friends," I muttered, and made my way past her into the kitchen. I was only punishing myself by fasting, I thought. She wouldn't change her mind and nothing would be accomplished by my fasting except my self-destruction.

I fixed myself some breakfast and Geraldine went off to dust and polish furniture while I ate. Not more than twenty minutes or so later, the phone rang again. I tried to get myself up and to it before she reached it, but suddenly she was a sprinter and got there just as I put the crutches under my arm.

"Yes?" she said with annoyance. She looked at me.

"Who is it?" I demanded.

"She's fine," she said. "She had a little accident and has her ankle in a cast so she won't be able to go anywhere for some time. No, I'd rather not have anyone visiting her for a while," she added. "Thanks for calling."

"Is that Doctor Marlowe? Is it?" I cried, but she hung up. "Why didn't you let me talk to her?"

"There's no reason to talk to her anymore. She's got nothing to offer you. Just be obedient, get better, and fulfill your responsibilities," she added. "Don't dillydally over your breakfast either. I want to wash that floor. You dragged down a lot of dust from the crawl space," she concluded and walked off.

I stared at the phone. Later, I thought, first chance I get, I'll call Jade. I returned to my breakfast and finished. Then I went to the living room. She practically flew back to her pail of water and mop and began to wash the kitchen floor. I sat there thinking. I had to have the rest of those letters. How was I going to get back up and into that crawl space now? I'd have to get someone to do it for me, I thought. Fat chance of that. She'd never let anyone in this house.

The pain was still fresh in my ankle, thumping harder and longer, forcing me to take another one of those pills. Before I knew it, I was drifting off, sitting in the big cushioned easy chair. When I opened my eyes, I could feel that hours had gone by. The sun was covered by a sheet of gray clouds. It made the house seem so dark and cold.

I didn't hear Geraldine come into the room. For a few moments, I didn't realize she was sitting there, too. Her back was to me and she was just looking out the window. She was so still.

"What time is it?" I asked.

Slowly, so slowly, it was almost like a dream, she turned.

"Why?" she replied. "Do you have an appointment?"

"No, I just wondered how long I've been asleep," I said.

"It's nearly twelve-thirty. I'll make some lunch," she added, and started to get up. It seemed to take more effort.

She looked tired and weak, more fragile than I could remember. When she stood, she had to catch her breath and steady herself for a moment.

"What's wrong with you?" I asked.

"Nothing," she said quickly. "I have all the work to do by myself now, that's all."

"I can help with some things," I offered.

She stood there gazing at me. Her face was caught in shadows so I couldn't see her expression, but just by the way she held her shoulders, I knew she wasn't pleased.

"I didn't want to fall, you know. But I wasn't going to stay up there all night."

"I don't know what's gotten into you," she said.

"Nothing's gotten into me but a desire to know more about myself. Why are you so against that?"

"I've told you. It's not the sort of stuff you want to know."

"I should be the one to decide that. It's my past mainly."

"Your past," she said with a thin, brittle laugh. She stepped forward and I now could see the cold, steely glint in her eyes. "Let me tell you some of it so you'll understand whose past it really was. She used me. You can't imagine a mother using a daughter like that."

"Used you? How?"

"In the beginning she would take me along. She knew that way my father would never have any suspicions if she did that."

"Take you where?" I asked, trying not to seem too excited or interested, for fear she would stop.

"To her assignations. Oh, she didn't have just one lover, you know, no matter what she wrote in those ridiculous letters, those fantasies she wanted you to believe about the

80

great love of her life. It all started when I was young. She would take me along supposedly to see a decorator or an architect," she said with that brittle laugh tinkling again. "What sort of decorator or architect worked out of his bedroom, huh? We'd go to a toy store and she would buy me something to occupy me while she did her dirties. I would be told to wait in the living room while Mommy dearest went to consult about redoing our house. Don't you think I could hear them sometimes, could hear their disgusting noises?"

"Didn't you say anything to her?" I asked, practically in a whisper.

"I didn't know what to say. I was too young to really understand, and besides, I was brought up to be obedient, to speak only when spoken to."

"Your father never found out?"

"Not until much, much later, not until you," she said with such disgust it made me feel more like a big germ than a person. "Even when she was in her forties, she was still misbehaving, only now I knew exactly what she was doing and exactly whom she was doing it with," she added, and started out of the room.

"But..."

"Stop," she commanded, spinning around on me. "Don't you see why I don't want to talk about it? It's better you never knew her as your mother. Who wants a mother like that? A slut, a tramp, a whore!" she screamed.

She stared at me a moment and then took a few steps back toward me.

"Why did I hide those things up in the crawl space? I'll tell you why. They're all spoiled, contaminated by her filthy hands, her pathetic attempts to make herself seem like the victim. Poor Lea," she said, wagging her head and twisting her lips, "poor, poor dear Lea forced into a horrible marriage with a handsome, wealthy, and respected man who only gave her the best things and tried to make her happy. Poor Lea with her servants and big house and cars and jewels and furs. Poor, poor Lea was denied...what?"

"Love?" I suggested, thinking about the letter I had read.

"Oh, love." Her sardonic smile wilted to be replaced by her dark look. "You don't go looking for love in the back of automobiles or in the bedrooms of strange men. Love is something that is nurtured, something that grows with time."

"Maybe she couldn't do that with a forced marriage."

"Nonsense. Any woman who is decent at heart and has respect for the right things can do that."

"You didn't want to get married, did you?" I pointed out. "That was forced on you."

"I did what had to be done," she said, straightening her shoulders firmly. "Thanks to her, I had to make great sacrifices, but I didn't do it for her. I did it for my father who didn't deserve being embarrassed and disgraced."

She paused to take a breath. It looked like she was in pain doing it.

"All right? Are you satisfied now? Can you appreciate me now? Will you be obedient?" she asked.

"I just want to have friends," I moaned.

"You will, but proper and normal ones. We don't need to bring any more turmoil into our lives, Cathy," she said with such a reasonable soft tone of voice that I had to look up. "It's just the two of us, now. Leave the ugly world out there and leave the ugly past where it belongs, buried," she pleaded.

I looked down. Maybe she was right, I thought wearily. Maybe my mother was loose and reckless and maybe I would become like her if I didn't listen. I had to agree that it certainly wasn't right to take your own daughter along when you met secretly with some lover.

"Won't you tell me where I was born," I begged.

"She went to our winter house in Palm Springs and stayed secluded there until you were born. Then you were left with a nurse for almost six months before Howard and I legally adopted you. My father fixed it all. It broke his heart, but he did what had to be done because he was a man of strength."

"So you know who my father was," I said.

"No," she said quickly, too quickly, I thought.

"But you said you knew what she was doing and with whom."

"Your father could be any one of a number of womanizers, I'm sure," she said, but I didn't think she was telling the truth. "Now let me go make us some lunch," she said. "It makes me feel disgusting even talking about this," she added and left the room. It was as if she had drawn out all the air with her.

I sat back, pondering it all. Should I believe everything she had told me? I still wanted, needed, to read those letters, I thought. The woman who wrote the first one couldn't be all that bad, could she?

Geraldine called me to lunch and I sat and ate a ham and cheese sandwich. I knew it had too much mayonnaise on it, but I was afraid to criticize her. All I had to do was complain about eating too much fat and calories and she would accuse me of obsessing about my figure and being attractive.

Could I be attractive? I had seen many pictures of the

woman I had believed was my grandmother when she was younger. She was a very pretty young woman. Did I resemble her in any way? Couldn't I be pretty, too?

"Our mother was very attractive though, wasn't she?" I asked. It was the first time I called her "Our mother." "Especially when she was younger."

"No. She distorted her good looks with all that makeup she wore."

"But she was pretty underneath."

Reluctantly, she agreed. To get her to say anything nice about our mother was like pulling teeth.

"Wasn't there ever a time that you liked her, loved her?" I asked.

"You won't stop talking about all this, will you?" she fired back at me.

"It's just natural for me to want to know," I said.

She thought a moment and sat back, nodding slightly.

"Of course I loved her when I was a little girl. What did I know? I was never once disrespectful to her, even afterward, even when I had..."

"What?"

"Had to pretend you were some strange baby. She would come to the house and stand beside me and gaze at you in your crib and talk about you as if you were someone else's child. I was supposed to pretend and go along with the whole effort to keep her reputation lily white, and I never once spit the truth back at her. It was on the tip of my tongue to do so, but I didn't. I swallowed all that bitterness and anger.

"Once, I saw my father sitting in his office, looking weak and crumbled. He didn't know I was looking in on him, and I thought: she's done this to him. She's taken a strong tower in the community and turned him into this shadow of himself. That was your real mother, a Delilah, a betrayer. You want to claim her? Go ahead, claim her and be damned with her," she said.

"I just want to know about it all," I moaned.

"Eat the apple, eat the fruit? The Lord said not to, but no, weak and foolish, we eat the fruit. We have to know the evil and then we suffer," she declared, and rose to take the dishes to the sink. It seemed to be more of an effort for her than ever.

"I can do that," I said.

"On crutches? You're sure to break something, but don't worry. As soon as you're able, I'll give you things to do. You'll make up for this," she threatened.

I sat there and watched her work. Did the bitterness she felt ever stop? Did she ever have a soft moment when she regretted the shape her life had taken? Was she ever sorry for all the hate and anger she threw back at our mother?

Not once, I realized, did she ever want to visit the grave site, not even to pay respects to her father. Surely, there were early memories she cherished. She couldn't want to bury everything.

My musings were interrupted by the sound of our doorbell. We both froze for a moment. Despite the legal agreement, we both lived with the fear of my father returning, defying the judge's decree. She wiped her hands on a dish towel.

"Probably one of those door-to-door solicitors trying to sell people something worthless," she decided. "I'll make short shrift of them."

Suddenly with real vigor and enthusiasm, she charged out to fulfill her mission. She actually liked being nasty to people, I thought. It reinforced her philosophy, her way of life, her conviction that most everyone and everything out there was horrid and deserved to be treated this way.

"We'd like to see Cathy," I heard Misty say, and I nearly forgot I had a cast on my leg.

I rose to my feet as quickly as I could and scooped the crutches under my arm.

"She can't see anyone," Mother told her.

"No," I screamed.

I had just stepped out of the kitchen and into the hallway as she was closing the door on Misty and Star. I was sure they had heard me and caught a glimpse of me because both their faces looked shocked for that instant.

She locked the door.

"Let them come in," I cried. "Mother, please. You'll see how nice they are."

"The nerve of them coming here unannounced like that. It proves what I've been saying. What sort of decent young lady would just barge in on someone, huh? No sort," she replied.

"Stop it. Let them in," I demanded, and made my way toward the door.

She stepped between me and the door, her eyes narrowed, her shoulders hoisted like some bird of prey about to pounce.

"Don't you dare open this door and call to them. Don't you dare disobey me. In fact, you get yourself upstairs and into your room for being insolent. Go on," she said, pointing her boney finger at the staircase. "Go."

"No," I said, and she stepped forward and slapped me sharply across the face.

It took all my strength to keep from falling to the side, but I managed.

"Don't you dare say no to me. Don't you dare. Go on!" she screamed. "Get upstairs."

I glared at her a moment. How ugly and twisted she looked to me now. How could I ever have called her Mother? Maybe, I thought, if I get upstairs and into my room quickly enough, I could open the window and call to them. I went up as fast as I could, but by the time I got to the window, there was no sign of either of them. It brought tears of frustration to my eyes. I lay my forehead against the glass and sobbed. Then I heard my door click shut. I spun around just as Geraldine turned the key in the lock.

"You can't keep me a prisoner. I will have friends!" I shouted. "I will. I will," I sobbed.

Weak and tired, I sank slowly to the floor and leaned against the wall. I shut my eyes and in moments, I was asleep.

I woke in pitch darkness. The clouds had thickened all afternoon and now it was raining steadily, the drops pinging against the window, sounding like someone tapping her fingernails against the glass. A streak of lightning lit the room for an instant and I remembered where I was and what had happened. Struggling to my feet, I leaned on my crutches and made my way to the night table to turn on my lamp. Then I sat on the bed and gazed at the clock. It was nearly nine. She hadn't bothered calling me to dinner. It was probably her way of punishing me further for daring to defy her.

Anger boiled inside me. I could feel it popping bubbles like a tar pit. I'm going down those stairs, I decided, and I'm going to call Jade this minute and she can't stop me. If she strikes me again, I'll hit her with my crutch. Fuming and refusing to be tired and defeated, I reached for the doorknob. Amazingly, it was unlocked.

I was surprised to see that there was no hall light on. It was too early for her to put the house to sleep, I thought. However, there wasn't even a light on above the stairs, something she insisted on having on in case she had to go downstairs for something during the night.

I found the switch and turned on the lights. Then I stood there, listening. It was deadly quiet, not a glass tinkling, no television or radio on. When I looked down the stairs, I saw that all the lights appeared to be off as well. Maybe she has gone to sleep already, I thought. Good. I didn't want to have to face her now anyway and I could call Jade without her knowing. I hated turning myself into a sneak, but it was her fault, not mine, I thought.

I started down the stairs, moving as quietly as I could, despite the crutches. However, the steps creaked. They were her steps, I thought, sentries reporting my whereabouts. I paused to listen, but I didn't hear her coming out of her room so I continued down. When I reached the bottom, I decided not to turn on any more lights.

I started down the corridor, barely permitting the crutches to tap on the floor. However, something unusual caught my attention as I started past the living room door. It was just a quick glimpse out of the corner of my right eye, but it made me hesitate. I listened again and then I returned to the doorway and peered into the living room.

A lamp was turned over on the table. Why? She would never permit such a thing, I thought, and stepped into the living room. I went to the standing lamp by the easy chair and turned it on. The light that lifted the darkness revealed her feet first. They were twisted and turned.

"Mother?" I edged forward. "Geraldine?"

When I came around the big coffee table, I saw her sprawled on her right side on the floor, an arm up against the side of the table, her face turned toward me, her jaw twisted as if she was trying to get something out from between her teeth, and her eyes wide-open but glassy.

For a moment I couldn't breathe; I couldn't move. I stared at her in disbelief.

"Mother?"

Slowly, with some difficulty, I lowered myself and reached for her hand. The moment I touched it, I knew she was gone. It was cold and the fingers were a little stiff. I drew my own hand back as if I had touched a hot stove, and gasped.

"Mother?"

My stomach felt as if it was doing flip-flops. I had to touch her again, to nudge her at the hip. Her body shook and her arm fell from the side of the table and hit the floor hard. Nothing else moved. She seemed to be staring angrily at me, accusing me. I could see her tongue was purple and her lips were blue.

"Oh, my God," I cried, and struggled to get to my feet. Nervous and shaky, I fumbled with the crutches and actually fell backward before I recovered and stood up. I stared down at her. Panic had nailed my feet to the floor and even the thought of taking a step seemed impossible. Finally, I turned away. For a few moments I headed in one direction and then another, spinning, crying, calling out for help. I knew I should get right to the phone and dial 911, but something kept me from doing it. Instead, I wandered mindlessly up and down the corridor, into the kitchen to the small den, back to the corridor and even to the foot of the stairs. For a few seconds, I contemplated returning to my room and crawling into bed.

I was afraid to look at her again. I diverted my eyes every time I passed the living room doorway. Then I started for the front door. I'll scream for help, I thought. I opened the door, but when I looked out at the night and the passing cars, I froze and stepped back, closing the door.

She's dead, I told myself. Geraldine's dead. Mother's dead. I'm all alone. How did she die? What happened to her? I thought I heard a sound from the rear of the house, the sound of the back door closing. Was it my father? Had he returned? Maybe he had been here and they had fought and he had hit her and killed her!

My blood turned to ice water. Once again, I couldn't move a muscle. I listened hard, but all I heard was the sound of the wind and some passing cars. Carefully, slowly, I made my way back to the kitchen and looked at the back door. It was shut tight and locked just the way she always kept it. No one could have gone out through it. That relieved me, but I was still shaking all over. What was I supposed to do? She was gone. I was alone.

Finally, I went to the phone, but not to call 911. Instead, I called Jade. She answered after only one ring.

"Hello."

"Jade, it's me. Cathy," I said in a hoarse whisper.

"Cat. How are you? Misty and Star told me what happened today. I was just on the phone with both of them, trying to decide what we would do next. She can't keep you locked up in there. I called Doctor Marlowe, too, and she said she had called and your mother told her you had some kind of an accident. What accident?"

"I fell and broke my ankle," I said.

"How did that happen? So she let you use the phone at

least, or are you doing it behind her back? Cathy? Are you still there?"

"Jade..."

"What's wrong? Tell me," she demanded. "We're your sisters. Cathy? We're here for you. You can trust us."

My throat seemed to have shut down. I couldn't get enough breath out to speak. I couldn't swallow. The tears were frozen at my lids. My hand shook terribly as I held the receiver to my ear.

"Cathy, talk to me. Cathy?"

"She's gone," I finally said.

"Who is? Cathy?"

"She's lying on the floor in the living room," I whispered as if I was afraid she would hear me even in death and be angry I had told someone about her.

"What?"

"She's dead, Jade. My mother, Geraldine, my sister, she's dead," I finally managed to say.

"What do you mean, dead?"

"I came downstairs and found her on the floor in the living room. She's dead. She died while I was upstairs asleep."

"Are you sure?" she gasped. "Maybe she's just asleep."

"No, she's not just asleep. She's cold and her eyes are stuck."

"Her eyes are stuck? You're not making sense. Did you call anyone, the police, 911?"

"No."

"How did she die?"

"I don't know," I whispered, actually looking around again.

"Was there any blood?"

"No, I don't think so. I'm not sure. I didn't really look at her."

"Maybe she's not dead then, Cathy."

I spun around because a rippling sensation at the back of my neck gave me the terrifying feeling that I wasn't alone.

"Cathy?"

"I don't know what to do," I continued in a whisper.

"All right. Stay calm. I'm on my way. I'll call the others, too."

"Should I call 911?" I asked.

There was a pause.

"Are you absolutely sure she's dead, Cathy? Are you?"

"Yes," I said. "I am."

"Then no," Jade said. "Don't call anyone yet. Just wait. I'll be right there. Don't worry. We're coming to help you, Cathy."

She hung up. I held the phone a moment and then I hung up and listened. The house was quiet. No one's here, I told myself. Be calm, I coaxed that part of me that wanted to scream. Then I went to get a glass of water and wait, my eyes turned inward, looking at a whirlpool of fear, spinning, spinning.

6

Burying Secrets

Jade was the first to arrive. When I opened the front door, she stood there gaping in at me, shocked by the sight of me in a cast and on crutches. I watched her limousine leave.

"Star told me she thought you were on crutches. How did this happen to you?" she asked, still not taking a step into the house.

"I was up in our crawl space looking through old cartons, searching for my past like you said I should when she discovered what I was doing and took the ladder away. I tried to get down and fell. I broke a bone in my ankle."

"She took the ladder away? Why?"

"To punish me for snooping," I said.

"And just left you up there? How cruel. Where is she?" she followed after a moment. We were still talking to each other in the doorway, but she gazed past me with tentative eyes as if she thought Geraldine might be lying right behind me in the hallway.

"In the living room. Like I said, I fell asleep upstairs. When I came down, the lights were all off. I found her on the floor," I said. "A lamp was overturned on a table, too."

"Really?" She gazed past me again. "You sure you're alone?" she asked. I knew what concerned her.

"Yes. I checked and the rear door is still locked."

"All right," she said, sucking in her breath, "show me."

I stepped back and she entered. I closed the door and led her to the living room. We both stood there looking down at Geraldine.

"I've never seen a dead person in person before," Jade said, impressed. "You're absolutely sure she's dead?"

"Touch her," I suggested. She stared a moment and shook her head.

"No, she looks dead enough." She stepped back and sat on the easy chair.

I continued to stare at the woman I had called Mother all my life, wondering why I wasn't feeling more sadness, why I wasn't bawling my head off. I guess it was because she still looked so mad at me, so mad at the world.

"Besides the lamp, were there any other signs of an accident or anything?"

I shook my head.

"You're looking at it all."

"Did you look at the rest of her?"

"Rest of her?"

"I mean, are you sure she isn't bleeding somewhere?" she asked with a grimace as if it put her in pain to even think about it.

I thought a moment and then went around behind Geraldine and lowered myself down.

"There's nothing," I said, and got back up.

"Maybe she passed out, fell, and hit her head or something," Jade muttered.

"Maybe. She wasn't acting right for days. I could see she was out of breath and even had some pain, but you know what I told you about her and doctors. She wouldn't ever admit to having a problem," I said. "She hated medicine and only took her herbal remedies. Actually, she was never very sick, but lately she looked pale to me often. Her lips are so blue," I added. "Otherwise she doesn't look so different. Her body's cold, of course," I rambled.

Jade raised her eyebrows, embraced herself, and looked toward the front door.

"Where are those two?" she asked, referring to Star and Misty. "There wasn't very much traffic. As soon as I hung up from talking to you, I called them and then I sent a cab for Star. Misty took her own cab. She's even closer to you than I am!"

I nodded and looked down at Geraldine.

"I tried to go on a fast in protest, but she didn't get frightened for me. I couldn't even last a day without food," I admitted.

"Protest? Protesting what?"

"Not letting me be friends with you, Star, and Misty."

Jade grimaced.

"She wouldn't let you be friends with us? What's wrong with her?"

"Nothing now," I said. I gazed at her. "She's dead."

Jade started to look a little pale to me, too.

"Are you all right?" I asked her.

"Me? Yes, of course. I'm just trying to stay calm and think straight." She clutched her hands and twisted her fingers a bit. "Where are they?"

"When I was up in the crawl space, I managed to read

one of my real mother's letters before Geraldine discovered me and took away the ladder. My real mother put a trust aside for me that I get when I'm eighteen. I never knew it," I said. "But then, there was a lot I didn't know, a lot I still don't know. I had to leave the rest of the letters up there. Maybe you can help me get them down now. We'll need the ladder, of course. It's back in the garage. Everything in this house has its proper place and must be returned to that place," I recited. Geraldine had drilled it into my brain.

Jade stared at me a moment and then looked back at Geraldine.

"She's actually dead," Jade said, shaking her head. "Wow." She stared a moment and then she looked up at me. "What? What about a ladder?"

I realized she hadn't heard a word I said.

We heard the doorbell ring.

"That must be Misty and Star," she said jumping to her feet. "Finally. Wait here."

She went out to let them in. I could hear them whispering in the foyer. They were there for at least a minute or so before they all appeared and gathered around me to look at Geraldine.

"Is she really dead?" Misty asked.

Star, unafraid, knelt down, lifted her wrist and felt for a pulse.

"She's gone for sure," she said. Without any hesitation, she moved Geraldine's head, looking through her hair and then the back of her neck. "No one hit her," she concluded. She looked up at me. "From what you told Jade about her being weak lately, I bet it was a heart attack."

"You have to have a heart to have a heart attack," Jade muttered.

"This is like a movie scene," Misty said. Her eyes were so wide that I thought her pupils might just pop out on tiny springs. "There'll be an investigation, the police, newspaper reporters, all of it!"

"Scare her some more why don't you," Star muttered, her ebony eyes brightening like hot coals. She stood up and looked at me. "How do you feel?"

I shook my head and embraced myself.

"The lamp was knocked over, but it's not broken. It's back where it belongs."

"What?" She looked at Jade who shook her head. "Cat, are you all right?" She reached out to touch my arm.

I shook my head.

"I feel numb," I said. "I don't even feel the pain in my ankle anymore."

Misty asked how I had broken my ankle and I repeated the story for them.

"What a mean thing to do to you," Misty said.

"I've got to go back in two days for another X-ray to be sure it's all healing right," I said, and laughed a thin, nervous laugh. "She thought they were just trying to run up a big medical bill. She didn't want to go back. Now, she doesn't have to."

I laughed again and that laugh became brittle, shattered, and turned into a sob. The sob ran on until I felt tears emerging. My whole body started to shake. Star put her arm around me quickly and helped me to the sofa. They all gathered around.

"Get her a glass of water," Star ordered Misty. She hurried out of the room. "You're going to be all right, Cat. Don't worry."

"I've been thinking a lot while I was waiting for you. Maybe…maybe it's my fault she's dead," I said, trying to swallow down a lump in my throat. Misty brought me the glass of water and I drank some quickly. "She got so angry at me. She was raging for the last couple of days. If she did have a heart attack, it's my fault," I insisted.

"No, no," Jade said, shaking her head. "She shouldn't have gotten angry at those things anyway. It's her fault. She probably ate her own heart out."

"Jade's right," Misty said. "My mother's always talking about stress making you sick and giving you wrinkles. That's what happened to your sister. She stressed herself to the point of breaking."

"She was meant to die," Star added. "It was her time. You can't blame yourself for that."

"I couldn't help with any of the housework and she hated that I made her relive the past. I kept asking questions she didn't want to answer. Telling me about the past was painful for her, too," I told them. Although they didn't look like they believed it or cared, they nodded as I spoke. It just felt good to keep talking so I related all the facts Geraldine had given me about our mother and her so-called assignations with different men. As long as I talked, I didn't cry.

"She should have told you everything years ago. You're not a child," Star said. "Granny says secrets can be like rats living in the closets of your heart, gnawing at you until you get sick."

"She got sick all right," Jade said, nodding at Geraldine's body.

"Who do we call?" Misty asked. "I mean, do we call the police first or an ambulance or what? Anybody know?"

"You call the police first," Jade said. "They have to investigate before they remove the body. It's an unattended death. Don't you watch any television?"

"You know I do," Misty said.

"They'll surely blame me," I said. "Maybe they'll want to put me in jail."

"That's silly, Cat. Stay cool," Star said.

She looked at Jade and Jade looked at Misty. Then they were all staring at me.

"More importantly, what's going to happen to Cat?" Star wondered aloud.

"Does your mother have any nearby relatives?" Jade asked.

I shook my head.

"There are some cousins, but they live on the East Coast I think. I don't even know their names."

"They won't care about her," Star said. "She's no more than a stranger to them."

"She can't call her adoptive father's family. That's for sure," Misty said.

Jade nodded.

"So what happens to her now?" Star asked. They were talking almost as if I wasn't even there.

"She's not eighteen yet," Jade said, putting on her official, adult face. "If there's no family to take her in, she'll go to foster care."

"What does that mean?" Misty asked before I could.

"It means she'll become a ward of the state and farmed out to some family until she's eighteen."

"You mean that she'll have to live with complete strangers?" Misty asked, astounded.

"No," Star said sarcastically. "They'll introduce her first. Of course, strangers. What do you think?"

"Oh," Misty said, turning to me. "Poor Cat."

"When she turns eighteen, her trust, all of it becomes hers and then she'll be on her own," Jade added, to soften the blow.

"Lotta good that does now," Star muttered. "She's got nearly a year to go."

Misty nodded and then looked back at Geraldine. When she turned to me again, I saw a new glint in her eyes.

"Who's your mother's, I mean your sister's closest friend?" she asked.

"She doesn't have any close friends," I said. "In fact, she doesn't have anyone I'd call a friend. She's never invited to anyone's home or invites anyone here. No one ever calls her. She has no one really."

"Had," Jade reminded us. "Had. She's gone."

"Besides," Star said, "just because someone might have been her sister's friend, doesn't mean they'd want to be responsible for Cat."

"I know, but what if…" Misty began, her eyes rolling as she shifted her feet and moved to the sofa, "we didn't tell anyone?"

"Huh?" Star said. "Didn't tell anyone what?"

"About…her," she said, nodding toward Geraldine's body. "From what Cat's saying, no one will miss her."

Star looked at Jade and me before answering Misty.

"You mean, keep her death a secret?"

"Yes, exactly. If no one knows she's dead, Cat doesn't have to be farmed out to foster care, right?"

"But…she *is* dead!" Star exclaimed. "How do you keep that a secret? Prop her up in the window? Misty, you do watch too much television."

"No, not exactly prop her up. One of us could parade around in her clothes once in a while so the neighbors don't get suspicious. If we need it, maybe we can get a wig that's close to her hair, too. I bet Jade's mother could get one for us."

"Oh, and what do I tell her? I need a wig to imperson-ate a dead woman?" Jade asked.

"No, you can say it's for a play or something. She won't check up on it, will she?"

"No, but—"

"Yes, we can do this," Misty said, getting excited. "Lis-ten, just listen for a moment," she insisted. "We don't tell the police and we help Cat. We can all take turns staying here. Why," she said, gazing around, "this house can be headquarters for the OWP's!"

Star looked at Jade who shook her head.

"What about money, stupid?" she asked.

Misty looked to me.

"Geraldine kept all our accounts up-to-date. I know where the books are. I know we have plenty of money in money market accounts, CD's, that sort of thing. She would talk aloud sometimes when she worked," I ex-plained, "lecture me about taking care of your own money yourself. She didn't even use an accountant. She did her own taxes. She said she learned all of it from her father."

"That's Geraldine, not you," Jade pointed out.

"No," I said. "I know a lot about it. I know I can copy her signature."

"Forgery?" Star looked at the others. "How do you know you can do that?"

"I did it a few times when I was too scared to show her something from school. No one questioned it. I would practice tracing it for hours and hours until I got it right. Many of the people who handle her banking and invest-ments never even saw her," I added, wiping my eyes free of tears. "She would speak to them on the phone or keep in contact with them through the mail. She hated going to their offices. It would mean she would have to tidy herself up and put on what she called a 'going-out' dress and spend money on gas."

"She doesn't have to spend it now," Star said.

"Yes, but Cat does. I don't know," Jade said. "What about your school when school starts up again? Won't they be wondering where she is?" she asked quickly.

I shrugged.

"She went with me at the start, but never again. They don't call the parents in. They send letters, sometimes make phone calls, but not often. They believe in handling all the problems themselves and not burdening the parents."

"You see!" Misty cried.

"I don't know," Jade repeated.

"What don't you know? It's a good idea, isn't it? Well? Isn't it?" Misty pressured.

Jade considered. Star watched her and waited. Then Jade turned and looked down at Geraldine.

"What about...her?"

"We bury her," Misty said, lifting her arms as if the answer was obvious.

"Bury her? Us? How? Where?"

Misty turned to me.

"What about your backyard?" she suggested.

"My backyard?"

"Yeah. Does anyone ever go there?"

"No, we're walled in and we don't have a gardener anymore. She thought it was an unnecessary expense," I said.

"Right," Misty said, "so the backyard will be perfect."

"Perfect? You're going to carry her out and bury her?" Jade asked incredulously.

"Well, not by myself. Star?"

"I suppose we could do it," Star said, musing. She

paused and turned sharply to me. "Do you have a Bible?" she asked me.

"Yes, right there," I said, pointing to it on the corner table by the sofa. "She read it often."

"What's a Bible have to do with anything?" Jade asked, her voice rising in pitch.

"I've been to enough funerals to know what to say. You read a psalm," she added. "Did she have a favorite?"

"I don't think so," I said.

"You're all crazy," Jade said. "We can't do this. We can't just bury her."

"Why not?" Misty asked.

"We can if Cat's got a shovel," Star said. "Do you have a shovel?" she asked me.

"In the garage," I said. "The shovels are kept along the wall, in their proper place."

"Get a clean bedsheet to use as a shroud," Star ordered.

"Wait," Jade said before I could move. "This is against the law, you know. You don't just bury someone without a death certificate."

"What choice do we have?" Star asked her. "You said yourself they'll send her away. Look at her, Jade. Do you want her to be forced to live with strangers. She had it tough enough as it was living here, didn't she?"

"Maybe we should talk to Doctor Marlowe," Jade suggested.

"What? You know as soon as you tell about her," Star said, nodding at Geraldine, "it's over. This is a secret we either all keep in here," she said, putting her right palm over her heart, "until the day we die, or not. Make up your mind now and forever, I say."

"I swear I'll never tell," Misty quickly agreed. "We can do a bond of blood or something, if you like."

Jade smirked.

"We don't need that silly stuff."

"It's not any sillier than what you did at your house with the candle," Misty countered, offended.

"We just don't need any ceremony," Jade said. "If we promise, we promise. Let me think a minute. You're moving too fast. This is so crazy." She turned to me. "Are you sure you didn't call anyone else?" she asked me, looking like she hoped I had.

"No. You were the only one I called. Who else would I call?"

She nodded. The other two watched her think.

"You really want to do this?" Jade asked me.

I looked down at Geraldine. She would be furious, I thought, but then I thought about the freedom and having the girls with me, all of us together, truly the family we coveted for so long.

"I think so," I said.

"Good," Misty chimed before I could have second thoughts. "We better get started. There's so much planning to do."

Star and Jade looked at each other and Star nodded.

"Well?" she asked her.

"Bury her ourselves? I'm wearing a Prada outfit," Jade moaned.

"So? If you ruin it, you'll buy another," Star replied. "We saw your closet, Jade. You probably have hundreds of outfits you haven't even worn yet anyway."

"What do we do first?" Jade asked, reluctantly.

"First we get the shroud and the shovel. I have the Bible here. Then we do the funeral," Star rattled off. She turned to me. "You get the bedsheet. I'll look for the shovel. Any lights out there?"

"No," I said.

"We'll need a flashlight."

"I just put fresh batteries in it," I said.

Jade raised her eyebrows.

"Fresh batteries? Wonderful." She studied me a moment. "Are you really all right with this?" she asked me.

I avoided looking down at Geraldine.

"I don't want to be sent anywhere," I said. "I'm tired of agencies and strangers."

"She's okay," Misty followed and put her arm around me to squeeze me and comfort me. "Stop driving her crazy."

"This isn't a game, Misty. I'm not kidding. It's illegal. We could all get into a lot of trouble. It's serious," Jade reaffirmed.

"I'm being serious," Misty cried.

"If we're going to do it," Star said, "let's do it or let's just all go home."

"No," I said quickly. "Don't go home. I don't know what I'll do. I'll run away. I'll—"

"All right, all right we'll do it," Jade declared. She took a deep breath and said, "Go get the bedsheet."

"I'll help you," Misty said, and followed me out. "You should make yourself a bed downstairs," she suggested as I worked my way up the steps. "At least until your ankle heals."

"Geraldine never liked the idea of anyone sleeping in the living room. She made me do it the other night but that was her way of punishing me."

"You're in charge of yourself. She's gone. She won't ever punish you again," Misty declared, almost gleefully.

I paused and looked down toward the living room.

"No, I suppose not, but if she could, she would send me to my room without supper, just for talking about this."

We continued up. I decided to take one of the bed-sheets from her bed, not mine. It seemed more appropriate to do so. When we entered Geraldine's bedroom, Misty gazed around, shaking her head with disapproval.

"It's so..."

"What?"

"Bland," she said. "And what's with that other bed? Why isn't it made?"

Geraldine's bed was made with the usual perfection, not a crease in the pillow or the spread, but my father's bed was stripped bare.

"It's where he slept. She wanted to feel he was gone, I guess."

"That's ugly. She could have left it made up," Misty said.

Of course, everything was glittering and clean: the dressers and armoire, the tables and the windows. Everything was in its place, not an article of clothing left out, not a drawer so much as slightly open. The window shade was down, the curtain closed.

"There's nothing to suggest a woman sleeps here," Misty continued as I located the bedsheet in the bathroom closet. "No flowery scent, no daintiness, and that plain white bedding...It's almost like a hospital room," she added.

I gazed around, considering what she said.

"I wasn't in here very often," I said. "She never let me help clean it, and even when I was a little girl, I couldn't come running in here if I had a bad dream. The door was always kept shut."

"It doesn't look like you missed much," she said. "You know it's strange, I have to keep reminding myself she was really your sister, not your mother."

"Me too," I said.

"I bet. Ready?"

I nodded and we returned to the living room where Star sat next to Jade on the sofa, talking. She had the shovel in her hand.

"I'll get the flashlight on our way out," I said. "There's a back door."

"That's good. I wouldn't want anyone seeing us carrying her out the front," Jade said. "They would think we murdered her or something."

"Okay, we have the sheet. What do we do next?" Misty asked Star, who had somehow become the one who knew the most about burying a dead body.

"Roll her up in the sheet," she replied and stood up. She reached out and I handed the sheet to her. "Move the table out of the way," she ordered. Misty and I did so and she spread the sheet out next to Geraldine.

Her eyes were still fixed on me, I thought. I couldn't look at her. Star went behind her and looked at us.

"Let's go," she said. "Roll her over."

"Ugh," Jade said, but got beside her. With her head turned away, she put her hands on Geraldine's back. Misty moved quickly to join them.

"Cat, you hold up the sheet on the end and as soon as she's completely on it, hand it over to me. Okay?"

With my eyes closed, I lifted the sheet and waited. My hands began to tremble. I could hear Geraldine screaming. *What do you think is going to happen now? Huh? I'll tell you. You're all going to get into big trouble, that's what!*

"I told you what would happen if you were friends with these girls. Look what they're getting you to do. Throw them out, now. Go on, tell them to go home."

They rolled her over and I opened my eyes.

"The sheet," Star said.

I handed it to her quickly and she pulled it snugly around Geraldine. Then they rolled her again and Star pulled the sheet tighter once more. Soon, Geraldine was completely covered, even her head.

"Okay," Star said. "Let's pick her up and carry her out."

"Lucky she's not too heavy," Misty said as they lifted her.

"I can't believe I'm doing this," Jade muttered.

"Get moving, Cat," Star ordered. I led them out, my heart pounding. I quickly located the flashlight and opened the back door. They were right behind me, struggling because Geraldine was so awkward a load.

"You're dropping your end!" Star snapped at Jade.

"Okay, okay," she said. "I'm not exactly used to carrying dead bodies."

They followed me out.

"Where?" Jade asked Star.

"Away from the house," Star said. "Over to the right is best, I think. Shine the beam there, Cat. Yeah, good," she said and we went about ten yards. "Okay, let her down. Damn. I forgot the shovel. Misty, go get it," she ordered.

"Why me?" she asked, looking back at the now empty house.

"Look, if you're afraid of going back in there alone, what do you think it's going to be like for Cat? You're the one who wanted to do this so much."

"Okay, okay. I'm just tired, not frightened," she explained. I knew it was a little lie, but I didn't say anything.

I looked down at the rolled up body and then around the yard. Fortunately, it was an overcast night. Anyone looking over our way wouldn't see much, I thought.

Misty must have run through the house. She returned in less than a minute and handed Star the shovel.

"I'll start," she said, "but we'll all have to do some digging. A grave's got to be deep and wide enough."

"I've never dug anything before," Jade complained.

"Like it takes a brain surgeon," Star shot back at her.

She pointed the tip of the shovel down and stepped on it to sink it into the lawn. It went in easily and then wouldn't budge.

"Rock," she said. "The ground's probably full of them."

"We can't do this," Jade moaned. "We're not laborers."

"You're right. It will be hard. You might break a fingernail," Star said.

"Very funny."

"There's a garden set in the garage, too," I said, remembering. "A small shovel and one of those claws to help get rocks out of the way."

"Misty?"

"Oh, no, me again?"

"Well, we can't send Cat with her crutches and all, can we? All she can do is hold the flashlight."

"What about Jade?"

"Where is it?" Jade asked me, sighing deeply.

"It's on the shelf to the right of the door," I explained. "It's where all the garden tools are kept."

She shook her head at Misty and started for the house.

"Well, we have to share the work," Misty cried. "It's only fair."

"Fair," Star muttered as she dug. "We're supposed to want to do things for each other and not worry about all that, remember?"

"I know," Misty said. "Boy, you really know how to dig," she added.

"Yeah, it's practically all I do these days, dig graves," Star quipped.

Jade returned with the garden set and Star told Misty to take the small shovel and dig around the big rock she had hit. She told Jade to use the claw and before long, the three of them were working on the grave, ripping up the earth and rocks, Jade complaining about how dirty she was getting her outfit and Misty worrying about calluses on her palms. Star made fun of them both.

"It isn't a joking matter. We'll have to come up with something to explain how we look if someone should see us when we get home tonight," Jade said.

Just then, I felt the first raindrop. Then another and another.

"Oh no," Misty cried. "It's starting to rain again."

"Work faster," Star commanded. They did but the rain started to fall faster too. I watched how the rolled bed-sheet grew more and more transparent. I thought I could see Geraldine's face clearly outlined in the wet cloth. It was as if she was emerging, pressing her face out so she could glare at me with hate and anger.

"This is too hard. It's going to take hours and hours!" Jade crabbed. "We shouldn't have started."

"Yeah, well we did," Star said, "so we have to finish it no matter what."

"My hair," Jade sobbed. "Look at me." She wiped her cheeks with the back of her sleeve and streaked her face with mud.

"Oh, well," Misty said, "I'll ruin another T-shirt and jeans. Don't laugh. These jeans are expensive."

Before long, the rain became a steady drizzle. No one said much. They grumped to themselves and worked.

"Isn't it deep enough yet?" Jade pleaded.

"No," Star said. "You want us to plant her so a foot pops up one day?"

"Ugh, how gross," Misty moaned. It made her dig faster, pulling out rocks and flinging them to her side.

I tried to keep the light steady. Sometimes, my hand shook so much, it made the light seem as if it was coming from a defective bulb.

"Okay," Star said nearly half an hour later, "I think it's deep enough."

"Thank God," Jade cried. They backed up.

"Don't forget, we have to cover her back up once she's in there," Star reminded them, "so don't relax too much. Who's got the Bible?" she asked.

"I'll get it," Misty said, volunteering before she was asked to retrieve it.

"I don't see why we need to read from the Bible," Jade said. "We're not clergy and it's raining harder."

"It's only right," Star insisted. "And you're already too wet for it to make any difference."

The rain began to ease up some, but by now, no one seemed to notice or care. Misty returned with the Bible and Star asked me to bring the flashlight around.

"Just shine it down here," Star said, flipping through the pages. "Granny and I went to Mary Dobson's funeral last month and the preacher read this at one point," she said holding the Bible up. Then she began, her voice softer, almost melodic.

"To everything there is a season, and a time to every purpose under the heaven: a time to be born and a time to die; a time to plant, and a time to pluck up that which is planted; a time to kill, and a time to heal; a time to break down, and a time to build up; a time to weep, and a time to laugh; a time to mourn, and time to dance; a time to

cast away stones, and a time to gather stones together; a time to embrace, and a time to refrain from embracing; a time to seek, and a time to lose; a time to keep, and a time to cast away; a time to rend and a time to sew; a time to keep silence, and a time to speak; a time to love and a time to hate; a time for war," she read lifting her head, *"and a time for peace.*

"Let her rest in peace," she concluded, "amen."

"Amen," Misty said.

"Amen," I said.

Jade, who stood there with her hair down, her makeup running, her face streaked with mud, smiled softly at Star.

"That was beautiful," she said. "Amen."

"Okay," Star said, handing me the Bible, "Let's finish it." She went around Geraldine and knelt down. Misty quickly knelt beside her. Reluctantly, Jade joined them and they rolled the woman who I believed to be my mother for nearly all of my life. She fell into the makeshift grave and disappeared.

"Good," Star said. "Now let's start putting the dirt back."

Jade groaned and they began. Nearly another hour later, Star patted down the ground and stepped back. She took the flashlight from me and ran it over the lawn.

"Anyone can tell it's been dug up. We'll have to plant new grass here."

"Not tonight, I hope," Jade pleaded.

Star laughed.

"No, not tonight, but it would have been good with all the rain."

"I've got some seeds in the garage," I said. "I'll throw them out later."

"Fine," Jade said quickly.

"We'll check it out tomorrow and decide what else has to be done," Jade said.

"Can we go inside finally?" Jade cried. "I dread looking at myself in the mirror."

"So don't and spare the mirror," Star said. Misty laughed.

We all headed for the back door. I was the last to enter. I paused and looked into the darkness.

If she hated me before, I thought, she'll hate me more now. She'll hate me for eternity.

I turned and entered the house. The door snapped shut behind me.

I felt like the only life I had known was over. Star had read the right verse from the Bible. It was a time to be born, a time to heal; a time to laugh and to dance. Finally, it was a time to love.

I hoped.

7

Terror in the Night

"**L**ook at me! Look at all of us!" Jade cried when we were inside and standing near the only full-length mirror downstairs in the hallway.

The four of us stood clumped together, gazing at our images. Our clothes and hair were soaked, our shoes were muddied, and everyone's face was streaked with grime.

"I can't go home looking like this," Jade moaned, and ran her fingers through her hair. When she saw the dirt on them, on the backs of them, and up her arms, she groaned again. "I look like the gardener!"

"So, we'll bathe and shower before we go home," Star declared. "Don't get so upset. You'll break out with a pimple."

"Star's right. And we can all just wash and dry our clothes," Misty said. "Can't we do that, Cat?"

"Sure," I said shrugging. "I'll put all the clothing in the machine. That was always one of my chores," I added. "We recently had the dryer repaired, even though Geraldine preferred hanging clothes on the line out back." I gazed at the floor. "We're tracking in tons of mud, too," I said.

It was funny how I kept thinking Geraldine still could hear every word spoken in this house, especially my words, and see everything we did as well. Her orders, complaints and criticism lingered on the walls and echoed through the rooms, reminding me we could bury her, but not her shadow or her voice.

"Stop being her and making us feel bad," Jade ordered. "She's gone."

"Oh, I didn't mean to do that. I..."

"Well, Cat's right. It's still a mess. Who's going to clean it up?" Star demanded. "You Beverlies?"

"We'll clean it up," Misty said. "First we should get out of these clothes so we don't drag mud any further around the house."

She pulled her T-shirt off, kicked off her sneakers, and began to undo her jeans, dropping everything in a pile right where she stood.

"I can't wash this outfit. It's supposed to be dry-cleaned only," Jade moaned. "It might shrink or stretch."

"So, if it does, just blame it on your maid," Star told her. "I'm sure you've done that before."

"I have not!"

"I have a pullover and a skirt you can borrow if you don't want to wash your outfit," I suggested, hoping to quench an argument before it began.

She thought a moment. I guess she was imagining herself in my clothes and wasn't pleased with the thought. She shook her head and began to get undressed, too.

"Just forget it. Wash it," she said.

As Star began to disrobe I left to get us all towels from

the laundry room. While I was in there I wriggled out of my wet clothes as quickly as I could.

"Hurry up with those towels, Cat," Jade hollered. "I need a hot bath. Do you have any bath oils, powders?"

"I think there's some left from what my father gave me," I recalled as I came back with the towels.

"Well?" she said. "Let's get moving. Don't you hear my teeth chattering? I'm freezing!"

Standing there all wrapped in towels, we looked like we were heading for the steam room in some resort. Laughing at the sight of us, maybe as a way of relieving all the tension and nervousness, they followed as I hobbled as quickly as I could back to the stairway and up, first to my room, where Star went right to the shower, and then to Geraldine's room where Jade began to run a bath. Misty found one of Geraldine's bathrobes and wrapped herself in it, waiting for her turn in the shower. I found the bath powder and brought it to Jade.

"This is good stuff," she remarked as she read the words on the box. "It has an herbal ingredient that's supposed to relieve aching muscles, and my legs ache. And just look at my fingernails," she suddenly whined, holding up her hand. "I'll have to go for a manicure first thing tomorrow."

I tried to look sympathetic for a moment and then left her mumbling and moaning.

While Star and then Misty showered, I took care of the clothes, getting them all into the washing machine. Then I put the plastic zip bag over my cast the way the doctor had showed me so I wouldn't get it drenched, and took my shower. Afterward, Misty, Star, and I gathered in Mother's bathroom and sat around the tub while Jade continued to soak, the foam up to and around her neck like a collar of bubbles.

"I can't get the chill out of my bones," she complained. "All that mud..." She shook her head and grimaced as if she had some in her mouth. "I think I swallowed some."

"It won't kill you, if you did," Star told her.

Jade brushed away some of the suds and looked at her indignantly.

"You might be used to dirt and grime clinging to your body, but I'm not."

"And what's that supposed to mean?"

"It means...it means I hope I never have to do anything like that again," she concluded, avoiding any confrontation.

Star's glare softened.

"My mother went to a spa in Desert Hot Springs where you pay to take a bath in mud," Misty said.

"Huh?" Star leaned back as if Misty had something contagious.

"It's supposed to be good for your skin."

"Well, this is different," Jade said. "The mud was cold and it was full of pebbles. I can still feel it in my hair!"

She sat up and asked for the shampoo. I asked Misty to get the shampoo in my room since it too was a special herbal blend that I'd received as a gift.

"Go on, spoil her some more," Star muttered.

"We've all got to spoil each other. That's a rule in the OWP's," Jade told her.

"Oh, it is, is it? You just make up the rules for all of us?"

"Excuse me. We'll vote. All opposed to spoiling each other say nay," Jade cried. No one did. She smiled at Star. "So moved," she said.

Star raised her eyes to the ceiling. Then she looked at me. I was staring at the floor, trying to keep my heart from periodically breaking out in flutters every time I realized what we had done.

"Are you all right, Cat?"

I nodded, and then I looked up and smiled at all of them. I never so much as had a girlfriend in my room talking to me. To have them all here, all of us together, helping and caring for each other like this, really made me feel like I had sisters. Sure I was all right. At least for now, I thought.

After she got out of the tub, Jade talked about a new skin cream her mother had brought home. It was designed to be applied after baths and showers.

"Water can make your skin dry, too, especially hard water. Our bodies have natural oils," she lectured, mostly to me, "so we shouldn't just dry and forget."

"I never put any of that on myself," Star bragged.

"Well, you should, before you turn into a wrinkly old prune," Jade told her.

"Girl, you make it up as you go along."

"I do not. If you don't want to learn anything new, you'll never grow."

"Spare me," Star pleaded. "All this wisdom so fast will wear out my poor, deprived brain."

Misty laughed. I couldn't believe I was smiling, too. For a while, as we brushed our hair and Jade babbled about waxing her eyebrows, how to use eye shadow to emphasize our eyes, and what lipsticks would complement our complexions, I completely forgot what had just happened and what we had just done. It was as though we were all in some girls' dormitory, filling our heads with only fluff, living in a cotton candy world where worries were as easy to pop as soap bubbles, and glitter instead of rain fell from the sky. How long would it last? I hoped forever and ever.

"I'd better get the clothes into the dryer," I said, realizing the time.

"I'll do it," Misty volunteered. She gazed at Star who looked pleased at her offer. "It takes you forever to go up and down those stairs. You really should set up a bedroom downstairs until you're better," she said.

Star nodded.

"Good idea."

"Maybe tomorrow," I said. "I'm all right. It's a short stairway."

Misty hurried off while Jade sat at the mirror and brushed her hair. How pretty she is, I thought. Can all the skin creams, makeup, herbal shampoos, and hairstylists in the world ever make me as pretty?

Nearly an hour later, Misty and Star went downstairs to bring up everyone's clothes. Jade's suit wasn't shrunk. As she had feared, however, it was stretched instead.

"I look like someone gave me a hand-me-down," she complained, holding out her arms to show us how the sleeves drooped. However, she had her hair looking as perfect as it had been when she had first arrived.

"Do you have any hot chocolate?" Misty asked me. "I feel like having some to calm my stomach."

"Me too," Jade said.

When we all went downstairs, I fetched the hot chocolate and gazed up at the crawl space door. Misty saw the direction of my gaze and understood instantly.

"I'll go get the ladder and go up there," she offered, excited.

"You're going to get yourself all dirty again," Jade warned "Can't it wait?"

"How dirty can I get and besides, Cat can't go up." She looked to Star for support.

"If she wants to do it, let her," Star said. "We don't need your permission for everything, you know."

"I didn't say you did," Jade shot back. Would these two ever stop dueling? I wondered.

"I'll be right back," Misty declared, and shot off.

I started to make the hot chocolate, when Star took over.

"Why don't you sit down and rest your ankle," she said, glaring back at Jade who sat filing her broken fingernail.

"I'm okay."

"I feel better doing something," Star responded.

We heard Misty banging the ladder on the doors and walls as she made her way into the house. Again, I couldn't help thinking how Geraldine would be screaming. Star went to help her and they set the ladder up in the pantry. Moments later, Misty was up and in the crawl space. I shouted up directions and she found the letters and dropped them into Jade's waiting arms.

"You want any of this other stuff?"

"No, not now, thanks," I said. She remained up there awhile going through it anyway.

"I love looking at old stuff," she declared as she began to descend.

"Are you going to read those now?" Jade asked, as she handed me the letters.

"Not right now," I said.

"They're private. She should read through them by herself," Star declared with understanding, and poured everyone a cup of hot chocolate. I thanked Misty for getting the letters. She started to take the ladder out but Star told her to just leave it there and have her hot chocolate first before it got cold.

"You're the one who wanted it in the first place. The ladder's not in our way or anything," she said. "Not that anyone's going to complain anyway," she added.

Once more I couldn't help but think about Geraldine raging about not putting things back where they belonged. I even looked to the doorway as if I expected to see her come storming in at any moment. I couldn't help feeling as if everything we had done had been only a dream after all.

The girls were quiet, watching me, sipping their hot chocolate and shifting their gazes from me to each other.

"What do we do now?" Misty finally asked.

"Go home and come back first thing tomorrow," Star said.

"What about, Cat?" Misty asked, nodding at me. "We can't just leave her here."

"You can come home with me, if you like," Jade suggested.

"Or me," Misty said.

"I can't compete with the Beverlies, but you can come to my little shack, too," Star said.

I looked from one to the other. If I chose one, would the others feel bad? Did they all expect I would choose Jade because she had the biggest, most luxurious house? Jade certainly looked like she expected that. If I didn't go home with her, would she be terribly disappointed?

"I'm too tired to go anywhere," I said. "I'll be all right."

"Are you sure?" Misty asked, her lips twisted into a frown. She looked around the room as if to add, "How can you want to stay here now?"

"Yes," I said. "I'll just do what I always do: go up to my room, close the door and go to sleep. I've got to be able to do it or none of this will work. I can't expect one of you to stay with me every night."

The girls looked at each other.

"Maybe I can stay tonight," Star suggested.

"No, don't get yourself into any trouble on my account," I said.

Jade's laugh was more like a high-pitched cry.

"Are you kidding? Now you say that? We just dug a grave in the backyard and put your dead sister in it," she said.

"That's great," Star said, practically leaping across the table at her. "Make her feel like it was only her who decided to do it."

"I don't mean that, but—"

"Then don't keep bringing it up."

"I'm not! Did I even mention it before this? I've been trying to forget it. I don't know how I'll sleep tonight."

"You sure know how to say the right things, don't you?" Star shot back at her and rolled her eyes at me.

"I'm sorry. I mean…"

"Maybe we're all just very tired," Misty suggested gently.

"Yeah, maybe," Star agreed. "All right. I'll get here as soon as I can tomorrow."

"We'll all get here as soon as we can," Jade said.

"Let's decide now on the schedule. I can probably get permission to sleep overnight tomorrow night," Misty said.

"I'll take the night after," Star said.

"Okay. I have the night after that," Jade added, obviously happy she wasn't going to be sleeping here that soon.

"We'll just keep up the schedule as best we can and invite Cat to our houses when we can't stay here," Misty decided.

"We'll try to not leave you alone too much," Jade said.

"You are right though, Cat, you've got to be able to be alone," Star pointed out.

I looked at them all, their concern, the fear on their faces.

"No," I said. "The truth is I've been alone most of the time anyway."

Star nodded. Misty looked sadder and Jade looked relieved.

"We should start cleaning up the house," Misty said.

"No, it's all right. I'll do it. Don't worry. It will give me something to do and help me keep my mind off things," I said.

"That's very sensible," Jade agreed.

"You would say that," Star told her. "Anything to get out of work," she muttered just loud enough for us to hear. Before Jade could react, Misty changed the subject.

It was decided that we would meet late in the morning and start to plan out all the details for the future, our future, the future of the OWP's.

Jade called for her limousine. It would take Misty and Star home as well. It was fortunate for us that Jade was so wealthy and had so much at her fingertips. Surely, I thought, it would help us later.

When we heard the limousine arrive, my heart skipped a beat. In moments they would all be gone and despite the brave front I had put up, I was terrified of being alone.

"I'll call you as soon as I wake up tomorrow," Misty promised.

They stood around me in the foyer.

"Okay," I said.

"We did the right thing," Star insisted. "You're not going to be farmed out to strangers now."

Jade didn't look as convinced, but Misty still managed to look happy and excited about it all, helping me to feel we were still on a big adventure and that the only thing that loomed ahead was fun and more fun for us. They each hugged me and offered me words of encouragement.

"If you need to, call me any time," Jade said. "You've got my private number and I can call my limo driver any time. I'll just send him to get you. Okay?"

"Thank you," I said.

I stood in the doorway and watched as they left and got into the limousine. Misty rolled down her window and popped her head out.

"Just go to sleep," she called. "Forget about it for now."

"Shut up," I heard Star tell her. I was sure she was worried about the driver hearing anything suspicious.

I watched them drive away and lingered in the doorway, afraid to go back inside; afraid that Geraldine would be standing there in the hall, dripping with mud and enraged, her eyes wild and full of fire.

"How dare you try to bury me!" she would scream and then fold her lips into that familiar cold smile to add, *"As if you ever could."*

Trembling so much that I thought my legs might collapse beneath me, I finally did gather the courage to go back inside. I couldn't help feeling that Geraldine was hovering over me, berating me for making such a mess. I quickly went to the laundry room, filled a pail with hot water and detergent and went about mopping up the floor. Then I returned to the kitchen and washed all the cups and saucers we had used. I wiped down the counters and the table, working all the while with my head down, scrubbing and scouring like someone ordered to sterilize the room, afraid that if I looked up, I would see her face, those hot and hateful eyes.

After cleaning up the kitchen, I struggled to put the ladder back in the garage. Most of the way, I used it like a crutch to keep the weight off my ankle. When that was done, I returned to the kitchen, picked up the packet of letters and went upstairs. I put the letters on my desk, yet strangely I couldn't bring myself to read them yet. Instead, I turned to cleaning the bathrooms, making certain that Geraldine's was spic and span—just the way she liked it.

I had intended to lie in bed and start another letter, but I was truly exhausted by the time I finished cleaning the bathrooms. Every part of me ached, even my neck and shoulders, and especially my leg, my ankle throbbing.

I prepared for bed and eagerly slipped under the blanket. When I lowered my head to the pillow, I closed my eyes and fell asleep almost immediately, but I didn't stay asleep. My eyes popped open and I stared into the darkness for a moment. I thought I had heard my door open and close. Was it part of a dream? Or was that what had woken me?

A chill started at the base of my neck and trickled down my spine like drips of ice water. In moments, my entire body felt frozen and numbed. I couldn't even raise my head from the pillow. All I could do was listen and wait. The floorboards creaked. I thought I heard what sounded like a skirt rubbing against a leg as someone crossed from the door toward my bed. Shadows darkened. I took a deep breath, closed my eyes and then with all my might sat up.

"Who's there?" I cried.

The rain that had fallen earlier had passed, but it had left dark skies and strong breezes in its wake. The wind whistled past the windows. A curtain trembled and then there was only a deep, dark silence. Slowly, I turned and gazed around my room. My eyes were accustomed to the darkness now and shapes became familiar. There was nothing unusual. Nevertheless, I reached slowly toward the lamp on my night table and switched it on. I blinked at the shock of light, but a blast of illumination revealed I was alone.

I allowed myself to take deep breaths again. My lungs seemed so tight, it took a while for my breathing to become regular. Still full of trepidation, I rose slowly, taking hold of my crutches and standing. I listened. The house was always somewhat noisy at night. Pipes groaned, floorboards stretched and tightened, the wind discovering every tiny opening and somehow threading itself through the hallways and in and out of rooms, weaving its body about like a snake made of smoke. Tonight, it wasn't as noisy and the stillness made me imagine a dark creature, holding its breath and waiting in the shadows.

Old habits die hard; before I went to bed I had closed my door just the way I had all my life. I made my way to it, opened it and gazed into the dimly lit hallway. There was no one lurking out there, no sound, nothing. It's all my imagination, I thought. Of course, it would work overtime tonight of all nights. Nevertheless, I couldn't keep myself from going next door to Geraldine's room. That door, too, was closed, just the way I had left it. I stood outside and listened.

This is so silly, so foolish, I thought. I'm frightening myself for nothing. She's gone. I'm all alone. I put my hand on the doorknob. I'll open the door and switch on the light and see she's gone, see that it wasn't all a dream. The girls were really here and we did bury her.

My fingers trembled as I turned the doorknob and opened the door. I stood there for a moment, gazing into the dark room. Then I found the overhead fixture switch and flipped it. Light dropped from the ceiling, washing over the bed, the chairs, the dresser and floors in a ghostly white. The bed was empty and there was no sign of anyone, of course. How ridiculous it was for me to even look, I thought, shaking my head as I turned off the light and closed the door.

I stood listening again, heard nothing unusual, and started back to my room. As I passed through my doorway, I stopped, the chill now rising from my naked foot, up my leg and into my heart. Slowly, I looked down. It was a cold, wet spot of mud. For a moment, I couldn't swallow. I couldn't even look at it.

It's just a spot I missed when I cleaned earlier, I told myself. We must have tracked it in and I just didn't see it. That's it. That has to be it.

But we had taken off our shoes and socks downstairs first, hadn't we? I asked myself.

The mud might have dropped from their hands and arms, I replied to myself, or maybe from my crutches. Where else could it have come from? Stop this. Stop it!

I hurried to the bathroom, scooped up a towel and returned to the spot, quickly wiping and drying it. I gazed around the room, searching for any others. There didn't seem to be any. Isn't that strange? a voice inside me asked. No, I said, no, no. It was just a dripping. Nothing. Stop. Stop! I screamed inside. I closed my eyes and embraced myself, squeezing myself as if to keep my fears from escaping my shaking body.

We buried her, I thought. We really did, but was it sinful? Would I be punished? Can her spirit rise and haunt me forever and ever?

I struggled to my feet, closed the door, and returned to my bed. This time when I lowered my head to the pillow, I lay there with my eyes open, waiting, listening. I lay like that almost until the first light of day before my eyelids slammed together like the doors of vaults and shut me in darkness and sleep.

The sound of a phone ringing woke me. It rang and rang and rang. I rose with great effort, every muscle in my lower back and my legs aching, and seized my crutches. The phone kept ringing. The closest one was in Geraldine's room, of course. I hurried to it. It continued to ring. I sat on her bed and lifted the receiver.

"Hello?"

"Oh, thank God you answered," Misty said. "I was beginning to get really scared."

"I don't have a phone in my room. She never let me have one," I said.

"Well, let's get one put in there. So," she added after a very short pause, "how did you sleep?"

"I didn't sleep much," I confessed.

"Neither did I. I just should have stayed. I worried about you."

"Thanks," I said. No one had ever said that to me.

"I'll be there in about an hour. Anyone else call yet?"

"I don't think so. They might have and I didn't hear the phone ringing," I said.

"I'll call them. Do you have any bagels? I like a toasted bagel for breakfast."

"No," I said, laughing. Who could think of eating at a time like this? Who, indeed, but Misty.

"I'll bring some. Did you...I mean, can you see out back? Does it all look all right?"

"I haven't checked. Oh," I said. "I forgot to spread seeds last night. I'd better do that today and water the ground."

"I'll help you. Wait for me," she said. "I'm getting up and getting dressed. My mother wanted me to go with her to lunch in Santa Monica, but I got out of it."

"Maybe you shouldn't have."

"Naw, it's all right. She really didn't want me along. She likes to be with her girlfriends and rag on men, and she can't do it as well when I'm there. See you soon," she added.

"Right."

I hung up and looked around the bedroom. Nothing was changed; nothing was disturbed. Despite my fatigue and nervousness, I was encouraged by Misty's call and returned to my room and got dressed to go downstairs and prepare some breakfast. It seemed so odd not to have my juice set out beside my cereal bowl already when I got there. Geraldine was always downstairs before me. It was still not home in my heart, not solid as a truth should be that she was dead and gone. I kept expecting her to appear and to start dictating my daily chores. Geraldine's litany of complaints and self-pity usually ran like a sound track while I had my breakfast.

"Don't slurp your cereal, Cathy. Watch that you don't drip on my clean tablecloth. Don't hunch over like that when you eat. You'll ruin your posture."

Those familiar admonitions circled my head like bees, buzzing in my ears. She didn't have to be here for me to hear them. When would they go away? Would they ever?

I went about setting the table for breakfast, expecting the girls might all come at once. More than ever, I was eager for their company, their chatter, and laughter. I was even looking forward to Star and Jade's verbal fencing.

When the phone rang, I froze and looked at it. Was it Jade? Star? Would either be calling to say she couldn't come? Would the excuses begin and would they all eventually leave me alone?

"Hello?" I said in a hesitant voice after I picked up the receiver.

"Mrs. Carson?"

For a moment I couldn't get myself to speak. My throat closed.

"It's Tom McCormick at the Unified Central Bank."

"Yes?" I managed, my voice cracking.

"You had asked me to let you know when the final wire transfer from Mr. Carson's account had been credited to your account. That was done late yesterday. Did you want me to have any of the funds shifted to your money market account?"

My throat tightened even more at the reference to my father.

"Mrs. Carson?"

"Yes," I said, realizing this was something my mother would have wanted done. "Please do."

"How much?" he asked.

I had no idea how much had been transferred from my father's account.

"Half," I told him.

"Half? Okay. I'll have that done for you. Thank you, Mrs. Carson," he added, and hung up.

Was that wrong? Should I have said to transfer all of the money? Did he think it unusual and did that make him suspicious? Or had I gotten away with it, the first test? I cradled the receiver and stepped back. Maybe I could be Geraldine when I had to. Maybe I would be all right. I stared at the phone, half expecting he would call back to confirm what he had been told, insisting this time that he speak with Geraldine. My heart thumped in anticipation.

The doorbell rang instead, making me jump. Was it Misty? What if it was...No, I thought. He wouldn't dare come back, would he? The bell rang again and again. I couldn't move. I heard a knock and then the bell. After another moment, I made my way to the front door, sucked in my breath, and opened it.

"Finally!" Misty cried. She had her arms filled with two large bags of groceries. She shot past me into the house. I stood there looking out at the street. It was quiet. No one was paying any particular attention to my house.

"Jade and Star will be coming along," Misty called from the kitchen. "Poor Jade didn't sleep much and has to do a lot of facial repair before she steps out. Star was making sure her brother was all right before she left. She's taking the bus."

Misty continued to unload her bags as I entered the kitchen. Then she turned and took a look at me.

"Ouch," she declared. "You do look like you had a hard night," she said.

"It was pretty awful." I was shocked to hear myself admit the truth.

I sat and told her about my waking up, hearing noises, checking it out, and finding the cold wet mud. Her eyes got wider and wider as I spoke. Then she turned and looked toward the backyard.

"Did you go out there this morning to see if...I mean..."

"Not yet," I said. "I couldn't get myself to do it."

She nodded, swallowed hard, and then started toward the back door. She looked back at me. I held my breath and then she opened the door and stepped outside. A moment later she returned.

"It's a mess," she said, looking relieved. "However, she's still where we put her."

I released the air I had trapped in my lungs and sighed, but I wasn't sure whether I was sighing with relief or with regret.

8

Sowing the Seeds

Even though Star came by bus and had to make some changes along the way, she got to my house before Jade. For some reason, Star didn't look as tired as we did from the night before. She poured herself a cup of coffee and bit on a Danish pastry as I told her about my difficult night.

"I was afraid it would be like that for you. We have to stay with you for a while," she insisted. She looked at the clock on the wall. "I thought we all agreed about that and the importance of being here. So where is our illustrious president?" she muttered, and sipped some more coffee. "Maybe she went to get her nails repaired," she added.

Minutes later we heard the doorbell and Misty went to let Jade in.

"Sorry it took me so long to get here," Jade sang as she swept through the kitchen doorway. She was dressed in another designer outfit, her hair radiant and shiny, and her nails freshly polished.

Star winked at me. Anyone could see Jade had spent

most of the morning at her dressing table, meticulously applying her makeup, turning herself from just another pretty girl into a teenage cover model.

"But I had a whopper of a nightmare last night and the moment I looked at myself this morning, I knew I couldn't leave the house without some major reconstruction," Jade explained.

She paused and looked at me, her face suddenly contorted in a horrid grimace.

"I dreamed your half sister dug herself out and came to my room. She looked like something from the latest Halloween movie. I had to smother my screams when I woke up. My nerves were so frazzled, I felt like they were all wicks on dynamite sticks," she rattled on breathlessly. Then she paused and collapsed on a seat.

"What a whopper of a nightmare," Misty muttered.

Jade knitted her eyebrows together and scowled.

"Tell me about it. Then I started to worry about us all being arrested and I couldn't get back to sleep for hours and hours. When I looked at myself this morning, I nearly passed out again. My eyes actually had bags under them! Can you imagine?"

"You poor thing," Star said.

Jade missed her sarcasm and got up to pour herself a cup of coffee instead.

"I just threw my outfit away," she continued. "No tailor could fix it and I didn't want to have to explain it to my mother."

She turned and looked at us sitting at the table, gazing down at us as if we were her private audience.

"How are you all doing?"

"Well, it's nice of you to ask," Star said. "Actually, I slept very well."

"You did not, you liar. No one could after what we did."
She studied me a moment, her eyes suddenly dripping
with sympathy. "Cat, I wanted to call you all night, but I
was afraid I'd frighten you. Are you okay?"

"No, she's not okay," Star said. "She had a really miserable night, too. Anyone can take one look at her and see
that. We have a lot of planning to do, Jade. If you can
come down from your cloud of self-pity long enough to
listen and think, that is," she added.

"Boy, you're in a good mood. Don't tell me you slept
well, cranky head." She plopped back in the chair and
sighed. "Okay, okay. Let's plan. Oh," she said before anyone could say anything else, "my parents have a big meeting today with their attorneys. It's all supposed to come to
an end, finally. Maybe my mother will have a big party to
celebrate. Consider yourselves invited if she does," she
said with a sweep of her hand. She was wearing new rings
on every finger of her right hand and a beautiful gold
charm bracelet.

"I'll put it right at the top of my social calendar," Star
said.

"You really think your mother would have a party?"
Misty asked.

"I don't know. She's capable of throwing a bash if she
feels she won."

"The bank called for my mother this morning," I said in
a voice so hollow and devoid of emotion, everyone
snapped their heads around to look at me. "Some funds
were wired in from my father's account, part of their set-
tlement, I guess."

"What did the bank want?" Star asked.

"The banker wanted to know how much to put in a
money market account. You make interest in that account

and it's something my mother always made sure she did," I said. "He asked how much to put in."

"He thought you were her when you talked?"

"I think so. I told him to put in half, but maybe I should have said more. The problem is I don't know how much was wired in."

"What did he say?"

"He just repeated it and thanked me and that was that."

"Good," Star said.

"It's not good. What if he calls and asks her to come to the bank to sign something?" Jade followed.

Everyone was quiet. New worries scribbling through the folds in our foreheads. I remembered something.

"I can tell him she's ill and to send it for her signature," I said. "I heard her do that once and they didn't question it."

"That's all right, but there'll be a serious problem when something has to be notarized," Jade explained. "You've got to be physically present and have a photo I.D."

"We'll worry about that when it happens," Star said quickly.

"I don't know," Jade said, shaking her head. "It's not going to be easy." She picked at a bagel. "Is this fat-free cream cheese?" she asked Misty.

"No."

"Great," Star said as she bit into her bagel.

"I don't like fat-free stuff. It's blah," Misty explained

"It's all right for you, but some of us have to worry about our figures." Jade pouted.

"Why is it all right for me?" Misty asked.

"You don't put on weight, obviously. That has to do with your metabolism," Jade continued in her characteristically haughty manner. "All of us aren't as lucky as you," she added.

Misty looked apologetic and hurt.

"I'm sorry. I didn't think of that."

"Fine," Star said. "We'll design a menu that pleases Jade, but for now, let's get to some of the important problems, if that's not too much trouble."

"Diet is important," Jade insisted. "And exercise. I'll be in charge of that," she volunteered. "Obviously, I know the most about it, so let me decide what to buy at the supermarket from now on."

"What don't you know the most about?" Star asked, leaning back and folding her arms. She could turn her eyes into small, ebony pearls and hold her lips in what looked to be half a smile and half a smirk of disgust.

"I'm just trying to make efficient use of our strengths," Jade defended.

"I want to be in charge of redecorating," Misty piped up before Jade could add anything to her own list of powers.

"Redecorating?" I asked. "What do you mean?"

"This house is gloomy. It needs color, life. It's going to be our headquarters, right? We should change the curtains, get some better lights, maybe paint some of the rooms. You don't even have any posters in your room, Cat! Who's your favorite actor? What singers do you like? Stuff like that."

"Oh," I said. "Right," I added, but I couldn't help agonizing about it. Geraldine had made such a point of my keeping my walls uncluttered, and she hated posters.

"Maybe we shouldn't change anything," Star said, seeing the look on my face.

"Why not?" Misty asked, bouncing in her seat.

"If someone comes in here and sees how different it is, they'll be suspicious."

"She's right," Jade said.

"But…" Misty looked so disappointed.

"No one comes here," I admitted. "No one will notice any changes. It's not that." I shrugged. "I just can't get used to not having Geraldine around saying no and bawling me out for even asking."

"Of course you can't," Star said. She turned to Misty. "Let's go slowly."

"But I'd like to see some changes," I asserted, and smiled at Misty. "Especially in my room. I used to dream that my walls were pink instead of that boring white, and I hate my bedspread and my pillowcases and my curtains. You're right. There's no personality in my room."

"That's true. We'll do all that, and you should have a television set and a phone in your room, too," Misty said, getting more and more excited. "Why don't we all go shopping today? We'll go to the mall and—"

"First things first," Star said, her face turning to stone. "We better fix up the yard back there. Just in case someone does come snooping."

"I am *not* doing any more yard work," Jade asserted. "I'm not about to ruin another outfit."

"Who told you to come here dressed up like you were going to a ball?"

"This isn't dressing up," Jade cried. "It's just…just being in style."

"Well, can we go to the mall afterward, then? I'd like to start doing things with this place," Misty pursued. "Okay?"

"I guess," Star said. "What about money?"

"Geraldine has one credit card," I said. "She never saw a reason to have more than one and she used it sparingly, always making sure she paid up before they could tack on any interest."

"Perfect. You probably have the whole limit to use," Misty said.

I nodded even though it put the jitters in me even to think about going through her pocketbook to get her wallet and the card.

"She always keeps a considerable amount of cash money in the house, too, but she never let me see where. I imagine it's someplace in her room."

"She didn't trust you?" Star asked.

"No, it wasn't a matter of trust with her. It was..."

"What?" Misty asked impatiently.

"She was protecting her privacy."

They were all quiet a moment.

"She sounds more like some stranger who treated you like a tenant," Jade said.

I shrugged.

"I never cared about that stuff before."

They were pensive again and then Star sprouted out of her seat.

"Let's stop wasting time. Where's the grass seed? Do you have a rake, too?"

"Yes," I said. I got up and headed for the garage. Misty followed and helped me bring it all out to the yard. Jade stood in the doorway and watched us as she sipped her coffee.

The yard looked bald in the spot we had dug up and the grass we dug up lay around in small lumps. First, Star raked the ground and smoothed it out well. Then we scattered the grass seeds and Misty turned on the hose and sprinkled over them. It was still hard to believe Geraldine was buried there. It was easier to believe she would pop her head out of an upstairs window and demand to know what we thought we were doing to her yard.

"You know what else we ought to do?" Star said, thinking and studying the yard, "we ought to buy a few plants and bushes for more cover. It still looks like a grave to me."

"That's why we have to go shopping," Misty insisted. "We've got the car."

"Cat can't drive her car with a cast on her, can she?" Star asked.

"I've got my license," Misty said. "I can drive us."

Star turned to me to see my reaction. Let Misty drive Geraldine's car? I gazed at the grave. If she heard, she would come busting out of the earth for sure, I thought.

"Well?" Star asked. She looked at Jade. "What do you think, President Jade?"

"If she has a license, what's the big deal?" Jade asked. "I have a license too, but I hate driving anything less than a sports car. However, I need some things myself and it's about time Cat had some more stylish outfits, although I'd like to work on her hair and makeup first. I guess I can bring her some makeup from my mother's company, though."

"Then it's settled," Misty said. "The OWP's take their first road trip."

"Cat hasn't said okay yet," Star reminded her.

They looked at me. I looked at the freshly dug earth and then I looked up at the increasingly blue sky. I had never gone shopping with friends. New clothes, my own television set? Why not? I thought. Why not really be free, finally, completely.

"All right," I said. "I'll go get the charge card."

Jade stepped back to let me enter the house.

"Want me to get it for you?" she asked.

"No thanks," I said. "It's all right."

Here we were planning to change so many things about Geraldine's home and I couldn't get myself to permit someone else to go through her personal things, even to fetch her pocketbook. When I got up to her room, I was still hesitant. Her pocketbook was where she always left it on the dresser. It was a big knitted black pocketbook that had once belonged to our mother. The snap was brass, worn and dull and the knitted strap was frayed. She liked to wear it over her left shoulder with the strap across her breasts so that the purse hung more to her front than her side. She told me there was less chance of someone mugging her or swiping it that way. On her small frame, it looked much too big for her, but style was not her concern. It was a practical pocketbook, one that could hold all she wanted to take along with her whenever she left the house.

I approached the dresser slowly. Many times, when I was much younger, I had a little girl's natural curiosity about my mother's things and once I had actually opened the pocketbook when she had left it in the living room. Before I could begin to explore however, Geraldine came flying in as if some unheard alarm had gone off in her head to warn her. She ripped it from my hands and slapped me sharply across the face. My cheek seemed to sting for a week, but I think it was more because of the shock than the actual blow.

"Little girls don't go snooping in their mother's things," she had yelled at me.

I didn't even know what snooping meant.

"Don't ever touch my things without first asking, hear? Curiosity killed the cat."

I sat there, terrified, rubbing my cheek, my tears stuck at the corners of my eyes. She was capable of hitting me again for crying. She had done it before. She hated the sight of tears. *"Most tears are crocodile tears,"* she'd preached. Again, I had no idea what that meant.

When I reached toward her pocketbook now, I still felt my arm and shoulders tighten, my whole body poised to jump back. Of course it was just my imagination, but the brass snap seemed to burn the tips of my fingers and I pulled my hand away. I closed my eyes and told myself to stop being afraid of silly things. How could I explain such behavior to the girls? They'd think I was really crazy and they'd all want to leave.

Holding my breath, I seized the pocketbook roughly and practically ripped it open. I found her wallet quickly and took it out, but now that the purse was open, I looked into it and immediately saw what looked like the stationery on which my real mother's letters to me were written. It was a sheet that was folded tightly. I plucked it out between my thumb and forefinger and then sat on the chair by the dresser and carefully unfolded it. It was a letter from our mother. I could tell that it had been folded and unfolded many times because the creases had produced small rips. The words looked like they were fading, too. It was as if Geraldine's eyes had worn away the ink.

My darling Geraldine, it began.

> *I know how unusual it is for a mother to be so beholden to a daughter. Children are normally far more indebted to their parents. The sacrifices you have made and are making for me only make me feel deeper love and affection for you. I realize it will be difficult for you, and at times,*

you might even hate me, but whatever you feel for me, I hope you will always feel love for your little sister and never rest her mother's sins on her shoulders.

Geraldine, I am not naive enough to believe that you are doing all this solely out of love for me or even respect for your father and a desire to protect him. I know you also hate me for having an affair and a child with the man you thought you loved and maybe even believed loved you. I know you think this draws you closer to him. I saw what you wrote him. I am sure it was just a young woman's infatuation. Believe me, he wouldn't have been right for you anyway, and I'm not just talking about family matters and the age differences. I know that he looked at you so dearly sometimes and unintentionally encouraged you, but he was a warm man, a thoughtful man.

Men, you will learn however, can be such silly fools. The smallest thing can titillate them and turn them into boys. I'm happy you're with Howard. He seems much wiser, and in the end, if you have to choose between a wise man and a doting lover, you'll always be better off with the wise man. Doting lovers stop doting; wise men are always wise. I'm better off with your father. I realize that now. I learned it too late. I know you will learn this important truth faster than I did and you will be a better woman. So when you kiss my daughter good night every night, think of me kissing you just for being there.

Love,
Mother

Kiss me every night? She never kissed me at night. And who was the man she loved, too, the man who was my father? Did she hate me for not really being her child with him? How could my real mother be so blind and so foolish as to expect Geraldine would love me as a mother should love a child? Geraldine used to say none are so blind as those who don't want to see. Was that the case here?

Why did Geraldine read this letter so many times and keep it with her always? What part of it did she cherish the most? I wondered, and perused it again. Was it our mother's expression of gratitude and love or was it the reference to my father? She carried it in her pocketbook, across her heart. She wore it like a badge or a ribbon. Did it mark a courageous act or was it her purple heart, her reward for a great wound?

Maybe she wanted to love me. Maybe she hated that part of herself that wouldn't permit it. Maybe it was painful for her to look at me and have my very presence, my life and my body before her, reminding her of what she had lost, what she couldn't have, reminding her of a great betrayal. Maybe in the end, she really did die of a broken heart.

I wanted to hate her, to remember her only as an ogre, but this letter made me feel sorry for her. Why did I read it? Even from the grave, she was chastising me. I could hear her.

"See, see," she was saying, *"I told you not to touch, not to snoop. When are you going to understand, Cathy? Stop moving the rocks, stop pulling back the curtains, stop pointing the light into the dark.*

"Leave the truth where it belongs, buried under a pile of sins."

"Hey," I heard Jade say from the doorway. "Are you all right?"

"What? Oh, yes," I said quickly, fumbling for the wallet and folding the letter. I stuffed it into my pocket.

"What's that?" she asked.

"Nothing," I said quickly.

Her face darkened with skepticism.

"We've got to trust each other, Cat. What we did together makes that very, very important," she said.

"It's just a lame apology," I told her, "an apology my mother wrote to Geraldine. I don't want to talk about it. The whole thing makes me sick."

"Okay, but when and if you do, just remember we're here for you."

"Thanks," I said. I put the pocketbook back on the dresser and held up the wallet. "I got it," I said. "And there's money in it, too."

She smiled.

"Then let's party at the mall," she declared, reaching for my hand.

I paused to close the door.

Even though she was dead and buried, I couldn't disregard her wishes. Bedroom doors had to be kept closed. Maybe so the secrets wouldn't slip out.

Or…

Slip in.

Misty was about Geraldine's size, so the driver's seat didn't have to be adjusted very much. Star sat up front with Misty, and Jade and I sat in the back, where there was more room for my cast.

"I've got to go to the hospital tomorrow," I said. "I'm supposed to have my ankle X-rayed again to be sure it's all right. If I don't appear, they'll call."

"So we'll take you," Jade said. "If anyone asks, we'll tell them your mother's under the weather."

"That's where she is all right," Star quipped.

Misty laughed and then she grew quiet and said, "I still can't believe we actually went through with it."

"Don't believe it," Jade suggested.

"Huh?"

"She's right, Misty. The more you think about it, the more chance you'll slip up. Let's make another OWP rule right away," Star continued.

"Ta da..." Misty sang.

"I'm serious."

"Okay, okay."

"Anyone who makes a reference to you know what from now on gets fined," Star declared in official tones.

"Fined? You mean, money?"

Star thought a moment and shook her head.

"No. The fine will be a punishment—whoever slips up has to do all the group's chores and fetching for the day." She turned and looked back at Jade, who raised her eyebrows. "I don't hear your vote, Jade."

"Yes," she shot back.

Star looked at me.

"Yes," I said with a shrug.

"Okay, okay," Misty said reluctantly, as if she could envision millions of trips to the shed or upstairs in the house to fetch this or that.

"Then it's unanimous. Shut your big mouths or else," Star concluded.

For a few moments, we rode in a dead silence.

"Let's begin at Fun Time in the mall," Misty requested. "They've got great stuff: posters, things to hang, black lights, everything! After that, we'll get new curtains for Cat's room and look for some new bedding."

She was so excited, she made me feel like it was nearly Christmas.

"That sounds good and then we'll go to Vogue City and check out some of the new clothes. Cat needs something decent for parties," Jade said.

"What parties?" I asked.

"Parties I'll have and parties we'll have at the club," she replied.

I smiled to myself. My house had become the club in their minds. Would it ever in mine?

Misty drove up to the entrance so I wouldn't have to walk that far. Then she parked while we waited. Minutes later, the four of us entered the mall and as we walked around the lower level, I could see the way we attracted attention. Jade and Star seemed very aware of the looks we were getting, especially from men.

"What are you looking at?" I heard Star mutter under her breath when two rather good looking, young black man stared our way. She gazed quickly at me. "Don't look back at them," she warned.

"What?"

"Keep your eyes focused ahead and get so you can see them out of the corners. That way they don't feel you're encouraging them to be bold, and if they say something to you, just pretend you didn't hear," Star advised.

"They're not looking at me anyway," I said.

"They will," Jade predicted, "when I'm finished with you."

It gave me a happy, excited feeling. My heart fluttered and my face got warm. She and Star had an electricity about them as if they were made of magnets, pulling and turning eyes their way with every step they took. I heard boys whistle and many tried to get our attention. Misty laughed.

Jade smiled at me.

"We break hearts," she said with pride. "That's what we do."

I had to laugh, too, but really at the thought that I could fill any boy with so much longing, he'd be crushed if I didn't pay him any attention. That was usually my fate, not the boy's. Maybe though, maybe what the girls had would rub off on me. I certainly felt more important just being with them.

At our first stop, Misty bought hundreds of dollars worth of decorations, posters, and pictures. I relied on their tastes and advice to make choices, embarrassed about not knowing who this actor was or that singer. Then we chose my new bedding and curtains.

After that, Jade rushed us into the clothing store and had me try on half a dozen different skirt and blouse outfits. She chose three that were very flattering then insisted I buy shoes too. Finally, we went to a Mexican restaurant for lunch. It was a bright, happy place full of people, chatter, and music. As soon as we sat in the booth, everyone began talking at once, or, I should say, they were all talking at once. I was content just listening, shifting my eyes, turning my head, spinning around to hear one story and then another. I felt like I had been turned into a sponge, absorbing their experiences, their times of fun, reliving their moments of excitement and pleasure.

"What will we do for dinner tonight?" Misty asked. "I vote for pizza."

"Pizza is so fattening," Jade said with a warning glance.

"Can't we start our healthy living tomorrow?" Misty pleaded for us all. "It'll be our first dinner in the clubhouse."

"Then it should be more special than just pizza," Star said. "I'll use Granny's recipe and make us Southern fried chicken and we'll have mashed potatoes and fried okra and black-eyed peas and—"

"Please, spare me," Jade said. "Fat city. Let's at least do Chinese. We can order from the healthier menu and get fun food that's not poisonous to our systems."

"My granny doesn't make poison," Star snapped. "Do I look unhealthy to you?"

"It's going to be late by the time we get everything home," I said. "Maybe it would be easier if we just order in tonight."

They all looked at me.

"Now I know Cat's strength," Star said.

"What?" Misty asked before I could.

"Miss Compromise, the Peacemaker. Okay, that's what we'll do tonight, but next time, we eat some home cooking," she concluded.

Jade looked satisfied and took out her pocket mirror. She shifted it to her right.

"See those two guys in the leather jackets in the booth back there," she whispered. "They were looking our way the entire time they were waiting to be seated. Any moment one of them is going to come over to say something."

Misty gaped.

"Don't make it so obvious," Star told her. She peered, too. "Grease balls," she decided. She smiled at Jade. "They're poor white trash, honey."

"I know, but it's fun to see what they'll do."

My heart started to pound because one of them did get up and start toward us. He looked like he was in his mid-twenties at least.

"Well, now," he said, "my buddy Carl and I were just admiring how you all get along so well. We thought now here's a group of young women who've got it together; cool, mature, good looking, fine representatives of the better sex. We were wondering if we might interest you in attending a party tonight. It's going to be great. We've got a live band and—"

"Just a minute," Jade said. She dipped into her purse and produced a small leather-covered notepad. I held my breath. She seemed to be seriously considering it. Misty sat with a grin on her face and Star just stared at Jade.

"Oh, I'm sorry," she said. "We're booked tonight. As a matter of fact, we're booked for the rest of our lives. But thanks."

He laughed.

"You sure?" he said.

"What are you, deaf or stupid?" Star asked him.

His smile faded. He looked back at his friend who was laughing at him, which made his face a darker crimson.

"Too bad," he said. "You're missing a good time."

Star continued to glare at him and he left the table to return to his buddy. Then Star broke the tension by laughing and so did Jade and Misty.

"He was cute," Jade confessed.

"So's a baby rat," Star said.

"How do you know who's right and who's wrong for you?" I asked.

They both looked at me.

"You'll know," Star said. "By the time we're finished with you."

They laughed again. I smiled and thought, I've got real friends, finally, and ironically, all because Geraldine died and left me alone. Was it wrong for something so good to come from something so bad? I was too nervous to care and maybe that was the biggest mistake of all.

9

Skeletons Out of the Closet

The telephone was ringing when we entered the house. I was holding open the door so the girls could carry in all the boxes, but I managed to get to the phone in time. The girls hurried to gather around me, anxious to hear who was calling. Was it the bank again?

"Hello?" I said, looking at them. After a moment I swallowed hard and said, "Just a minute, Doctor Marlowe."

I put my hand over the mouthpiece.

"She wants to talk to Geraldine. What will I do? What should I say?"

"Tell her your mother said she has nothing to say to her," Jade dictated. "Go on," she urged, "and make it sound truthful."

I took a breath and did what she suggested.

"I'm sorry, but she won't come to the phone, Doctor Marlowe. She has nothing to say to you."

That wasn't really a lie, I thought. She has nothing to say to anyone.

"She's not doing the right thing, Cathy. You need your follow-up visit. There are too many loose ends," Doctor Marlowe insisted. She sounded like she wasn't going to be satisfied until she spoke to Geraldine.

"I'll speak to her about it, Doctor Marlowe," I promised, "and I'll call you as soon as I can."

"You know I'm right, Cathy. We should do what's best for you." I thought she was going to end the conversation but then at the last minute she spoke again. "I understand you had some sort of an accident?"

"I'm fine," I said, maybe too quickly because there was a long pause.

"Have you seen or heard from the other girls?" she asked. The tone of her voice suggested that she already knew the answer.

"Yes, we've been in touch with each other," I admitted.

"I'm happy about that. I really do think you're all good for each other. Please don't let too much time go by before I hear from you," she urged.

"I won't, Doctor Marlowe. Thank you for calling," I said and hung up.

"Well?" Star asked.

"I don't know. She sounded like she believed me. She wants me to convince Geraldine I should return for a follow-up and call her soon."

Jade looked thoughtful.

"Cat could go back to see her, pretend she's convinced her mother to let her go. Maybe that would end it," she mused aloud.

"Too dangerous now," Star said. "You know how smart Doctor Marlowe is. She'll take one look at Cat and know everything. She's bound to ask difficult questions."

"Maybe she won't call again," Misty hoped.

"We'll stall as long as we can," Jade agreed, but a dark cloud of concern had moved in over our excitement, threatening to rain reality down on our efforts to create an oasis of fantasy in this desert of hard, sad times.

"I'm getting started on the redecorating," Misty declared. "I refuse to let anything depress me."

She attacked the project with her characteristic explosion of energy. Before long, we were all contributing in one way or another. Star and Jade rearranged furniture in the living room while I hobbled along beside Misty and helped her hang pictures and posters. She also set up the new CD player and the speakers. While we worked, we listened to the new CD's we bought and for the first time ever, rock music flowed through this house. Whenever Jade and Star passed Misty and me in the hallway, they were singing and dancing, and before long, we were all in the hallway, even me with my cast, singing, swinging, and swaying to the rhythms.

"I can't wait for our first party!" Misty cried.

"Who will we invite?" I wondered aloud.

"We'll be careful and take great care about who we choose," Jade said. "We should discuss every suggestion and make a rule we all have to accept anyone someone suggests, okay?"

"How are we going to do that?" Star asked. "I don't know your friends and you don't know mine."

"We'll talk about them and do the best we can," Jade insisted.

"Let's not worry so much about everything," Misty piped up. "Let's just have fun for a change."

"Hmm," Star grunted. She looked at me and then shook her head. "Don't worry about Doctor Marlowe; don't worry about the bank. Don't worry about this and don't worry about that. Maybe we should be calling ourselves the OWW's then, Orphans Without Worries."

Misty laughed. Star looked at Jade and then they both laughed, too. It was good; it was good to hear that sound in this house, a sound so alien to my home, I was always taken by surprise whenever I heard it here.

Our work continued. On the way back from the mall, we had stopped at a house and garden supply store where Star chose some plants and bushes to cover the grave while Misty and Jade picked out the paint for my room. We bought all the rollers and pans, too. Then Misty said we should think about painting the hallways as well. We talked about doing something with the house lighting. Geraldine always kept it dim, the fixtures loaded with low wattage bulbs to save on energy costs. Misty wanted us to buy some tinted bulbs, but Star thought it would make the house look too much like a bordello. In the end we agreed on a lighter shade of blue for the hallways and Misty, who seemed inexhaustible, decided to start on that while Star went out back to finish dressing up Geraldine's grave with the plants and bushes we had purchased. We were going to hang my new curtains, too, before the end of the day.

Jade was the first to grow tired of the work and began to complain about being hungry so we planned what we would order in from the nearest Chinese restaurant. Then they each called home to say they were staying at my house for dinner. Only Star's Granny was actually home to receive the call. Jade's mother was at a dinner meeting already and Misty's mother had left word with her answering service that she was going to a movie with one of her girlfriends.

"I thought you were getting permission to stay with her overnight anyway," Star reminded Misty.

"I was. I mean I will. I thought it would be easier to ask

from here and not have to answer any questions about it," she explained.

"Well, Granny said I can stay for dinner," Star declared, and then looked to me, "but only if you promise to come to our house for one of her home-cooked meals. I told her you would and she said tomorrow night. One thing about my granny, she doesn't dwell in the world of fluff. None of this 'we'll do lunch or dinner' stuff. If you say you will, she pins you down to being real. You can stay over, too," she added.

Jade and Misty both nodded with looks in their eyes that told me how much they wished they lived in Granny's world rather than their own.

"Do you have anything to drink here?" Jade suddenly asked. It was as if just the suggestion of something dark and unpleasant had to be kept out any way possible.

Misty's eyes widened. She looked clownish. Her cheeks had dabs of blue paint on them and there was a streak under her chin.

"Yeah, something to drink. That's a real good idea," she seconded.

"Drink? You mean, alcohol?" I asked Jade.

"I know you have milk and cookies," Jade quipped.

"Oh. I think there's some liquor in the pantry," I said. "I don't know what it is. My father was the only one who drank it."

Jade went to look and returned with the report that we had half a bottle of vodka and nearly a full bottle of gin. She had the vodka in hand.

"I'll make everyone screwdrivers," she announced, "and we'll relax before dinner."

Misty went to wash up and I called in our dinner order, putting it on the charge card. All the shopping, the work, the music, and laughs really had made me feel better. Not once during the day had I had a chance to relive the night before. As long as we kept occupied and excited, we didn't dwell on what we had done and what it all meant. Bigger questions like how would we manage to continue all this once school had begun again and we were all occupied with our own little worlds didn't even come up. For now, we were all on a roller coaster and no one wanted to do or say anything that might bring us to a dead stop.

After Misty returned from cleaning her hands and face, we gathered in the rearranged living room. I had to admit it looked brighter and gave the impression of being bigger by not separating the chairs as far from the sofa. We pulled the curtains fully open and let in the twilight, which threw a hazy glow of pink and yellow over the otherwise dull brown walls. Star and Jade sat on the sofa while Misty and I chose the easy chairs. It was when we had stopped and relaxed that we all began to feel the fatigue settle in. We sat there quietly for a few moments, sipping the drinks. I didn't taste the vodka, but I knew from my previous bad experience of drinking rum and Cokes that it can sneak up on you.

"Did you read any more of your real mother's letters to you?" Jade asked me.

"No. I was too tired last night."

"What did she tell you in the first letter besides the stuff about your trust fund?"

"Not that much," I said. "She made it sound like she wasn't in love with her husband, Grandpa Franklin. She said she arranged for Geraldine to adopt me so that I would be close to her always, to keep me in the family."

"Some family," Star muttered.

"She found another letter in Geraldine's pocketbook

today, too," Jade told Star and Misty, who sipped their drinks and looked at me with interest. "An apology or something, right?"

"Yes," I said. I reached into my pocket and produced the letter. "She doesn't say exactly who my real father is, but she suggests Geraldine loved him and maybe wanted him to be her husband."

"So it was probably someone younger than your real mother if Geraldine was interested in him too," Jade conjectured.

"Maybe," Star said. "Though Geraldine could have been in love with someone's grandfather, too, the way she thought."

"Actually, the letter suggests that my real father *was* older than Geraldine," I added.

"Do you think your father's name is in the other letters then?" Misty asked.

I shrugged.

"How can you be so calm about it? Don't you want to know who he is?" she asked.

"Sure she does," Jade answered for me, "but you should know from our experiences at Doctor Marlowe's that we don't just rush headlong into any of this. It's too traumatic."

"But maybe when she finds out, she can go to him and maybe he'll want her to move in with him and be his daughter finally," Misty said in her dreamy tone of voice again. Actually, it sounded more like something she wished for herself.

Star shook her head.

"You do live in Never-Never Land, don't you? That's the last thing her real father wants to happen. He's probably got his own family and wife and how do you think they'll feel learning about Cathy, huh?"

"Oh," Misty said. Then she smiled. "So what? We're here now. You don't need anyone else. Still," she said after a moment, "if it was me who didn't know who my real father was and I had a chance to find out, I'd be very excited and anxious to do it. I wouldn't wait."

"Cat isn't you," Star said. "So shut up about it already."

Misty looked glum for a moment and then brightened.

"Let's talk about our first party. When should we have it?" she asked.

"We're having it now," Star said.

"No, I mean with boys," Misty insisted.

Star looked at Jade.

"Not until we've got everything the way we want it," Jade said, as if it was the most obvious fact of all. "When the time comes, we'll tell whomever we all decide to invite that Cathy's mother has gone away for the day and we have the house."

"We don't want to invite too many people," Star cautioned, "and we better be sure no one makes it sound like an open party or we'll get all sorts of riffraff."

"Let's just invite boys. Four of them," Jade suggested. "Who needs any more competition, not that I'm afraid of it or anything."

Star laughed and drank some more of her screwdriver.

"I'm not! It's just...not prudent to invite other girls at this time," Jade insisted.

"Prudent? I like that. What do you think, Cat? Should we just invite boys?" she teased. "Is that prudent?"

"I don't know," I said. "You girls know about the only party I ever went to, really, and you know what happened to me," I said, gazing at my drink.

They nodded, all looking both sad and angry for me as they recalled the story I had told them at the group therapy session. I had been given too much rum and Coke to drink and some boys had taken advantage and groped me while girls I thought were my friends looked on and laughed.

"Nothing like that is going to happen here," Star assured me. "We won't let it."

"That's right," Jade insisted. "We'll always look out for each other."

I smiled. I really did feel safer now, even safer with them than I had felt with Geraldine. And that's what family was supposed to do for you, I thought, make you feel secure, let you know that there are people who care about you and want to protect you and love you. We'd be friends forever and ever, and there was nothing I wouldn't do for them and nothing they wouldn't do for me. It wasn't just the vodka that made me feel warm and comfortable now. It was their smiles and their laughter and their promises.

We could believe in the promises we made to each other easier than those our parents made to us. Because we were all veterans of disappointment, we knew how painful it would be to disappoint each other. What better guarantees were there than the ones born out of mutual pain and respect?

"To the OWP's," Misty cried, holding up her glass as if she could read my very thoughts. "One for all and all for one!"

"To the OWP's," we joined, and drank down our drinks.

Jade started to prepare another for all of us as the dinner arrived. We were just beginning to feel very good and be happy. The best was yet to come, I thought. My friends had helped me bury all my disappointments, forever and ever.

Was I being too optimistic? Was Misty rubbing off on me? Was I turning into a dreamer? What if I was? Anything was better than what I had been, I thought. This was like being born again and there was no turning back now, never.

Geraldine could rise from the grave; she could haunt this house; she could turn shadows into shapes and hiss her displeasure from the darkest corners. She could glare at me from behind my eyes, from my deepest, darkest memories, but she wouldn't turn me around. You always wanted doors to be shut, Geraldine, I thought. Well, this time, I'm slamming them shut on you.

Maybe it was the vodka talking, but I felt brave and strong. I drank another and I sang along with the girls whenever they burst into song. We ate everything in sight and then collapsed on the sofas and in the chairs, laughing at our appetites, not caring about the loudness of the music or the noise we made. It felt so good to do it, to have the freedom, but I couldn't help gazing up at the doorway and thinking about Geraldine. It was just habit. She wasn't gone long enough for me to not feel afraid.

"What are you looking so worried about?" Jade cried at me. "Stop looking behind your shoulder. She's gone. She's a potted plant!" she declared, laughing. Her eyes were glazed. "I ruined an expensive outfit helping to plant her," she added, the vodka definitely speaking now.

Star immediately sprung up, her finger pointed.

"You did it," she accused. "You spoke the unspeakable and you are fined."

"What?"

"Am I right?" Star asked us. "We made the rule in the car. We all voted, right?"

Misty looked timid, but nodded.

"She's right, Jade."

"So, what am I supposed to do now?" Jade shot back at Star. "Go to my room?"

Star straightened up and smiled.

"You clean up, girl. That's your punishment," she said.

Jade's mouth dropped open. She looked at me and then at Misty. Neither of us would dare contradict Star.

"Fine," Jade said, rising and sobering quickly. She wiped her cheeks as if to wake up her face and then she headed out to the kitchen. We watched her saunter along mumbling about washing dishes and ruining her brand-new manicure.

"We'll bring her down to earth yet," Star declared with a smirk. "We'll bring her right down to earth with the rest of us."

Misty called home to tell her mother she was going to spend the night with me, but her mother had still not returned from the movies.

"She must have gone someplace afterward with her friend," she said. "I just left a message with her answering service. It's actually easier this way. Half the time, we talk to each other through that answering service anyway. I'd feel strange not having it between us." She looked around and then turned to me. "Where will I sleep?" Before I could suggest anything, she declared, "Not in your half sister's room."

"I'll sleep on the sofa and you can sleep in my room," I said. Her eyes darkened with thought. She glanced up the stairway and shook her head.

"No, it's not fair to take your bed. I'll sleep on the sofa."

"You're just afraid to sleep upstairs," Jade said, laughing.

"Well, it's all right for you to sound so brave. You're not sleeping here tonight. I am."

"It would be easier for Cat to avoid going up the stairs," Star said. "Didn't we tell her that?" she reminded Misty with an impish smile.

Misty looked trapped.

"We can both sleep in my bed," I said. "It's big enough, if that's all right with you."

"Yes," she said quickly, seizing the suggestion. "Of course it's big enough and it'll be more fun. We'll test out your new bedding and hang your curtains, too."

Jade and Star looked at each other and laughed.

"Well, we'll both feel better," Misty added, nodding. "Tomorrow, we should do something with your half sister's room, like rip it apart and start over again. We'll get every trace of her out of there just the way my mother got every trace of my father out of our house after they separated. And we'll paint it, too, a color she hated."

"That's just about everything but white," I said.

"All right," Jade said, growing serious. "Do what you want, you two. I've called for the limousine to pick up Star and me and take us home tonight. It'll be here any minute. In the morning we'll meet here and start thinking about planning our first party and stuff," she said.

"Don't forget, Cat, you're coming to my house for dinner tomorrow night and you're staying with me," Star told me. "We don't have to worry about ghosts there," she said, teasing Misty.

"There's no ghost here. Stop it," Misty moaned.

Star and Jade laughed.

When the limousine arrived, Misty and I watched them leave. Misty looked like she wished she was leaving with them.

"You really don't have to stay with me," I told her. "I was all right last night. I'll be all right tonight."

"We decided and that's it," she insisted. "I'll be fine and so will you. We can talk and talk until we pass out," she said. "We'll be fine."

"I'm afraid I don't have anything really nice for you to sleep in," I said. "Just cotton pajamas."

"That'll do, although I'll probably look like I'm floating in them. I don't know why I don't grow," she complained. "I think my hormones went on vacation right after I turned twelve."

"You're perfect," I said, laughing. "You're..."

"Don't you dare say 'cute,' " she warned me, her right forefinger jabbing the air.

"Petite," I risked. She turned over the word in her mind, smirked and sighed.

"I guess I'll look twenty years younger than I am for the rest of my life. My mother says that's a blessing I'll first realize the day I turn thirty. But until then," she said, "it's a curse. C'mon. Let's go hang the curtains."

We turned off the lights and started up the stairs.

"Maybe you'll read me one of your mother's letters afterward," she said. "Unless you think they're just too personal."

"I don't know what they are," I replied. Then after thinking a moment, I added, "After the things we told each other at Doctor Marlowe's and after what we've pledged to each other, nothing's too personal anymore, anyway."

She paused and looked at me on the stairs.

"That's how I feel," she said, "only it's nice to hear you say it. It's nice to know you believe it."

"I do," I said.

She looked emboldened and happy, and began charging

the rest of the way up the stairs with no hint of fear or trepidation in her stride.

"Well, if Geraldine's ghost is in this house, we'll throw her out," she vowed, and continued up to my room.

I watched her climb the stairs and realized that this was the first time ever I had had a friend sleep over. Geraldine never approved of the idea, nor did she approve of my sleeping over at someone else's house. She might certainly wake up from the dead to haunt us tonight. But let her, let her come. We're ready for her, I thought.

I hoped.

After we hung the curtains and changed the bedding and we were both snugly under my blanket, I reached for the pile of letters and pulled out the next one. Carefully, I unfolded it. The paper was so fragile and crisp from age that I had to be gentle. It would take only the smallest amount of pressure for it to tear.

"*Dear Cathy,*" I read aloud.

> "*I assume by now you have read my first letter. I do hope you will have read all of them before we get a chance to talk privately. Of course, I will want to answer all your questions. I know you will have many. I would if I were you.*
>
> "*I imagine the first question that comes to mind is why I went ahead with the birth. The moment I set eyes on you, of course, I was happy I had. I can't imagine a world without you in it now.*"

"That's nice," Misty piped up. "Remember when I first began in the group therapy session and I jokingly said my parents tried to give me back, but it was too late? I have

165

no doubt that if they had a chance now to have a child all over again, they wouldn't. At least she wanted you even after you were born," Misty pointed out.

I nodded and returned to the letter.

> "Relationships between men and women are very complicated, Cathy. I know this is something you will learn for yourself. I only hope I might still be around to help you get through some of the more difficult times. I'm not sure Geraldine is equipped for the kinds of crises a young girl might experience."

"Boy, was she right about that!" Misty cried.

> "As I said in my first letter, my parents, especially my mother, really believed I would learn to love Franklin, but love has to come from a deeper place, a place other than your brain. You don't study someone and memorize his every mannerism and his habits so that you can please him and call that love.
>
> "Whether we like to admit it to ourselves and others or not, we women need real passion and affection in our lives. We like to feel good, to be petted and fussed over. It's nice to see a man's face light up when you enter a room. It's heartwarming to see he is willing to show you how much he does love you. Unfortunately, Franklin was never capable of that. He is a good man, a moral man, a considerate man, but he's not a passionate man. Maybe it was wrong for me to let my eyes wander, to let my heart have a louder

voice than my conscience and my brain, but I did.

"Sometimes, I let myself believe Franklin knew what I was doing. It helped me to think that he did, to imagine that he even condoned it because he recognized that my lover provided something for me that he could never provide. I told myself Franklin just wants me to be happy and he is willing to look the other way if that means I'll be happy. Perhaps it was only foolish hope or, as I have said, a way of rationalizing my infidelity, but I let myself believe it.

"I want you to learn from this how important it is to give yourself to a man you can truly love and who can truly love you in all respects. Settling for anything less will lead to lifelong unhappiness, deep frustration, and eventually disaster in one form or another. Just look at me as an example.

"I was so reckless about my affair that I didn't take the proper precautions. I think now that deep in my heart I didn't want to. Yes, as horrible or as shocking as that may sound to you, I wanted my lover's child growing in my womb. Maybe it was my way of confessing and if you are a really moral person, even if you can get away with a sin, you will have a great need to confess it. Eventually, you must. Remember that, Cathy. Never fool yourself into believing you can escape your own conscience. It's a voice that dies only when you die, and you will hear it in your sleep as long as you live."

I paused because my throat had tightened, and I looked at Misty who was lying there so still, listening, her eyes fixed on the wall, her face full of anticipation. She realized I had stopped and turned to me. We stared at each other a moment.

"Don't even think it," she warned. "It's not a sin; we didn't kill her or anything. We did what we had to do to protect you. What difference does it make where she rests in peace or who knows?"

I nodded, but my chest felt so full, so heavy with the guilt I wanted to believe would go away.

"It's a beautiful letter. I agree with what she said about love. Don't stop reading. There's more, isn't there?" she asked hopefully.

"Yes," I said. I looked at it again and continued.

> *"I think I can actually pinpoint when you were conceived. It was on a rainy Friday. Franklin was out of town on business and your father came to the house. Shall I tell you now who he is? My fingers tremble with the pen in hand. Will I cause more trouble, hurt more people? Do you have a right to know? Of course you do. Whatever happens as a result is my fault only. Never, never blame yourself for anything.*
>
> *"Your father was Franklin's much younger brother Alden. He was actually only five years older than Geraldine. Does that make it sound like I robbed the cradle? I hope not. The truth is Alden was emotionally wiser and older than most of his contemporaries, although he was a disappointment to his parents and especially to Franklin, who was the hardest on him—even be-*

fore he knew Alden and I had become lovers. Alden didn't want to be confined to a business career. His love was music, composing. He played the piano beautifully and many a night, he performed only for me.

"In college he majored in music, and won many awards. He earned a small living tutoring, giving private lessons, but he had no ambition to be wealthy and powerful. He was a beautiful man: poetic, romantic, a dreamer I suppose, and he was very handsome. I expect you will inherit his good qualities, Cathy. I really do.

"However, by the time you begin reading these letters, I don't suppose you will know all that much about Alden. The family wasn't proud of him as they should have been and they refrained from talking about him if they could. It was as if his personal creative ambitions were considered a sign of madness. Perhaps he was a little mad, but all creative people are. I found his disregard for material wealth and for all the things Franklin and his family found important to be charming. He was refreshing, as refreshing as a warm but crisp late summer breeze, and he had a smile that could melt the hardest, iciest heart—yes, even Geraldine's.

"He spent a lot of time with Geraldine. He tried to get her to play the piano and she did take lessons from him, but I think she did it more to be in his company than out of any love of music. She did passingly well, but the moment she found out about us, she stopped the lessons and hasn't put her fingers to keys ever since.

"I know Geraldine felt more betrayed by Alden than she did by me. Her deep love and affection for him soured into jealousy and hatred. It got so she wouldn't speak to him unless she absolutely had to and she avoided him as much as she could. She didn't even go to his funeral.

"I expect you know about his death of course, but you will have known it only as a family tragedy and not, as you now do, as the death of the man who was your true father.

"The tears are rolling off my cheeks so fast, I think I have to stop for a while. I wanted to tell you about our wonderful night together, the one in which you were created; however I'll save that for the next letter.

"Love can be so painful sometimes that I envy Geraldine for being so hard. She once told me bitterly that she didn't need to love anyone or have anyone love her. I know she was just speaking out of anger and disappointment that she had never met anyone who loved her dearly, passionately, but there are times when I wish it had been true for me.

"And then I think how lonely she must be and I feel absolutely dreadful for her. The truth is every time I look at her, I think of my own guilt. I am partly responsible for her misery and all the beautiful music and true feelings in the world can't erase that from my heart. It's a scar.

"You, you are the only hope I have for redemption. Be wonderful, be someone full of love and compassion, and never stop searching until

you find someone who fills your heart with so
much joy you can hardly breathe without him
beside you.
  "I'd like to know I was responsible for that.
                                    "For now, Mother"

I put the letter down and looked at Misty. She was wiping the tears from her cheeks.

"That was beautiful," she said. She sat up and gazed at the letter. "So now you know who your father is or was, I should say. What do you know about him?"

"Hardly anything," I said. "Geraldine never talked about him and there isn't even a picture of him—that I know of, that is. I know where he is buried and I know he was killed in an automobile accident and he was supposedly drunk. That's what she means by a family tragedy."

I paused and shook my head.

"I don't even know what he looked like."

"Wow. Well, we've got to search high and low tomorrow for pictures, okay?" Misty said.

"What? Oh, yes."

"Maybe there were some in one of the cartons up in the crawl space," she suggested.

"Yes, there were old pictures in a cigar box."

"I'll go back up and get everything down. We'll have a good time exploring," Misty said. She thought a moment. "That was strange, that part about Geraldine. Your mother made it sound as if Geraldine was in love with Alden too, but Alden was her uncle. Surely, she didn't expect to marry her uncle. I guess she was just terribly disappointed in him for having an affair with her mother. Men can let you down in so many ways," she concluded.

I nodded, folded the letter carefully, and put it back with the others.

"You're not going to read another one?"

"I'm tired," I said.

"Me too. It's been a great day though, lots of fun, right?"

"Yes," I said.

I reached over to turn off the light.

"You know, you closed your bedroom door even though we're the only ones in the house," she said.

"Just habit. You want to open it?"

She thought a moment.

"No, it's all right. I guess."

I turned off the light. We lay there in the darkness, both of us with our eyes open. When I glanced at her, she looked like she was listening.

"Your house creaks a lot," she said. "Right?"

"Just the wind," I said. "It's an old house."

"Right."

"Good night, Misty. Thanks for staying over."

"Night."

She turned over. There was a sound from below even I didn't recognize. I could feel her body tighten beside me.

"Is that the wind?" she asked. "Cat?"

"I guess," I said.

"You guess?"

"Yes," I said. "It's only the wind."

"Somehow, in the darkness, it's harder to be brave," Misty said.

"Do you want me to leave a light on?"

"If *you* do," she said.

I smiled, got up, and turned on the light in my bathroom, closing the door just enough to let some illumination into the bedroom.

"Better?"

"Sure," she said. "Night."

"Night."

"Your mother," she said. "I mean your real mother. She sounds very nice."

"Yes."

"Too bad you can't do what she wished and meet her now after you have learned the truth. It's not fair. None of this is fair," she added. She reached back to squeeze my hand once and then she fell asleep.

I smiled to myself.

Fair, I thought. What an illusion that was for all of us. But at least I have friends, I thought. I'm not alone. And I'm not afraid of what's to come.

10

❦

Geraldine's Secret

Once Misty and I fell asleep, we slept through the night, comforted in knowing we were beside each other. I didn't have any nightmares either. The next morning Misty was up before me, exploding with her characteristic energy, talking about having breakfast and getting started as quickly as possible on continuing to redo the house, or as she now called it, "the club."

While we were having breakfast, both Star and Jade called to say they were coming over as soon as possible. Jade sounded as if she had just woken, but Star's voice was full of energy. By the time they arrived, Misty and I had already painted most of the hallway.

"We found out who her father was," Misty told them almost immediately. "It was in the next letter. Her mother's brother-in-law, Alden. You were right, Jade. He was a younger man. He's dead though, killed in a car accident, a DWI," she added, without stopping for a breath.

They both looked at me, waiting to see my reaction.

What was I supposed to do? I wondered, or what was I supposed to feel? I never knew him, never even recalled seeing him or speaking to him. How could I feel sad or disappointed or anything?

"As soon as I finish this," Misty continued, "I'm going up into the crawl space. We think there might be pictures of him in one of the cartons and I'll bring the other stuff down so Cat can put whatever she wants in her room. Finally," she added.

"I'm glad you're making all these decisions yourself," Jade snapped at her.

"I'm not making them myself. Cat and I talked about it last night, right, Cat?"

"Yes," I said, but Jade still looked annoyed.

"We should share important information immediately," she said.

"What did you want us to do, call you last night?" Misty asked, holding her brush up and away like a torch. We had spread newspaper on the floor to catch any drips. It was a good idea because we had paint all over our clothes and splattered on our faces, too.

"Of course you should have called. You know we were all concerned and interested. It was her assignment to find these things out and report back. Did you forget all that we pledged and did at my house?" Jade chastised.

"I'm sorry. Boy. This is worse than being in school and living with those rules."

"Either we're together or we're not," Jade snapped.

I looked at Star. Usually, she would have something to say to ease any conflict or challenge Jade, but she remained quiet.

"Damn all these family secrets," Jade said. "They fall like rain around us."

She marched toward the kitchen. "I'm making some coffee," she muttered.

"What's the matter with her? Her mascara run or something this morning?" Misty asked Star in a whisper.

Star stepped closer to us to speak softly.

"Her parents finally settled their divorce late yesterday. Her father suddenly decided to give up fighting for full custody. He's building a new house and he's met someone new, someone who has a daughter about Jade's age and a son in college. They're going to move in with him. It all came as a surprise, even though it must have been going on for quite a while," Star explained.

"Oh," I said. I looked toward the kitchen. "No wonder she's made that remark about family secrets falling like rain. But I thought she hated their bickering over her and she would be happy when it was settled."

"Yes and no," Star said. She looked at Misty. "It's nice to be wanted a lot by both your parents, even under those circumstances. I think it gave her a sense of security. Now that's it's over, her mother is talking about having a small celebration," she continued, still in a whisper, "but Jade doesn't want any part of it."

"I don't blame her," Misty said. "I hate it when my mother is happy about something in the divorce going her way." She stared after Jade for a moment and then turned to Star. "Sorry we didn't call you last night when we made the discovery. As I said, Cat read another letter and—"

"Oh, I don't care about that, and I don't think she's really upset about it either. Let's just get to work. I think it's a good idea to rip your sister's bedroom apart and turn it into something nice," she told me. "The way we're feeling it'll be good to rip anything apart," she added, and laughed.

Jade returned and looked at the repainted walls.

"You're doing sloppy work," she criticized. "You're supposed to put tape over the places you don't want to paint."

"Here," Misty said, handing her the brush, "do it right while I go up into the crawl space."

Jade looked at the brush and then stepped back as if it was the most disgusting, vile thing she had ever seen.

"I'll pass on that," she said. "Especially with what I'm wearing."

"Put on a pair of Cat's pants and one of her sweatshirts," Misty suggested.

"Just go about your business and stop bossing me around," Jade snapped back at her. She gazed at the paint and grimaced with more disgust. "I'm having coffee at the moment," she added, and hurried back to the kitchen.

We all laughed and then Star took over for Misty while she went to set the ladder up in the pantry. When she was ready, she called to us and Star helped her hand down the cartons. We carried everything into the living room.

"Look at this doll!" Misty declared holding up the one with the battered head and face. "Someone took her frustrations out on it, I guess."

"Gee, I wonder who," Jade said. She sifted through the clothing. "Some of this stuff still has tags on it. It was never used."

"She told me she didn't want to give me any of it," I explained. "She said my mother was just trying to buy my love."

"They do try that," Jade said, her eyes small and angry, "and we let them most of the time. My father has decided he wants to buy me a new car with his own money. It's supposed to make me feel better about his decision to spend the rest of his life with another woman, another family. Maybe Geraldine had the right idea putting all this up in the attic."

"I don't think that was right," Misty said softly. "Cat probably could have used these things."

I sat with the cigar box in my lap and opened it slowly, taking out the first picture. It was a photograph of Geraldine seated at the piano and a man standing and smiling beside her.

"This must be Alden, my father," I said, and they gathered around. "According to what my mother wrote in her letter to me, he gave Geraldine piano lessons."

"He's good looking," Misty said. "You have his nose and mouth."

I looked at other pictures. Most of them had Geraldine in them as well as my father. One was torn. Someone obviously had been ripped out of the picture.

"I don't think we have to work hard to guess who was standing there next to him," Star said.

"Why don't you do the same thing?" Jade suggested. "Cut Geraldine out of one of the better pictures of him and put the remaining photograph in a nice frame?"

"That's right," Misty said.

I stared at the face of the man who was supposedly my father, my mother's lover. He was handsome, with light brown hair that waved just enough to be perfect. His eyes looked like they sparkled with laughter.

"Nice smile," Jade said. "You should smile more, Cat. That will be your smile, too," she said. "Poor Cat," she added putting her hand on my shoulder, "you found your father and lost him almost at the same time." I felt her body stiffen and looked up at her. "Believe me," she said, "it's easier that way, Cat. It's easier than losing him years and years later."

"You didn't lose your father," Misty told her. "You'll still spend time with him, won't you?"

"Right. Quality time," she said with her mouth twisted as if she had bitten into a rotten apple. "I know the drill well. He'll have his days and he'll try to crowd a week or a month into them while he looks over his shoulder to see what his new wife and family are up to. Thanks, but I think I'd rather be in Cat's position. At least she is past the pain."

"Still, not to let her know about her father until now was cruel," Misty insisted.

Jade shrugged. She was feeling so bitter, it seemed like nothing would put a smile back on her beautiful face, a face where smiles belonged, where they blossomed.

Star took the pictures from my hands and returned them to the cigar box.

"Enough of this sad reminiscing. I think now we're all in the right frame of mind to go upstairs and do that room," she said. "Ready?"

"Yes," Jade said, straightening.

"Absolutely," Misty said. "Let's get to it."

I started to shake my head.

"It's too late to turn back now, Cat," Star said. "Roll up your sleeves and follow us. Forward," Star declared, and they headed out of the living room. I did follow, not knowing what to expect next, but feeling as though I was a train, doomed to follow the tracks no matter where they led.

The girls began by tearing down the bland, white curtains and stripping Geraldine's bed. Then they argued about what color we should paint the room.

"It's got to be either pink or a light blue," Misty insisted.

"I say we paint it black," Jade suddenly suggested.

"What?" Star said. "Black? Are you crazy? A room painted black?"

"It will be our ceremonial room," Jade continued, walking around the room. "We don't need it to be a bedroom. We'll clear out all this thrift shop furniture and we'll buy pictures and things for our organization."

"Like what?" Star asked.

"I have some ideas, some good ideas," she said, nodding. "Trust me." She turned to us. "Well? Don't you want a ceremonial room? We'll use it for our special meetings and for our private talks. No one will be permitted up here but us. That's a cardinal rule of the OWP's."

"You and your hideaways," Star remarked. Jade stared at her, waiting, impatience firing up her eyes. "Okay, okay, I agree."

"Misty?"

"Sounds...interesting," Misty said.

"Cat?"

"What are we going to do with the furniture?" I asked.

"We'll give it to the Salvation Army or someone. That's the least of our worries. If we're going to rid this house of Geraldine, we should do it right," she insisted. She nodded and smiled as she looked around. "It will be a perfect special place. Let's get started. Misty, go with Star and get plain, flat black paint, gallons, and more brushes and rollers and pans," she ordered. "Cat and I will empty the dressers and closets and pack up the clothing, except what we think we might need for some reason or another. You were right when you suggested one of us might have to parade around in Geraldine's clothing occasionally.

"Well?" she said when no one moved. "Do we need to take another vote or what?"

Misty looked at me and I looked at Geraldine's bedroom. Black? All the furniture given away? It would be as if she never had existed. I nodded.

"Be careful with the car," I told her. She smiled and looked at Star who raised her eyebrows.

"I don't know what you have in mind, Jade, but it better not be something weird," she warned.

Jade laughed.

"Like what we've already done isn't weird, right?" She stopped smiling. "We've got to keep building ourselves, building our confidence, building our union. We're better than the families we were born into," she said. "Better together."

"I like that," Misty declared. "Better together. A new slogan. I'll get us all T-shirts that say it."

Jade nodded.

"That's it, Misty, now you're thinking like an OWP. Well, Miss Star?" she asked her.

Star shook her head and laughed.

"Are you going to help paint, Miss Beverly Hills, or just watch us work?"

Jade reached for Geraldine's robe that was hanging on the inside of the closet door. She slipped it over her clothing and turned back to us.

"Absolutely," she said.

"Okay. Let's go, Misty, before she realizes what she promised."

They hurried out. Jade turned to me. Geraldine had that robe so long, I couldn't remember when she didn't. I would never even think of putting it on, but Jade had no reason to have my inhibitions.

"Let's start on the drawers. We don't want to throw out anything valuable," Jade said, and I joined her as she pulled out the top dresser drawer and began to pluck Geraldine's clothing like she was plucking feathers. She dropped them almost immediately, as if they were all diseased, and the pile began to build on the floor. When she reached the third drawer, she stopped and turned to me.

"Whoa," she said, "what do we have here?"

"What?"

Slowly, she brought out an exquisitely embroidered sheer silk bra designed with underwire cups.

"It must have done wonders for her nearly nonexistent bosom," Jade said, holding it up.

I shook my head.

"She never wore that," I said, astounded.

Jade tossed it to me.

"There's more here," she said, and reached into the drawer, this time coming out with a velvet and satin one-piece undergarment. It had push-up underwire cups, removable pads and a thong bottom. Jade held it up. I shook my head. "I've seen this in either Victoria's Secret or Frederick's of Hollywood," she said.

She tossed it to me and plucked out another skimpy bra, more thong bottoms and a chic maillot in a burnout dot pattern made of spandex. There were also two tanksuits with mesh midriffs, one in light gray and one in black.

"I never saw her wear any of this," I said. "I don't understand. Why is it here? How?"

"Maybe that's why she wanted the door always closed," Jade said, and cleaned out the drawer. "She had her own fantasies after all, Cat."

Jade's eyes narrowed as she looked at the nightstand. She glanced at me and marched over, pulling on the handle. The drawer didn't budge.

"It's locked," she said. "Where would the key be?"

"I don't know. Maybe her pocketbook," I said, and went to it. I turned it over and emptied the contents on the small dressing table. There was no key to any drawers, just keys to the house.

Jade shrugged.

"What do we care now?" she said, and went into the closet. She emerged with a metal shoehorn in hand and shoved it into the crack of the drawer, trying to pry it open. While she struggled, I looked through Geraldine's jewelry box and some other small boxes for the key. I turned when Jade moaned that she wasn't having any success. The shoehorn bent before it budged the well-locked drawer. She sat on the floor, frustrated.

"I'll have to go downstairs and get a hammer and a screwdriver or something," she said. She started to rise and stopped. I saw a smile break out over her face.

"What?"

"Well, lookie here," she said, reaching under the bed. "She's got a key dangling on a string that's tied to the bedsprings."

She reached under and brought it out. The string was long enough to reach the nightstand, and sure enough fit the lock. Jade turned it and looked back at me. I shook my head. This was all a surprise to me.

"I have no idea why she locked it," I said.

She opened the drawer and I hobbled over to look into it with her.

"Figures," she said, nodding.

"What's in there?" I asked.

"You don't know?"

I shook my head.

She reached inside the drawer and then held up a stack of books and magazines.

"Pornography," she said. "And sex manuals." I raised my eyebrows and she added, "With pictures."

My eyes widened. To discover that Geraldine read these...it was so shocking, I wondered if I wasn't dreaming this whole thing.

"No."

"Yes," she said, smiling. "Your precious Saint Geraldine had a whole secret life here. While she wouldn't let you own a bathing suit or wear shorts or clothes she thought might look too tight, behind closed doors she was Miss X-rated. What a hypocrite."

Jade tossed the books and magazines onto the pile of clothing.

"Nothing will surprise me now," she said, and started on the closet.

I stood back, still stunned. What did all this mean?

"Get in here," Jade called.

I entered the closet. She was standing in the corner. She had pulled away most of the garments and there, well hidden behind them, was a small safe.

"I don't suppose you know the combination," she asked me.

"I didn't even know it was here."

"This isn't going to be easy to open," she said. She knelt down and searched around the safe. I drew closer. "Go back and search that night stand drawer. Look for numbers written on anything," she ordered. "Since she kept it locked, we might have a shot."

I took everything out of the drawer slowly and inspected it. There was a small flashlight, some over-the-counter medicines for colds and headaches, a box of cough drops, a pen, a pair of reading glasses, a small pair of scissors and a back scratcher, but no slips of paper, and no pads. There was nothing written on the pad by the phone either. I returned to the contents of her pocketbook and sifted through it all carefully.

"Nothing," I told Jade when she emerged from the closet.

She stood there with her hands on her hips, thinking.

"We've got to find the combination," she said.

"It's going to be like searching for a needle in the haystack," I told her.

"Maybe. We've got to think like her. I saw this movie once where the detective tried to become the killer, get into his mind, to track him down," she said.

I smiled. She was sounding more like Misty, but at least the search had inspired her and washed away her expressions of gloom and doom.

"She was confident that you would never come in here. That door doesn't even lock," she said, nodding at the bedroom door. "Once it was shut, it was as good as locked, though. Yet, she did lock the nightstand. Why? Maybe because your adoptive father slept here," she answered herself, just like Geraldine used to do. "Chances are he never knew the combination to that safe either."

"Do you think he knew about the other stuff?" I asked, nodding at the sexy undergarments and the books and magazines. She thought a moment and shook her head.

"No, I don't, especially after what you've told us about both of them and their relationship." She gazed around the room and shook her head. "You're right," she said. "If she wrote it down on something, it could be anywhere, maybe even in a different room. Still, we should give it a try," she concluded, and started to inspect behind furniture and under the bed. She even pulled out the drawers and looked behind them as well. I did as much searching as I could and after about a half hour of ripping things apart, we both stopped and sat on the mattress, discouraged.

"It's got to be someplace really obvious," she thought. She gazed up at the light fixture and then looked at the windows and ran her eyes over the walls. "Once, at school, when I was afraid I might forget my locker combination, I went into the girls' room and I wrote it in tiny numbers on the wall in the first stall. Let's inspect the walls," she decided and rose. I took the opposite wall. We practically had our noses to them.

"What are you two weirdos doing?" Star asked from the doorway.

We had both been concentrating so hard, neither of us heard her and Misty come in and up the stairs. They both stood there gaping at us, bags in hand.

"We're looking for the combination to the secret safe I discovered in the closet. I thought Geraldine might have scribbled it on a wall."

"Secret safe?" Misty asked.

"I discovered a few other surprises too," Jade said, nodding at the second pile on the floor.

Star approached it slowly and then knelt down and examined the garments. She picked up the books and magazines, too.

"Are these what I think they are?" she asked Jade.

"None other," Jade said. "Geraldine was Madame X-rated herself, apparently. Behind closed doors, of course."

"Wow," Misty said gaping. She looked at me.

"I never knew any of it," I said.

"What would make you think she wrote a combination to the safe on the walls?" Star asked.

Jade explained her theory and the next thing I knew, all four of us were going over every inch of the room, searching for numbers. After about twenty minutes or so we stopped, Star declaring it was stupid.

"Can't we just break it open?" she asked.

"Go look for yourself," Jade said, and she did, returning with her head shaking.

"No way without dynamite," she said. "Do you have any idea what's in it?" she asked me.

"I didn't even know it was there," I said, "much less have any idea of what's in it."

"The way to find out what's in it," Jade said, "is to open it."

"Really? Why didn't I think of that?" Star asked Misty. She widened her eyes and looked from one to the other. "If we drop it from the window on a big rock, maybe it will break open."

"I doubt it," Jade said.

"Well, we can't spend all day looking for numbers," Star declared. "We should be getting some of this painting done. Don't forget," she told me, "you're coming to my house for dinner and staying over."

I smiled and nodded.

Jade groaned her frustration and stood staring down at the nightstand for a moment. She sifted through the cough drops and medicines, studying the labels.

"Where would she keep numbers?" she muttered.

"Mix the paint, Misty," Star ordered. "We got you your own roller, Miss Jade," she said.

Jade didn't turn. She kept her concentration on the nightstand. Then she picked up the flashlight and turned it in her hands.

"Any time Miss Beverly Hills is ready to help do what she wanted all of us to do is fine," Star sang.

Jade looked at her and pointed the flashlight at her.

"I'll beam you out of here if you don't shut up," she warned, and flicked the flashlight on, only it didn't go on. She shook it and then threw it on the bed. "You're lucky it doesn't work."

"Geraldine was fastidious about keeping everything working. Remember her obsession with our inventory," I reminded them.

Jade stared at me a moment, and then she smiled and picked up the flashlight. She unscrewed it quickly and looked at the cap. Then she broke into a very wide grin and held up a tiny slip of paper.

"That's why it doesn't work," she said. She unfolded it. No one spoke for a moment, waiting. "It's the combination," she declared. "Clever."

She nodded at me and we followed her back into the closet where she knelt before the safe and began to work the numbers from the little slip of paper. There was a click. She looked up. I drew closer, and she opened the safe door.

The first thing she held up was a very thick stack of money wrapped with a rubber band.

"All fifties," she announced, flipping through it. "There's a lot of money here...thousands, probably."

"Good," Star said. "I was afraid we were going to have to raise the club's dues."

Misty laughed and Jade reached into the safe to produce a velvet sack. She emptied it on the floor. It was filled with rings, bracelets, earrings and two expensive looking women's wristwatches, all of it sparkling with diamonds and rubies.

"I bet all that belonged to your mother," Misty told me.

"Yes, I suppose it did. Geraldine never wore any rings and even hated wearing a watch. She never wore earrings either," I said.

"It all belongs to you now," Star said.

"There are documents, too," Jade said, continuing her search. She opened them as she pulled them out and described them. "Deed to the house, their wedding certificate, some savings bonds, sizeable too," she added.

"So Cat's rich," Star said. "Now let's get back to work. Cat and I have to leave in about three hours or so."

"Wait," Jade said. "There's something way in the back." She extended her hand and came out with an official looking envelope. She gazed at me and then she turned it and opened it, pulling out some documents.

"Well?" Star asked.

"It's adoption papers," she said.

"Well, there's no surprise there. We know Cat was adopted, right?" Star asked.

"Right," I said.

"This *is* a surprise," Jade said, nodding her head. She turned the papers our way. "They're not Cat's adoption papers."

"Huh?" Star said.

"They're Geraldine's. According to this, Cat, she isn't even your half sister. Your mother adopted her."

"What?"

Jade continued to read.

"She was adopted here in California." She looked up at me. "It's official. She's not really related to you."

"Good," Star said quickly. "She's better off not having even the slightest blood tie to that witch. You're okay with it, right, Cat?" she said, putting her arm around me.

I didn't know what to say. All these surprises stunned me. I felt like I was being turned around and around by each different discovery until the whole world was topsy-turvy.

"I don't understand. It has to be some sort of mistake or confusion. Someone put the wrong name on the papers. It should have been my name."

Star glanced at the papers and handed them to me.

"Read it for yourself. It's stamped and signed and her name and the date are in a number of places. No one made any mistakes."

I studied the document. It was true.

"She never even...suggested such a thing," I muttered. "No one did."

"And there's nothing in the letters you've read yet that suggests it either," Misty added.

I looked at her and nodded.

"Maybe it's coming up in the ones that remain," Jade said softly. She stood up. "It doesn't really matter all that much anymore anyway," she said. "She's gone. You've got to put the whole ugly past behind you."

"I never saw any resemblances between the two of you anyway," Star said.

"Oh, my God," Misty cried, her eyes wider. We looked at each other. "She could have married Alden. He wasn't really her uncle. No wonder she was so upset about it."

"Yes," I said. "Yes." So much was beginning to make sense to me now.

"Here's the money," Jade said, handing it to me, "and your mother's jewelry. You might as well keep it in your own room now." She closed the safe and locked it again.

I took it all and gazed at the documents and then I left the closet and sat on the naked mattress. They all came out and stood before me, waiting. I glanced at the pile of sexy clothing and then at them.

"I never knew anyone, I guess. No one was who they were supposed to be. Everyone lied."

"It's been the same for us," Jade pointed out. "The only difference is it's stopped for you." She looked at Star and Misty. "Not for us."

Everyone was quiet, lost for a few moments in her own dark thoughts. Star was the first to emerge, and as usual, channeled her anger into energy.

"Are we going to paint this place or just sit around moaning and groaning about ourselves? I thought we didn't need anyone else anyway."

"Right," Misty said.

Jade nodded.

"Right."

"Then let's get started, Princess Jade," Star said, and thrust a roller in her hands.

"We need music!" Misty cried, and rushed out to turn on the stereo. A minute or so later, the sounds rocked the house. Star twirled with her roller in the air and Misty shimmied up to her. The two of them lip-synching the song. Jade and I roared.

Secrets fall like rain, she had said.

Maybe Star was right: my storms were over.

Or maybe, maybe they had just begun.

11

❧

Exposed

For all of us the revelation of family secrets and lies made the world seem less and less solid. It was as though the very ground we walked upon could become thin ice at any moment. We would fall through, screaming and crying until we hit rock bottom, forced to confront another ugly truth about ourselves or our lives. Even with a warm, secure and loving family, young people my age struggled to find the answer to the haunting questions, "Who am I? Who am I supposed to be?"

After it's all over, the early childhood, a chain of birthdays woven with candlelight, piles of presents, voices of relatives singing and praising your promise and future, after the years of schooling, fitting yourself into different size desks, memorizing, reciting, reporting, and performing for jury after jury of teachers, counselors, and administrators, you still feel inadequate, alone, vulnerable, and naked in a world that can be unforgiving and terribly demanding.

Sometimes, you cling to your family like some ship-wrecked passenger clutching a lifesaver, but when you look into their eyes, you see their impatience and their expectation. You hear what they're thinking: you should be swimming on your own by now. You'll only drag all of us down if you don't.

If you're lucky, really lucky, you find someone to love who will in turn love you and the loneliness and fear is greatly reduced. Often, it seems from what we've all experienced, you can make the wrong choice and just when you thought it was safe enough to let go of the lifesaver, you're tossing and turning and on the verge of drowning again.

But what if you've never really had a loving family? What if all your birthdays were treated as minor inconveniences and all your presents were grudgingly shoved your way? What if all your candles were snuffed too quickly and whenever you reached for that lifesaver, you were tossed a deflated tube and left to struggle on your own?

And what if after you had come through the darkness and finally looked for the light and for hope and promise, you found only a prism of lies twisting and turning, making you dizzy and sending you spinning in a whirlpool of memories you now knew were all illusions? Into what stream, what pool would you dip your hands to wash your face in smiles? Where would you go to hear the melody of laughter? What place in yourself would you reach into to draw out some happy moment to share even if you did find someone with whom you could share?

How would you know the difference between yourself and your shadow? Would anyone blame you for stopping and asking everyone, every passerby, every acquaintance, every stranger the same question? Do you know who I am? Do you know where I can go to find that out?

I had a mother who was captured only in a small pile of letters. I had a father who was someone frozen in old photographs, a face without a voice, a hand without a touch, eyes that never saw me and ears that never heard me. I had parents consisting of twisted and knotted ribbons of deception, who even deceived each other.

My friends and I had begun to unravel all the ribbons and make the painful discoveries. My mother was not my mother. She was my half sister. My half sister was not my half sister. She was a complete stranger who had no past herself. What if one day, one moment early in my life, she had stopped and turned to me and said, "Cathy, it's time you knew the truth so that we can all live in a solid world, a world without thin ice."

What if she had given me the most precious gift of all? My real name, my identity, an opportunity to be someone and know the difference between my shadow and myself? What kept her from doing that? Who was she punishing? Or was she merely so full of hate that any act of love was beyond her?

Tied and bound by death she lay in the cold, dark earth behind our house like some piece of buried evidence that would easily convict all those who had helped create her. It was best not to think of her. Oh, do not think of her, Cathy. Run your hand over your forehead, I told myself, and wash the memory away as you would some ugly stain. Think of yourself as reborn. Light new candles, Cathy the Cat. Turn them against the darkness.

I thought all these things as I worked mechanically beside my new sisters. They chatted and laughed, sang and giggled, and filled their ears and eyes constantly so as to keep out their own demons. Geraldine used to say "Work hard so you don't think about unpleasant thoughts." She was right about that, although I was sure she never dreamed I would think of her as one of those troubling thoughts.

"All right now," Jade cried, interrupting my reverie as she turned around and looked at our work.

The whole room, even the ceiling, was a flat black. She, Star, and Misty had moved the furniture out, taking the beds apart first and then removing all the drawers from the dressers. The room was completely bare. All the furniture and clothing was in the hallway near the stairs.

"Tomorrow, I'll call the Salvation Army," Jade said. "They'll come by to pick up the furniture and the clothes." She looked at me. "Is there anything of hers you don't want to give away?"

"No," I said, without any hesitation.

"Good." She inspected the door closely. "Can this be locked somehow?"

"Why?" I asked.

"This room will be our sanctuary, our temple. We don't want anyone in here, even by accident," she explained.

Star looked at the door too.

"You'll have to replace this knob with one that locks then," she said.

"Okay. I'll pick up a new knob on the way here tomorrow," Jade promised.

"Let's get going then. It's late," Star said.

We went to clean up and I put on something nicer than a pair of jeans and a sweatshirt to wear to Star's house. Then I packed a small bag for my overnight stay. I couldn't help feeling anxious about it. I had never before stayed overnight in anyone's home but my own.

Jade called for her limousine and ordered the driver to take us to Star's after he had dropped off Misty and her, but I couldn't help trembling a little as I locked the front door and left. Jade sensed it the most, I thought.

"It will get easier and easier each time," she whispered. "Before long, you won't even give her a passing thought." She squeezed my hand and we all got into the limousine.

I clutched my overnight bag on my lap like I would a parachute and stared ahead.

"I hope you're both going to follow OWP rules and not eat too much fattening food," Jade told Star.

"When you have her over at your house, you'll be in charge of the menu. Your buffet wasn't exactly a Jenny Craig spread. Anyway, I'll thank you not to tell me and my granny what to have for supper," Star retorted. She shook her head at me.

"I'm just trying to—"

"Run everybody's life?" Star sang.

"Oh, what's the use? You can help only those who want to be helped," she told Misty, who raised her eyebrows. "You know that you didn't wash off all the paint. You've got a black streak on your left temple. How did you get paint there?"

Misty shrugged.

"If my mother asks, I'll tell her I helped paint a dog-house or something. Stop worrying about everything."

"From the way it looks," Jade said, "I'll be the only one who worries about anything. What time will you be back tomorrow?" she asked Star.

"Let's see," Star said slowly, "after Cat and I get our toe-nails done and we have our skin treatment, we'll do lunch at the Polo Club and then—"

"All right, you idiot, just tell me when you want me to be over," Jade moaned.

Star glanced at me, shrugged and said, "About noon, I suppose."

Jade made arrangements to pick up Misty and then they were both dropped off. Now that Star and I were alone in the limousine and heading for her home, I really grew nervous.

"Will your granny ask me lots of questions?" I wanted to know.

"Probably," Star said. "Don't try to lie. She's got some kind of built-in lie detector."

"Great. What will I do if she asks about Geraldine?"

"Tell her everything but her fortunate departure and subsequent burial," she instructed. "Don't worry. She's not nosey. She's just concerned. Thank goodness for that," she added, and gazed out the window. "Without her, I wouldn't know what to do. Rodney would probably end up in some orphanage and I'd become a lady of the street."

"You wouldn't really, would you?"

"Cat, when all you have is what you have, you don't have any other choice sometimes. But forget it. We have it all now. We have each other," she added.

"Yes," I said. "We have each other."

Star's granny had an apartment on the first floor of a building in Venice Beach. Because of the apartment's location in the building, it had a rear entrance to a small patch of land covered with an anemic lawn, spotty and, according to Star, often cluttered with garbage of one sort or another.

"My granny takes it on herself to keep it as cleaned up as possible. A few times I caught her carrying away old tires. I don't know where she gets the strength and it doesn't do any good to bawl her out for it either. She just shakes her head and says 'What has to be done, has to be done.' That's Granny," Star explained as the limousine pulled to the curb.

Star's neighborhood looked seedy and worn, some of the small homes in desperate need of whitewashing, their sidewalks cracked and chipped, their gates and walls broken, some with doors dangling on rusted hinges. Every once in a while, there was a house that was well kept; at least Star's granny wasn't the only one trying to maintain the grounds and the building.

"Granny says we're too close to the ocean here. The sea air eats away at everything."

What a contrast to Jade's estate, I thought. Star was right. We were all from different planets.

We got out and entered the building. Someone had scribbled graffiti on the wall with a thick marker.

"Uh-oh," Star said. "That's new. Tomorrow morning, Granny will be out here scrubbing. Don't say anything about it," she warned me, and she rang the buzzer. "I forgot my key," she explained.

A moment later, her brother Rodney opened the door for us. Star had called him a string bean and she was right. Even though he was about eight and a half years younger, he was already only a few inches shorter than she was. He had her nose and eyes, but I could see that whatever innocence and softness he still possessed was well hidden beneath his cautious and distrusting eyes. He lifted the left side of his mouth and tilted his head to shout back.

"It's just Star and her friend," he cried.

"You say 'Hello,' Rodney," Star lectured. "That's what you do first, and you don't go shouting who's here. You introduce people," she added, with a biting sharpness that actually made him flinch.

"Sorry," he said. "Hello."

"This is Cathy."

He nodded at me and I said hello, but barely loud enough to hear myself. It brought a tiny smile to his lips.

"Did you break your leg?" he asked.

"No, just fractured my ankle."

"Oh." He looked disappointed. Then he turned and sauntered down the short hallway, lifting his shoulders with pride. He stopped at the doorway of the kitchen.

"Star's back," he said, and stepped away for us to enter.

Granny Anthony wiped her hands on a dish towel and turned to greet us. The aroma of her cooking filled my nostrils. Despite the worn, tired look of all the furniture, the floor, the appliances, and even the walls, I could see how well kept and clean her kitchen was. She beamed a wide smile at us.

"Welcome, honey," she said.

Star's grandmother had smooth, rich skin with just the tiniest wrinkles at her eyes and at the corners of her mouth. Her big, round eyes were full of warmth.

She wasn't more than five feet four inches tall, but she held her head high and proud. She had smoke gray hair brushed back and tied neatly in a bun.

"Thank you for inviting me," I said.

"Are you in any pain, dear?" she asked me.

"No, I'm fine."

"Good. Y'all make yourselves at home. We got fried chicken, mashed potatoes, black-eyed peas, corn on the cob, and a peach pie Rodney helped me bake."

"Did not," Rodney said quickly, embarrassment filling his eyes.

"You cut the peaches, honey," she insisted.

"That's nothing," he said, glancing at me.

"Without cutting himself," Star contributed. "That's good."

"Oh, he never cuts himself, Star. Don't go teasing him."

"Okay, Granny. C'mon," she said to me. "I'll show you where to leave your things. I'll be right out to set the table, Granny."

"Done," Granny announced. "Rodney did it."

"I didn't do all of it," he protested. Helping with domestic chores obviously made him very self-conscious.

"Thanks, brother," Star told him, and reached up to run her hand through his hair, but he jerked away quickly and she laughed.

No matter how she teased and admonished him, I thought, it was easy to see the love between them. Already, I was jealous. The warmth among them was palpable. I welcomed the opportunity to be washed in it.

Star's room was very small and crowded. Pieces of furniture touched. It was possible to approach her bed only from one side because of the tiny space between the one dresser and the bed frame. Rodney's cot was against the other wall. He had a poster of Michael Jordan above his bed. That and a few other sports pictures were all the decorations. Even his dreams were rationed in this room, I thought sadly. I also imagined he had just about outgrown the cot.

"Just drop your overnight bag on the dresser," Star instructed. She went to her narrow closet and sifted through some of her garments. "I'll just change into this dress," she said, holding up a maroon tank dress that reached mid-calf. "Granny expects it," she whispered.

"Oh. Maybe I should have worn something nicer," I thought aloud.

"No, that's fine. Why don't you wash up while I change," she said and pointed out the bathroom in the hall.

A few minutes passed and then I heard a knock on the door.

"Can I come in?" Star asked.

"Sure, I'm just fixing my hair." I answered, and opened the door for her.

"Sorry about the intrusion," she said as she washed her hands and then started to tie back her hair. "Our mansion only comes with one bathroom."

"Maybe I should have put on some of that new makeup Jade brought me," I said.

"Not for Granny. She hates when people put on airs and she'll let them know, too. You're fine," she said. She gazed at herself once more and then we went out to the small living room where Rodney was watching television. He glanced at us and then looked back at the set.

"What did you do all day, Rodney?" Star asked him.

"Nothing. Played some hoops with Sandy in back of the school for a while," he added.

"Did that Cokey come by again?"

He hesitated.

"What happened?" she asked before he could even think of something to make up.

"Same thing," he said, without looking at her.

"This kid about Rodney's age works for a drug dealer and tries to hook his friends," Star explained.

"Rodney's age?"

"Yeah. He flashes his wad of money and tempts other people, right, Rodney?"

"I dunno," Rodney said.

"But Rodney is smarter than him. Right, Rodney?"

"Yes," he said quickly.

"Because he knows if I ever catch him with that stuff, I'd turn him into the police myself, right, Rodney?"

"I didn't take nothing," he snapped at her, and then looked at the television set.

"I hope not," she muttered. "I hope not," she whispered to me.

We went into the kitchen to see if there was anything we could do.

"Everything is just about ready," Granny Anthony said. "I hope you came with a good appetite, child," she told me.

"I didn't have much lunch," I said.

"Oh? Why not?" she asked.

"I was so busy today. We're redoing some of my house. Ourselves," I added. "Sometimes, when you're so involved, you forget to eat."

Granny laughed.

"Isn't that the truth. Okay, Star, you take in the bowl of mashed potatoes."

"Can I help?"

"Oh no, no. You got enough to do with those crutches. Rodney Fisher," she cried.

He popped into the doorway quickly.

"Need some help here, child."

He rushed to his grandmother's side to help her and Star bring out the dinner.

Everything was as delicious as the aroma had promised. I couldn't believe how tasty the chicken was. When I was offered more, I was unable to resist. I looked at Star who knew I was thinking about Jade and her plans to have us all eat healthy.

"Don't worry about it," she muttered.

"So, how's your momma these days?" Granny Anthony asked. "Has the commotion settled down some?"

"Yes," I said, hoping my voice didn't shake.

"You girls all have had it hard from what Star tells me, but she says it's all going to be okay. When you're young, you can hold a lot on your shoulders if you have a mind to. Just remember, child, at the end of every storm, there's a bright sky and sometimes, a beautiful rainbow. Keep your eyes fixed ahead and nothing will seem too hard."

"Where's your rainbow, Granny?" Star asked sharply.

Granny Anthony patted her hand.

"It's coming, child. It's coming."

"So's Christmas."

"Now don't you go and mumble discouragement, Star. Half the time we make our own dark clouds and wonder why there's so much rain falling on our heads. Does your mother work, Cathy?"

"No, ma'am."

"But you all are taken care of?"

"Yes, ma'am," I said. "For now."

"That's half the battle, half the battle. Rodney, you're not wiping your hands on your pants, are you?"

"No, Granny," he said, his eyes wide.

"Or my fancy tablecloth?"

He shook his head.

"Well, you're wiping on something, and your napkin's still folded."

"I'm not wiping on anything, Granny," he protested.

"He's been licking his fingers dry," Star said, coming to his rescue. "Thanks to your good cooking."

"Oh, this is just an ordinary meal," she said. She sat back. "When I was a lot younger, I made some real fancy dinners. My husband was alive then and we had people in and out of our house day and night. Banquets is what we had, real banquets."

"This is a banquet as far as I'm concerned," I said, and she smiled. Then she turned serious.

"Is your mother a good cook?" she asked.

"She never cooked anything fancy," I replied, still skating around the truth.

"Even when your daddy was there?" she followed.

"Cathy doesn't like talking about those days, Granny," Star interceded.

"Oh. Sure. I understand. It's a shame though. All you children not having a real home life. It's a shame."

"We'll survive," Star muttered.

"Sure you will. Why shouldn't you? More mashed potatoes, honey?" she asked me.

"Oh, no. I'm stuffed like a turkey," I said, and she laughed.

"She's been hanging around you I see," Granny told Star.

"I wish I had some nicer quarters for y'all to sleep in tonight. Rodney's going to take the couch tonight."

"I am?" he asked.

"You can't be in the same room as the girls, Rodney."

"Oh," he said.

"I hate to put anyone out," I said.

"Rodney isn't put out. He likes sleeping on the couch. Some nights, he falls asleep there and I don't have the heart to wake him," Granny said.

We all laughed, but Rodney turned away, embarrassed.

It was a great feeling being there among them, eating the wonderful food, feeling their love and warmth. When we had first driven up, I had felt sorry for Star, even ashamed for her, but now, I felt sorrier for myself, and even for Misty and Jade.

"This house isn't anything compared to some of the places I slept when I was a young girl," Granny told us and described some of her experiences when she traveled with her parents years and years ago. Her language was colorful, vivid, and when she talked, I could almost feel what she felt reliving the events.

We were having a wonderful time. I actually put all the events of the last few days behind me. I didn't once think about Geraldine, about the letters and the discoveries. If I could move in here with them, I thought, I would, and I'd be willing to sleep on the couch each and every night to do it, too.

Granny had us in stitches describing a cousin of hers whose father was an undertaker and who actually took a nap in a coffin. His father brought in some customers and when they looked in and he opened his eyes, there was bedlam.

My stomach hurt from laughing. Rodney had tears streaming down his face and Star was radiant with happiness, too. Suddenly, in the middle of all that, there was a loud rap at the door. We all stopped. Granny looked at Star.

"Who would that be?" she asked.

"I'll go see," Rodney said, taking the reins of his budding manhood before anyone else could rise.

We all waited as he went to the door and opened it.

"My God Almighty!" I heard a woman exclaim. "Is that you? Look how you've grown!"

"Oh, no," Star said, looking at Granny and then at me. "It's her."

"Who?" I asked.

"My mother," she said, and we all looked up at the doorway with anticipation.

I didn't expect a woman as pretty nor with as nice a figure as the woman who entered. Her hair looked recently trimmed and styled and she wore what at first looked like a new and expensive skirt and jacket outfit. On closer inspection, I saw the stains in the material. She wore matching two inch square heel shoes that were scuffed and worn down.

Star's mother carried a small suitcase that looked like it had been tossed from an airplane.

"Well, look here, I'm just in time for dinner," she declared.

Both Granny and Star just stared at her.

"Doesn't anybody want to say hello and tell me how happy they are to see me?"

"We didn't know you were coming," Granny said with the corners of her mouth dipping into a frown. "We're surprised."

"Neither did I till yesterday." She laughed. "What a trip."

"We thought you were with Aaron's cousin Lamar. Where's he?" Star demanded. It was the first thing she had said to her mother, no hello, no smile, nothing.

"I don't know and I don't care. That fool is a loser, and I don't invest my time in losers. I'm starving, Mama," she added to change the subject, and moved quickly to the table. "Aren't you going to get me a plate?" she asked Star. Star glanced at me and then rose with reluctance. "Who are you?" she asked me.

"She's my friend," Star said from the kitchen doorway.

"I guessed that much."

"My name is Cathy," I said.

"What happened to you?" she asked, pointing at my leg.

"I had a bad fall and fractured my ankle. I'm okay," I said.

"Hmm. I suppose my daughter told you all sorts of bad things about me," she said, throwing a look toward the kitchen door.

"Are you back for good?" Granny asked, changing the subject.

"Of course I'm back, Mama. I'm here, aren't I?" She grimaced and looked like she was going to cry. "I had a very bad time, too."

"Uh-huh," Granny said, nodding with her round eyes growing smaller.

"I did. I tried my best to do good and make a home so I could send for my kids, but people lied to me. Promises were made and then broken minutes later, but still, I tried."

Star returned with a dish and her mother began to serve herself.

"Thank you, honey. You look pretty. I guess your granny's been taking good care of you two."

"Better than you did," Star said sullenly.

"Now there, go on," her mother said, sitting back, "jump all over me when I'm down and out."

"You've always been down and out, Mama."

"You hear that and in front of her friend, too. You talk this way to your mama?" she asked me.

"Leave her be," Star ordered.

"What am I doing to her?" She gazed at me and I looked down.

"I'll start on the dishes," Star said abruptly, and started to clear off the table.

"You could wait until I'm finished," her mother said.

"Leave them, Star, honey. Go on with your friend. Me and your mama have some catching up to do. Rodney, you're excused. Go watch television with the girls," Granny said.

"C'mon," Star told me, and we went to her room. As soon as she closed the door, she apologized. "I had no idea she would pop in on us like that."

"It's okay."

"The problem is she'll be sleeping in here with us."

"Oh," I said. "Well, then, maybe I should go home."

She stood there thinking a moment.

"We'll both go. If I was left alone in this room with her, I don't know what I'd do. Maybe I'd smother her in the middle of the night." Her words were angry, but she just looked sad. "I'm sorry about all this."

"It's okay. I had a great time with your grandmother," I said.

She nodded.

"Do you have money for a cab on you?"

"Yes."

"All right. I'll call one for us. I don't like leaving Granny with the dishes so I'll try to help her clean up," she said. "You want to stay here a moment or go join Rodney in the living room?"

"I'll wait here, but I would like to help, too."

"She won't let you. You're our guest," Star said, and slipped out.

I sat on her bed and gazed around the small, dark room. How hard it has to be for her, I thought. No wonder she seems so angry all the time. I guess I would be too, I concluded. She wasn't gone long.

"I called us a cab," she said. "Mama's not upset about having the room to herself. It's best we leave."

"What about Rodney?"

"He'll be all right sleeping in the living room. The way it looks, that's going to turn into his bedroom. I don't hold out much hope of my mother getting any sort of decent job and finding us a place to live. I'm too mad to think about it all right now. Let's just get out of here."

"Is your grandmother upset?"

"She'll be fine. Mama's still afraid of her," Star said. She smiled. "Misty will be happy. You and I are going back to sleep with the ghost. We'll call her and Jade when we get to your house," she added. "Sorry this turned out this way."

"I'm fine with it," I said. "Don't worry about me."

When we emerged, I saw how Star's mother looked small and remorseful. Granny Anthony had been quietly taking her to task and bawling her out for her lifestyle, I imagined.

"I'm sorry you had to go to some mental doctor," her mother told Star when we appeared. "Mama just told me some of it."

"I'm not sorry," Star said. "At least I learned how to deal with you."

"I was hoping you and I could be friends again, honey," her mother said.

"When were we ever friends, Mama? I was only a burden to you."

"Well, I've changed, honey. I'm different. You'll see."

"Right," Star said. She kissed Granny.

"It was a wonderful dinner, Mrs. Anthony. Thanks again," I said.

"You're welcome, honey. Be careful out there, hear?"

"Yes, ma'am."

I stopped at the living room door to say goodbye to

Rodney. He suddenly looked his age. His mother's shocking appearance had turned him back into a little boy.

"Just stay out of her way tonight," Star told him, "and be a help to Granny."

He nodded and looked at the television set, but I didn't think he heard or saw anything. His eyes were glassy and full of fear.

The cab was waiting for us outside. Star hurried me to it and we gave the driver my address.

"The faster I get away from her, the better I'll feel," Star muttered.

Minutes later, we were out of her neighborhood, but what she was trying to leave behind, was still wrapped around her, making her stiff and quiet. All the memories and pain could be resurrected in seconds, I thought, and nothing prevented it from washing over her and leaving her like someone drowning in a sea of nightmares.

All the way back to my house, she muttered about her mother, reliving some of the events she had revealed in our group therapy sessions. I sat silently, waiting for her temper to cool. Just before we reached my house, she stopped talking and pressed her forehead to the window.

"I'm sorry, Star," I said, and touched her arm. She reached back to take my hand.

The house was pitch dark when we arrived. I had forgotten to leave on a light, even in the hallway. The whole house reeked of the paint we'd used. We should have left a few windows open, I thought.

"I need something cold to drink," Star declared when I turned on the hall lights. "Then we'll call Jade and Misty and tell them that we're here."

"Okay."

I followed her down the hallway to the kitchen. As soon

as I turned on the light, we both stopped dead in our tracks and stared. The rear door was wide open and it was obvious from the chips of wood on the floor that it had been forced. Star turned to me and shook her head.

"It can't be. No," she said.

My heart was pounding so hard, I thought my chest might just explode. I actually couldn't speak. My throat was that tight and my feet felt nailed to the floor.

Star moved first, slowly, glancing back at me, and then reaching the door and opening it further.

"Get that flashlight," she ordered. "Cat, c'mon."

I think I whimpered like a mouse.

"Cat!"

I moved as quickly as I could to the drawer, seized the flashlight, and thrust it at her. She took it quickly and aimed the beam outside, running the light quickly toward Geraldine's grave. I inched up beside her and, leaning on my crutch, gazed out. Nothing had been disturbed. I think we both released a lung full of boiling hot air.

"For a minute I thought we were in a Stephen King movie," Star said, and then turned to the door with more scrutinizing eyes. She ran her fingers along the jamb. "Whoever did it just pried it out without concern. You've been burglarized, girl."

"What did they take?" I wondered aloud.

We looked at each other and both thought about the safe.

"Jade closed it and locked it again, but we took the money and the jewelry out," I reminded her. "And I took it with us to your house in my purse. All we left inside the safe were the documents."

Star led the way through the house, up the stairs, and into what had been Geraldine's room. We paused in the closet doorway and I pulled the chain to turn on the over-head fixture. Again, we both gasped.

The safe was gone.

"Whoever it was couldn't get it open and decided to just carry it off and maybe blow it open someplace else," Star imagined aloud.

"It was heavy."

"Yeah, but not that heavy." She gazed around the empty room and freshly painted black walls. "What else could they take?"

"I don't know. There isn't much that's worth a lot," I said.

Nevertheless, we went to check my room. This time I gasped aloud when I opened the door. My room had been torn apart: dresser drawers opened and emptied, my bed-spread pulled down and cast on the floor, the mattress pushed off the bedsprings, the closet open and clothing tossed about.

"Who would pull a bed apart like that? No burglar I know," Star remarked. She stared at me as my eyes widened with a terrifying thought. Then she nodded. It was as if she could read my mind. "You think it was him?"

I couldn't keep the tears from escaping my lids. They were cold tears, tears of fear rather than tears of sorrow.

"He must have come by, seen the house was dark and tried to get in. Geraldine changed the locks after she threw him out because she was worried he had an extra key somewhere."

"So he broke in the back and came up here because he knew about the money, probably," Star continued. "When he couldn't get into the safe, he just carried it off." She gazed around my room. "Why did he tear your room apart? What else was he looking for?" she wondered.

I started to shake my head and stopped, shifting my eyes guiltily away.

"What?" she cried. "Damn, girl, don't be keeping secrets from me now, not after all this!"

I nodded, fighting to get the breath to speak. She waited, impatiently.

"Remember when I told you all about the trip he took me on, that time up in Santa Barbara?"

"Yeah, sure," she said. "So?"

"I was ashamed to talk about the pictures. It was so hard telling about it as it was. I thought it wasn't necessary to give all the details."

"What pictures?"

"Of me. He made me pose. He had one of those instant cameras. Then, he...he didn't want to keep the pictures on him or anywhere he thought Geraldine might find them, so he made me hide them in my room and promise to let him have them whenever he wanted to look at them. He told me they were beautiful pictures and he was proud of them."

I shook my head so vigorously, the tears flew off my cheeks.

"Okay, okay, don't go crazy on me," Star pleaded. "Where are they? Did he find them?" she asked, gazing at the room.

"I don't know," I said. "They're in the bathroom in the cabinet under the sink. Geraldine cleaned this room after I went to school, but I knew one place she would never go, one thing she would never touch," I said, walking to the bathroom.

The cabinet doors were opened.

"Did he find them?" Star asked when she stepped up behind me.

Resting my crutches against the cabinet, I bent down and reached in, bringing out a box of sanitary napkins.

Star smiled.

"Geraldine never would look in there, huh?"

I shook my head and pulled out the napkins. Between the third and fourth were the pictures. I held them up and smiled.

"Serves him right for not thinking like a woman," she said. Her smile faded quickly. "Now get rid of them. Tear them up and flush them down the toilet where they belong."

"Yes," I said, and did exactly what she said. "I guess even after Geraldine threw him out and everything, I was still afraid and just pretended these didn't exist," I said as I tore them to shreds.

"He's got to be one sick man to come in here and tear this place apart just for those." She thought a moment. "Maybe he was afraid they might be used as some kind of evidence against him. That's probably what Jade will tell us," she concluded.

"Do we have to tell the others about them?"

"Not if you don't want to," Star said, "but, Cat, I'm beginning to really believe we should trust each other. Completely," she added.

"Yes, you're right," I said. "It's good to stop lying, at least to each other."

I rose and gazed around my room.

"I better start fixing this up. We have to sleep here tonight," I said.

Star laughed.

"I'll go call the girls and then we'll do what we can with the rear door."

She started out.

"Star?"

"Yeah?"

"Do you think he'll be back?" I asked. "I mean, he's got to be wondering why Geraldine's room is painted black, why all her furniture is out in the hall."

She thought a moment and nodded.

"Yeah. He'll be back," she said. "We'll have to talk about it and decide what to do, but for now," she said, looking up at me, "he's not about to talk to anyone. After all, he wasn't supposed to be here, and he broke in and stole the safe. I'm sure he's really confused and doesn't know what to do himself. For the time being, that's good for us."

"Yes, but I'm worrying about *after* the time being," I said. "I mean, we can't call the police or anything now, right?"

She nodded, but offered no words of encouragement. Then she left and I turned back to my room.

What sort of rage, what sort of madness drove him to do this? I wondered.

And when would he be back?

12

Wedding Belles

Star let Jade and Misty in and they rushed through the house to look at the back door. Then they came pounding up the stairs to my room. I had most of it put back together and I was working on the bed.

"What went on in here?" Jade asked. "Why did he tear the room apart?"

I looked at Star and then explained about the pictures.

"They're down the toilet now," I concluded.

"Good, but why would he break in?"

"He could have been watching the house and could have seen me leave with Star," I conjectured. "We shouldn't have left it all dark. When no one answered the doorbell and he saw no lights were on inside, he decided to break in, probably to get his hands on the money."

"Star says he took the safe?"

"It gone," I said. "He probably took it because he couldn't get it open."

"Either that or it walked out," Star added.

"Lucky we took the money and jewels out of it. You still have them, don't you?" Jade asked me quickly.

"Yes. I took them with me when I went to Star's house for dinner and they're still all in my purse."

Misty was the first to realize we had returned from Star's house early.

"I thought you were sleeping over. What brought you back here?" she asked.

"My mother," Star replied, and described her mother's dramatic sudden entrance and return to their lives. "I guess it's more like I'm running away than just coming back here," she told us.

"Wow," Jade said, and plopped on my yet-to-be straightened bed. "All this just when everything was going good."

"What will we do? Her father has seen everything," Misty moaned.

"Not everything," Jade reminded her.

"How can you be sure?"

"If he knew anything, he would have called the police by now, wouldn't he?"

"But the house, what we've done," Misty said. "He could tell someone."

"He just can't go complaining about what we've done in the house. He wasn't supposed to be here and he broke in and he stole the safe," Jade said. She looked at me. "Right?"

"Yes," I said. "That was a major part of the agreement: he wasn't supposed to come here ever again."

"But he did and he might come back," Star reminded us.

"Or call and ask for Geraldine," Misty suggested. "He's got to wonder what's going on."

"So? We'll just have Cat tell him that redoing the room was Geraldine's idea, if he asks."

"Redoing it black?" Star pointed out with a skeptical grimace.

"Geraldine's weird, isn't she?" Jade said.

"Was weird," Misty corrected.

"Was. He'll believe it. He has no choice," Jade insisted.

"And if he demands to speak to her?" Star wondered.

"To do what? Confess about the break-in? Stealing her safe? No, I think he's going to keep his distance and maybe just give up," Jade said. Her voice had a ring of hope, even prayer in it.

We were all silent. I glanced at Star who sat on my desk chair and stared down at the floor now. I had been so preoccupied with my problems, I had forgotten about hers.

"What are you going to do about your mother returning?" I asked her.

"What can I do? I'll go back in the morning and see what she's up to. She's not going to want to take responsibility for her children, if she can help it. That's my bet and my hope. I would rather Rodney and I went on the road."

"Your granny wouldn't agree to your mother moving in with her now anyway, right?" Jade asked.

"What choice does she have?" Star asked with a shrug. "Rodney and me, for that matter, are still her legal children. You're always playing the lawyer, Jade. You know all about that stuff."

"Let's just wait and see," Misty offered. "Everything has a way of working out in the end."

Star shook her head and looked at her.

"You sure you haven't got a head full of bubbles instead of brains, Misty?"

"I'm just trying not to be depressed," Misty cried defensively.

"Yeah, well, that's easy for you Beverlies at the moment."

"It is not. You don't know anything about anything," Misty accused.

"I know you have a comfortable, warm place to sleep tonight," Star muttered, "and you can get your parents to give you practically anything. Just like Princess Jade who's getting a new car from Daddy."

"And I told you where he can put that car," Jade said.

"Yeah, but you'll take it anyway," Star said dryly. Jade didn't deny it.

"You just don't know everything, Star. You just don't know all about us just because you heard stuff in the therapy session," Misty insisted, her eyes glossing over with hot tears.

"I know enough," Star insisted.

"No, you don't!" Misty screamed. Her hands were clenched into little fists that she pounded against her thighs. "My daddy is marrying his girlfriend Ariel Airhead this Saturday and he wants me at the wedding. My mother is very upset about it and doesn't want me to go. I feel like tearing myself in half and sending one half to the wedding and another to...to hell!"

We all just stared at her, too shocked to say anything.

She wiped the tears from her cheeks with quick flicks of her hands.

"You know that this month was supposed to be their twentieth anniversary. They were going to redo their vows. We were all going to be a happy little family forever and ever. Well, Daddy's going to take vows all right, only with a new bride."

"I'm sorry," Star said softly.

"Damn, damn, damn," Jade chanted. She looked up at the ceiling. "One thing after another! When does it stop?"

"It doesn't," Star said. "Don't you get it? It doesn't stop until we turn our backs on them and walk away...completely."

Misty sniffled and nodded.

"Let's make some coffee and think," Jade declared. "We've got to find ways to help each other otherwise..."

"Otherwise what?" Star asked.

"Otherwise," she said looking at me, "there was no point in burying Geraldine."

With our heads bowed, we paraded silently down the stairs to the kitchen, me holding up the rear with my hobble. When I started to make the coffee, Star interceded.

"Sit down, Cat. I'll do it. The Beverlies expect to be waited on," she added. We couldn't tell if she was being serious or trying to lighten the mood.

"You know, I'm sorry your mother came bursting in on you, Star, but taking it out on us isn't going to help," Jade said.

"Yes, thank you for your advice, Doctor Marlowe," Star replied with a smile, letting us know she wasn't mad.

I looked across the table at Misty whose eyes were bloodshot. She stared at the wall as if she didn't see or hear anything. Look at us, I thought, we're crumbling. Whatever made us think we could help each other? Geraldine was right. Sick people can't help sick people.

For a while, no one spoke. The silence was heavy. Then Misty snapped out of her daze and looked at me sharply.

"When we were up in your room, I didn't notice your letters," she said. "I remember you had them on the dresser."

Star and Jade fixed their eyes on me as I thought and then shook my head.

"Me neither. He must've taken them."

"Why would he take them?" Jade asked, her mouth turned down with disgust. "How sick is he?"

"Sick enough," Star said. "I'll go back up and look."

"I'll help," Misty said, rising.

The two left and Jade fetched the coffee cups and took out the milk. She tried to keep my mind off things by describing some of the new clothing her mother had bought in anticipation of her big celebration. She was talking with nervous energy, reminding me of how she was at our group therapy sessions, especially toward the end when she described her attempted suicide with sleeping pills. Then she poured us both some coffee. We heard Misty and Star come down the stairs. One look at them told me they hadn't found the letters.

"Maybe he gets off on reading other people's private stuff," Star said.

"Maybe he didn't know all of it himself," Misty suggested. She looked to me.

"I don't know what he knew. He never mentioned anything to me."

"Well, we can't do anything about it now. Let's concentrate on what we can do," Jade said firmly. She poured Star and Misty their coffee and sat.

"So? What can we do?" Misty asked.

"Move on with our plans. In the morning I'm picking up some things for our private room. If you want, I'll pick you up first," she said to Misty.

"Okay."

"We still have a lot of fixing up to do around here. I'll sleep over tomorrow night," she told me. She looked at Misty. "When did you say your father was remarrying?"

"This Saturday and it's a church wedding, too, with lots of guests!"

"We'll all go with you," Jade said.

"You will?"

"Why not? Star?"

"Fine with me, but I don't have anything fancy to wear."

"I have just the dress for you," Jade said. "I'll bring it here. Cat needs something nice, too. Tomorrow afternoon, I'll have the limousine take us to Camelot's on Sunset and we'll get her something outstanding."

"That's nice, thanks," Misty said, her face filling with her characteristic cheer and vivacity.

"I'd better do some more work on Geraldine's grave," Star said. "It's lucky he came around here at night. We might get other visitors. It still looks too much like what it is. I'll do it in the morning before I go home." She sipped some coffee. "If I don't get back here later in the day, don't wait around for me," she added.

"Is there anything we can do for you? Maybe we should all come to your house," Jade wondered.

"No, it would just make Granny nervous and all. She'd be afraid my mother would do or say something embarrassing. We'll see," she said.

The silences were long and deep between us. When we sipped our coffee, we peered over the cups at each other, all of us sensing the tension in the room. How fragile our confidence really was, I thought. For me the doubt worked like a doorway to the darkness from which Geraldine could emerge, her face twisted in a smile of derision, her eyes like two candle flames. Her hatred and anger shot up from the ends of her dead fingers, twirling and streaking through the earth and into the house to crackle and spark in the rooms and hallways and to remind me that she wasn't far away. She was never far away.

"Are you all right?" Jade asked me. "Cat?"

"What? Oh, yes," I said.

"Let's finish straightening up," she said. "What do we do about the back door?" she asked, nodding at it.

Star inspected it and then went out to the garage to get some tools. We all watched her work.

"One of Mama's boyfriends once broke in our door like this," she said. She fixed the lock so it worked at least well enough to get the door closed.

"That doesn't look very secure," Jade said.

"Let's face it," Star told her, "if someone wants to get in, they'll get in no matter what."

"You don't have an alarm system?" Jade asked me.

"No. Geraldine never wanted one, I guess."

"Maybe she was too mean to be afraid," Jade muttered.

"Or too stupid," Star said.

Jade and Misty stayed for another hour or so, talking about our future plans, fantasizing trips and big parties, working their imaginations hard to drive back the fear and anxiety we all still felt. When they left, Star and I finished fixing up my bedroom and the bed, and then decided we would go to sleep and not even bother watching any television. The thing about emotional exhaustion is you don't realize how heavy it is until you stop moving and lower your head to the pillow, I realized. Then, you feel like you'll never get up.

"You don't think he'll come back tonight, do you, Star?" I whispered when we were both in the bed.

"Naw. He's got to be one confused man. I bet his jaw just about dropped to the floor when he saw all the furniture in the hall and then looked in on Geraldine's room and saw what we did. That Jade, she's a piece of work. Who knows what she's planning to do in there tomorrow, but one thing's for sure, it won't be any new Beverly Hills fancy decor. Jade and her private places."

"We all need them," I said.

Star was quiet a moment.

"Yeah, I guess," she said. "Trouble is, someone's always busting in and ruining it."

"Maybe that won't happen this time," I said.

"Maybe," she said, but not with any confidence.

"Night," I said.

"Sorry I couldn't have you over, Cat. Maybe some other time," she said.

"Sure. There'll be other times."

She didn't say yes.

The future was more of a mystery than ever, despite our optimistic dreams.

In the morning Star went out to rake the grave some more and make the area look less and less like a cemetery plot. We called her a cab and I gave her the money to go home. I gave her enough for her to also get a cab in the afternoon.

"I'll try to be back," she promised.

Now that my father had returned and done what he had done, taken what he had taken, I was more afraid of being alone than ever, but I tried not to show it. Nevertheless, I was at the front window watching and waiting for Jade and Misty most of the time. It was a partly cloudy day. Every time the sunlight tried to warm and brighten things, a cloud seemed to rush in and shut it off. The dreariness made me feel even more alone. When that big limousine finally appeared, I breathed a sigh of deep relief and quickly went to let Jade and Misty in. Their arms were filled with packages. The chauffeur followed carrying a fairly large oval mirror.

"You can leave that right here, thanks," Jade told him. He placed it just inside the door. As soon as he returned to the vehicle, Jade turned to me.

"Everything all right?" she asked me. "No more visitors?"

"No one. It's been quiet. Star said she'll try to return late this afternoon."

"Good."

Jade's chauffeur returned with a rolled up rug and left that beside the mirror.

"Let's get to work," Jade told Misty as soon as he left. They began carrying things up the stairs to our private place. I followed.

"What did you two buy?"

"You'll see," Misty said, smiling.

They went down to bring up the rug and then the mirror. First, they rolled out the rug and placed it in the center of the floor. It was a tightly woven wool rug with red and black stripes. Jade placed the mirror low on the wall to the right so that when we were sitting on the rug, we could see ourselves. After that she unwrapped two pairs of brass candelabra, placing them at opposite ends of the room. Misty filled them with tall, black candles.

Jade had also bought what she called New Age meditation music CD's. They played one while they worked. There were posters and pictures of strange, ethereal scenes, some with clouds and water, some with stars and streaks of light. There was incense to burn and chimes Jade hung just over the doorway, and Misty put in the new doorknob and gave me a key.

"We'll get more decorations," Jade said after hanging the pictures on the walls. "I didn't want to take too long.

Well?" she said, gazing at everything, "what do you think so far?"

"It's different," I said, looking at the rug and the candles in the naked, black room. They had even painted the windows.

"Wait until Star sees it all," Misty said. "It gives me an eerie feeling, but I like it."

"It's got to be meditative, spiritual," Jade explained.

"Why did we have to paint the windows?" I asked.

"We want to leave the loud, noisy, troubled, rotten world out there when we all gather in here."

"How do you know about all this?" I asked her.

"My mother was into it for a while. She joined one of those meditative groups shortly after she and my father started their divorce wars and it seemed to help her, but then the organization asked for more donations and she found out her spiritual leader was buying up prime property in Westwood with the money, so she quit, but I liked the music and I read her pamphlets and got more out of them than she did, I think.

"In here, we won't be afraid to expose our deepest feelings to each other. That's what makes it sacred, so remember to always keep it locked so no one else sets foot in it. Okay?"

"Yes," I said. Maybe it would work, I thought. Maybe we would have a special place, a true escape.

We heard the phone ring and I picked up the receiver. The phone had been left on the floor. It was the doctor at the hospital wondering why I hadn't shown up for my X-ray. He wanted to speak with Geraldine.

"Oh, I'm sorry. She's out, but I'll be right there," I said.

"It's important we check how that's healing," he emphasized. "I thought your mother understood."

"She did; she's just been sick," I said, thinking of the first possible excuse. After I hung up, I told Jade and Misty about the forgotten appointment.

"Don't worry about it. Let's get over there."

"I'll drive," Misty said, and we went downstairs. Jade remembered to call Star to let her know where we would be should she arrive. She listened for a moment and then hung up.

"She doesn't sound too happy. She said it was all right because she wouldn't be here until dinner. Rodney was upset. Her mother took him along supposedly to shop and he ended up in a bar with her."

"Maybe she'll drink herself to death and solve the problem," Misty muttered.

Jade and I gazed at each other, both thinking the same thing I'm sure. It was sad that Star's and her brother's happiness and even safety depended on their mother being gone and out of their lives.

We got into the car and headed for the hospital. It took us nearly two hours to get my X-rays done and the doctor to look at them. He was obviously concerned that Geraldine wasn't there, too. I said she was running a fever.

"But I thought you told me she was out before," he reminded me.

"She had gone to the doctor who prescribed medicine and told her to rest," I said.

He still looked annoyed and suspicious, but said I was healing fine.

"I want you back next week. Have your mother call me the day before," he ordered and wrote out his name and number. I thanked him and we left.

"What will I do next week?"

"He won't remember her voice. I'll call and pretend

I'm Geraldine," Jade said. "We'll be fine. The important thing is your ankle's coming along well. Now, let's go to Camelot's and get you something for Misty's father's wedding. Shopping is the best way to get rid of worries," she added.

"Something a Beverly would say," Misty quipped. She thought a moment and then smiled and said, "Funny, but when Star's not with us, I feel like I have to say what she would say."

"We're all becoming part of each other," Jade explained. "Let's hope it's only the good parts."

We all laughed. I was beginning to be afraid we wouldn't find any reason to, but we did have a great afternoon. Little did I or Misty know that Camelot's was an offbeat clothing store, selling what they described as "Mythic Clothes." The shop was scented with incense and there was music not unlike the CD's Jade had purchased for our special room.

The first dress Jade insisted I try on was a gown of stretch velvet. It had gold metallic trim and pointed sleeves. I thought it looked like a costume on me, but that was nothing compared to what I looked like in what was called the Goddess dress, made of crinkled silk with a gold metallic corded belt. After that I got into the Fairy dress, a silk chiffon with a handkerchief skirt and separate top that tied at the shoulders. It was pale lavender and both Jade and Misty decided it was the one I should buy. I kept laughing at my image in the mirror and thinking how wild Geraldine would be if she saw me in it.

"You really are a pretty girl, Cat," Jade said after she came up beside me, put her arm around my shoulders, and her head against mine. We both looked at me in the mirror. "Soon you'll be breaking more hearts than me," she whispered.

Could I? Could I really? I wondered as I stared into the mirror.

"Let's get the Goddess dress for Star," Jade decided. "In fact, let's all buy something here. I'll do the velvet gown. Misty?"

"Okay. They'll all be perfect for Daddy's new wedding."

She considered, and chose a crinkled silk tunic with a V-neck and a crinkled silk skirt in teal. Imagine the sight of the four of us when we entered that church, I thought, but I was sure making a scene and stealing the moment was exactly what Misty hoped we would do.

We ended up spending a little more than a thousand dollars.

Geraldine is surely spinning in her grave, I thought, and half expected to find the earth churned up when we returned to the house. On the way home, we stopped at Misty's so she could pick up her clarinet. She wanted to play for us after dinner. We were determined to have a good time and put away all the dark events.

To my surprise, Star loved the dress when we showed it to her after she arrived. We all put on our new clothes and paraded around the house.

"Perfect clothes for our first session in our special place," Jade declared, and led us up the stairs where we were to light the candles, turn on the music, sit on the rug, hold hands, and touch each other's spirits.

"If Doctor Marlowe could see us now," Star quipped, and we all laughed. Our laughter was truly like music, music to drown out any storm.

Jade gave us our first lesson in meditation and whether

it was my imagination or not, I did feel the tension leave my body. Afterward, we all helped make a great pasta dinner with a spinach and goat cheese salad to start. Jade had brought wine from her mother's house. We sat around the table, talking and enjoying each other.

Jade insisted that our mythic clothing had turned us all into goddesses and we each described the magical power we would most like to possess. Misty wanted to be invisible and spy on whomever she wished. Star wanted to fly. Jade wanted to turn men into love-hungry slaves. I said I wished I could live in a castle with walls that kept out all sickness and unhappiness.

"That's what this house will be," Jade declared.

When the meal ended, Misty put on a CD and we cleaned up to music. After that was done, we went into the living room to relax and Misty performed for us on her clarinet.

The melodies from Misty's clarinet were as meditative as Jade's New Age CD's. Jade, Star, and I all closed our eyes and let ourselves drift. I know I felt as if I was floating on a cloud.

When Misty stopped playing, she sat in a lotus position in front of us. No one spoke for a few moments.

"I'm glad you're all going to be with me on Saturday," she said. "No matter what, I can't think of my father as being married to someone else, standing up there and promising someone else he'll love her forever and ever. It makes me feel...like I don't exist anymore, like he's just erased his past and everything and everyone in it, even me."

Star reached for Misty's hand, and then Jade's, and I held Jade's and Misty's hands. We sat there, linked. Nothing else needed to be said.

After a moment we all stood up.

"Tomorrow," Jade decided, "we'll get back to fixing this place up so it's more like a party house. Maybe we need more dramatic lighting, even some new pieces of furniture, more pictures, lots of stuff!"

"Back to the stores," Misty declared, holding her hand up high as if she held a sword.

"Beverlies," Star muttered, "think shopping solves everything."

Misty, Jade, and I looked at each other and then roared.

"What?" Star said.

"You said it before," I told her.

"Huh? When?"

"Through Misty," Jade said, and we laughed again, only harder.

"You're all crazy," Star said. She thought a moment and then added, "Thank God for that."

The rest of the week went quickly. Jade stayed that night and Misty returned for the following evening. The next day the Salvation Army came and took Geraldine's furniture and clothes. It went a long way toward helping me feel she was truly gone for good.

We had meditation sessions every night and had fun cooking and talking. Star felt pressured to remain at home for Rodney every evening. She told us her mother had gotten a job as a waitress in a bar on the beach and was already keeping very late hours. Because she woke Rodney up when she came home, stumbling over furniture, Granny convinced her to sleep in the living room and let Rodney go back to his cot.

Finally, it was Saturday, Misty's father's wedding day. Jade had her limousine pick us up. Misty said her mother was furious about it because we were making it into such a big event by buying new clothes. She had no idea what the rest of us were wearing. If she had seen us all together, she might have reversed her opinion. The moment the four of us entered the church, the entire wedding party spun their heads around. Jade was carrying a magic wand that worked on batteries and lit up a light at the end. She had bought a sequin laden headband for Misty to wear and gave Star very ostentatious costume jewelry. She gave me a large, ruby colored glass necklace on a thick silver chain.

Misty's father looked confused as we marched down the aisle to take our seats up front. I was sure Misty hadn't told him she was bringing us. Our dramatic entrance was followed with a wave of murmurs from the guests. Her father's friends and Ariel's family and friends didn't know whether to laugh or cry out in protest. We could see it in their faces, but we didn't stare or smile at anyone.

Jade had given us our marching orders before we had arrived.

"Don't look at anyone. Keep your face forward, your eyes fixed on the bride and groom, and look very serious. We're there to cast a spell for Misty."

"What spell?" Star asked. "What crazy thing are you talking about now?"

"A spell to protect her from any further unhappiness," Jade replied.

"I love it," Misty cried. The fantasizing kept her from letting sadness and pain into her heart.

"And just how are we supposed to cast a spell?" Star asked.

"As soon as the minister begins, I'll lift my magic wand and move it first to the right and then to the left. When I do that, everyone move with it shoulder to shoulder, understand?"

"Where do you get all of this stuff?" Star asked.

"A dream vision I had last night," Jade said.

"I love it," Misty repeated.

My heart was pounding because I couldn't believe Jade would go through with it, but she did, even lighting up the bulb, and we all did what she had asked. Then she lowered the wand. The minister had paused to watch us, and Misty's father and Ariel turned to us, too. Misty's father's smile disappeared, but he turned back to the minister and the wedding ceremony was performed.

Almost as soon as he could, her father approached us.

"What is this, Misty? Who are these girls? Why did you all come dressed like this? And what were you all doing? Ariel is upset. Did your mother put you up to this?"

"No, Daddy. These are my friends and we wanted to bless your new marriage so it doesn't fall apart like your first marriage and make everyone unhappy," Misty recited as if she was reading from a children's storybook.

He turned so red, I thought we'd see steam come out of his ears. Then he nodded.

"I thought you would act a lot more maturely about this, Misty. I'm disappointed."

"Me too, Daddy," she said. "It doesn't look like our magic is working."

"Okay. All right. I see what you're up to. We'll talk about it later," he told her, giving us a plastic, cold smile, before leaving us to greet his other guests.

"I don't think your father appreciates us, Misty," Jade declared. "Let's skip the wedding reception and go dancing at the Kit Kat Rave Club on Melrose instead."

"Good idea," Misty said. She looked after her father for

a moment, her eyes filling with tears, and then she marched ahead of us up the aisle. We followed, Jade dipping her wand at people like some bishop imparting blessings. When she lit the bulb, they either flinched or gasped. I hurried along behind them as quickly as I could, eager to get out of the church.

In the limousine, Jade revealed that she had snuck a bottle of vodka and some orange juice out of her house.

"A little of this will put us all in the right frame of mind," she announced.

"It don't always work that way," Star said. We knew she was referring to her mother.

"It will for us because we're not going overboard, Star. We need to have a good time," she added pointedly, nodding slightly at Misty who was looking small and very sad as she watched the wedding party departing.

Star's eyes darkened with understanding and Jade fixed the drinks. She turned the music up too, so by the time we reached the dance club, we were all feeling happy. I had never been to anything like the club before, but it seemed to me that we weren't dressed too differently from most of the other girls who were there. Everyone looked like they were wearing costumes.

As soon as we arrived, they immersed themselves in the lights and the music. I understood why Jade called it a rave club. Everyone seemed worked up into a frenzy. I could feel it even sitting at the table and watching. Jade made me get up with my crutches and do what I could with one good leg. Everyone around us thought it was amusing. It was as if we had jumped into the ocean and we were being carried out to sea in a wave of hysterical pleasure. Soon we were all screaming and laughing. Sometimes, I was dancing with a strange boy, sometimes with one of the girls. It was the same for all of us, but we never really got to meet anyone. The music was too loud to hear anyone speak. We danced for an hour without stopping until Jade decided she was thirsty. We returned to our table and ordered soft drinks.

"How do you like your father's wedding reception?" Jade shouted to Misty. It was the only way to be heard, even away from the dance floor.

"I love it. Can't wait until they cut the cake!"

Jade laughed. Star and I joined in, but I didn't feel like we were really laughing. It was more like we were crying. We sipped our drinks, the music rushed over us, the lights spun colors over the crowd of revelers, but that old stubborn and determined demon of depression found its way to our table, casting his shadow. I could see it in everyone's faces and feel it on my own.

"I have to get home," Star shouted into Jade's ear. "I want to help Granny tonight."

Jade nodded, paid the bill, and led us out to her waiting limousine.

Even inside the car and away from the noise, my ears still rang.

"I think I'm going deaf," I moaned.

They all laughed at me.

"I guess it's your first time in a dance club," Jade said.

I nodded.

"I usually bring some earplugs," she told me.

Misty leaned against Jade, her eyes closed. Jade put her arm around her and looked at Star and me.

"Girls," she said, "it's time we stopped mourning our dead families. Good times are all we should think about. Tomorrow, at our meeting, let's start presenting some candidates for our first party."

Misty perked up.

"Really?" she asked.

"I think we're almost ready," Jade said. "Star?"

"Right," she said. "But remember what Jade said. We're not inviting any other girls. We're being prudent."

"All right, stop teasing me," Jade begged.

"Why Princess Jade, don't tell me you're sensitive after all," Star said. "Don't tell me you're admitting any weakness."

Jade's face grew dark and serious.

"I've already done that, Star. We all have."

She lifted her toy wand.

"Now it's time to wish it all away," she said.

Everyone watched her wave the wand like someone trying to hypnotize us. Star started to laugh, but Misty suddenly sat up.

"I think it worked," she cried, smiling as if she really had been touched by something magical.

"Me too," Jade agreed. She looked at Star.

"Absolutely felt it," Star said.

They all turned to me.

"Yes," I said. "It's a new beginning."

We were all quiet. I gazed out the window at the city streets as we wove our way back through the darkness of our troubled thoughts, searching for the promise of tomorrow.

13

New Beginnings

"**D**avid Kellerman," Jade began.

She had a picture of herself, two other girls from her school, and three boys down at the Santa Monica Pier near the merry-go-round. We were all sitting in the living room for another of what we were now calling our OWP meetings. This one was called to organize our first party.

"This is David," she said, pointing to the tall, dark haired, slim, good-looking boy who stood behind her in the picture. She paused in front of each of us for a moment with the picture and then stepped back, looking very proud and satisfied and obviously expecting us to have an immediate similar reaction.

Star glanced at me and raised her eyes toward the ceiling.

"So?" she said.

"David's father is one of the principal owners of the Ascot Theater, which translates into free tickets and good seats to rock concerts all year. He lives in Woodside Village, right near Century City, which is probably where we would live if we didn't live where we do."

"You want to invite a boy to our party so you can get free tickets to rock shows?" Star pursued.

"No, silly. I can afford the tickets, and I probably could get pretty good seats, too."

"So?"

"Well, he's good looking, isn't he?"

"Let me see that picture again," Star replied, curling her fingers at her fast and furiously.

I looked at Misty, who covered her smile with her hand. We both knew Star was teasing Jade. Nevertheless, Star studied the picture as if she really was considering David's good looks. She shrugged and handed the picture back to Jade.

"His eyes are too close together. Granny says never trust a man whose eyes are close."

"Oh, pleeeze," Jade cried. "His eyes aren't too close and that's just some old wives' tale, superstition."

"Don't disregard superstitions. There's a lot of wisdom in them," Star insisted, wagging her finger at Jade.

Jade looked at us.

"What do you two think?"

"What else can you tell us about him?" Misty asked.

"Yeah, what else?" Star followed. She sat back with her arms folded under her breasts and pressed her lips together as if she was really sitting in judgment on some jury to decide the future of Jade's romances.

"He's had this thing for me forever," Jade said. "Up until now I've been polite, but noncommittal."

"You mean you've been teasing him," Star said.

"No," Jade said. "I have not."

"So why didn't you ever go out with him? You sure

you're not just playing with him?" Star asked, shaking her head with disapproval.

"No, I wasn't playing with him. I don't do that... much," she added with a coy smile. She looked serious again. "I didn't think he was sophisticated enough for me, but he's matured and, despite what you think, become quite handsome as he got older."

"I didn't say he was ugly," Star relented.

"The point is he'll value an invitation from me and respect it and us, and he knows how to behave at a party," she continued. "I've been thinking seriously about going out with him and this will make for the best opportunity to see if he and I jell."

"Jell?" Star asked, her eyebrows hoisting. "What are you doing, making jam?"

"Laugh if you want, but I think he makes for an excellent candidate and that's my choice. Well?"

Star shrugged.

"I don't have any objections," Misty said.

"Cat?"

"I guess he's fine," I said, glancing at Star.

"Fine," she agreed.

"Thank you," Jade said, and sat. "So? Who's next?"

"I was thinking about asking Chris Wells," Misty announced, "but I don't have a picture of him."

"Just describe him," Jade said.

"He's only a little taller than I am, cute and shy, with long blond hair he's always brushing away from his eyes. Deep blue, by the way," she added. "I've had a crush on him for a long time, but I always felt he looked at me as if I was five years old or something."

"So why do you want to invite him?" Star asked.

"Well, lately, he's been different," Misty revealed with

a suggestive smile. "He lives nearby and on at least two occasions, he stopped by when I was outside. Once, when I was washing the car and once when I was reading a magazine. He talked a lot and stood there watching me, and the way he looks at me now is a lot different. You know how sometimes a boy has an expression on his face that makes you feel naked? It's something like that. I think he was this much away from asking me on a date," she added, holding up her thumb and forefinger.

"Why didn't he ask?" Star questioned suspiciously.

"Like I said, he's very shy," Misty said. "Which I like," she quickly added. "Too many boys think they can say anything they want to you, even if you're a complete stranger. Chris is...the sensitive type," she decided after a moment.

"Maybe he's so shy and so sensitive, you'll scare him when you invite him," Star said.

"Maybe she won't," Jade interjected. "Does he hang around with a nice crowd or what?"

"Yeah, his friends are okay," Misty said. "My mother likes his family, if that means anything."

"Snob city," Star muttered.

"We're just trying to reassure ourselves, and do due diligence," Jade defended.

"Do what?" Star asked.

"Check their backgrounds so we don't invite the wrong people," Jade explained. "Isn't that why we're having this meeting?"

"Excuse me, I forgot." She turned to Misty. "Do you know his blood type?" she asked.

"What?"

"We should also get a urine sample," she continued.

"Very funny," Jade said. "Who do you want to invite, big shot?"

Star laughed and threw an impish glance my way before settling back.

"Remember when I was telling you about Lily Porter's cousin, Larry?" Star asked.

"No," Jade said.

"Passed right over your head or below your nose?" Star asked her, eyes blazing.

"I forgot, all right? We haven't exactly been doing nothing these days," she explained in a high-pitched voice.

"I remember," I said. "He's in the army, right?"

"That's right, Cat. Good. How did you remember with all that's going on?" she asked, giving Jade a side glance. "Must be you think of something else besides your nail polish."

"That's not fair," Jade cried.

"All right, I'm sorry. Anyway, he's coming home on Tuesday and I'm going to meet him and I was thinking," she said, smiling, "if he's all he looks like, I'd invite him."

"That sounds good," Misty said. "He'll certainly be mature being in the army and all."

"Oh, he's mature," Star said, smiling. "He's twenty."

"Twenty? Why, he's closing in on social security," Jade quipped, seizing the opportunity for payback. "Why go out with such an old man?"

Star glared at her a moment and then broke into a smile.

"Okay, one for you," she said.

Their attention turned to me.

"Who do you want to invite, Cat?" Jade asked.

"I don't know anyone," I said.

"Isn't there anyone you'd like to know?" Misty asked.

I shook my head.

"I don't know anyone well enough to invite to a party. I mean, there are boys I wish I knew, but I've never said two words to any of them."

Everyone was silent.

"In that case I would like to suggest I ask David to bring his cousin Stuart along," Jade said. "They're together quite often and Stuart is good looking, too, and very polite."

"A blind date?" Misty asked.

"Cat wouldn't mind, would you, Cat?" Jade asked me.

"I don't want to ruin it for everyone else," I said.

"You won't. I know for a fact that Stuart doesn't go out that much and he's not going with anyone. He's just right for you," Jade insisted.

"Who are you? Cupid?" Star asked.

"It's our first party. If they don't get along, it's not the end of the world, you know." She turned back to me. "Stuart's about David's height with darker brown hair. He looks a little like Christian Slater and he's very intelligent, an A-plus student."

"Then he'll think I'm stupid," I said.

"No, he won't. Why should he? You don't do badly in school," Jade countered.

"I haven't done well this year. I missed a lot of school, as you know."

"You're not looking for a job, Cat. You're just meeting some brainy, spoiled, rich kid," Star said. "This isn't going to be an audition or anything."

"Don't listen to her. Stuart's not spoiled," Jade said. She shot one of her sharp, hot looks Star's way. "You don't even know him."

"He's rich, he's spoiled," Star insisted. "But that's okay. That's fine," she said, holding up her hands. "I'm getting used to spoiled people."

"I feel sorry for this Larry," Jade said, shaking her head. "After he meets you, he'll wish he was back in boot camp."

"Is that right? Well, let's just wait and see where he wants to be after he meets me. He might even go AWOL just to keep me happy."

"Oh, brother." Jade stared at her and then they both laughed. Misty smiled at me.

"This is beginning to sound exciting," she said. "Right?"

My heart had begun to race with the thought of being on a blind date. If they all had a good time and my date didn't, I would be like the lead weight I was afraid I'd be and the party would be ruined. It seemed so important to them, too.

"Okay then," Jade said, "we've got our list. Now let's plan the party. I want this to really go well for all of us, and," she said, gazing at me, "especially for Cat."

"Amen to that," Star said.

We talked about the menu and then had a small argument about having liquor. Misty and Jade wanted it; Star thought it might make for trouble.

"Especially if one of us drinks too much," she pointed out. "Something might be said that we'll all regret," she warned.

"That won't happen," Jade insisted.

"When you're having a good time and there's music and stuff, you just can't help it sometimes. All one of us has to do is make one little mistake..."

"You're making it sound terrible and dangerous just to have a good time here. It's why we're doing all this," Jade declared, holding up her arms. "If we can't have fun— mature, intelligent fun—what's the use?"

"I just want us to be cautious, is all," Star replied.

All of us were quiet for a few moments.

"The boys are going to be looking for booze," Jade said. "We have the house to ourselves, all this freedom, they'll think we're nerds or something. Do you think your army boyfriend is going to want lemonade?"

"Maybe we should just have some beer," Star relented.

"Beer? I hate beer!" Jade moaned. She looked at me. "Do you like beer?"

"I haven't really drunk much," I said.

"See?"

"All right," Star said, "have booze, but don't blame me if it goes bad."

"It won't," Jade maintained. She thought a moment. "I'll make this punch drink and I won't put in that much."

"You mix booze with stuff and you get sick faster," Star said.

"Brother."

"I'm just telling you. Unfortunately, I know about it," Star reminded us.

"Okay, we'll be extra careful," Jade promised. "Music," she said. "I'll bring some of my new CD's." She looked around. "I think we should fix up this room, move out some of this furniture so we can dance."

"Call back the Salvation Army?" Misty asked.

"No, not give it away. Just move it someplace for the night," Jade explained. "Maybe we can put some of it in the dining room."

"Okay with me," Star said. She looked at me and I nodded.

"We've got the date, the time, the menu, and the plan. It's going to be a great first party," Jade declared.

Misty smiled and I tried to look optimistic.

"Just one more thing," Star said, leaning toward us.

"What?" Jade asked.

"Let's be sure to keep everyone out of the backyard. Just in case I didn't do all that good a job."

"You did. Stop worrying," Jade chastised.

Star leaned back.

"Granny always tells me an ounce of prevention is worth a pound of cure."

"Spare me all the wisdom," Jade moaned.

"That's your trouble, Jade. Someone already did that."

Misty and I almost laughed and then stopped because neither Star nor Jade was smiling. It would take more than one good party to make us forget who we were and why we were brought together. Maybe, we'd never forget long enough to have a good time after all.

As far as forgetting went, it was just about impossible for me to not think about my father and fear his return. Not an hour of a day went by when I didn't pause to listen more closely to a sound I had heard in the house or a car that seemed to have pulled into my driveway. I gazed out of the window so often anyone passing by would have wondered if I was being held prisoner or something.

However, despite the storm clouds that always seemed to hover on our horizon, the closer we drew to the night of the party, the more excited we all became. Star's initial meeting with Larry turned out better than she had anticipated. Larry not only wanted to see her again and said he would come to the party, he called her every day thereafter and took her to dinner one night. Jade reported that David Kellerman was very excited about the invitation and then called to say his cousin was even more eager to come and to meet me, which put me in a panic.

Jade took control of my makeover, but would any hairstyle, any makeup, any new clothing have much of an impact on my appearance? I was still clumping around with a cast on my leg, of course. And what about my limited and troubled experiences with boys? Would I quickly make a fool of myself and ruin the evening?

The day before the party, Jade took me to her hairstylist. She spent most of the time trimming my hair evenly and complaining about the job my last stylist had done. I was too embarrassed to say it had been Geraldine. After that, she cut my hair in a shortish, graduated bob. My hair was then blown dry and sprayed with a gloss lacquer. I had never had anything like it done before.

"Now that's an up-to-date hairdo," Jade cried, and when I looked at myself in the mirror, I felt my heart skip.

Was that really me? It changed my whole appearance. I no longer looked dragged out and tired. It was so difficult to think of myself as attractive. Geraldine's admonitions against vanity resonated like a drumbeat in my head.

"What are you looking at, Cathy? Are you going to fall in love with your own face, too?" I could hear her ask.

Back at the house, Jade experimented on my face with different shades of makeup, eyeliner, and lipsticks while Star and Misty sat in judgment, everyone arguing about the results.

"That makes her eyes too large."

"That's too much of a contrast."

"You're ruining the graceful line in her lips."

My face was smeared, painted, and changed so much, my skin began to feel raw. Finally, they all agreed on a shade of lipstick that flattered me and everyone decided the rest of my makeup should be subtle.

Misty wanted us all to wear our mythic clothes again, but Jade had a new designer dress she wanted to wear and she insisted I go with her and buy something new, just for the party.

"I always buy something new whenever there's an occasion," she told me.

She decided I looked very good in a black strappy gown, even with my leg in a cast. It had a low neckline, one that would have driven Geraldine to paint an A on my chest, but Jade insisted that I stopped being ashamed of what she called my "assets." In the end I relented and bought the dress.

Jade had brought over a selection of clothes for Star to try, and Star settled on a low cut Anna Sui dress, augmented by a push-up bra. Jade insisted she wear high-heeled sandals, which Star happened to have.

Misty was going to wear a tight Betsey Johnson minidress in a floral print with high-spiky heels. She had a pair of her mother's large gold loop earrings she wanted to wear, too. Jade thought they were boring, but Misty obviously still used her mother as a role model for some things and ignored the criticism.

Late in the afternoon of the day of our party, Jade insisted we go up to our special room to meditate. Just having the three of them around me, all of them talking, sometimes all at once, hearing their laughter while we primped and preened, made me feel comfortable and happy enough. Meditating seemed unnecessary, but Jade had this idea that under our "glossy, perfect surfaces," as she put it, "ran an undercurrent of nervousness and hysteria."

"We've all made good progress with Doctor Marlowe," she said, "but it would be foolish and naive of us to believe we were four stable females. Each of us still has a stick of dynamite under our hearts and the wicks could be lit at any moment, sometimes because of the smallest, dumbest things."

She was talking mostly about herself, but it really did apply to each of us. No one objected or argued with her. We marched into the room quietly, all of us in our bathrobes. We had bought four thick white terry-cloth robes the day before at the department store, among other things, to always keep at the clubhouse, as my home was now called.

We gathered in a circle on the rug. Jade lit the candles and closed her eyes as she reached out for Star's hand and Misty's, who both reached out for mine. A continuous stream of New Age music ran under our thoughts. First, we had our long moments of silence, reaching deeply into ourselves, then Jade began a chant, a prayer, wishing for us to have happiness, to become free of our pasts, our demons, and shadows, to blossom and flourish in our renewed and newly nourished souls.

Afterward, I did feel as if all my fears and horrible memories had been driven down into some deep and dark vault inside myself, locked up and shut away so I could be free to be fresh and new and hopeful. As we started to dress, however, and I looked at the clock ticking toward the start of our party, I couldn't keep the tension and nervousness from crawling back into me.

"What does a boy expect from a girl the first time they meet like this?" I asked my far more experienced sisters. Everyone paused and, after glancing at each other, turned to me. Star was first.

"I'll tell you one thing, Cat. You don't throw yourself at him, even if he looks like Mr. Perfect. The more you hold back, the more they want you and the higher you go in their eyes. I didn't even kiss Larry good night the first night. I let him peck me on the cheek, but none of that suck face stuff minutes after 'How do you do?' " she advised.

"Oh, spare me," Jade said.

"I'm not lying." She nodded at me. "When I did kiss him, he thought it was gold," she said, smiling. "The more you like someone, the more you want him to respect you. Isn't that true, Princess Jade?"

Jade's skeptical smirk evaporated and she nodded.

"She's right," Jade said. "But, look, don't build this up too much in your mind. Try to relax and remember he'll probably be as nervous as you are, maybe more. You've got to project some confidence. Think about your smile. Make it small but soft and sincere. Don't laugh and giggle after everything he says. Boys can tell when you're trying too hard to please them and believe it or not, they think less of girls who do that. Not that they don't want to be pleased. They just want it to be sincere."

"Don't stare at him all the time, either," Star said. "Make him feel you're not even interested in him in the beginning. Make him work for it."

"The important thing is you've got to look confident even if you don't feel confident," Jade said. "Walk with your shoulders back, like this." She demonstrated. "I took a whole course in charm," she added before Star could laugh.

"How is she gonna do that on crutches, Jade?" Misty pointed out. I could tell she was listening intently to their instructions too.

"Well, do the best you can," Jade told me, "and drop your eyes once in a while. Make sure you speak slowly and pause dramatically between sentences to hold his attention. And most important of all," she said, her own eyes small and determined, "if he isn't right for you or if he doesn't appear to care for you, don't let him see your disappointment, Cat. Keep your tears behind your eyes. Besides," she said with a laugh, "you don't want to smear your makeup."

"There's so much to remember," I complained.

They laughed.

"We're not saying you have to think about it like some lines in a play or something," Star said. "It'll all come naturally after a while."

"I'd kiss on the first date," Misty piped up, "if I wanted to and I liked the boy. It doesn't mean he'll think less of you," she insisted. "I might even do a little more."

"Oh, you would, would you?" Star challenged.

"Yes," Misty said. "I'm not saying I will tonight, but I might."

"Misty's not all wrong," Jade said. "A lot depends on the guy, I suppose. Maybe there are no rules that always apply, just some things to keep in mind. The most important thing is to be honest."

"Excuse me," Star said. "You're always honest with the guys you date?"

"You can flirt a little," Jade admitted, "but don't try to be someone else just to get him to like you. Okay?" she asked Star.

They looked at me.

"I'm not sure I'm not more confused now than ever," I said, and everyone laughed.

"You'll be fine," Star assured me. "If he doesn't like you, he isn't worth it."

"She's finally right about something," Jade said.

Star stuck out her tongue at Jade. Then we all returned to dressing and putting on the finishing touches. In fifteen minutes, the doorbell would ring and the boys would begin to arrive. A party in my house! Not in my wildest imaginings did I think this would ever happen. Geraldine certainly never imagined it.

Could the dead hear what went on around them? Was death like chains and gags? Was she being tortured and frustrated in her grave? Was it her punishment? I shuddered to think that maybe we were being cruel or evil. Perhaps our histories, our troubles had turned us into something we never anticipated.

Downstairs, Jade put some finishing touches on the cheese and crackers, shrimp plate, and chips and dip. Then she prepared her spiked punch. The three of us stood and watched her and glanced at the clock.

"Wait a minute!" Star suddenly exclaimed. Jade turned.

"What's wrong?"

"We never told each other what we told the guys about why Cat had the house to herself."

"Oh, no," I muttered. What a time to finally remember to compare details, I thought.

"All I said was we had my friend's house for a party because her mother was gone for the night," Jade said. "I didn't tell David anything about Cat's situation. What about you?"

"Yeah, I said that, but I said her parents, I think. I don't know if I just said mother. I can't remember," Star said.

"How can you not remember what you said?" Jade nearly yelled. "What were you, drunk?"

"Don't be stupid."

"Well, how can you not remember?"

"I said...mother. I didn't say parents. No, I wouldn't have said parents."

"Are you sure?"

"Yes. I'm sure."

"Damn, you must be love struck," Jade chastised. "Not sure, sure. Misty, what about you?"

"I didn't tell him anything. I just said we were having a party at Cat's. He didn't ask any details and I didn't think to tell him any. What do I tell him if he asks?"

"Say what I said. Her mother's gone for the night."

"What about her father?" Star asked.

"No father," Jade said. "Her father...died." She widened her eyes. "Killed by a drunk driver when he was only in his late twenties. That's partly true, isn't it?"

"Everyone got it?" Star asked.

My heart was pounding. What a big mistake we had almost made.

"Okay, it's settled then."

"Wait. What did her father do?" Star asked.

"I don't know. What?" Jade asked, looking my way.

The clock was ticking.

"My father was a musician," I said, remembering my mother's letter. "He taught music at...at..."

"UCLA," Jade inserted.

"UCLA," I said. "My mother is still not over it, even after all these years."

"Where did she go tonight?" Star asked.

We all thought.

"To her sister's in...Phoenix," Misty said. "I have an aunt there."

"Fine. Everyone got it?" Star asked.

"I guess nobody said anything about this, then," I said, indicating my cast.

"Just tell them you tripped on the stairs. You're a klutz," Jade decided. "It's better than saying you fell from the crawl space above the pantry. Then you'd really have explaining to do."

They all nodded just as the doorbell sounded.

"Talk about just making it at the bell," Star muttered, and went to answer the door.

Larry was the first to arrive. Star said that made sense; the army taught him to be punctual. He was a strikingly good looking six-feet-three-inch young man with firm wide shoulders. He looked very handsome in his army uniform and stood with a calm, deliberate air about him.

Star introduced him, and his first question was what happened to my leg.

"I came down my stairs too fast one day," I said quickly.

"Anyone ever tell you that you look a lot like Will Smith?" Jade asked him to change the subject.

"No, ma'am," he said. "Most compare me to Denzel Washington."

"Ma'am? Please just call me Jade," she said. "Next thing I know you'll salute me."

"I'm the only one he's saluting tonight," Star joked, and Larry laughed. "C'mon, I'll get you some of Jade's wonderful punch," she told him. Jade glanced at Misty and me when Star threaded her arm through Larry's and led him into the living room.

"She's full of beans," Jade whispered. "They've already slept together."

Misty's eyes bulged.

"I can tell those things," Jade insisted.

David and Stuart arrived next. Both wore dark sports jackets and slacks. David looked as he did in the picture, only more handsome. Stuart was good looking, too, but looked very serious. He had an air about him that made him seem older, wiser.

Everyone was introduced in the living room and Jade put on some music. The boys liked her punch. Stuart got me a glass and we sat on the sofa. Misty was near the door, anxiously awaiting Chris's arrival. I could see by the look on her face that she was afraid he wasn't going to show.

"How long have you been wearing the cast?" Stuart asked. He had a deep, resonant voice. Very manly, I thought.

"Not long. About ten days," I said.

"I broke my wrist once. When I was ten, I fell off my bike and tried to break the fall with my hand straight out. It was pretty painful. Does your ankle still hurt?"

"No, it's fine."

"Jade told my cousin that you're attending St. Jude," he said.

"Yes." I wasn't sure if she had told them I hadn't attended much this past year, but I guessed probably not.

"You know Guy Davis? I think he goes there. He'd be a junior."

"No," I said, "but that doesn't mean anything. I didn't make a lot of friends there."

"Oh? How come?"

"I don't know," I said. I sipped my drink and looked down, but I could see him smiling. Was that a dumb thing to say? I wondered.

"I don't have all that many friends at school either," he revealed. "I'm not in any sports or clubs. Most days I go straight home from school and hang out with my younger brother Judson until our mom gets home."

"What about your father?" I asked quickly.

"He died. Heart attack. He had a problem with a heart

valve that required surgery. We thought it went okay. So did the doctors, but... it didn't."

"I'm sorry. How long ago was that?"

"Three years ago. I kinda feel I have to take up some of the responsibilities," he added, looking down at his glass of punch. "It's why I don't get out much, I guess. David's always after me to do stuff with him. He's a popular guy at school and on the basketball team." He paused, sipped his drink, and looked around. Misty was still hovering near the door. "What about your parents?" he asked. "Where are they tonight?"

"My mother went to visit her sister in Phoenix," I recited.

"And your father?"

For a moment I felt my throat close. It seemed so wrong to lie to Stuart, whose father really died. Mine did, too, and technically, I suppose, I wasn't lying, but I was about to pretend I had known my father. Star, who was half listening to our conversation, paused in talking to Larry and looked at me.

"My father is gone, too," I said. "He died in an automobile accident."

"Oh, I'm sorry. David didn't mention that."

"Maybe he doesn't know," I said.

The doorbell rang and Misty practically flew out of the room. Moments later, she appeared with Chris at her side. He was cute, but it was also easy to see from the way his eyes shifted and his smile flickered, that he was as shy as she had described. Misty led him straight to the spiked punch.

Jade turned the music up, and she and David began to dance. Almost immediately, Star and Larry joined them and then Misty tugged Chris onto the floor as well. Stuart and I remained seated on the sofa, watching.

"I feel silly dancing with this," I said pointing to my cast.

"That's okay. I'm not that great a dancer even without a cast on my leg."

We both laughed and watched the others.

"My cousin's a good dancer," he leaned over to tell me.

"Yes, he is."

"Star's pretty good too," he added.

"I think I should start cooking the meatballs," I told him. "We're making subs and they'll need a half hour or so."

"Oh. I'll come with you," he said, surprising me. "I've become something of a cook," he told me as we walked down the hallway to the kitchen. "My mother works and sometimes, I make our dinner."

I nodded and he watched me drop the meatballs into the pan of sauce.

"Mind if I taste?" he asked.

"No. Go ahead."

He dipped a spoon into the sauce, tasted it, and looked pensive.

"What's wrong?"

"Nothing. It's delicious," he said. "Just enough garlic, too."

I laughed.

"I just followed a cookbook."

"Well, you followed it very well," he said. He gazed around the kitchen and stared at the back door. Star's repair of the rebroken door wasn't very good. It still looked quite chipped and battered around the lock. I saw the way his eyebrows tilted toward each other as he wondered.

"We should get back to the party," I said. "I'll just let this simmer."

"Sure," he said. "How long have you lived in this house?"

"All my life."

"It's cozy," he said, "but the pictures and some of the decorations surprise me."

"Yes. My mother and I just did some of it because we got bored with how the house looked."

He nodded and gazed up the stairway.

"How many bedrooms?"

"Two," I said.

When we looked into the living room, we saw that slower music was being played and everyone was dancing closely. Misty looked very happy and gave me an impish little smile as she tightened her embrace around Chris. For a long moment Stuart and I remained in the doorway, watching.

"How did you all meet?" he asked. "You're all going to different schools and live in different parts of the city, right?"

Once again butterflies of panic fluttered in my chest. There were just too many lies floating around us. One or the other was bound to crash and send up question marks and create suspicions. The best thing to do, I concluded, was stay as close to the truth as possible.

"We all had the same therapist," I told him. "Doctor Marlowe."

"Oh." He nodded and looked at them. "I saw a counselor too, after Dad's death. Did it help you?"

"Yes," I said.

"Me too." He smiled. "It's good to have someone to talk to," he said, "someone who really listens."

I nodded.

"You wanna try it?" he asked, nodding at the dancers.

"I'll be clumsy," I said.

"So will I. We'll be a perfect couple," he said. He smiled, but with such sincerity, I lost my inhibitions in a moment. It was as if he could fill me with confidence simply by directing those hazel eyes at mine. Our eyes locked as if we were both about to journey through them into our very souls, touching each other deeply before retreating like two people who suddenly snap out of a hypnotic state.

He gently took the crutches from me and placed them against the wall. Then he put his arm around my waist and held me as if he would keep me from falling off the edge of the earth. I never would have thought it, but I actually forgot I had a cast on my leg. We moved about the room with almost as much grace and ease as the others. I saw how the girls were all gazing at us, each with a soft, happy smile on her face. None matched the smile on my face, however.

When the music changed and became upbeat, we didn't retreat. We were all swinging and laughing. In fact, I became so involved with my dancing, I nearly forgot about the meatballs. Stuart reminded me.

"I'm one of those men who could be won over with food," he whispered.

I laughed, but he looked like he really meant it. He and I then returned to the kitchen and prepared the sandwich platters.

"We're a team," he declared. "You make them up and I'll serve them."

Finally, we joined the others and all of us sat around eating and talking. David asked Larry questions about the army and Germany, and even Misty's Chris, who had been so quiet all evening, asked questions. Afterward, everyone helped clean up and for a while, we all just sat around, talking about schools, music, and movies. I could see the curiosity building in Stuart's face as I revealed that I hadn't seen this or done that. I could almost hear him ask, "Where have you been?"

Where had I been? While everyone else was out there, experiencing life, doing things, Geraldine had me practically imprisoned in her own unhappiness and depression. It wasn't hard to understand why I had at first welcomed my father's unholy affections.

Jade and David started to dance again and soon after Star and Larry joined them. Jade looked like she was trying to outdo Star for a while and then everyone just stopped, exhausted. It was getting late, anyway.

It had been decided beforehand that Misty was going to stay over with me. When the party ended, Star left with Larry, and David decided that he and Stuart were going to take Jade home. Chris lingered. I could see Misty really liked him.

"If you're tired," she whispered, "just go up. I'll come up later." She glanced at Chris who sat on the sofa trying not to look conspicuous.

"Oh, sure," I said.

I went out with David, Jade, and Stuart to say good night. Star and Larry had already left.

"I really had a good time," Stuart told me. "I'm glad I let my cousin talk me into it."

"I'm glad too," I said.

"You're a nice girl," he said. "Easy to talk to and not full of yourself like so many girls I meet these days."

"Thanks," I said.

Jade and David were waiting patiently in the car and involved in each other. My heart started thumping. What was I supposed to do? Look like I wanted to kiss him good night? Encourage him? Just stick out my hand? Was a handshake okay or silly for a girl?

Before I could ponder the questions long, he leaned forward and brought his lips gently to mine. His eyes were closed, but I kept mine open. It was a quick kiss, almost too quick to be considered anything.

"Good night," he said.

"Good night."

He lingered very close to me.

"I'd like to call you tomorrow. Maybe we can go for a ride or something and have some lunch at the beach," he said. "How's that sound?"

"Good," I said. It sounded more than good.

He smiled, turned to go to the car, paused, and then returned to me.

"I've been out of it so long, I guess I kissed you good night like someone would kiss a relative. You probably think I'm a clumsy fool."

"No, I—"

He embraced me and kissed me harder on the lips, holding me longer, sending a hot shaft of excitement up my spine and around my stomach.

"There," he said. "That's more like it, right?"

All I could do was nod. He smiled softly, squeezed my hand gently and left for the car. Before he got into the backseat, he waved.

"I'll call you midmorning," he promised and got in. I watched the car back away. Jade waved.

"Great party!" David called back to me. I waved to him, too, and remained on the walk as the car moved down the street. Just before it reached the corner, its headlights washed over an automobile parked on the right.

My heart stopped and started.

It looked exactly like my father's car and there was someone sitting inside. I saw his silhouette just for a second. I couldn't move. The car's lights went on; its engine started and it pulled away, disappearing like some short but horrifying nightmare, into the darkness.

I caught my breath and hurried back into the house. I wanted to tell Misty, but the lights were out in the living room. The music was low and I knew she certainly didn't want to hear or see me at the moment. She especially didn't want to hear anything unpleasant tonight.

No matter how close we all got to each other, some burdens would be my own, I thought. I carried this one up to my bedroom with me and closed the door. I had wanted to go to sleep dreaming of Stuart's warm eyes, but instead, when I closed my own, I could see only my father's eyes shining through the darkness like some predatory animal's, waiting patiently, hovering, confident that soon, soon he would get what he wanted.

14

Caught in the Act

Misty didn't come up all night. I fell asleep waiting for her and woke up once during the night and realized she wasn't beside me in the bed. I listened for voices below, heard nothing, and concluded she might have left with Chris. However, when I went down in the morning, I found her curled up on the sofa. She had a blanket partially wrapped over her and I could see she was wearing only her bra and panties. Her dress was draped over the back of the sofa. Chris was gone. I didn't wake her. I went into the kitchen and started on breakfast. Just as I sat at the table, she appeared in the doorway with the blanket around her like a toga.

"Hi," she said after a big yawn. She shuffled to the coffeepot and poured herself a cup. After she took a sip, she smiled and said, "Great party." She paused when I didn't respond. "You had fun, didn't you? I saw how close you and Stuart were most of the night."

"Yes, I did have fun and he's very nice," I said.

"Well, why are you so glum looking then? Are you mad at me for spending more time with Chris?"

"No, of course not," I replied.

"So?" She sat and sipped her coffee. "What is it?"

"I think my father was out there last night, parked across the street. It looked like his car and his silhouette when he pulled away. He left right after David drove off with Stuart and Jade."

"Maybe you just imagined it was him," Misty said. "You're nervous about it since the break-in. I mean, why would he just sit in his car across the street and then leave when they left? That doesn't make sense, does it?"

"I don't know. He was probably stunned by what he had discovered in here when he broke in, and now he is spying on the house. Seeing I had a party surely sharpened his curiosity. He knows Geraldine would never permit it."

She thought a moment and then shrugged.

"What's he going to do about it?"

"I don't know."

"He's supposed to stay out of your life. He's got to be afraid you'll call the police if he comes around, so stop worrying so much. You'll get a wrinkled brow and Stuart might not like that," she teased.

I blushed and she laughed.

"Guess what," she said, leaning toward me, her eyes full of glee. "Chris isn't as shy as I thought." Her eyes brightened even more in anticipation of my reaction.

"What do you mean?" I asked instead.

"What do I mean? He didn't leave until about an hour ago," she said, and stopped as if she had drawn dots on a page that I was supposed to connect in my own mind. "I didn't exactly chain him to the sofa," she added. "Understand?" She laughed. "I think I'll make some toast," she said, rising. "So," she continued as she worked, "how far did you two go?"

"How far?"

She turned and raised her eyebrows.

"Yes, how far? Did you take the advice of our two leaders and make your kisses seem like gold?"

"Oh. He kissed me good night," I revealed.

She continued to stare at me, waiting.

"What?" I asked.

"That's it? You two were dancing very closely at one point, and you did spend a lot of time with him in the kitchen, I noticed."

"We were preparing the food."

"Uh-huh," she sang.

"That was it," I assured her. She still looked skeptical. "He's calling me this morning. He wants to take me to the beach and then to lunch."

"That's nice. I'm going with Chris to the Santa Monica mall this morning. He wants me to help him buy his mother a birthday present. I wonder where Star and Larry ended up last night," she added after the toast popped up.

"Larry was very nice," I said. "All the boys were."

"It's our new aura," Misty declared with dramatic flair. "Jade was right. Our spiritual sessions have wrapped a ring of charm about us that attracts only handsome, nice guys. See how we're all glowing!"

She laughed, and I wondered if she really believed it or was just having fun and teasing me.

Just under an hour later, Stuart called and arranged to pick me up by eleven. We still hadn't heard from Jade or Star. Misty helped me clean up the house, but criticized me for being too vigilant about it.

"You act as if we're going to have an inspection. Geraldine's not coming back," she emphasized. Then she showered, dressed, and was ready for Chris when he came.

"Would you like to go with us?" he asked after Misty and I greeted him at the door.

"She can't. She has a date," Misty sang. "Cat's on the prowl," she told him, and followed it with a long meow that made us both laugh. "I'll call you later," she cried out as she left the house.

I returned to my room and spent the rest of my time in front of my new vanity mirror trying to decide if I needed a darker lipstick, more makeup on my cheeks, or less eye shadow on my lids. It all made me so nervous, I finally just washed my face and put on the same lipstick I had on the night before.

I had bell-bottom jeans to wear that would go over my cast, but I hated how I looked in them. My hips were too wide. Instead, I chose one of my new skirts, a blouse, and a cardigan sweater, which I didn't button. Searching through the bag of jewelry Jade had discovered in Geraldine's safe, I found a gold bracelet and a gold ring with diamond baguettes that fit my pinky finger. When the doorbell rang, I quickly sprayed on some of the cologne Jade had brought me and then started down the stairs, hating how clumsy I looked with this cast and crutches. Even so, I couldn't remember when I was more excited. This was really my first date.

Leaning on my crutches, I pulled the door open only to face a deliveryman from Federal Express. My expression of disappointment hoisted his eyebrows.

"Geraldine Carson?" he asked.

For a moment my throat closed and I couldn't utter a sound. In an instant, I made a decision.

"Yes?" I said, pretending to be Geraldine.

"I have a delivery," he said, showing me the big envelope. "Please sign here," he said, offering me a clipboard and pointing to a line.

I visualized her signature and tried my best to do it right even at a moment's notice. The messenger didn't care or ask for any identification.

"Thank you," he said.

I forced a smile, thanked him, and stepped back, quickly closing the door. For a few seconds, I just stood there trembling with the envelope in hand. Swallowing down a lump in my throat, I went into the living room, sat on the sofa and studied the envelope. There was no indication as to who had sent it. Maybe it was just the hospital or the bank or even Doctor Marlowe, I thought. I took a deep breath and tore it open.

A sheet of paper was taped to two slices of cardboard. First, I read what was on the paper.

Dear G——
Your so-called innocent is not so innocent after all. There's blame to be shared.

He didn't sign it, but I recognized my father's handwriting. Slowly, I pulled the two pieces of cardboard apart and the picture fell on my lap. It had obviously been taken with a telephoto lens the night before. It had definitely been he in that car parked across the street. The shot caught Stuart and me kissing the second time, the long and romantic kiss. We were under the lights and clearly identifiable. I had been so dazed by the kiss that I hadn't felt his hand at the side of my breast. I know he didn't mean to grope me or anything, but it was just the awkward way we embraced when he had rushed back to give me "a real kiss."

If Geraldine were alive and looking at this, I thought, she would have found this photo damning. Whatever privileges she had granted would have been revoked. I could almost hear her shouting over my shoulder.

"In the street! You kiss someone like that in the street and in front of our home for anyone to see?"

Why had my father done this? What did he want? I thought and thought until a cold, terrifying reason reached the surface of my confusion. Could it be that he was actually jealous? That he didn't want to see me with anyone else? Was he hoping this picture would turn Geraldine against Stuart and have her forbid me from ever seeing him again? Did he revel in the commotion and the dissension he would create in this house? He wanted her to keep me locked away. Maybe he hoped I would hate her so much, I would turn back to him.

Whatever his reasons, another chilling thought occurred to me. He would be spying on me all the time. He might even be out there this very moment, I thought, out there with his camera, waiting, hoping to catch me in some compromising act so he could have more to use in his drive to turn Geraldine into an even worse ogre.

What was I going to do? I had to talk to the others to tell them about all this and get their advice. I went to the phone and called Star. Her granny answered and said Star and Larry had taken Rodney to the zoo. I thanked her and then I called Jade. Her answering machine came on and I left an urgent message. I imagined that she was still in bed, but would call me soon.

When the doorbell rang, I realized that in my turmoil I had completely forgotten about Stuart. It was just a little after eleven. For a moment I spun about in a fluster, the picture still in my hand. I didn't want him to see it. I shoved it under a magazine in the living room and then went to the door. He had rung again.

"Hi," he said. "I didn't mean to rush you, but I wanted to be sure you had heard."

"That's okay," I said.

"Are you ready?"

"Yes." I gazed back into the house as if I somehow still expected Geraldine to appear, especially after the picture had been delivered, and then I hurried out, closing the door behind me quickly.

As soon as I did step out, I paused, leaned on my crutches, and studied every automobile in the street. My father's car wasn't there, but maybe he had a different car, or maybe he had hired someone to follow me and take pictures. All sorts of scenarios ran through my terrified imagination. Stuart sensed my anxiety.

"Anything wrong?" he asked

"Oh, no," I said. "I was just looking to see if Misty was gone. She just left to go shopping with Chris," I added quickly, but I was never a very good liar. Geraldine had eyes that locked on mine and forced me to be truthful most of the time. She was always prying, checking, reconfirming.

"Do you have to be back any specific time?" Stuart asked as we went to his car and he opened the door for me.

"No," I said.

"So your mother's going to be away today, too?"

"Oh, yes. She called and said she was staying over another night, maybe even two."

He nodded, smiling.

What would I do after two days? I wondered. I needed

to talk to Jade or Star desperately. We had to come up with some sensible explanation. Hopefully, Stuart wouldn't keep asking me about Geraldine.

"I thought I'd take you to Laguna Beach," he said. "It'll take us a little over an hour, if that's all right."

"Yes, fine," I said.

"I had a great time last night," he continued as he started the engine and backed out of the driveway. I looked back, studying all the cars down the street, waiting for one to start up and follow. "I guess I've been shut up in my house of responsibilities too long. I almost feel like a guy traveling in a desert who reached an oasis. You're the oasis," he added.

His words made me blush and I didn't know what to say. I started to laugh and stopped, recalling Jade's advice about giggling stupidly after something a boy had said.

"Jade says the trouble with most people she knows is that they don't balance their lives with fun and work. Star accuses her of putting too much emphasis on fun and says she doesn't know the meaning of work." Stuart laughed. Was I talking too much already, sounding like a little idiot?

"I guess you girls are all getting along pretty well, despite the differences. That's terrific. Most of the girls I know at school stay in their safe little cocoons, their own little cliques. I guess you all have something in common."

"Yes, we do."

"I kind of lost contact with my best friends."

"Oh, too bad."

"It's okay," he said, smiling. "I'm back. I'll have best friends again. I hope you'll be one of them," he continued.

I didn't know what to say to that. It just about took the

breath out of me. I didn't want to just say sure or of course I will. I wanted to sound sincere and smart.

"It takes time for people to become real friends," I finally said.

"You're right. I'm glad you feel that way, too. All I mean is I think you and I can be friends and I hope you feel the same way about me. Jeez," he said, shaking his head. "I must sound like the biggest jerk spouting off like this. I'm sorry."

"No, you don't. Really," I said, amused and encouraged that he had the same fears about himself.

He looked at me with those warm, trusting eyes and I smiled at him.

"Let's wait until the end of the afternoon and then you'll get another chance to tell me I don't talk too much," he said. "You look great," he added as if he had just looked at me.

"Thank you."

I turned and looked straight ahead, my heart thumping. What a beautiful day loomed before us: the sky was a soft blue with just a few small puffs of clouds dabbed against it. We soon saw the ocean glittering as if there were mirrors floating on the surface, the breakers fresh and exciting. Sailboats appeared, popping up like props on a perfect set. The world can be beautiful, I thought. I can be happy, can't I? I can put all the sadness behind me for a while. Please, I told my nervous conscience, take a day off.

Stuart and I got to know each other much more during the trip. He told me about his ambitions to pursue a career in medical research.

"I really started to think about it after my father's

death," he explained. "Some day I'd like to be responsible for discovering a cure for the heart problem he had and preventing what happened to my family from happening to others. I know this might sound silly to you but sometimes I think of it as a way of getting revenge."

"That doesn't sound silly at all," I told him. "Anger often pushes us to do more, to work harder."

He nodded and gazed at me.

"You sound pretty smart. I bet you do really well in school, huh?"

"I have and haven't," I admitted. "This past year's been difficult."

"Sure, I understand," he said. "I nearly dropped out after Dad died. I kept thinking I should just go and get a job and be my mother's main support. We're fine as far as money goes, but I just felt responsible. Gosh, listen to me talking about these problems. You've got to be thinking I'm a deadly serious person who doesn't know how to relax. Sorry."

"It's all right," I said, laughing. "It's nice to have a sensible conversation, too."

"Right," he said. "Do you like wraps? I know this great little place on the beach that makes a bunch of different kinds..."

"Wraps?"

"You don't know what they are?"

"No," I said. Why did every answer I gave seem like a terrible revelation? He could easily tell I've practically been incarcerated most of my life.

"Oh. Well, they're like tortillas wrapped around chicken, salads, meats, cheeses. They're fun. You'll see," he said.

"I'm sorry I don't know about them."

"No, that's great. It's more fun for me because I can enjoy your discovery, too," he explained.

It was nice the way he made me feel comfortable about everything. Before we arrived at the beach, I really relaxed and even stopped gazing surreptitiously out the rear window and in the side mirrors to see if we were being followed.

Stuart parked as close to the beach café as possible.

"I don't want you to have to walk too far," he said, but I protested.

"Don't worry about that. I'm fine. It doesn't bother me if it doesn't bother you to move slower."

"I'd rather move slowly," he said. "I hope this day goes on forever."

Once again, I felt the heat rise to my face. I blushed so much after the nice things he said that I was sure he thought I was a walking thermometer. We paused to go into the shops along the way and some interesting art galleries. He decided he just had to buy me a necklace of hand-painted tiny seashells. After that we went to lunch and I did enjoy the wrap sandwich.

Afterward, we found a place on the beach where we could sit and watch people playing volleyball and we could look out at the sailboats. I never thought about the time. What a luxury that was. Most of my life, I worried about each passing minute whenever I went anywhere because if I didn't get home on or before Geraldine had expected, I would have to undergo a vigorous cross-examination. It just wasn't worth it. Now, without that hanging over my head, it was as if a great weight had been lifted. I could laugh and talk and enjoy myself. I felt free and that sense of freedom opened doors I had kept locked in my mind for as long as I could remember.

When Stuart talked about his youth, his favorite things, his fears and hopes, I could do the same. Sometimes, we started to talk at the same time. We'd stop and laugh, and he'd always insist I go first. We had a great deal to look at and enjoy, but we ended up looking at each other more and concentrating on ourselves far more than anything around us. We could have remained at my house for all it mattered, I thought, and then I thought that maybe it took the trip, the new surroundings, the sun and the water and the laughter around us to help us both become less inhibited.

Whenever there were periods of silence between us, I remembered my fear and gazed around, searching for signs of my father. I didn't see anything to suggest he was nearby, and toward the later part of the afternoon, Stuart went to get us something cold to drink. We had decided to make dinner at my house when we returned. He was calling his mother to let her know. He said he wanted to prepare a pasta meal and show off his culinary talents. We envisioned the others coming over as well and it sounded like a good way to keep our fun day rolling on and on into the evening.

I sat there feeling so warm and happy. In the sand I traced a heart and smiled to myself. My eyes shifted forward after a shadow fell over me and I saw a very familiar pair of feet. When I looked up, he was smiling down at me.

"How did you hurt your leg, Cathy?" my father asked with a tone of concern.

Because the sun was directly behind him, I couldn't see his face that well. I squinted, my heart suddenly pounding like a prisoner would pound on a wall.

"What are you doing here?" I asked instead of answering.

"Walking on the beach. It's a public beach. What are you doing here, Cathy?" he countered, now with a note of amusement.

"Leave me alone," I moaned, cringing back.

"You didn't tell me how you hurt your leg?"

"I fractured my ankle."

"How?"

"I fell."

"I wouldn't let you fall, Cathy. I'd always take better care of you. I always did," he said, and turned away to walk up the beach just as Stuart was returning.

"Who was that?" he asked, handing me my cold lemonade.

"Nobody," I said quickly.

"Nobody?"

"Someone asking me directions to someplace. I couldn't help him," I added. I watched my father turn off the beach and head for the street. Stuart stared after him as well.

"Are you all right?" he asked, kneeling down beside me again.

"I'm just getting tired I guess," I said.

"Sure. Let's head back. I want to stop at a grocery store and pick up a few things for our dinner. Okay?"

"Yes," I said.

"I hope you had a good time."

"Oh, I did, Stuart. Thank you."

"Great," he said, helping me to my feet. We started for the car. I tried not to watch my father walking away, but it was difficult to just ignore him.

Stuart gazed at me curiously when he opened the car door for me. Then he looked toward my father, too, squinted with suspicion, and got into the car. We drove in silence for a while.

"I really enjoyed myself today," he said finally. He smiled at me. "Thanks for coming along."

"Thanks for asking me."

"That was the easy part," he said. His smile had a way of wiping the anxiety out of my eyes and my heart.

He reached down for my hand and held it a moment. I moved closer to him and we rode on in a softer sort of silence as if both of us were afraid of ending a magic moment.

After Stuart bought some groceries, we returned to my house. I half expected to find either Star or Jade there, but the house was empty. I went upstairs to freshen up while Stuart started on the dinner. He wanted to make a pasta sauce and prepare some shrimp.

While I was upstairs, I phoned Jade, who was so breathless when she answered, I thought she might have been on a treadmill.

"Oh, Cat," she cried, "I've been calling you all day. We've got to get you either an answering machine or an answering service ASAP. Where have you been?"

I told her about my date with Stuart, but I quickly went on to the photograph and to my not-so-accidentally meeting my father on the beach.

"I've got to think about this," she said. "If you call the police and complain, they'll only ask to speak with Geraldine."

"I know. What do I do?" I asked with some panic.

"Stay calm. That's the first thing. I need to think more. He knows he's breaking his agreement, but he probably thinks you're doing things behind Geraldine's back and won't tell on him or something. It's complicated. Why doesn't he just leave you alone? Have you spoken to Star?"

"Not yet," I said. "When I called, she was out with Larry."

"Hmm. Well, let's schedule a meeting of the OWP's tomorrow late in the morning."

"What about tonight?"

"Oh, I promised to go to the movies with David tonight, and I don't want to cause anyone to become suspicious about us," she added, but I had the sense that it was more like she didn't want to give up her date.

"Okay," I said.

"What are you doing tonight?" she asked, and I told her that Stuart was making dinner.

"We were hoping to have you all over."

"Oh. Maybe another time. David's taking me to one of my favorite restaurants on Melrose. Maybe Star will come or Misty," she added. "Tell them about our meeting. And don't worry too much. It will be all right," she insisted.

If only that all it took was her saying it, I thought.

As soon as I hung up, I called Star. Rodney answered and then called her to the phone.

"Sorry I didn't call you today yet," she began immediately, "but I had a big blow-out with Mama. She was drinking, of course, and when she met Larry, she started to be disgusting and flirt with him. It made me sick with embarrassment and I let her know it. Granny came home and it was a horrible scene. Mama ran out of the house and I hope she stays away for good. I'm supposed to meet Larry's mother and father tonight, too," she wailed. She was complaining and crying so much, I didn't have the heart to tell her about my problems, but I knew I must.

She listened and then after a moment of silence said, "I just knew that man was going to be more trouble. I could try to come over later," she said, "but it might be hard with me going over to Larry's house and all."

"I know. I understand," I said. "I'll be all right." I told her about Jade's plan for a meeting and she said she would be sure to be here. "Maybe Misty will spend another night with you," she concluded.

When I called Misty, however, all I got was her answering machine. I left an urgent message and then finally went to my bathroom to freshen up. I couldn't stop the trembling inside myself. Seeing my father like that so suddenly on the beach, hearing his voice and what he had to say had sent sharp shivers through my body. A montage of bad memories exploded in my mind. It brought tears to my eyes and for a long while, all I could do was sit on the edge of the bathtub and embrace myself as if I were two people, one trying to comfort the other.

I didn't realize just how long I had been upstairs until I started to change my clothes and looked at the clock. It had been well over an hour. I rushed to cover up the redness around my eyes and tried to get myself to look calm and relaxed. I had put on one of my new skirts and blouses. After one final brushing of my hair and after putting on fresh lipstick, I started downstairs.

It was so quiet, I thought Stuart might have given up on me and left.

"Stuart?" I called. "Sorry, I was so long."

I made the turn at the base of the stairs, but stopped at the entrance to the living room. He was sitting on the sofa and looking rather odd, I thought. His head was slightly tilted and his eyes were glazed and full of confusion.

"Hi. Sorry. I got on the phone and you know how that can be when girls talk. It doesn't look like any of them will be coming tonight. Maybe Misty. I haven't heard back from her yet. Anything I can do?"

"The sauce is simmering," he said. "I've got dinner under control, but there is something you can do," he added.

"Oh." I went farther into the living room. Smiling, but anxious, I asked, "What?"

"You can explain this," he said, and held up the photo I had left under the magazine.

My heart felt like a yo-yo, falling, falling, falling until it almost touched the bottom of my stomach and then jerking up again only to bounce and wobble. Words fell over themselves clumsily in my mind as I tried to develop some sensible answer. My mouth actually opened and closed without my making a sound.

"Who would do this?" he asked.

I wondered if I could somehow ration the truth the way someone lost in the desert might ration her water. There was that part of me that didn't want to ration anything and that part of me that wanted to just gulp it all and stop pretending I could survive anyway.

"I didn't mean to snoop or anything," he continued, uncomfortable with my silence. "I was waiting for you and just started to look at this magazine when I found the picture."

"I'm sorry," I said, "I didn't tell you everything about my family."

"I don't mean to be nosy. It's just that...this picture...it's weird to find it like this."

"I know." My thoughts were gathering, straightening up like bowling pins. I nodded and sat across from him. "My mother recently got divorced," I said. "I had a stepfather and he's the one who took that picture. He sent it here today by Federal Express."

"Why?"

Jade's parents' divorce battle came to mind first. It gave me fodder for fabrication.

"My mother and he fought over who was a better parent and he was just trying to prove she wasn't as good as she thought she was. They're still going to do legal battle over custody and responsibility for me."

"He thought this was terrible?" he asked, holding up the picture.

"I guess. I didn't tell my mother I was having a party."

"Oh," he said. "So he thinks he caught you having a wild time behind her back and he's blaming her for leaving you alone?"

"Something like that," I said. "I'm sorry you're in the middle of it."

"No, that's all right."

He looked somewhat satisfied and I breathed with relief.

"It was just strange to come upon this. Do you see him much anymore?" Stuart asked.

"No. Well, yes. I saw him today," I said, deciding to use every opportunity I had to bring in truth.

"What? When? Before I came?"

"No. He was the man on the beach I said was nobody. I'm sorry I didn't tell you who he really was."

"You mean you just accidentally met him there?"

"I don't think it was accidental," I said.

Stuart's face grew tight and serious as his eyes darkened. Suddenly, he looked at the window.

"He's spying on you. Is that it?"

"Yes," I said. "If you want to leave, I'll understand," I said.

"No. That's stupid. He's just being stupid. How long after your real father's death did your mother wait before remarrying?"

"Not long."

"And how long were they married?"

"Nearly my whole life. I never knew my real father," I admitted.

"Oh," he said, nodding.

"I'm sorry I didn't tell you all this."

"No, you don't have any reason to apologize. Why should you have told me? I was a complete stranger."

"I don't mind telling you now," I said, "and I did feel bad deceiving you into believing something else."

He smiled.

"I'm happy you trust me now. Don't worry about your stepfather. When your mother comes back, if she has any doubts about you, I'll be an expert witness as to your good behavior."

I laughed, but then I thought what am I going to do about Geraldine never coming back? I had never dreamed I would meet someone who would complicate things like this. I never imagined I would want someone here always and to do that, I would have to explain Geraldine's absence. How many lies could I tell and when would the weight of them collapse around me and leave me broken and alone again?

"Well," he said, slapping his hands together, "I don't know about you, but I'm getting hungry." He glanced at the picture. "And I kind of like this picture. Mind if I keep it?"

"No," I said, smiling.

"We look really good together here. It looks like a scene in a movie. Maybe we'll do it again in a better light so he can get a better picture," he added. "It's no sin to kiss someone you like very much. He's done it, hasn't he?"

"What?" I said, losing my breath as if someone had

punched me in the stomach. Of course, Stuart was talking about something completely different, but still, it took me by surprise.

"Kissed someone he liked. He liked your mother once and kissed her and I bet he had a girlfriend or two. What is he, a monk or something?"

"Oh. No," I said. "Hardly that."

"So that's that. Let's forget about it and enjoy our dinner. At least, I hope you'll enjoy it."

"I will," I promised.

"Madame," he said, standing and bowing. "Might I escort you to the dining room?"

"Thank you," I said, laughing.

He put a hand on my shoulder as we walked into the dining room. He had set the table and put a candle on it.

"Wow," I said. "I guess I was upstairs a long time."

"Not a minute wasted down here, however," he said. "Just take your seat please," he said, pulling out my chair.

"I should help," I complained.

"Not tonight," he insisted.

I sat and he went into the kitchen. Moments later, he returned with plates of salad.

"I found a bottle of wine in your pantry. Is it all right for us to open it?" he asked.

"Yes, of course," I said.

I watched him open the bottle and then pour me some.

"To the beginning of something wonderful," he said, holding his glass up to mine, "and I don't mean only this dinner."

Our glasses clicked and we both sipped our wine, our eyes locked on each other.

Truth, I begged, stay outside a while longer. I promise when it's time to call you in, I will.

15

Truth or Consequences

Misty didn't call back until Stuart and I had finished dinner and were standing side by side in the kitchen, washing the dishes. He insisted he help with the cleanup.

"Sorry I didn't call earlier, but I just came home and found your message," Misty said. I could tell by her excitement and how fast she was talking that she didn't want our conversation to last too long. "What's happening?"

"I have a lot to tell you," I said. "I was right about what I had thought this morning," I said in a softer voice.

"What was that?" she asked. She sounded as if she was distracted.

"Are you alone?" I asked.

"No," she said, following it with a giggle.

"Me neither," I said.

"Oh. Who's there?"

"Stuart," I said, glancing at him. He smiled at me.

"Good for you. Star and Jade there, too?"

"No."

"Oooooh," she said. "Back in the kitchen?" she teased.

"Did you hear what I said about this morning?" I snapped at her. "What I told you was true."

"I forgot what you said this morning. I can't think very well right now anyway. I'm a little occupied," she added. "My mother is out again, which works fine for me."

Frustrated, I decided to give up on telling her any more at the moment.

"We're having a meeting late in the morning tomorrow," I said. "Jade wanted me to tell you."

"Okay. I'll see you then. Be careful," she added, this time with a more serious tone. "You don't want you know who to know anything about you know whom."

"Right," I said.

"I don't know what gave me the idea Chris was shy," she concluded, laughed, and hung up.

"Everything all right?" Stuart asked immediately.

"Yes. That was Misty. She's falling in love," I said dryly.

Stuart laughed.

"It's in the air," he said, waving the sponge around his head. I laughed, too. It worked like a detergent, washing away all the anxiety.

When we finished cleaning up, we went to the living room to watch television, but neither of us could find anything we really cared to see. We talked continually over the sound. I complimented him again on the dinner and then, right in the middle of a sentence, he suddenly leaned toward me and kissed me softly on my lips. My unspoken words fell into the pond of warmth that overtook my body. We kissed again, and then he kept his lips close and twirled a strand of my hair around his finger for a moment.

"Sometimes," he said softly, "when I look at you, I think you're just like a little girl. There's something so innocent and fresh about you, and then I listen to you speak or see the depth of understanding in your eyes and I think you're so much older than you look."

"Really?" I asked with concern.

He smiled.

"It's not something that turns me off, Cathy. It's something that turns me on. You're full of mystery and surprise. You're interesting."

"I am?"

"Yes, you are, very much so. Even your kisses are intriguing," he said. "For example," he said, kissing me and then sitting back and thinking. "That time your kiss was full of wonder. I can almost feel your indecision."

"Indecision?"

"Should you kiss me back as hard and as long, or not? You seem to want to, but you're the first to stop, and then..." He kissed me again, softer and then harder and longer, and I felt my whole body warm and open like a blossom in the sun. "Then," he continued, whispering, "you manage to touch me deeply. Who are you?" he asked, his eyes so close and so fixed on mine, I could barely think. "I want to really know you, Cathy," he continued, "deeply, fully. I hope you feel the same about me. Do you?"

"Yes," I said quickly.

"Good." He kissed me again, this time his lips moving off mine and over my chin, down to my neck. I leaned back on the sofa.

His hand moved up the sides of my body and over my breasts. I felt him undo the top buttons of my blouse and quickly bring his lips to the exposed top of my bosom.

"Good touching," I heard my father whisper in my ear. I couldn't help but stiffen beneath Stuart's kisses.

"It's all right, Cathy," Stuart said. "I really like you a lot."

"Yes," I said. "I like you, too."

"Good, good." His lips were on my bosom again and his fingers undoing another button and another until he was able to separate the sides of my blouse. He lifted me from the back of the sofa gently and brought the sleeves down my arms until my blouse was off. I kept my eyes closed and felt his lips touching me everywhere while his fingers unclipped my bra.

"It has to be loving and gentle," my father instructed. *"No groping like some sex-starved animal. Every touch is full of passion but respect. Like this, see? See the difference?"*

"Yes," I said aloud as Stuart's fingers moved my bra away and he brought his lips to my budding nipples. He took it as my approval, but my mind was reeling through time, remembering, confusing moments from the past with what was happening now.

"You're wonderful, Cathy," he said. "A promise, fulfilled. Do you like me, really like me?"

"I do, Stuart."

"Do you trust me? It's important, Cathy. First, we've got to trust each other. Do you?" he pursued.

"Yes."

"Because I'll never disappoint you. I promise," he said.

"Beware of their promises," my father advised. *"It's like pulling on a string and pulling with expectation that something wonderful is at the end, but when it's all there, you find nothing, nothing. I promise to always cherish you, they'll say."*

"We're good together, Cathy," Stuart said. "It's something you can easily tell, you can easily feel. Do you feel it, too, Cathy?"

"Yes," I said.

My father's touch always made me feel safe, I thought. When I was little, it was all I had, the only affection I enjoyed. Why shouldn't I have surrendered to it, rushed to it, welcomed it? I can't be blamed, can I? Stop looking at me with those eyes of accusation, Geraldine. Even now, even under the ground, you're looking up at me.

I turned my head and then my body to avoid any more of Stuart's kisses and caresses.

"Are you all right?" he asked.

"I don't like doing this in this room," I said.

"I understand," Stuart said, but instead of retreating as I expected, he slipped his hands and his arms under me and then, as if I didn't weigh anything at all, he stood up with me cradled in his arms like a child.

"I'm too heavy," I protested.

"You're a feather tickling my heart," he said, and kissed me on the ear and the neck as he turned and walked with ease out of the living room. He started up the stairs, steady, strong. My head rested against his chest.

My father sometimes carried me this way when I was little, I remembered. He'd nuzzle his face in my hair and lick the back of my neck so that it tickled, and then he'd laugh. He did it again when I was older.

"Remember when I used to do this?" he'd asked me. I couldn't help but giggle. Then he'd moved his tongue down my neck and over what were my emerging breasts at the time, lingering on my nipples. *"Good touching,"* he'd whispered. *"See how nice it feels."*

"Which room is yours?" Stuart asked, pausing with me

in his arms when we reached the upstairs hallway. I nodded at my door, and he opened it and carried me to my bed. He lowered me softly on to it and then he stood up and took off his shirt. I watched him unzip his pants and slide onto the bed beside me. We kissed, a very long kiss with his tongue touching mine. The only light came from the hallway.

His fingers found the zipper on my skirt and lowered it. Then he sat up and slipped it down. As if every naked part of me was like a magnet to his lips, he kissed me quickly on my stomach and then moved down with kisses until he was at my waist, fingering my panties.

"Stuart..." I whispered.

"It's all right," he said. "I'm a Boy Scout." He leaned over the side of the bed, picked up his pants, dug into his rear pocket to get his wallet and then pulled out the protection.

I started to shake my head and he put his finger on my lips and I stopped.

"It's all right," he said, "especially when two people find something as special as we have. I want you. Don't you want me?"

"They'll touch you here," my father said, *"and you'll lose your ability to think. You'll be on a merry-go-round. Your head will be spinning. Is it spinning now? Is it?"*

"Yes," I said.

Stuart brought my panties down. In seconds, he was there, naked and hard, pressing forward, his kisses clearing the way. I kept my eyes closed, thinking, what if I can't ever love anyone because of my father? I've got to do this. I've got to love someone. I've got to relax and be unafraid and prove to myself that I can.

"Cathy, Cathy, Cathy," Stuart was saying. My legs began to relax and then I opened my eyes.

She was standing in the doorway, her hands on her hips, her face full of disgust as she nodded.

"I'm dead only a little while and this is what you do," I heard her say. *"Disgusting."*

"Close the door," I cried.

"What?"

"Please, close the door, Stuart."

"But there's no one in the house."

"Please."

"Okay, sure," he said, rising. He slipped off the bed. She was still standing there, glaring until he closed the door.

When he returned, I let my head fall back on the pillow. He was there again, bringing himself to me and then into me. For a moment we both were still, holding onto each other. He kissed my eyes.

It's different. It's real. It's love, isn't it? I asked myself and then I told myself it was. Good, good, good.

A steam of "Yes" passed through my lips. Stuart was moaning his pleasure and his promises, but I could hear only my own cries of glee. I can love someone, I thought. I glared into the darkness as we continued to rush toward each other, covering ourselves completely in a blanket of passion. My father's voice was drowned out by my cries of pleasure, and Geraldine's face faded.

Tonight, I thought, I'll bury you both.

Stuart and I lay together in my bed for a long time afterward, neither of us willing to end the moment by rising and remembering that there was a tomorrow and we would have to stop touching for a while. Finally, he rose, went to the bathroom and then started to dress.

"How are you?" he asked. "I didn't hurt your leg or anything, did I?"

"No," I said, laughing. "I thought I hurt you with my cast."

"Never felt a thing. To do with your cast that is," he added. "It's getting late. I have to go home," he said regretfully. "Anyone staying over tonight?"

"No."

"I wish I could, but..."

"It's okay," I said.

"Maybe I can tomorrow night," he offered. "That is if your mother is still going to be away." He stopped buttoning his shirt and thought a moment. "Did she ever call you today?"

"I called her," I said quickly. "When I was up here earlier."

"Oh. And?"

"She will be away tomorrow, too," I said.

"Oh, great. I'll call you in the morning to tell you what time I'll be around, okay?"

"Okay," I said.

"I hate leaving you," he said. "Wait a minute. I carried you up here. I'd better go and get your crutches."

"I can get around all right without them."

"No. Don't do anything that might lengthen your recuperation," he warned. "I have plans for us running on the beach someday soon."

I laughed and he left to get my crutches. I rose and put on my robe. Moments later, he returned with my crutches and I decided to go down to see him leave. He turned at the door.

"I had a great time," he said. "This was about the best day I had in a long time."

"Me too."

"You're sure you're all right?"

"Yes, I'm fine," I said.

He kissed me good night and left. I watched him get into his car and pull away. I waved and then looked at the street. It was dark and quiet, but still I sensed I wasn't alone. I stepped back quickly and shut the door, locking it with the safety bolt. Then I went to the kitchen to get a glass of water. The phone rang just as I got there. I stared at it. It rang again and again.

Maybe it's Star, I thought. She did say she would try to come over later. I lifted the receiver and said hello.

"I want to speak to Geraldine," he said. "Why doesn't she ever answer the phone when I call? I called all day. Where is she?" he demanded.

"You're not supposed to be calling here," I said. "She told me you're not."

"Put her on."

My heart was thumping so hard that I started to lose my breath.

"We know you broke into the house and stole the safe. Why did you take my letters, too? They're mine. I want them back," I demanded.

"What's that? Someone broke into the house?" he said. I could almost see his smile.

"I know it was you."

"Why didn't Geraldine call the police and ask them to question me, huh?" He waited for my answer, but I had none. "What's going on there, Cathy?" he asked with suspicion now dripping off his words. "She wouldn't let you have a boy over there this late. Where is she?"

"Leave me alone!" I screamed, "or I will call the police."

"Put her on. I have legal business to discuss. I can call her for that. Go on, ask her."

Oh, God, I thought looking about helplessly. What do I do? I literally turned around, struggling to come up with some solution.

"She's not here," I finally told him.

"Not there? This late? Ridiculous. Where is she? You're lying. Put her on. I'll keep calling," he threatened. "I'll come over there. I have a right to do that. I don't have to break in."

"She's in the hospital," I blurted. "That's why she didn't call the police. I haven't told her what you did yet."

"What?" It gave him pause. "What do you mean? Why is she in the hospital?"

"She had a problem with her heart and the doctor wanted her to stay and be observed for a few days. She told me if you came over here, I was to call the police immediately."

"What hospital?"

"I'm not supposed to tell you. Her doctor doesn't want anyone calling her or visiting. Even I have to limit my visits," I said.

He was quiet a long moment.

"If she finds out what you're doing in her absence, she'll get even sicker," he said.

"Leave us alone!" I cried and then hung up and held my breath, waiting to see if he was going to call back. He didn't, but then I thought he might deliver on his threat and come to the house. I went around turning off all the lights and then I sat at the front windows and watched the street and the driveway. I sat there for hours, my eyes closing on their own sometimes. I know I kept drifting off because suddenly I would shudder and awaken.

He didn't come so I made my way upstairs, and after making sure my door was closed and a chair was up against it, I went to bed. It didn't take long for me to fall asleep, but I tossed and turned all night, waking periodically in a terrible sweat, listening for sounds and then falling back asleep like someone in a coma. By the time morning came, I was more exhausted than I would have been if I had managed to stay up all night, I thought.

I moved slowly, lethargically, washing, dressing, and going down for some breakfast. I wasn't very hungry and barely nibbled on some toast with my coffee. Stuart called to see how the rest of my night went and if I was all right.

"I'm just a little tired," I told him, "but otherwise, fine."

"I can't wait to see you again. I have a few errands to run for my mother and then I'll be over for the whole day and if you want, the whole night. I've already told her I might do that."

"What did she say?"

"My mother treats me like an adult now. She just says the motherly things like 'Be careful' and 'Be sure.' I'm both," he insisted.

How wonderful, I thought, to hear him say that, and how wonderful for him to have a mother who was so caring and understanding.

"Okay," I said. "I'll see you later."

Shortly after I ended my conversation with Stuart, Jade, Misty, and Star arrived. Jade had used her limousine to pick them up. Despite the dark storm clouds that loomed over us, they were buoyant and happy, all talking at once about their dates the night before.

We sat around the table in the kitchen having coffee.

Misty took out some of the bagels we had in the freezer, toasted them and set them out with jam.

"My mother met some other slob," Star told us. "She was talking today about leaving again. See these fingers," she said holding up both hands with her fingers crossed. "I'm keeping them that way all day."

"You met Larry's parents, I understand?" Jade said.

"So?"

"That's what I wanted to ask," she retorted.

"They're nice. He's got an older brother who is a computer engineer working for some software company in California. Larry's working with computers too, and he plans on getting into that career when he gets out of the army. And as soon as he's established he wants to get married and start a family."

"It sounds like some serious plans are being put on the table," Jade said.

"Maybe."

"Really?" Misty cried.

"I didn't say anything's for sure," Star quickly added. "We just talked in general. You've all done that too."

"Not about that subject," Jade insisted. "I don't know if I ever want to get married and have children."

"I think Chris and I will be going together for a long time, maybe forever and ever," Misty announced. "He's a lot like me."

"That's no good," Jade said. "You want a man who complements you but adds, not duplicates."

"He adds," Misty said indignantly.

"What does he add?"

"Can you all just stop this for a moment?" I screamed.

Their faces froze after they turned to me.

"I'm glad you're all having a good time and you've all found the loves of your life, but we have a big problem."

"I still don't know what this is all about," Misty protested.

"I tried to tell you last night on the phone, but you were too wrapped up in your romance," I said, surprising even myself at how sharp I sounded, but I had been patient even though my stomach felt as if it were filled with killer bees.

"That's not fair. Besides, you had Stuart here. You weren't exactly playing checkers all night, were you?"

"Stop. Let her talk, Misty," Jade said. "I'm sorry, Cat. We've all been in storms of disappointment so long and so much. We're just overreacting to some good times."

"Well, what's it all about?" Misty demanded.

"My father. I told you he was out there spying on me the night of the party. He took a picture of Stuart and me kissing good night and sent it to Geraldine by Federal Express."

"He did?"

"And yesterday, he followed us to the beach and approached me when Stuart went to get me something to drink."

"Did Stuart see him, learn who he was?" Jade asked quickly.

"Not then. I told him later."

"You told him? Why?" Star asked.

"Because he found the picture under a magazine. I had hidden it quickly and poorly when he arrived to take me to lunch and the beach. He was shocked, and wanted to know who would take it and why."

"What else did you tell him?" Jade asked. They all looked like they were holding their breaths.

I described my fabrications and they listened, Jade nodding. Then I told them about his phone call last night and what I had said to my father to get him to stop asking for Geraldine.

"That's good. You did the right thing," she said. "You were smart. I guess we're all getting to be good liars. Look at the good teachers we've had for parents."

"But what do I do now?" I asked.

No one spoke.

"He'll call again and again, and he *will* come here," I said.

"She's right," Misty moaned and sat. "What are we going to do?"

"We're in trouble," Jade agreed. "I knew we shouldn't have buried her. I knew it."

"Well, what do you suggest now, we dig her up?" Star quipped.

"Maybe."

"Are you crazy?" Star nearly screamed at her. "Besides, you were the one who pointed out that Cat would end up in some foster home."

"That's better than prison," Jade mumbled.

"We'll all be arrested," Misty muttered.

"Take it easy, Misty," Star told her.

"What do I tell Stuart about Geraldine after today? He'll wonder why she isn't home," I pointed out.

They were all quiet a moment and then Misty looked up quickly.

"Maybe you should break up with him," she said.

"What?"

"That's it. That will solve everything. Just get into an argument and throw him out. Then you don't have to worry about what he knows and what he doesn't."

"I don't want to do that. How would you like me to tell you to get rid of Chris now?"

"I don't have to worry about him discovering any secrets," she replied.

"That's not fair, Misty," Star said.

"Well, what is she supposed to do? What are we supposed to do?" she cried, her eyes wild. "Maybe I should go ask my father for advice or you should ask yours, Jade. Or you should ask your granny, Star."

"Calm down," Jade said. "Give us all a chance to think."

"Stuart's coming here today," I said. "He wants to stay over tonight."

"That's just great," Misty said with a frown.

"Well, why did you have a party here and invite the boys and get me a date?" I shouted back at her.

She stared at me. Then she looked at Jade.

"We're losing it," Jade said, and stood. "Everyone upstairs to the room."

"What?" Star said. "What good is that?"

"Just do it," Jade snapped. "We need to get calm."

Star rolled her eyes, took a deep breath, and stood up.

"C'mon, Princess Jade has spoken," Star told us."

Misty glanced at me and then stood up. I rose and the four of us made our way up the stairs to the special room. We gathered in our circle. The candle was lit, the music turned on. Jade closed her eyes and held out her hands. Everyone did the same.

"Clear your minds of the turmoil," Jade prescribed. "Concentrate on your breathing."

After a moment, Misty moaned.

"It's not working. I can't stop thinking about getting caught."

"Try harder. Don't talk for a while. Just breathe in and out, in and out."

"Oh, this is stupid," Misty complained after another moment.

"All right," Jade said. "What are our problems and how can we solve them? No hysterics," she warned.

"We've got to decide what to do about Stuart," Star said. "If he is going to be coming around here, he's just naturally going to want to know where her mother is."

"There are only two choices," Jade said. "We either let Cat tell him the truth or Cat ends the relationship before it's started."

"It's already started," I said.

"How can we even think of telling him?" Misty asked. "What if she breaks up with him two days later? He could tell someone and then what?"

"She's right," Star said.

"I'm not planning on that happening," I said.

"You don't plan these things. They happen. Right, Jade?" Misty asked.

"Yes, that's true." She looked at me. "What do you want to do, Cat?"

"I want to tell him."

"But suppose it frightens him off or he thinks you're crazy for doing it?" Misty asked.

"She's right again," Star said.

"Cat's too inexperienced to get so involved with a boy. We shouldn't have let it happen," Misty chastised. She looked at me. "He's your first real boyfriend. You shouldn't get so serious so fast."

"I don't think we should be lecturing each other about relationships," I said.

"We know more than you do," she insisted. "Tell him

you're getting too serious. Tell him you need to take a break. He'll call for a while and then he'll give up and go look for someone else."

"I don't want him to look for someone else," I protested.

"You've got to make the sacrifice for the good of the OWP's," Misty demanded.

"What?"

"You wanted our help. We gave it to you. We made you part of our group. Now it's time for you to do something for us," she said.

I looked at Jade. She remained silent. Star's eyes narrowed with thought, but she didn't disagree.

"We still have to think about her father," Star said.

"We can eventually call the police. Misty can do what we planned and put on Geraldine's clothes one night. She'll parade in front of the window and he'll think it's her," Jade said. "Then, if the police call him, he will be frightened off and will stop."

"That might work," Misty thought aloud. "Where's the dress?"

"We left it in the closet," Jade said, nodding toward it.

"Does she need the wig?"

"Not if it's done at night and from a distance. Geraldine's hair was about her shade," I said.

"Okay, that's settled. You see," Misty told me, "if you will just be cooperative and willing to help the OWP's, all will be fine. We can go on without worry. In a week or so, we'll have another party and we'll find another boy for you to meet. If you like him, we can pretend Geraldine's going to be away longer this time, maybe a week or even two!"

I shook my head.

"You can't be serious."

"I make a motion Cat get rid of Stuart today for the good of the OWP's," Misty said.

I looked at Jade and Star. Neither opposed it.

"You're all thinking of yourselves, protecting yourselves, keeping your new boyfriends."

"That's not entirely true," Jade said. "We don't exactly have all that many choices here."

"I want to tell him the truth. He'll keep our secret," I insisted.

"It's not only your secret," Misty said. "It involves and endangers all of us. You have no right to make that decision on your own. It has to be an OWP decision. Am I right, Jade?"

Jade nodded.

"I have a motion on the floor," Misty continued.

"Why do you think you can trust him, Cat?" Jade asked.

"I have a motion!" Misty cried.

"This is on the motion," Jade snapped at her. "Cat?"

I looked down and thought.

"You all know what my life was like with my father and Geraldine. You all know what went on, what he did to me. The first time Stuart touched me, I cringed. He felt it, but he didn't get angry or discouraged. He was gentle and sensitive," I said.

Tears began to burn under my lids, but I held them back and continued.

"No matter how hard I tried, I couldn't keep the memories of my father out of my mind when I was with Stuart. I could even hear my father's voice over Stuart's. I thought this is the way it will be all my life. I'm spoiled goods," I said, looking up at them.

Even Misty started to soften.

"But something happened last night, something very special and precious. Stuart's voice suddenly overpowered my father's and I could feel him being pushed out of me, shut out of me. I could love someone and someone could love me, and maybe that's more important than worrying about the truth and Geraldine and everything else," I said. "I think I'd even be willing to go to prison now, if I had to. I'll just say that I did it all myself. No one has to worry."

For a long moment, no one spoke.

"I think we should trust Cat's instincts on this," Star said, nodding. "Let her tell him. Jade?"

"There's no point in doing all we're doing if we don't allow ourselves to change and grow in new directions. Doctor Marlowe might even be happy about it," Jade added with a smile.

We all looked at Misty.

"All right," she said. "Maybe I was being too selfish, worrying about my own love life. I'm sorry, Cat."

We hugged.

"Do you want to tell him today?" Jade asked.

"I should. I can't think of another lie about her."

"Maybe we should all be there," Star suggested. Jade looked at me.

"It's not a bad idea, Cat. Then we'll leave you alone with him."

"All right," I said. Now that they had agreed, I began to feel nervous about it. Jade sensed it and reached out again.

"Hold hands," she ordered. She lowered her head and we clasped and lowered ours. "Deep breaths, clear your mind, refresh your spirit. We've got to call on each other, strengthen each other."

The music played. The candle burned. Minutes went by and the tension was drained from our bodies.

"We're going to be all right. We're going to be fine," Jade concluded.

Before we left the room, Misty tried on Geraldine's dress and paraded about.

"What do you think?" Jade asked me. "Remember, it's from a distance."

"She is about Geraldine's height," I said, "but we should fix her hair so it looks more like Geraldine's. And you have to hold your shoulders more stiffly," I instructed Misty.

"Okay, you'll do your first performance tonight," Jade told Misty.

"It's creepy," Misty said. "I feel like one of Stephen King's twisted characters."

"That was Geraldine," I muttered, and they all laughed.

Misty took off the dress. Jade blew out the candle and turned off the music. She paused and looked back as we stood in the doorway.

"See," she said, "it is our special place, and we'll always be special to each other."

All I could do was hope and pray she was right.

16

❧

The Bonds of Fate

"Hi," Stuart began excitedly as soon as I opened the door. He came in quickly. "I thought you might want to go to a movie tonight. We could have dinner at Yin-Yangs which is right near the movie and..."

He paused when he saw all the girls sitting in the living room.

"Oh, a meeting of the sewing circle, huh?" he joked. When no one laughed, he looked at me with surprise.

"Anything wrong?"

"We all want to talk to you, Stuart," Jade said. "Please come in and sit." She nodded at an empty chair.

"What's going on? Say, aren't you meeting my cousin later? He said something about taking you to the beach club for dinner tonight. Star, Misty, hi," Stuart continued as he walked into the living room. He glanced at me and sat. "So? What's this all about?" He smiled. "Planning another party?"

"It's about us and about Cat," Jade replied with a sternness in her voice. She turned to me. We hadn't discussed just how we were going to go about this, but I assumed we would all speak.

I sat to Stuart's right, facing him, but I didn't say anything.

"We're not a sewing circle, but we do have sort of a club," Jade continued.

"We call it the OWP's," Misty said.

"OWP's?" Stuart smiled. "What's that?"

"Orphans With Parents," she explained. He looked even more confused.

"Excuse me? How can you be an orphan if you have parents?" he asked. Every time he spoke to one of them, he glanced at me.

"Without going into great detail, Stuart, we all met at a therapist's office," Jade continued.

"Yes, I know," he said. "Cathy told me that."

"Oh?" Star said.

"That's all I told him," I quickly added.

"She didn't reveal anything about anyone, if that's what this is about," Stuart confirmed.

"It's not exactly what it's about," Jade said. "But it's no secret that we've all had problems with our parents. Mine, as you know, are concluding a divorce. Misty's are divorced and her father remarried recently. Star's father deserted his family and her mother did the same."

"She came back the other day, but I'm hoping it's not for long," Star interjected.

"And Cathy's parents are divorced," Stuart said, "and still battling over who's the better parent. I know it's unpleasant. It's great that you're all friends and can help each other. OWP's," he said to Misty. "Okay. I guess it makes sense in a way when you have a divorce in a family."

"It makes sense in a lot of ways," Misty replied.

"Cathy's parents aren't exactly divorced," Jade said. "That's not the problem Cat is dealing with here today."

"Huh?" He looked at me. "I don't understand. She told me they were."

"Cathy, why don't you…"

"My parents haven't got a formal divorce yet. Actually," I said, "to begin at the beginning. My mother is not my mother. She's really my sister. We were both adopted. She and my father adopted me because my real mother had me out of wedlock late in life."

Stuart just stared as if my words were like fish floating around his head, too fast to catch and hold.

"I didn't find this out until relatively recently and only after my father was prohibited from having anything to do with me."

"But I thought you said they were struggling over custody and—"

"I didn't tell you the whole truth."

"Why not?" Stuart asked. He thought a moment and then asked, "Why is he prohibited from seeing you?"

"Why would a father be prohibited from being near his daughter?" Jade asked as an answer.

"I don't know."

"Think," Jade ordered. "Use your X-rated imagination."

He did and then his face registered his conclusion. He quickly looked at me.

"You mean that he abused you?"

Even now, even after all the therapy with Doctor Marlowe, it was still difficult for me to do much more than nod.

"Her sister, who pretended to be her mother for years and years, wasn't exactly easy to live with either," Star said. "She was never really involved with Cat and wasn't there when Cat needed her the most."

"*Wasn't* easy to live with?" Stuart caught. "Isn't she still here, playing the role of mother?"

"She's dead," Jade said. Her words fell like small bombs among us.

"Dead?" He looked at me and at them, and shook his head. "But I thought she was visiting a sister or something." He shook his head. "I don't think I understand any of this. What's going on, Cathy?"

"Before anything more is said, we need a promise from you, or more to the point, Cat needs a promise that what we're about to tell you, you'll keep secret for as long as necessary," Jade told him. "If you feel you don't want to know any more, we'd understand. Even Cat would, right, Cat?"

"Yes," I said. "I'm sorry about all this, Stuart. I wish I could have told it to you another way, but..." I looked at the others. "They're all involved now, too. They had to approve of telling you."

He sat back, a look of confusion moving to a look of fear that snapped him forward.

"Wait a minute. You're not going to tell me you...all of you are responsible for her sister's death or something, are you?" he asked with a tremble in his voice.

"No," Star said firmly.

He let out a breath and relaxed.

"Thank God for that," he said.

"But we did something that isn't exactly legal afterward," Jade said.

"Afterward? Yes, how did she die?"

"She had a heart attack and died right here in this room," Star said.

"So there was a funeral and everything?"

"There was a funeral," she said, looking at us, "but not exactly what you would expect."

He kept shaking his head.

"I still don't understand. What I would expect?"

"Cat has no real relatives, Stuart. She's just a little over seventeen so she can't legally be on her own," Jade explained. "With an abusive father and no close family, she is a prime candidate for foster care. We thought if we could keep her mother's death a secret until she was eighteen, she'd be all right. She has trust funds, and for now she's capable of taking care of herself in every way. We're determined to help her do that."

"Keep her death a secret? What are you all telling me, that no one but you people know her mother is dead?" Stuart asked, leaning forward.

"Exactly," Jade said. "And now you," she added. She looked at me. "Cat wanted us to tell you. You should be flattered. She hasn't been able to put her trust in many people. None of us have, for that matter, but for reasons known only to her, she has decided to place her fate in your hands, too."

"I see," he said, sitting back. He thought a moment, his eyes blinking rapidly. Then he looked at Jade and me, and sat up again. "If her death is still a secret, where exactly is she? I hope not in the freezer."

"She's in the backyard," Star revealed.

"And she had a proper burial with a reading from the Bible and all," Misty said.

He raised his eyebrows.

"You buried her in the backyard?"

"Exactly," Jade said. "And it wasn't easy."

"Are you absolutely sure she was dead?" he asked.

How many times had I had that nightmare? I thought, and from the way the others looked after the question, how many times had they?

"Yes, absolutely," Star said firmly. "She had no pulse. She was blue and stiff and cold, and even Jesus couldn't raise her," she said.

"The backyard?" he repeated, gazing toward the back of the house.

"It doesn't look like a grave," Misty said. "Star worked hard on that. If you want, go look for yourself and tell us where you think she is," she said proudly.

He stared at Misty as if she and the rest of us were all crazy. A faint smile creased his lips.

"Is this for real or are you all having fun with me?" he asked.

"Hardly," Jade said with a face that could be mistaken for granite. "Cat's already told you how terrible her father is behaving."

"Then he doesn't know about...your sister being dead?"

"No," Cat said. "He called last night and I told him she was in the hospital."

"He broke into the house, too," Misty blurted. "He broke in through the back door."

"What? When? Why?"

"A few days ago. We think he was after money that was in a safe in her sister's closet."

"Among other things," Star muttered, glancing at me.

"He took the safe, but we'd already taken the money out of it," Jade told him.

"So that's why that back door looks like it does," he

said, more to himself than to us, and nodded. "What are you going to do when he finds out about...I don't know whether to call her your mother or your sister."

"That's been her problem, too," Star muttered.

"I just call her Geraldine now," I said. "We're hoping that he'll stay away because he'll think she'll call the police. At least he's afraid of her."

"But you told him she was in the hospital. What's to stop him from just coming over here, even right now?" Stuart asked.

"We're going to pretend she came home. Misty is going to dress like her. Cat says they're about the same size," Jade told him.

"You mean she's going to impersonate her?"

"Exactly," Jade said. "It will be dark so we think she can do it."

Stuart shook his head, glanced at me and then at them.

"This is nuts."

"It's what we have to do to protect her. Are you going to help us?"

"What do you want me to do?" he asked.

"Keep your mouth shut about it for starters," Star said. "Think you can do that?" she added. "Cat does. Cat's the one who has all the faith in you," she told him.

He looked at me.

"If it's for her and it's what she wants, of course," he said.

I smiled.

"Actually," Jade said, thinking aloud, "it's good that you're in on this with us. It will give Cat more security to have you around."

"In on this?" He paused. "Doesn't anyone call for her sister? Doesn't anyone come visiting?" he asked me.

"No. She didn't have any friends and conducted almost

all her business over the phone. She hated going out of the house."

"And no family?"

"Just cousins who never call, never write," I said. "She never called or wrote them either."

"But there's your father out there," he reminded us.

"As we told you, he's supposed to stay away. If he comes around, you can chase him off," Jade said. "Threaten to call the police."

"Sure," Stuart said skeptically. "I'll scare the hell out of him. What does he do? Doesn't he have a job?"

"He's an executive in a stock brokerage firm and he can do almost anything he wants," I said. "He's often away from his office, visiting with clients."

Stuart smirked. "This isn't going to be easy."

"It has been up to now," Star said dryly.

We heard a car horn sound in the driveway. Stuart's head snapped around, his eyes wide.

"That's only my limousine," Jade said. "We've all got some things to do today, but Misty is coming back here tonight for a little while. By herself," she added. "You see, Cat is going to bring her mother home from the hospital tonight."

"Huh?"

"I'm going to get into the clothes, fix my hair like Geraldine's and wrap something around me so I'm mostly hidden," Misty explained.

"We were thinking you might be the one to drive them," Jade said.

"What? Me?"

"You'll leave with Cat and return with her sister."

"You can even be a kind gentleman and help her into the house," Star said. "In case you're being watched."

"You don't have to do it, if you don't want to," I told him quickly.

"I could be the one to drive them, too," Jade said, "but we just thought since you were already here, it would also make it easier for her father to believe Geraldine would permit you to be here afterward."

"You think he'll be out there tonight?" Stuart asked, gazing nervously at the window.

"Cat believes he's watching the house often," Jade said. "You already know that he followed you two all the way to the beach yesterday."

He sat back, looking glum.

"So?" Star demanded. "Are you in or what? Stuart?"

He looked up sharply.

"I said if it's what Cat wants..." he replied, but looked quite thoughtful and troubled.

"Good," Jade said, standing. She glanced at her watch. "I've got to go."

"Wait," Stuart said. "If Misty is going to impersonate Cathy's sister, she can't come here. I mean, Misty can't be seen coming here, nor can she be seen leaving for the hospital with us. If two people leave, obviously three have to return."

"That's right," Star said. "He's right."

"I'll sneak in through the back door," Misty said, "just in case, and then I'll hide down in the back of the car when you leave."

"Back into the driveway and Misty will get in from the garage," Star said.

"Sounds like you've all been studying spy movies or something," Stuart said.

"We do what we have to do to help each other," Jade told him. "It's an oath we've taken."

"Oath?" He started to laugh and stopped when he saw Jade's face harden with determination.

"For us, promises usually don't have any meaning, whether they're sworn oaths, vows at the altar, or written contracts. But what we tell each other does have meaning," she said with such authority and assurance, even Stuart looked impressed. Star smiled and Misty looked delighted.

"That's who we are," she said. "OWP's. For now, you're an honorary member."

"For now," Star muttered. "We'll see how he does."

"Okay, let's go," Jade said. "I have some important things to do before David comes over for a swim this afternoon." She paused and looked at Stuart. "You can't tell him or anyone else any of this," she warned. "No one else knows."

"I understand," Stuart said.

"See you later, Cat," Misty said. "Don't worry. I'll do fine as Geraldine."

"I'll be checking on you afterward," Star said. "I'll call."

"Thank you," I told her.

We all hugged and then I watched them leave and get into the limousine. Out of habit now, I studied the street. I didn't see him, but I didn't have to. I felt him.

When I returned to the living room, Stuart was still sitting in his chair, his head down, his hands pressed together like someone in prayer.

"I'm sorry, Stuart. I didn't mean to get you involved in all this, but the choice was either to tell you or..."

"Or what?" he said, lifting his eyes to me quickly.

"Say or do something that would drive you away so I wouldn't have to continually come up with some lame excuse for why Geraldine isn't home," I said.

"Well," he said, standing, "I still can't believe you guys did this and in the backyard?"

I nodded.

"I've got to take a look and see for myself before I really believe it," he said.

I followed him to the back door. He opened it and stepped out, looking over the yard. The day was mostly overcast with the occasional sunlight drawing dreary shadows over everything.

"The fresh seeds and freshly planted flowers give it away. Right?" he said, nodding at the grave.

"Right. After a little while it will be hard to tell though."

"Maybe."

"You should have seen us out here that night. It wasn't easy to dig a grave."

"I bet," he said, shaking his head. Then he looked at me, his eyes narrowed and troubled. "So you're really on your own? You really have nobody now?"

"I have the girls and I hope I have you," I said.

He looked toward the grave again.

"This is crazy, Cathy. I said what I said in there in front of them, but now that I see this and realize what's happened, you can't go on with this. It really is illegal. I don't think any of you actually thought this out."

"But you told them you'd help, Stuart."

"Even if you all are somehow able to carry it off until you're eighteen, how are you going to explain this when you have to? You know, they'll dig her up and they'll do an investigation to see if she died naturally or whatever. If there is even the slightest suggestion or possibility she didn't, the four of you could become murder suspects."

"Murder suspects! She just died, Stuart. She had a heart attack."

"How do you know that? None of you has a medical degree, Cathy. Do you know how that's determined? I do. Remember, I told you I want to go into medicine. They have to do an autopsy and they examine the heart. They can tell if it's been damaged. What if it hasn't?"

"Why else would she have died?" I moaned. I wished we weren't having this conversation ten feet from Geraldine's grave. I could almost see her smiling beneath the ground.

"There are lots of causes of death." He thought a moment and then he turned to me and put his hands on my shoulders. "Cathy, what if she was depressed about all this and she took her own life? What if she swallowed some pills or something? Don't you see? Someone might think you put the pills in her food and then you and your girlfriends, all troubled and disturbed so much they had to have therapy, buried her to hide what you did."

I shook my head.

"No, no that's not what happened. I couldn't have done something like that," I cried.

"But I bet you've wished it, haven't you?"

"Maybe," I admitted.

"So someone who doesn't know you obviously could think it." He stepped back. "No," he said. "Now that I've seen this and thought about it, I realize you have to go in there and call the police and tell them what you did."

"No, Stuart," I said, the tears streaming out of my eyes and zigzagging down my cheeks to my chin. "I couldn't do that. They're my friends, my best friends. I can't betray them. We're all in this together."

"Yeah, I know. The OWP's. You're not children anymore you know. The next thing you'll all tell me is you have a clubhouse."

I looked up sharply.

"Oh, this house is your clubhouse?"

"Yes, in a way," I said softly.

"Cathy, this is all insane. You're going to be in big trouble."

I shook my head.

"You promised them, Stuart. You said you would help."

"I know. I know, but the reality is you can't keep this up for months and months. Something's going to happen. Your father will eventually figure out something's not right. Don't you see? You've got to call them back and get them to go to the police, and if they won't, you've got to do it yourself. That's your sister in the ground there!"

I shook my head vigorously.

"No, that would be a horrible betrayal."

"What's more important?" he asked. "Loyalty to them or doing the right thing?"

"Loyalty to them," I said firmly, and stepped back, out of his reach.

"It's not going to work," he insisted. He looked back at the grave and shook his head.

"You promised," I said through my tears. "I talked them into trusting you," I moaned. "I thought you really cared about me, wanted to be with me."

"I do," he said. "That's why I'm telling you all this." He stared at the ground. "Let me think. Oaths, clubs, OWP's, Jesus."

I felt a wave of anger and hardness come over me.

"Don't think about it anymore. You can go home now, Stuart," I said, grinding back my tears with my closed hand. I wiped my cheeks and straightened up on my crutches. "Just forget everything we've told you and go home. You don't have to help us, help me, and get yourself into trouble, too."

"I didn't say I wouldn't help you," he muttered. "I'm trying to help you now. Think of yourself."

"I'm going back inside," I said, and turned away from him. As quickly as I could, I went through the house and into the living room where I sat in what had always been Geraldine's chair. A few moments later he appeared in the doorway, his shoulders slouched, his eyes directed down.

"I really do want to help you, Cathy, and I don't want to leave you. I like you a lot, but I've got to think about my mother and what this would do to her on top of everything she's suffered. There's my little brother to think about, too."

"Go home to your mother and your little brother, Stuart."

He raised his head.

"I mean, I'm willing to stay with you, to drive you to the police if you want."

I forced a smile.

"Thank you, Stuart. If I decide to do that, I'll call you," I said.

"Cathy, you're just not thinking of the consequences," he insisted.

"Really? What are the consequences, Stuart? Are they worse than the consequences I've suffered merely by being born into this nightmare? Jade told you to use your imagination, but no matter how good your imagination is, you can't even begin to understand. Despite my father, these past days have been the first days when I felt, I believed, I could be someone with her own identity, someone who could love and be loved. My disturbed friends, as you called them, helped me to do that and never once really thought about what risks they were taking. We really are special. You can laugh and make fun of us as much as you like, but we're the OWP's," I said.

"Cathy..."

"It's all right, Stuart. I really do understand what you're going through. I know now that it would be unfair to ask you to do anything like this. I'm not upset with you. You do have responsibilities to your mother and brother."

He looked relieved.

"I mean, I'll be happy to stay with you and if you want to do what I said, help you to do it. Until then, I swear," he said, raising his hand as if he were in court, "I won't talk about any of this. If something happens later on, I'll say I didn't really believe it or something, but if I'm part of the impersonation effort and the cover-up, that becomes impossible."

"I understand," I said. "I really do."

He stared a moment.

"We could still go to the movies," he said. "If you'd like."

"That's okay. I think I'd better just rest."

"And think over what I told you," he added, nodding. "I hope you'll come to your senses and convince the others to do the same. Then call me and I'll come running over here, Cathy. I will. That's a promise," he swore, raising his right hand.

I don't think there was a word I hated more.

"Thank you, Stuart," I said nevertheless.

He came to me, kissed me on the forehead as if kissing me on the lips would somehow put an evil spell on him, and then he turned and walked out. I heard the door open and close. The silence that followed roared in my ears.

Misty had been so right, I thought. I had grasped the

first chance at love. I wanted something that wasn't there so much I refused to heed the warnings. Desperately, I needed to prove to myself that I was capable of loving someone despite what my father had done, and that desperation and my inexperience had blinded me to reality. I felt as terrible about what I had done to my girlfriends as I felt about what I had done to myself. I dreaded the phone call I was going to have to make to them.

Saddened, I went upstairs and entered our special room. I sat on our rug and lit the candle. Then I closed my eyes. Was Stuart right? Should we tell the police what we had done? Could we get into such deep trouble that everyone would suffer just to help me? I had wanted my freedom and my friends and a normal life so much, I was willing to do almost anything, believe in almost anything, and try almost anything. How I wished I had someone older and wiser to talk to, someone who would listen. I was greatly tempted to call Doctor Marlowe, but to do anything without all the girls agreeing seemed to be even a greater wrong.

The room wasn't working for me. It was no good without the others, without their spirits and energy combining with mine. I blew out the candle and started out of the room, even more despondent than when I had entered. Suddenly the phone rang. Maybe the room does work, I thought. It had to be Jade, Star, or Misty. They had felt my trouble. I had reached one of them with my cry and now one of them was calling. Hopefully, it was Jade. She would be the most sensible now, I thought.

"Hello," I said anxiously as soon as I lifted the receiver.

"You're lying," he said. "I've called every hospital in Los Angeles and she's not registered at any of them. Where is she?" my father demanded.

I tried to speak, but my throat felt as if it had closed up.

"Did she tell you to give me that cock n'bull story?" he demanded.

"It's not a lie," I finally managed. "You didn't call the right hospital and I told you she didn't want you to call or see her. I'm going to get her later today. She's being released," I said. "I'll tell her you called and called, and I'll tell her you broke into our house. I'll tell her how you've been following me and spying on me. I'll tell her everything today. Leave us alone!" I screamed at him.

I slammed the receiver down so hard, the cradle nearly shattered. For a few moments I just stood there gazing at it, my heart pounding as I gasped for breath. Then I sank slowly to the floor, and sobbing, called Jade.

She answered with a laugh.

"Shut up," I heard her tell someone. "You're such an idiot. Hello," she said, and laughed again before I spoke.

"Jade."

"Cat? What's up now?" she asked with a groan.

"I'm sorry," I said through my sobs.

"I can't understand you. What's wrong? Why are you crying? Cat?"

"I'm sorry, Jade. I made a mistake. Stuart...doesn't want to get involved. He left," I said.

"Oh, great. I had a feeling this would happen. We shouldn't have listened to you. Damn."

"I'm sorry, but I do believe him when he says he won't tell anyone."

"Sure. Boys are such creeps."

"We have another problem," I said. "My father just called and demanded to speak to Geraldine again. He said he called every hospital in Los Angeles. I told him I was picking her up today and slammed the phone down."

"Brother," she said.

"I'm sorry. What should I do?"

"Nothing. You'll have to drive, it's a good thing you didn't break your *right* ankle. I'll send Misty over later just as we planned, so under the cover of darkness you can do exactly what we planned and hopefully that will throw him off. It's Cat," I heard her say. "Stuart's not driving you."

"Misty's there?"

"Yes, she's here with Chris. He and David are waiting for us at the pool. We're all going swimming. She'll have to figure out her own excuse to get rid of him for a while. Do you think your father's out there now?"

"I don't know. I'm scared," I said. "Stuart thinks we could be arrested on suspicion of murder. I don't want to get you all in trouble. I came up to our room. I'm here now, but it's not working for me."

"What? You're in the room?"

"It's not working."

"Cat, take it easy. You're getting hysterical."

"I lit the candle. I tried to meditate and calm down and…"

"All right. All right. I'll send Misty over now to be with you. She'll be there as soon as she can."

I heard her groan in the background.

"She's going to hate me. I know she wants to be with Chris."

"It'll be all right. I'll talk to her. She'll do what she said," Jade added, lowering her voice to a conspiratorial whisper. "She'll come in through the back. Unlock the door and just wait for her. And Cat, try to stay calm. That's the most important thing now."

"I'm sorry. It's all my fault."

"Let's not do that," Jade nearly yelled. "Let's not start blaming ourselves. They're always trying to pass the blame onto us somehow. Just wait there, calmly. Damn them," she said.

I wasn't sure who the them was at this point, but I was afraid to utter another sound.

"Okay," I said in a small voice, and hung up the phone.

Trembling so badly, I clung to my crutches as I made my way out of the room. I didn't know where to go. Suddenly, going downstairs and being alone seemed terrifying. I went into my bedroom instead and closed the door. It was where I went and what I did all my life when I was afraid. I would crawl onto my bed and pull my legs in and hold myself and close my eyes and wait for the waves and waves of anxiety and trepidation to go away. Sometimes they did immediately and sometimes it seemed to take hours. I would fall asleep and wake and still be trembling.

Geraldine never came to check on me, even when I was very little. It got so whenever my father did come to see if I was all right I welcomed his hands.

"There, there," he would say, *"let's get our little girl to feel good again."*

All my unheard, unvoiced screams were trapped in this room. I imagined them bubbling under the surface. The walls had absorbed them like a sponge. They could, at any sudden moment, explode in a cry so powerful, the whole house would go up in a cloud of dust. Some wind would come along and blow it all away so that it would be as if it had never existed, me and my sister and father along with it. The world would be so much better off, I thought.

I tried to close my ears as well as my eyes because sounds were rising up through the floors. I could swear I heard the vacuum going. Geraldine was there, cleaning, hating the dirt and dust, mumbling to herself about something she had read or seen that confirmed her dark, dreary view of people. Maybe I shouldn't have hated her so much. She had been betrayed too, I thought. Now I could understand why she was so hardened and bitter. Whom could she believe in?

Was that the sound of water running? Was she washing a floor, rinsing a table, doing windows? And that now, was it the droning of the television set, locked on one of her electronic preachers, confirming her dismal visions? Did I hear footsteps on the stairs? I tightened my eyelids and squeezed my body. She was whispering through the door.

"I told you. Now you see that you reap what you sow. You slept with him. You let him touch you. You're dirty deep down into your very soul. You can't scrub it out no matter how long you soak in a tub or shower or rub. Anyone can look at you and see. Sin is in your eyes. You let him touch you."

Whom did she mean, Stuart or my father?

The whispering became unintelligible. It was just the constant sound of air flowing through her dried lips. I put all my strength of concentration on the image of a single candle flame and watched it flicker and flicker until it drifted into the tiny spiral of smoke and was gone.

A loud rapping sound snapped open my eyes. I listened, my heart thumping. Had all I had imagined been true? There was a tinkle at the window and then a thump on the wall. I rose, puzzled and terrified, but I made my way to the window and gazed out. Misty was below. I opened the window quickly.

"What are you doing? You didn't leave the back door unlocked."

"Oh, I'm sorry," I said. "I fell asleep."

"Hurry up. It looks like it's going to rain," she ordered, and went around to the back of the house.

I moved as quickly as I could and made my way down the stairs, through the house and to the door. She burst in, closing it quickly behind her.

"What happened? Don't you remember our plan?"

"Yes, I'm sorry. I didn't realize how long I had been asleep."

"Jade told me what you said. I knew we shouldn't have trusted him. Did you break up?"

"I guess," I said. "I don't expect him to come back."

"You're better off," she said. "I'm never going to fully trust any man, even the man I marry, if I marry. What good are promises and vows, even with a priest holding his hand over you both? I feel sorry for Ariel. My father will probably break her heart, too.

"Did he call again?" she suddenly asked.

"You mean my father?" She nodded. "No."

"Well, let's get started. I promised Chris I'd meet him at seven-thirty. One good thing about Chris is he never asks many questions. Where's the dress?"

"Upstairs where you left it," I said.

She hurried ahead. After she put it on and fixed her hair the way I had described Geraldine's, we got into the car. She sat on the floor in the back.

"Are you sure you can drive?"

"Yes," I said, even though I wasn't. I couldn't stop the trembling inside me. When I took hold of the steering wheel, it helped, but my breathing was so rapid and short, I was afraid I would make some terrible error and have an accident. Then what would we do? How would we explain anything?

"Go, go, go," Misty urged. "I'm not exactly comfortable down here."

"Okay."

I started the engine, opened the garage door.

"Oh, no," I said. "It's raining hard."

"That's good. It'll be more difficult for him to see us," she said.

Right, I thought, but it's harder to drive, too. I headed out slowly. As I left the driveway, I glanced around quicky, searching for signs of my father. A car more than halfway down the block did look like his.

"I think he's there. I think he's going to follow us."

"Try to lose him if he does," Misty coached from the back.

I watched the rearview mirror. Raindrops made the window look like shattered glass.

"It's hard to see in this. I can't tell if that car is his."

"Forget about him, Cat. Just drive to the hospital."

"What hospital? We never decided!" I cried in a panic.

"Take it easy," she said. She gave me directions to Saint John's and we drove on.

During the whole trip, I never knew if he was right behind us or not. I made so many turns and took a number of side streets. We drove to the hospital, parked, and waited for as long as we thought it would take to get Geraldine checked out. I watched for any signs of him, but saw none. After what we thought was a sufficient time, we drove away with Misty in the front seat.

The rain fell in periodic torrents and then slowed to a drizzle. It was like that in Los Angeles. It could be raining hard ten blocks away and almost not raining where I was. When we arrived at the house, I closed the garage door behind us before either of us got out. Then we went to the living room and Misty took Geraldine's chair. I had her back to the window and opened the shutter just enough for someone to see her silhouette.

"I'll pretend to get you some tea," I said.

"Don't pretend. I could use a cup of something hot."

After I brought it to her, she sipped it and smiled.

"So? How do I look?"

"I don't know. I guess from across the street you look like her."

"I'll sit here another twenty minutes and then I'll walk out and leave through the back. Of course, I'll change first," she added with a laugh. "It's creepy, but if it works, he'll keep his distance."

"We hope," I said.

"Don't worry about Stuart. You'll have a new boyfriend in a week. I've got some ideas already. Jade wants us to have a meeting about all this tomorrow night," she added.

"Okay," I said, "but don't worry about getting me a boyfriend."

I gazed through the shutters at the street. Maybe he wasn't there. Maybe all of this was for nothing. I suppose we'll know soon enough, I thought.

"I'm going to heat up some soup," I said. "Be right back."

"It's all right. I'm fine," she told me.

At the doorway I gazed back at her. She was sipping her tea and gazing through the shutters. From where I stood, she did look like Geraldine. How many times had I seen her in that chair sipping tea and gazing out at the street? What went through her mind? What did she see? Did she envision a way out or did she imagine walls keeping her forever imprisoned in her terrible disappointments?

I could actually still see her, hear her, even smell her.

INTO THE GARDEN

People don't die, I thought, until the memory of them is gone. How foolish I was to think that we could roll her into the ground, cover her up, and be free of her.

Geraldine and I would be joined forever and ever. We shared the same silences and heard similar voices. I was with her even now in our mutual garden of sorrow.

17

Daddy's Home

Maybe it worked, I thought. Hours passed and my father hadn't called, nor did he dare to come to the door. Actually, I hadn't heard from any of the girls, either. Finally, close to ten P.M., Jade phoned to see how things were. I heard music and laughter behind her. She told me she was at an exclusive beach club with David.

"Have you spoken to Star?" she asked.

"No."

"I tried to reach her earlier to tell her about Stuart, but she went somewhere with Larry before I could reach her, and I didn't want to leave any message with her grandmother. She's spending more and more time with him."

"So she doesn't know about Stuart?"

"Not unless Misty's spoken to her since I tried. I'm planning for us all to meet tomorrow night. Misty told you, right?"

"Yes."

"Another crisis meeting," she said, "but what's new about that, huh?"

"Maybe Stuart's right," I said sadly. "Maybe we made a big mistake and we'll all get into terrible trouble."

"Don't get yourself all depressed, Cat. We'll figure it out. We always do," she said. "I've got to go. David's waiting. Stuart hasn't said anything to him, apparently. I'll call as soon as I'm up and around tomorrow morning. However, the way it's going that might be tomorrow afternoon," she added with a laugh.

Minutes after I hung up, Misty phoned. She said she and Chris had just come out of seeing a movie and they were stopping to get some slices of pizza.

"Anything happening?" she asked breathlessly, sounding like she was hovering over the receiver so Chris couldn't hear our conversation.

"No. Jade called and said she hadn't spoken yet to Star. Have you?"

"No. It's all right. We'll call her in the morning. You all right?"

"Yes," I lied.

I didn't want to say or do anything that would take away from their fun. If I hadn't insisted on our telling Stuart everything, I would have probably been spending the night with him and having fun, too, I thought. At least there would have been one more night or maybe two. I'm my own worst enemy. Geraldine used to say that. She might have been right at least about one thing.

"I need a favor," Misty said.

"What?" What could she possibly want from me? I wondered.

"I was going to bring Chris to my house tonight afterward, but my mother shocked me by having a small house party. Apparently, she has a date, too. Since my father's marriage, she's been looking for a boyfriend. Just for spite, I think."

"What's the favor?"

"I want to bring Chris over in about an hour. Do you think that would be all right even though you have no one to be with?"

"I don't know," I said. "It's not that I care about not having a date, too. If my father is out there and really believes we brought Geraldine home, he surely would wonder about it. Geraldine wouldn't let anyone within a foot of our door after ten and hopefully, we've got him believing she's here. Wouldn't we risk all that?"

"He can't be parked there all day and night," she said.

"I didn't think he was there the night he took the picture of Stuart kissing me," I pointed out.

"We could come in through the back door," she said, "like I did."

"But how would you explain that to Chris?"

"I'll just say a neighbor complained about our party or something and you don't want your mother to know. You promised her no more parties or guests. Like I said, he doesn't ask questions. We'll stay in the living room. You don't have to wait up or anything. Just leave the back door unlocked," she said.

The thought of doing that sent a chill down my back, but then I realized my father could easily force it open anyway if he wanted to.

"Okay," I relented.

"And Cat?"

"Yeah?"

"Don't tell Jade or Star. It doesn't involve them," she said.

We don't keep secrets from each other, I thought, but I knew why she didn't want them to know. They might very well be upset at her for taking such a chance.

"I won't lie if they ask," I warned.

"No, I'm not asking you to. Just don't volunteer the information. Okay? If none of this is okay, I'll understand," she said.

"No, it's all right."

Actually, the thought of having someone else in the house tonight was comforting, even if they were totally involved in each other and practically forgot I existed.

"Don't wait up," she repeated, and hung up.

After I unlocked the back door, I went into the living room to watch television, but I didn't really see anything. The tube blinked and brightened, flickered with people. All the voices merged into one unintelligible hum. When I gazed around, I suddenly felt terribly lonely. It made me think of all the elderly people who sat in houses day and night, looking at the world through a television window. If they turned and looked out their house windows, nothing seemed much different after a while. What was real and what wasn't was hard to distinguish.

I closed my eyes and tried to think about Stuart, tried to remember our wonderful day and night, but already his face and his voice were sinking into the mire of lost remembrances. We hadn't had time to build a strong enough place for our memories to be safely stored. Had I imagined his smile, his wonderful words, his touch, and kiss? What had been real and what hadn't? Maybe none of it was. Maybe I had wanted it so much, I dreamed it all.

Worried still that Misty and I might not have done well, or that my father hadn't seen any of it, I tried to stay awake until she and Chris arrived, but try as I would, the terrible drowsiness was like water rushing over me, drowning me until I dropped deeper and deeper into a nightmare. I was rushing through a hallway full of cobwebs, breaking one after another, fleeing from someone whose footsteps grew louder and louder along with my growing panic. The cobwebs got thicker and harder to break. Soon I was struggling to get through one. The threads stuck to my arms and my legs like gum. I was becoming more and more tired, stumbling now, until finally, I fell forward into a large web and just hung there, unable to move my arms or my legs.

When I looked down, I saw I was naked. The shadow coming after me grew darker and closer and then, I woke up, screaming. The sound of my own voice terrified me. I waved my arms and fell back in the chair, stunned that it had all just been a dream. I was soaked with sweat, too. My heart was a parade drum, marching my blood around my body in rhythmic thumps. It took a few minutes to get my breath.

It was still very quiet. Misty and Chris hadn't arrived. Actually, I had been asleep only a few minutes. Misty probably didn't want me to be down here when she and Chris arrived anyway, I thought. She made a big point of my not waiting up. I rose and started upstairs. I was going to soak in a tub and then try to sleep. Tomorrow, they would all be here, and we would start again and solve all our problems.

I went up and ran the tub. While I was soaking, I heard music below. I listened for a while, imagining them either dancing closely or kissing on the sofa. Misty was so happy she had found someone she liked and whom she believed liked her. I was envious, but not jealous. Each of us deserved some good luck, I thought. I had half hoped that Stuart would have rethought it all and decided I was too important to him to just give up, even over something like this. Maybe tomorrow he would show up and tell me just that. Then I imagined Star telling me to stop being a dreamer. "You're hanging around with Misty too much," she would say.

What kind of people don't dream, don't wish, don't live in fantasy at least once in a while, however? How droll and dreary their lives must be. Even Geraldine must have had her dreams, must have fantasized that the man she had loved, my real father, would have come by and told her she really was the one he wanted. In her mind she would have lived a fairy-tale life. How she must have resented me, the very embodiment of the death of her fantasy, the period that ended her "Once Upon a Time..." abruptly and forever.

It was strange how now, after her death, I was beginning to understand her more and more, and even sympathize with her. Once again, I thought that if she had been wise enough to give me the truth long ago, she and I might have become real sisters and both of us might have had some happiness together.

The music was still playing when I got into bed. I lay there listening to it. Occasionally, I thought I could hear their muffled voices and some laughter. Then, the music stopped and it grew very quiet. I turned over, closed my eyes and soon fell asleep.

When I rose in the morning and went down, I expected to find Chris and Misty asleep on the sofa, but they were already gone. Either they had left very late the night before or very early this morning, I thought. There were two glasses on the coffee table, both still with some orange juice. I smelled them and thought there was vodka in them as well. They had left a blanket crumbled on the sofa. I folded it and put it in the closet and then I took the glasses to the kitchen. I didn't have much of an appetite so I just had a slice of toast and jam with a little juice.

It looked like it was going to be a beautiful day. From what I could see, there wasn't a cloud in the sky and barely a breeze. I stepped out back and looked at Geraldine's grave. The rain from the night before had settled in and around it, making it more discernable. It looked like the ground had sunken some, but it also looked like some of the seeds of grass had begun to sprout. Very soon it would be covered and not so obvious, I thought.

As I stood there, I heard the doorbell ring. For a moment I didn't move. It was far too early for Jade, and Misty surely was still sleeping. We had never spoken to Star. Who would be there this early? It rang again and again. With my heart thumping, I went back through the house and first looked through the front window. I didn't recognize the car in the driveway, but when he stepped away from the door I spotted Larry in his uniform and breathed with relief. They rang again and I went to the door as fast as I could now.

"Sorry," I said, opening it, "I was out back."

"You were? Why?" Star asked, her eyes wide with suspicion. She was carrying a bag of groceries.

"Just getting air," I replied.

"Oh, good. We brought some breakfast," she began as she stepped in.

"Good morning, Cathy," Larry said.

"Good morning. You brought breakfast?"

"Yes. Larry and I spent the night up the coast, but neither of us was hungry when we woke up, so I thought we'd buy some fresh bagels and stuff and stop here on the way home. I figured you might be alone or is someone else here?" she asked with an impish grin.

I was reminded that she didn't know what had happened the day before.

"No, I'm alone," I said.

"Mind if I turn on the television?" Larry asked.

"No. Go ahead," I told him, and he went into the living room. Star and I went to the kitchen.

Before I could even begin to tell her what had happened, she put down her bag of groceries and hugged me.

"Oh, Cat," she cried, "I have so much to tell you. I really do think my luck has changed."

Without taking a breath, she continued.

"I never really believed in that love-at-first-sight stuff. Movies are movies, but in real life, people are lucky if they fall in love after being together for years and years. I mean, who in her right mind except some soap opera freak is going to believe that you look at someone who looks at you, and in that moment your heart flutters and your blood races and you just can't wait to throw yourself into his arms forever and ever? Huh?"

Me, I wanted to say, but I was afraid to say or do anything that might slow down her train.

"But that's exactly what's happened here, Cat. You remember what I told you girls when I set eyes on Larry's picture, right? Already, something was happening to me. I didn't want to make all that big a deal of it. How many times has my mama been in love? Every man she started with after my daddy took off was the perfect new man, her knight in shining armor, each of which turned out to be a disappointment in shining tin foil." She shook her head in disgust.

"So when it comes to believing in anyone, especially a

man who drapes all these promises over you like some expensive furs, I said to myself, that will never happen to me. If I ever marry, it won't be for some glass of foam called love. It will be sensible and then, maybe someday, I'd look at my man and think, we have something, right?

"Wrong," she said before I could even nod. She finally took a big breath and then smiled and pressed her hands to her breast and gazed up at the ceiling. "Larry and I, we have something akin to magic, Cat. You know how you get comfortable when you settle yourself in a nice warm bath. I don't mean one of Jade's fancy smelly baths, but just an ordinary, warm tub?"

"Yes," I said.

"Well, every time I'm with him, all the time I'm with him, I feel that way. I feel...comfortable and warm, and most important of all, Cat. I feel safe. Oh, I know what Jade's going to say," she added quicky, making a sour face. "She's going to tell you all that I fell in love with a uniform, that the uniform makes me feel safe, but believe me, Cat," she interjected with a soft, coy smile, "I've been with him when he's out of his uniform and it doesn't change a thing. In fact, I feel it all more. Understand?"

"Yes," I said.

"Good. I knew you would. Of all of us, I knew you'd be the one to understand first and best," she told me. "Now here's the good part," she continued, pulling a chair out and sitting, "Larry and I haven't just been pawing over each other these past twenty-four hours. We've been thinking and talking and planning sensibly. I'm going to finish high school and he's finishing up his stint in the army and getting all his training. He's already got a good job lined up with his cousin, and what we're going to do is get married right after I graduate and he's out of the army. The most wonderful thing of all is he wants us to take Rodney in with us, too. It would lift some burden off Granny who, as you know, isn't exactly healthy and strong enough to raise another family. These are years she should be enjoying without daily worries. Larry sees that, believes that. He's as good as he is handsome, and I do believe he loves me more than any man will," she concluded.

She waited a moment for my reaction.

"Wow," I said. "It does sound great, Star. I'm happy for you."

"Right," she said. "You can consider me engaged, even though he hasn't gotten me a ring yet. He will real soon and then maybe, we'll have an engagement party, huh? We could even have it right here!"

I nodded, but I didn't look as enthusiastic as she would have liked.

"What's wrong?" she finally asked. "Something's happened, hasn't it?"

"Yes," I said. I sat, too.

Star waited patiently, but she read my face and nodded.

"Something to do with Stuart, huh?"

"I'm sorry," I said. "Everyone was right. He got cold feet right after you all left yesterday. He wanted me to call the police and confess what we did, and he said he couldn't help us and get involved. He did promise he wouldn't tell anyone though," I added.

"Sure," she said.

"I can't blame him, Star. He was worried about his mother and his little brother."

She raised her eyebrows at that.

"You know his father died and he feels he bears responsibilities for them."

"Maybe," she said, nodding. "Okay, so we don't really need him anyhow. If he keeps his trap shut, we'll be all right." She thought a moment and then looked up. "Did Misty go through with the plan anyway?"

"Yes."

"Who drove?"

"I did and we went to the hospital and back. She sat in the chair by the window."

"Think your father saw it all?"

"I don't know. He hasn't called again."

"Then it worked," she concluded.

"I hope so, but we don't know for sure that he was out there watching. Jade's called a meeting tonight."

"Tonight? What time?"

"I don't know. Around dinner, I guess," I said.

"It's Larry's last night here. We're planning on going to a nice dinner somewhere special," she moaned.

"Oh. Well, maybe we can get Jade here earlier then."

"Yeah. That's what we'll do. I'll make her come about three, even if I have to go over there and drag her over."

"I'm sorry, Star. I don't want to make anything difficult for you."

"No, no," she said, shaking her head. "We're all in this together. There won't be a problem," she assured me with a smile. Then she stood. "Let's make some breakfast."

"I already ate, but I'll have coffee with you."

"Good." She turned and went to work while I sat there hating myself for being the one OWP with the most serious and troubling problems. All I could do was make things more difficult for them and ruin their chances at happiness. Soon, I thought, they'll all hate me as well.

* * *

When Larry came to the table, he and Star did seem like the most lovey-dovey couple I had ever seen. They were unable to keep their hands off each other. If she would get close enough to him for him to lean over and kiss her, he would, and when they handed each other things, their fingers lingered around each other's and their eyes locked on each other's eyes. I almost felt like I was intruding just being at the same table. They talked about their future as if they were alone. Larry was planning on flying Star to Germany during the holidays this coming year.

Finally, they looked at me as if they just realized I was there, too. Star laughed about it, but Larry looked embarrassed. Afterward, she and I cleaned up the kitchen and he returned to the living room to watch TV.

"I'm going to have a nice church wedding," she told me. "His parents would want that, and I'm not going to invite Mama," she added firmly. "If she came, she would only ruin it, and that's one event, she isn't going to ruin, no ma'am."

"What if she comes anyway?" I asked.

She thought a moment and shook her head.

"She won't. I'm not about to tell her either. Besides, she's gone again and maybe for good this time. Even Granny hopes so, and she's her daughter. She just thinks it's best for everyone all around."

"That's sad," I said.

"It's not Granny's fault. She did what she could to bring her up right. Some people," Star said, turning to me, "are just bad inside, Cat. They're like spoiled apples. If you keep cutting out the rotten parts, you'll end up with nothing but some seeds. It's not worth the effort. Shine the good ones," she advised, and then she stopped and smiled and hugged me.

"Thanks. I've got to go home for a while, but I'll be back with the others at three. I'll take care of Jade myself," she promised.

Larry said goodbye. He didn't think he would see me again before he left for Germany. He gave me a kiss on the cheek and a hug and said he looked forward to when we would all be together again. I watched them leave, feeling both sad and happy at the same time. Larry certainly appeared to have put the joy back into Star. I couldn't recall a time when she looked more radiant and alive. I was happy for her, but I also knew that some day she and Larry would be off and we'd probably drift far apart.

As if Geraldine's spirit slipped into me, I looked with critical eyes at the house right after they left. Maybe to keep myself occupied and not think of things that would make me tremble inside, I decided to vacuum and dust and wash the kitchen floor. As I worked, I imagined her beside me urging me to use more elbow grease or to concentrate on what I was doing. Whenever I completed something, I considered how Geraldine would react, and occasionally, I would go back and either polish, dust or vacuum the same spot over again.

After housecleaning, I started on clothes. I set the machine and turned my attention to the refrigerator. If the girls were here and saw me, I knew they would think I had gone mad, but the more I worked, the more I found to do. It seemed an easy way to pass the time and for the first time I considered that this might have been the very reason Geraldine had made the house her whole world. Maybe it was the only time she didn't feel lonely and defeated by her life.

These thoughts brought back images of her I had stored in a different place in my memory. In them I saw her sitting and staring out the window or standing alone in the backyard and looking west toward the ocean, as if she could see something way out there that had caught her interest and longing. I saw her pausing over some vase or some otherwise meaningless artifact and turning it around in her fingers as if she had found a valuable jewel. Never once did I think it might hold some cherished memory for her. All I thought was she was inspecting it for a smudge or dust.

All I had learned about her and myself had served only to make her more of a stranger. And yet, I wondered what her life would have been like without me. I recalled the day I had forced her to tell me about my adoption. She had told only a partial truth. She left me believing I was her half sister, that we shared the same mother, when all the while she knew she had been adopted as well and we had no blood relationship. Yet, she wanted me to believe we had. Surely that must have meant she wanted me to believe we were still close in a way. She wasn't ready to tear us completely apart. Could it be that she needed me after all? That even in her meanest, most insensitive moments, she needed me?

Loneliness was another kind of starvation. With no love, no friendship to feed her soul, Geraldine withered away inside herself. Her spirit had died long before her body. Surely this was why she didn't try to get the medical attention she knew in her heart she needed, and depended entirely on her herbal remedies even when they weren't really working.

Eventually Geraldine had become just another shadow sliding along the darkened walls of our home, shying away from the sunshine, from anything bright and warm, retreating from the sound of other voices, blocking out smiles like some vampire terrified of the illumination which would only, in the end, destroy her.

Her heart ran out like an old clock. She made no attempt to wind it or restore its batteries. She finally welcomed the silence, the stilled hands. She turned to reach back for her lost spirit and joined it in whatever place she was destined to rest forever and ever.

With every wipe of the cloth, every spray of the disinfectant and dip into the detergent, I stopped hating her a little more. For a few moments in time, I had become her and I understood her, and just as she had, I hated what had created the creature she had become.

All these thoughts exhausted me more than the actual work had. I made my way back upstairs to rest a while and then freshen up for our OWP meeting. For an hour or so, I dozed on and off, finally waking to what I was sure was the sound of footsteps below. I looked at the clock. It was only one-thirty. Perhaps Misty had decided to come earlier, I thought.

I rose, washed my face, and fixed my hair, straightened my blouse and skirt and then made my way downstairs. We had so much to talk about now, so much to do and decide. In many ways this was the most important meeting of all, I thought, and I was anxious to get it started.

When I descended the stairs, however, I didn't find anyone in the house. It was quiet and nothing had been disturbed in the kitchen. How strange, I thought. I guessed I had imagined the footsteps. There was still a good hour and a half before the girls were supposed to arrive anyway. Then, I heard the sound of footsteps again, but this time, they were coming from the stairs. I held my breath a moment and listened hard. Yes, the stairs creaked. My eyes went to the back door. I had forgotten to lock it after I had rushed in to greet Star and Larry.

I felt like there was a small fire in my chest, the flames licking at my heart, and the feeling melting my breath until I actually had pain in my lungs. Trembling, I made my way back into the hallway and looked at the stairs. My father had just turned into the corridor. He stood there, smiling at me.

"What have you been up to, Cathy?" he asked.

I didn't think I was capable of getting the words out, but they came rushing up, regurgitated out of my heart.

"You're not supposed to be in here. You better get out now," I said.

His smile widened.

"Let's you and I have a quiet little talk first, Cathy. Come along," he beckoned with those long, spidery fingers of his. "In the living room, the much changed living room," he added, still smiling.

His face looked thinner, darker, the lines deeper, and his eyes seemed vacant and filled with shadows. He wore one of his black sports jackets, but he didn't have a tie on and his jacket and pants looked creased enough for someone to believe he might have slept in them. I hadn't noticed how long and stringy his hair was when I saw him on the beach that afternoon. I had been too shocked by his sudden appearance, and he had been standing with the sun blazing behind him, his face shadowed. This disheveled appearance was very unlike him. Usually, he was immaculately dressed. It frightened me even more to see him like this.

"I'd advise you to come in and sit with me, Cathy," he followed, his voice full of a heavy threat.

There wasn't very much else I could do. I hobbled

along into the living room. The closer I drew to him, the more my heart pounded. It was as if it had become a Geiger counter and he had turned into pure radiation. I placed my crutches beside me and sat on the sofa. He stood in the doorway a moment and then he went to the window and gazed out.

"Where are your girlfriends today?" he asked.

"They'll be here very soon," I said. "And they all know you're not supposed to be here. They'll go for the police."

He turned, his face stern, his lips tight.

"I doubt that very much, Cathy. Very much. Yes, I broke in here the other night. I couldn't understand why your mother was behaving like she was and I needed to get some things. Imagine my surprise when I saw what had been done to the house and to your mother's room. I left thinking maybe she had gone mad and was redoing it in some bizarre fashion. When I saw that old, cheap furniture out in the hall, I thought finally she's letting go of something. Maybe her attitudes about what's valuable and what isn't had changed and she wouldn't be as penurious.

"God, how she drove me mad with that 'a penny saved is a penny earned' crap. If I heard 'waste not want not' one more time, I think I would have gone mad. It got so I heard it in my sleep!" he cried, his hands turned up as if he was pleading his case in front of some jury.

"I knew she had hoarded every nickel I ever gave her and was ever given to her. She had a lot in that safe of hers. You know she never trusted me with the combination? What kind of a marriage is it where the wife wouldn't give her husband the combination to the safe in their bedroom, huh?

"I'll tell you," he answered for himself, much like she

would have, "not much. It was never much. I was a fool to have let myself be talked into it."

He smiled.

"I found the letters in your room. You've read them, I suppose."

"Only the first two," I said. "You had no right to take them."

"Only the first two? I see. Well, you know enough about yourself and her then. The other letters are full of apologies and promises and all that phoney stuff that was never to be. You didn't get the safe open, did you?" he asked suddenly, his eyebrows hoisted and poised.

"Yes, we did," I said.

"We did? Oh, you and your girlfriends, huh? Of course. So you know the rest then. You know your mother was really adopted, right?"

"Yes," I said.

"Do you know that I never knew it?" he asked. "That's right. They kept that from me. From *me!* They probably thought I might think again about marrying her or something. I wish I had.

"Never marry for money and comfort, Cathy. In the end you might have some money, but you won't have the comfort you so cherished.

"It was you, you only who gave me any comfort," he said in a softer voice, a voice that sounded as if it was filled with tears and pain. "When she took you away from me..." He paused as if he was all choked up and turned away for a moment. I saw his shoulders rise and fall.

He gathered himself and when he turned back to me, there was no longer even a trace of softness in his face.

"She had no right, no right. I was the only one who ever

gave you any affection, who sympathized with you, who cared for you. I was the one who gave you toys, wanted you to have things. She stopped me all the time. She was jealous of our relationship from the start. She'd rather you were alone, suffering, crying, than have me. What kind of a mother was she to you?"

He paused again and smiled.

"Yes, Cathy, was. When you told me she was in the hospital, you had me for a little while, even though I knew she would hate to be in any hospital," he added.

For a moment he stared, and I stared as his words twisted and turned in my mind, tying themselves in a knot. The smallest, slightest chill started at the base of my spine.

"She was a remarkably healthy woman. I think her meanness made it so. No disease, no germ dared to locate in her inhospitable body. You know how rare it was for her to even have a cold. In all the years we were married, she never went for a physical exam or any of the regular checkups most women have. I kept thinking some day she'll have cancer and she won't be able to stop it, but not her, not even cancer dared invade her skin and bones.

"I was convinced she'd outlive me, maybe even both of us, and she might have, too. You see that, don't you? You think she'd ever have let you have a normal relationship with anyone? You think you'd ever have a boyfriend or do any of the things you wanted to do?

"Remember, it was I who bought you that party dress. Remember?"

He paused again and looked over the room.

"You girls are something," he said. "Those pictures out there," he continued, nodding and laughing. "She's spinning in her grave. Right, Cathy?"

I couldn't talk now. My whole body felt frozen. I couldn't even feel my heart beating.

"So what would she do to protect herself, to keep up her health besides eat like a bird and clean this house for exercise? Just those herbal remedies, remember?"

He reached into his jacket pocket and took out a bottle.

"This was one of her favorites." He looked at it and read, "Pycnogenol." He nodded at it. "I made fun of her all the time, but she was happy about it because that meant I wouldn't take it and she had more for herself."

"Why do you have it now?" I asked. My voice was so thin and small that I didn't recognize it when I spoke. It was as if someone else was in the room with us, asking the question.

"Oh, I didn't want it here any longer," he said. He paused and looked at me hard. "It's the real reason why I broke into the house that night. I didn't realize she had changed the locks on me. I had to break in when I thought you were all away."

"Why?" I asked.

"Why? I was afraid she might have finally convinced you to use this stuff, too, for one thing. For another, I didn't want anyone else to look at it...closely. You might have noticed there were different kinds of pills in the bottle—though I doubt you would have guessed they were strychnine," he added. "It was sort of a game of Russian roulette I played with her, waiting for the day she would take the right pill. I had a half dozen in here, resembling her precious herbal wonder. I guess it's safe to say now that she did, right?

"Cat got your tongue, Cathy? I remember her asking you that occasionally." He started to laugh and then stopped.

"I was able to check to see if you were telling the truth

about the hospital simply by checking on my hospitalization plan, Cathy. She kept that because I had to pay it. To be admitted to any hospital there had to be contact made with the plan, even after an emergency, and none had been made, and as you know, I called every hospital anyway. So I knew you were lying, and when you went through that charade to pretend to go get her, I nearly had a heart attack from laughing. I must say your girlfriend did a nice job sitting in this chair, looking like Geraldine.

"Tell me," he said, "where did she die? Were her eyes wide open, was she grimacing in pain? She was in rigor mortis pretty quickly, right?"

I felt as if I was shrinking, melting, and soon I would disappear in the sofa. Movement, speaking, even breathing seemed out of the question. He didn't notice. He put the bottle back into his pocket and smiled again.

"When you began to do things I knew Geraldine would adamantly forbid, I began to suspect she was indeed gone, but then I thought, if she was, why weren't the police here? Why wasn't someone calling me?

"And then, after I had been here and seen what you and your girlfriends had done and were doing, it came to me. What a wonderful surprise!" he said.

"At first," he continued, "I thought you had just packed her up and taken her someplace and then I saw the changes in our backyard and realized what you and your girlfriends had accomplished."

"You...killed her?" I finally asked.

"No. I helped her out of her misery because that's what she was in...misery. And she had no right to take you from me like that. None. She was just being vengeful, taking out her miserable life on me. On us," he said. "We were happy for a time before she destroyed it, weren't we?"

"No," I said, but my answer was weak and I was terrified. If he had heard, he decided to pretend he hadn't.

"It's over now, anyway. We can forget about it all. But we can't stay here, Cathy. Don't worry. I have a nice surprise for you. Guess what I did. I bought a houseboat. That's right. I don't know if you'll remember when I took you to the marina one afternoon and you were so intrigued with the sea and with the boats, and then we went on that houseboat one of my clients owned. Remember that? You thought it was a fun idea to live on the water so you could move your house around whenever you wanted to. Remember?"

I shook my head even though I did.

"Sure you do. Anyway, we have it now. We're going to have such a good time," he said. "Just the two of us, away from all this, and anytime we feel like it, we'll move." He laughed. "Isn't it wonderful?"

"No," I said. "I won't go with you."

His smile softened and then faded. The dark, gruesome face that replaced it was very frightening because I hadn't ever seen him so angry.

"Sure you'll go, Cathy. If you don't," he said, "you and especially your friends will be in a great deal of trouble. You girls buried her, not me," he pointed out. "And when they come and dig her up and examine her, they'll think you and your girlfriends killed her, too. They'll all go to prison. Do you want that to happen?"

My eyes began to fill with hot tears, so hot they burned under my lids. I shook my head.

"Good," he said, clapping his hands. "It won't happen then. You go upstairs and pack a little bag. Take what you want for now and we'll come back in a few days and get more. Eventually, we'll take whatever we want from the house and then one day, we'll have a convenient fire. Maybe Geraldine will be consumed in it. I'll figure it out for us, don't worry, and none of your friends will be in trouble. Until then, let's start to enjoy our houseboat.

"Oh, it's so much fun, Cathy. You can't imagine what it's like to wake up and smell the sea every morning. It stirs up your appetite. You'll be able to make me breakfast. It will be wonderful. Just what Geraldine would have hated to see," he said, laughing.

"Okay." He continued moving toward the front door. "Now that I know what is happening here, I'll bring the car around. You go upstairs, pack your stuff and I'll be right along."

He crossed the room and leaned down to kiss me on the forehead.

"I'm here for you again, sweetheart. Daddy's back."

His hand brushed some strands of hair from my face and then he walked out.

When he closed the front door behind him, it was as if a clap of thunder had sounded through the house, shaking my very bones.

What evil had we buried when we buried Geraldine?

18

Treacherous Waters

For a few moments I was actually unable to move. Every muscle in my body was frozen with fear. I couldn't even take a deep breath because I felt as if I had as much earth on my chest as Geraldine had on hers. The air around me was thick and heavy, too. Tiny electrical charges crackled and sparked. I closed my eyes and prayed all this had just been another nightmare, but when I opened them again, I realized, of course, that it had been real. He was here and he was coming back for me.

What was I to do? With the speed of lightning, different options passed through my mind. I could get up and go out the back to hide or maybe escape over the wall. But where would I go and what would that solve? I could do what Stuart had told me to do and call the police. How would the girls feel about that? What would I have done to them? I could stay here and plead with my father, maybe try to bluff him with threats, but I was never good at that sort of thing, and I was far too fragile now to put up anything resembling a convincing facade.

If I didn't do what he wanted, he would call the police himself and all of us would be in big trouble. I could envision even the girls wondering if I hadn't been the one to put the poison in Geraldine's jar of herbal remedies. At minimum there would be significant enough suspicion to have a long and painful investigation. All of them would be in big trouble and now, when they were all having such a good time finally. Larry might change his mind about marrying Star. David would certainly stop seeing Jade, and Misty would lose her new boyfriend, too. All this would happen, not to mention it would wrench their families' lives even further apart than they were.

Just thinking about Star's granny, how kind she had been to me and how fragile she was, made me shudder at the possibilities. How much were they supposed to bear? Their own problems had ruptured their relationships and their home lives. They didn't need mine, too.

I had no real choice. I had brought them into all this. I couldn't be selfish and cause them all this grief. It was too late to think about myself anymore. I had given that up when I had called Jade and told her Geraldine was dead. I should have called the police immediately. Should have, could have, hindsight, the moans and groans of the guilty and stupid, Geraldine used to say. "When you're drowning because you were careless or foolish, wrap an excuse around yourself and see how long it keeps you floating."

She was right. It was too late for excuses. None would keep me from drowning.

Leaning heavily on my crutches to pull myself up, I rose and started toward the stairs, walking, I'm sure, like some convict heading for the electric chair. Visions of my future made me numb. I was mechanical, taking one step after another, holding onto the railing as I ascended. When I got to my room and gazed around, I couldn't think of anything I wanted to take.

For a few seconds, I contemplated suicide. I could go into the bathroom, lock the door, cut my wrists and put them in a sink filled with hot water. Maybe before he got the door opened I would die. But then what? Would the girls be safe? He would be free to say whatever he wanted, wouldn't he? He would tell the police I couldn't live with what I and the girls had done. They might even pity him, not me, not us!

All I could come up with finally was the hope that if I gave myself some time, I might think of something. For now, there was nothing to do but follow his orders. I filled a small overnight bag with necessities. Before I was finished, he came charging up the stairs.

"How we doing?" he asked, his face flushed with excitement.

"I don't know what to take along," I said.

"Don't worry about it. We can come back from time to time and get whatever you want." He clapped his hands together, rubbing the palms as he walked into my room and looked at everything, smiling.

"I like the changes you made: new curtains, bedding, pictures, but wait until you see the houseboat. It's luxurious, everything Geraldine hated and thought opulent or ostentatious. I've got oak cabinets and paneling, with solid oak trim throughout, chrome faucets in the bathrooms, a Sub-Zero refrigerator, a deluxe sound system, big screen television set." He laughed. "She thought she knew where all my money was, but I was smart," he added, pointing to his temple with his right forefinger. "I envisioned this day would come and I stashed money in places she couldn't ever find. She thought she was so perceptive when it came to that, checking on every penny. That was her biggest trouble: thinking she was smarter than me in every way."

He saw I was just standing there staring at him and he blinked and glanced once more at the room. Then he laughed.

"What the heck did you girls do with our bedroom? What's that supposed to be in there, huh?" He brought his face closer to mine. "Is something weird going on here, something you want to tell me?"

"No, nothing weird. It was our meditation room, where we went to calm down and think and be..."

"What?"

"Together," I said. He'd never understand what OWP meant, and he might even get angry, I thought.

"Right. Well, you won't need that sort of thing anymore. Let's get going," he said. "I want to get some things from the garage. I'll meet you outside."

He left and I gazed at the clock. The girls would be here in less than an hour now and they wouldn't find me. What would they do? I wondered and it occurred to me that they might do something that would get them into trouble. I had to leave them a note. I was positive they would go around back to get into the house so that would be the best place to leave it. Not sure what to say, I started to write.

> *Dear Jade, Star, and Misty,*
> *I'm sorry I can't continue with things the way they are. I'll be all right if you all would simply concentrate on yourselves now and find happiness. Please just turn and walk away and forget*

everything. Don't come back to the house. Don't try to call me or find me. I love you all and appreciate everything you've all done for me, but now it's time for you to do things for yourselves and your own families. Please, please, please, for my sake, do what I ask.

Love always,
Cat

It was the first time I had ever signed my name like that. It brought tears to my eyes. I quickly folded the note and headed downstairs. I could hear him opening and closing cabinets in the garage, so I made my way back to the kitchen, found Scotch tape in the drawer where it was kept and taped the note to the outside of the back door. I put the tape on doubly thick to be sure the wind wouldn't blow it off.

"Cathy?" I heard him call.

I closed the door softly. If he found the note, he would be angry, I thought. Almost tiptoeing, I returned to the front of the house. He was at the front door.

"Where were you?"

"I was very thirsty, so I got a drink of water," I said.

He stared, his eyes darkening with suspicion.

"Did you call someone?"

"No," I said quickly.

"If you did, you'll only make things harder for everyone," he warned.

"I didn't call anyone. I swear," I said.

He considered and then he smiled.

"No, I don't think you did. I think you want to be with me now. I know you realize I'm the only one who really cares for you, right? Isn't that right?" he insisted.

"Yes," I said. I tried to swallow after I said it, but my throat wouldn't open.

"Good. Well," he said, looking at the house, "let's bid this prison good riddance once and for all. Need help?"

"No, I'm fine," I said. There were tears under my lids, but I was holding them back. If he saw me cry, he would get enraged for sure, I thought. I lowered my head and started out. He held the door open for me and then he shut it hard, took me by the elbow and guided me to the car. He put my small overnight bag in the back, closed the door, and got in. For a moment he just stared at the garage.

"Remember when I made that dent?" he said, nodding at the place on the garage where he had backed the car into it. "She wouldn't let me fix it. She wanted it to remain there forever as a way of reminding me I had screwed up, like some scar. I was always tempted to do it again for spite." His brow folded and then relaxed when he turned to me. "That's all behind us now. Think of it as nothing more than a bad dream. It's time to wake up and be happy."

He started the engine and turned on the radio.

"Remember how she hated my playing the radio loud and especially hated it if I put it on one of those stations that played contemporary music? 'How can you concentrate on your driving with all this racket, Howard? Lower it,' she commanded, like some general.

"Orders. She loved to give orders." He laughed. "I bet she's giving Satan orders now and he's wishing she was good enough for heaven. Maybe he thinks she's another way to punish him, huh?"

He put the car into reverse and backed us out.

"Look at that sky. It looks even better down by the

ocean, Cathy. The water makes it seem...I don't know, bluer. I suppose there's some reason for it."

He started away. I looked back at the house. Suddenly, it didn't look half as bad as it always had. Suddenly, it looked like an old friend, deserted, left to wither and die alone with only the echo of our voices and our footsteps reverberating and evaporating, leaving it in silence and darkness, a monument to the troubled, sad family it had somehow served despite the tears, the cries, the moans, and small prayers for mercy that were the measurements of my desperate little existence.

My father seemed to blossom with light the farther we got from the house. He talked continuously throughout the trip to the marina, describing some of the things he had been doing since he had left our home.

"I actually did much better at work. I made a lot of money these past few months, Cathy, and I lucked out with the houseboat. I had this client who had just bought it, hardly used it, and lost money in some stupid investments. I saw a chance to get something for nearly half the original cost and pounced. The kitchen is bigger than the one in the house!

"It's got a nice living room and two bedrooms, not that I expect we'll have any guests sleeping over anytime soon. I want us to spend lots and lots of time together without any outside interference. We've got to get to know each other all over again, Cathy. The truth is, honey, we just have each other in this world. You know what I think of my family. I couldn't care less of what they thought of me, never did.

"You don't even have to go back to school if you don't want to. I'm thinking seriously of taking a year off. I can afford it now. I could do some business from time to time just to keep my hand in things, but we could travel. You know, we could go up the coast to Canada. Wouldn't that be something? There are some beautiful things to see, places to go.

"That's what I like about this new home...it's got freedom written all over it, and you know how trapped we both were back there with the warden."

He glanced at me and nodded.

"I know all this is strange and new to you, but you'll be surprised at how quickly that will change. You'll become a sailor. Now about that ankle...what else has to be done?"

"I'm supposed to go back for another X-ray the day after tomorrow," I said. "If I don't, the doctor will call."

"We'll go back. What's the big deal? Until then, we'll take it easy on you. No housework for my princess for a while, huh? I'll do the cooking tonight, too. I've become a good cook, Cathy. The truth is I was always a better cook than Geraldine, but she wouldn't stand for the spices and the seasoning, so we had to put up with bland food and pretend everything was hunky-dory."

"I never heard you complain about her food," I said.

"What good was it to complain about anything? Would she change anything? Would she deviate from her religious observance of her schedules and methods? No, a complaint just made things more miserable for us, for you," he said. "That's why I stayed and I put up with all her crap. You! I knew how she would take out her anger on you, so I kept my mouth shut.

"But that's all past us, Cathy. Let's make a pact to try to forget about it. Let's start all over, okay? Yeah," he said, liking his idea more and more, "let's do this. Let's pretend you and I are completely different people now. Don't think of me as Daddy anymore. Think of me as the man who will protect and keep you happy forever and ever. In fact, I want you to call me Howard from now on, from this minute on, okay?"

I knew why he wanted that. It put a small buzzing in the base of my stomach, making me feel like I had a large fly there trying to find its way out.

He turned up the radio, sang along, and smiled at me.

"Wait until you see our new home," he declared. "I can't wait to see your face."

He had the houseboat docked near a place called Fisherman's Village in Marina del Rey. The boat was bigger than I had imagined. He said it was nearly forty-five feet long. As we got out of the car and made our way to it, he continued to describe it, telling me it had twin inboard engines. The deckhouse featured a ten-foot long dinette, an inside control station, and a bar. The galley was a full-fledged kitchen open to the deckhouse and adjacent to the bar. There were big windows providing lots of light.

He was proud of the outside area with its full walk-around decks, covered bow with a lounge seat, plus a huge sundeck and flying bridge control station with back-to-back seats. He seemed to know a lot about the boat, rattling off so many details, it made my head spin. I knew he was trying to impress me.

I was surprised at how roomy it was inside and how large the main bedroom was. It had a queen-size bed, carpeted floors, dressers, and a large built-in armoire. There seemed to be as much closet space as we had in the house.

"Just make yourself at home," he said. "Look around, explore, and then go up and sit on the deck, and enjoy the sea air," he told me. "I'm going over to the supermarket. I thought we'd have a special dinner tonight, filet mignon. I'll get us an apple pie and some ice cream for dessert. I know how you liked that whenever she let us have it," he said, and then slapped his hand over his mouth as if to stop any more words from emerging.

"Oops, my fault. I know, I know. I mentioned her and the past. You've got to stop me, Cathy, as soon as I do that. Okay?" He laughed. "You look stunned. It's beautiful, I know. You're going to be very happy here, very happy.

"I'll be right back," he said, and went off to the supermarket.

I hobbled around looking at it all. I was surprised and even a little frightened by how many pictures of me he had. Apparently, he had taken many with him when he left the house and more when he had broken in. When I opened the armoire in the master bedroom, I discovered my mother's letters at the bottom, just behind pairs of his shoes. At least he hadn't destroyed them, I thought, and took them out. Then I went onto the deck, sat in a chair facing the outlet of the cove, and pulled the next letter from the pile. It was better than just sitting around and waiting for the world to fall on me, I thought. I had to keep my mind on something or I would go mad with fear.

My darling daughter, she began this one.

> *Yesterday, I had the first sense that I might have made a serious mistake by giving you over to Geraldine. When the idea of having her and Howard adopt you was presented, she offered no resistance nor even suggested the slightest unhappiness about it; yet today I discovered that she has yet to give you some of the things I bought you. When I confronted her about it, she told me you weren't ready to receive things and you wouldn't appreciate them.*
>
> *That wasn't why I bought them for you. I*

wanted to do things for you from the start and to always do things for you. I explained that to Geraldine, but she seemed hardened, different, almost as if she had undergone some serious change in her personality. To be honest, she actually frightened me a little. Her eyes were so small and dark when I spoke to her.

Your grandfather doesn't think anything of it. He says she's just adjusting to having an infant in the house. Of course, he might be right. I hope he's right, but as silly as it might seem right now, I wanted you to know why I haven't been visiting you as much. Geraldine makes it more and more difficult for me, discouraging me, telling me not to come today or finding some reason for me not to come tomorrow.

And she hasn't been here for weeks, months actually. She's turned down almost every invitation, finding some excuse or another why she or she and Howard can't make it for lunch or dinner. I've even offered to take them both and you, of course, on a vacation with us, but she's becoming something of a hermit.

Howard complained to me about her a few days ago. He was here discussing a business investment and he stopped in the sitting room to talk to me about her. He says he can't even get her to go out to dinner anymore. I don't know what to make of it all. I'm worried.

Of course, I will call and try to visit as much as I can. Maybe it will all pass. Maybe Franklin is right: it's just a temporary adjustment to having a child for whom she must care and nourish.

That is a demanding responsibility and not everyone has the same reaction to it.

    Howard is very unhappy, too. I told him I would do what I could, but then he went and said something to Geraldine about our conversation and now, this afternoon actually, she accused me of conspiring with him against her. Whatever I do seems to be wrong and to only make matters worse.

    I wanted you to know all this. Isn't it silly? You're still an infant and I'm talking to you as if you were old enough to understand. Oh well, these letters are meant to be read when you can understand and I'm just trying to give you a sense of your history, our history.

Love,
Mother

Every time I read that word, I felt a deep longing inside me. I was truly the orphan in our group. I had never known a real mother, nor father, for that matter. Right now, I felt like I was just a shell. It didn't matter what happened to me. I was as light and as empty as a shadow anyway. The only thing left for me to do was keep anyone else from suffering because of my horrible fate and destiny.

The letters that followed all described an ever-widening chasm between my mother and Geraldine. In one letter my mother concluded that Geraldine was doing everything in her power to keep her from me. She described a terrible argument in which Geraldine accused her of all sorts of things, using words she had used when she had described her to me. She called her a slut and a whore. My mother claimed she even offered to take me back, but Geraldine wouldn't hear of it. What would it make her look like if she gave me up like that, she wanted to know. She blamed my mother for ruining whatever future she had, whatever hope for love and happiness she had. My mother wondered if Geraldine might not be right. I sensed that my mother went into a deep depression. Her letters became painted with apologies. I could almost hear her wailing and moaning as she wrote long sentences of mea culpa. Suddenly, I had become the embodiment of all her sins and my very existence was meant to serve as a constant reminder.

No wonder she had drifted away and I had seen so little of her after a while. It was both because Geraldine wanted it that way and because she herself had difficulty looking at what she considered her sins. I began to wish I had never found the letters and read them. My father had done me a favor by taking them. I wanted to toss them over the side of the boat.

Someday, I thought, I'll toss myself over as well, but not yet, not until enough time had gone by to ensure my friends would be safe.

I fell asleep in the lounge chair and woke when I felt a little chill and realized the sun was so far west, shadows were stretching over me. I could hear my father working to music below. A short while afterward, he came up to announce that dinner was ready.

"I knew you would enjoy sitting up there," he said as I started into the cabin. He saw the letters in my hand. "Oh, you found those, huh? I wanted to throw them away, but I thought I'd leave it up to you what to do with them. They are yours and Geraldine had no right to hide them from you. See," he added, "I'm going to treat you like the adult you are."

"I wish you had thrown them away," I muttered, and put them aside.

He stepped back so I could get a full view of the dinner table. He had candles lit and the table set with salads, French bread, and a bottle of wine.

"How do you like the china? Geraldine would never even dream of spending what I spent on dishes," he added quickly, and laughed. "Pretty, isn't it?" He lifted up a plate to show me the design.

"Yes," I said.

He pulled out my chair.

"Mademoiselle Cathy."

I looked at him, smiling, beaming, behaving like a schoolboy, oblivious to everything he had done and everything that was wrong with what we were about to do. He was fully caught up in his fantasies now and I was afraid of doing anything that might shatter the illusions.

I sat and he poured the wine.

"Can you imagine her sitting here watching me give you a glass of wine? I do. I imagine it," he said with a very strange, twisted smile on his lips. He nodded at a chair against the wall. "I see her there. I see her bound and gagged. Her eyes are bulging with anger. See her?" he asked me.

I couldn't help but look at the chair. He was nodding at it.

"Her face is bright red and the veins in her neck are popping like they always did when she got really enraged. She's struggling against the ropes. Stop struggling, Geraldine!" he screamed.

I jumped in my seat. He was staring at the chair with a mask of anger over his face that would rival Geraldine's if she really was there.

"You can't stop any of this now, so you might as well sit back and enjoy it." He turned to me. "Drool runs out of the sides of her mouth and down her chin like it would on some mad dog. But," he said, suddenly smiling again, "that won't stop us or even bother us in the slightest, will it? The more we enjoy ourselves, you see, the worse it will be for her.

"Good," he added and sat. "That's fresh goat cheese on the salad," he pointed out, and poked his lettuce with his fork, stabbing it and bringing it to his mouth. "Go on, eat," he ordered.

My stomach felt as if it was filled with rocks, but I forced the food into my mouth and chewed.

"This isn't cheap wine," he continued. "It's French, a merlot recommended to me by one of my more sophisticated clients. That's the good thing about dealing with people of great wealth, Cathy, you learn a lot without having to spend all that money on your own education and experiences. She," he said, nodding at the chair, "used to mock my work. She would say that making money on someone else's money is not honest work. When she was frustrated or angry at me, she would call me a financial pimp," he said, laughing. He looked at the chair. "A pimp, nevertheless, who made her financially comfortable." He stared a moment, and then looked at me and smiled. "You haven't tried the wine. Don't be afraid. Try it," he said, and I sipped it. "Well?"

"It's very good," I said, not knowing what would be good and what wouldn't.

"I know. Everything we do is going to be first class from now on. First class!" he screamed at the chair. Then he paused for a moment as if his brain had shut down, his eyes becoming a little vacant.

I didn't move a muscle. His face was so rigid, it frightened me more. I could hear the meat under the broiler.

"Should I look at the steak?" I asked, simply because the silence was terrifying.

"What? Oh, no. I'll do that. Relax. Rest. Recuperate," he said, and jumped up. "You like yours pink, right? Just like I like it."

He took out the meat and set up our platters with new potatoes and string beans.

"I made sure they gave us the best cut," he bragged, and brought the dinner plates to the table. "Go on, cut into it and let me know if it's done enough for you."

I followed his orders, tasted the meat, and nodded.

"Great, huh? Everything will be, forever and ever. I bet she's hungry," he said, nodding at the chair. He blinked when I just stared at him. "Or, I mean, she would be if she was really here. Of course, that's what I mean." He laughed. "I'm so happy that I get carried away sometimes. Don't think anything of it, honey. I'm in tip-top shape." He shoved a thick chunk of steak into his mouth and chewed it vigorously, savoring the flavor and moaning about the pleasure of a good piece of meat.

I ate because I knew if I didn't, he would be very upset, and from the way he jumped from high moments of happiness to hot moments of anger, I was afraid of disturbing him. It was better to let him travel up and down the highways of his own emotional journey and just keep as quiet and as unobtrusive as possible, I thought.

My heart had long since pounded itself into a state of numbness. Sometimes a look of his, a touch on my hand, a sudden jerky motion toward me would start it thumping again, but I didn't think it was possible to get my blood pumping around my body any faster than it was pumping now. I took tiny breaths, not only because I was afraid I might just pass out, but because my chest felt as if it was being held in a vise that tightened and tightened with every passing moment.

I ate all that I could force into myself and then I declared I was so full, I would burst.

"But you have room for our pie a la mode, right?" he asked, looking like a little boy who might be terribly disappointed if I said no.

I nodded.

"Always room for the fun things," he declared, and scowled when he looked at the chair. "She was like the fun police or something, ready to pounce on anything that gave us pleasure. You know, she was the only person I ever knew who couldn't be tickled. I used to try, just to torment her, but it never worked. She didn't have a soft, sensitive spot on that granite body of hers. She had so many calluses on her palms. She could have sanded wood with them."

He rose and started to clear the table. Almost by instinct, I began to help.

"No, no," he cried when he saw me gathering the plates. "You don't do anything, remember? I'll tell you what," he said, glancing at the chair. "Let's have dessert later, much later. For now, you go into the bedroom. I have a surprise for you there. Put it on," he said.

"A surprise?"

"Yes. Go ahead. I'll be in after I do this. Go on," he urged, gesturing toward the master bedroom.

Trembling so badly, I almost couldn't manipulate my crutches, I turned and walked into the bedroom. There, spread over the bed, was a stretch silk lace chemise. When I held it up, I realized I'd be as good as naked in it. Lengthwise, it just reached mid-thigh.

"Put it on!" I heard him shout. "I'm sure you'll look great in it. I bought it a few days ago and can't wait to see you in it."

I just stared at it. Memories of his long fingers exploring my body while his lips were close to my ear whispering words of love and affection returned in a flood, washing over me, weakening my legs, and leaving me limp and trembling. I had to sit on the bed. I closed my eyes and tried to catch my breath.

"Hey," he said, coming to the door. "Don't you like it? It was expensive," he added. "Go on, put it on. Go on," he said more firmly. "Or, do you want me to help you?" he followed. "Is that what you want? I'd like that."

"No, I can do it," I said quickly.

"Sure you can. She'd pop her cork if she could see you in that," he added, and returned to the kitchen.

Slowly, I undressed and then put on the chemise. I felt so naked, I shivered and embraced myself. When I heard him behind me, I turned. He was standing in the doorway with a dining room chair in his hands, holding it in front of him.

"I like to imagine her in here with us, watching and fuming, don't you?" he asked, and put the chair against the bedroom wall. "You look better than I imagined. You're a beautiful girl. I know she never wanted you to know that, but you are.

"Well now," he said as he started to unbutton his shirt, "here we are in our own new home. What could be better than this?" he said.

Midway down his shirt, he stopped and listened. I hadn't heard anything because there was too much thunder in my ears coming from the raging storm within my heart, but now that he was silent, I did hear what sounded like footsteps above. That was followed by a loud, hard knocking on the door.

"Who the hell is that?" he asked. "Just a minute," he said, buttoning his shirt and moving quickly out of the bedroom and through the boathouse. I sat back on the bed and waited, my whole body feeling as if I had been tied and bound, too. I gazed at the empty chair.

I heard a male and then a female voice and my name. My father raised his voice and began to yell. Then I heard some scuffling, more shouting and moments later what sounded like a chair being overturned. I rose and went to the door just as a woman who looked about thirty came hurrying toward me. She was wearing a police uniform.

"Cathy Carson?"

"Yes?" I said.

"Are you all right?" she asked.

I looked past her and saw a tall, dark-haired man in a suit hovering over my father. He spun him around and placed handcuffs on his wrists.

"It's okay, honey," the woman said. "You're going to be all right."

"What?" I asked, full of confusion. "What's going on?"

Before she could respond, I looked past her again because I heard more footsteps on the steps. I saw Doctor Marlowe coming toward me quickly. I fell back on the bed unable and unwilling to stop the tears from bursting free. Doctor Marlowe sat beside me quickly and embraced me, holding me tightly to her.

"It's over," she said. "Finally, it's over."

Epilogue

The girls had gone for Doctor Marlowe. After they had
read my note, they had a meeting and concluded they had
to tell her what we had done and what danger they believed I was in. It was Dr. Marlowe who guessed that my
father was involved and called the police, who tracked us
down at the boat. They took a great chance for me, and I
will forever love them.

After I dressed, Doctor Marlowe and the policewoman
questioned me about what my father had done, how he
had blackmailed me into going off with him. I broke into
hysterical tears many times during my description of it all,
but Doctor Marlowe helped me get it out and talk, and
then I told the policewoman what my father had said he
had done to Geraldine. I remembered he had taken the
bottle of herbal pills and put it in his jacket. She searched
and found it, and later, when they confronted my father
with it, he confessed.

That didn't excuse us from what we had done. We were

still brought before a judge and lectured. Doctor Marlowe seemed to be the only one who understood and supported us. Jade's and Misty's parents hired high-priced attorneys to help, even though they didn't seem to do that much. Star and I just had Doctor Marlowe, who in the end, appeared to have the most influence with the judge. The others had families, legal guardians, to assume responsibility for them, but I had no one now.

Once again, Doctor Marlowe stepped forward. She volunteered to be my foster parent. She and her sister were going to take me into their home. I resisted until she assured me it was something her sister really wanted to do.

"Emma needs a companion. I'm far too busy to give her the attention she deserves, Cathy. Don't worry. You'll be earning your keep," she promised.

Beggars can't be choosers, Geraldine would remind me, but I couldn't have had a better choice.

Both Doctor Marlowe and I discussed my final year of schooling and decided I should return to the public school system. She wanted me to live as normal a life as was possible, to meet people, to do the things girls my age were doing. Under her guidance and Emma's encouragement, I actually participated in some extracurricular activities. I tried out for the school play and got a good part.

Jade, Star, and Misty came to see me perform and afterward, we all went out together for pizza. We had kept in contact most of the year, despite Jade's mother's attempts to keep us apart. She blamed most of what had happened on Star, Misty, and me, telling Jade we were bad influences. How could her daughter do such a thing as bury a person?

Jade was as defiant as ever, even after the court proceedings, and her mother quickly reverted back to her regular lifestyle. Jade adjusted to her father's new life as best she could and seemed to get past another crisis.

Misty's father did break up with Ariel before the year was over. She said nothing made her mother as happy as that did. In the end though, Misty seemed to feel sorrier for him than herself or her mother. She said he seemed lost and confused and she started to spend more and more time with him.

"We're actually getting to know each other, finally," she told us.

Larry and Star planned their wedding. In June, right after graduation, they were married in a church, just as Star had wanted. Larry got a good job, too, and Rodney came to live with them in their home in Encino. The three of us went there for dinner one night in July and we had a great time together. Soon the three of us would be off to college.

Jade was admitted to Boston University. She said she wanted to go to school as far away from her home as she could and was disappointed she wasn't accepted at Oxford. Misty was accepted at Berkeley in San Francisco, and I entered UCLA. I would live at home with Doctor Marlowe and Emma, at least for the first year.

Late in my senior year, my house was sold and the money was added to my trust. I took everything from the house that I wanted, which wasn't all that much. When I told the girls, they took a ride with me because I wanted to visit the house one more time. It wasn't that I was all that nostalgic about it or that I wanted to relive some happier memories. I just felt I owed it a final visit.

It seemed already to be a tomb. The emptiness, the cold shadows were really what greeted us. I walked through it, gazed out the windows, went to my room and stood by my bed remembering my lonely nights and my ugly times with my father, but also my time with Stuart.

Do you leave yourself in a home that you've spent so much of your life within? I wondered. Will the next inhabitants sense my presence here, or will fresh paint, new carpets, and furnishings erase all the history? What is a house anyway? It can't keep its secrets in the shadows forever and ever. Windows are thrown open, new voices and new laughter chase out the gloom.

All of that is scattered in the wind and hopefully will find no new home, I thought.

Misty came up beside me and hugged me.

"Say goodbye forever and ever," she whispered.

Star agreed and Jade waved her magic wand, the one we had taken to Misty's father's wedding. She had brought it along because she said we never stop needing magic.

"Be gone forever all you sad moments," she cried.

We all laughed and then turned away and walked out. As we drove off, I glanced back and imagined Geraldine in the window, looking out, dreaming of her own escape. In the end she was buried beside her adoptive parents and Alden, her one and only love. Maybe, that was her escape.

"We're all going to be fine, just fine," Jade declared. "In fact, we can retire the OWP's. It's served its purpose," she said.

No one disagreed.

"But that doesn't mean we won't be together forever," she promised.

We all promised.

But we knew what promises were. It didn't matter. What we had together, we would always have. Time and new people, new friends and new loved ones couldn't take that from us.

Our candles would burn forever in the darkness of our precious memories.

And our flowers would bloom in the garden every spring, every year, forever and ever.

Goodbye would never really cross our lips.

Read all the books in the Wildflowers series by V.C. Andrews®

Misty

Star

Jade

Cat

Pocket Books